The Chinese Time Machine

Also by Ian Watson & published by NewCon Press

Beloved of My Beloved (*with Roberto Quaglia*) (2009)
Orgasmachine (2010)
Saving for a Sunny Day (2012)
The 1000 Year Reich (2016)
Assassin's Legacy (*with Andy West*) (2018)
Assassin's Endgame (*with Andy West*) (2018)
The Monster, The Mermaid, And Doctor Mengele (2021)

The Chinese Time Machine

Ian Watson

NewCon Press
England

First edition, published in the UK April 2023
by NewCon Press
41 Wheatsheaf Road, Alconbury Weston, Cambs, PE28 4LF

NCP 301 (hardback)
NCP 302 (softback)

10 9 8 7 6 5 4 3 2 1

ISBN: 978-1-914953-46-0 (hardback)
978-1-914953-47-7 (softback)

Front cover by Mabel SustanciaGris
Typesetting by Ian Whates

Contents

For Guapa, my better reader.

The Chinese Time Machine

1st Trip: *Brave New World*, by Oscar Wilde

The two travellers, Mason and Sharma, already visited the village of Berneval-le-Grand on the north coast of France by air-taxi in the year 2050 for reconnaissance purposes, and now they return in the year 1897 in a covered carriage pulled by a pair of shabby black horses. In 2050 the air-taxi vehicle flew from Oxford over the automated English farms then directly across the sea. In 1897 the two men leave their time apparatus in the otherwise vacant warehouse where they emerged in the port of Dieppe and hire the carriage with its coachman for the 10-mile journey to the village, which will take them two hours through chilly drizzle. One good thing about the poor weather is that scarfs legitimately hide a subvocalising mouth as regards use of the lingo necklace with synthvoice; the burly coachman shouldn't think that they are weird ventriloquists.

The coachman sits outside, up top, cloaked against the poor weather. Inside, Mason and Sharma are private.

Another benefit of the weather: Oscar Wilde ought to be indoors on such a day, which will become the day of the writer's disappearance, if all goes well. The day of the beloved author's rescue from the aftermath of spending the two horrible years in prison, in Reading Gaol.

While their journey towards Berneval-le-Grand proceeds at less than twice a person's walking pace, Mason speaks up with enthusiasm: "I can't wait to show Oscar his stained glass memorial in Poets Corner in Westminster Abbey!" Mason inclines his holographic watchpad, its face blank and black for the moment. Here in 1897 there is, of course, no Cloud to link to – the only clouds hereabouts are big low layers of slow grey vapour – but the watch is loaded with a mass of images with which to woo Wilde.

"Erm, the memorial in the Abbey shows –"

"– that his reputation will recover hugely! That his nation will adore him in times to come. To have his name in Westminster Abbey where kings and queens are crowned, after being a criminal in a gaol cell."

"Wilde's country was Ireland," says Sharma, "not England."

Sharma's family, four generations back, emigrated to England from India. Sharma's Mom and Dad only ever spoke a little Hindi, and Sharma himself only English. These days few such citizens fly back to their countries of origin for family holidays, nor are there low-cost flights for tourists. The carbon footprint! The rising seas! The air-taxi from Oxford to 2050s Berneval-le-Grand and Dieppe was approved only because the Time Institute in Beijing insisted on a fast modern recce to the intended extraction site in case something unforeseen becomes obvious. Only one journey with destination Dieppe and environs can ever be made in the world of 1897. There's no possibility of practising. There's only one chance of extracting Oscar Wilde. Today's the chosen day. Dieppe is as close as they wish to materialise.

"Excuse me," continues Sharma, "but that piece of stained glass in Westminster Abbey clearly indicates the year when Wilde *dies* – only three years from now."

"Not if he comes with us."

If Oscar Wilde goes to live in the future, the overwhelming *probability* is that he will write an ultimate, world-inspiring masterpiece. The quantum-computing viewers only show foggy glimpses of alternative time-lines, but in all of those glimpses the cover of a book by Oscar Wilde is visible in various editions, a novel which the Oscar Wilde who died in Paris in 1900 never wrote, a novel which according to the words plainly visible on no less than three covers '*electrifies our world and brings a new age in literature*'. Those are crucial words. Already beloved worldwide, due to being rescued Wilde will become epochal.

Across the damp green terrain outside, farmers' families and helpers are harvesting apples from laden trees, to become cider. Cows graze. Plenty of grass for cows. Does no one realise about all the methane in cows' farts and the madness of raising animals where veggy crops can grow instead? Of course not. Far too soon for that.

"*If* he comes with us? He'd be a fool not to leap at our offer. A fortunate future for him, maybe many more years of life. Surely a Nobel Prize, because he'll still be alive to receive one."

"If he's a fool, then I plug him with an amnesia dart, preferably while he's seated. He forgets all about us, and his ultimate masterpiece is never written. But we're almost certain that won't happen."

Foolproof, really. On this drab damp day Wilde will hardly be out visiting anyone. By now the villagers with whom Wilde joked and chatted have mostly turned against this posh and charming, but fairly penniless, English gentleman who they now know used a false name to hide from them his notoriety as an offender against morals. Not that Wilde's sins of the flesh are seen as so terrible in France, but he should have taken up residence in an arty part of Paris just for instance.

Or else he ought to have stayed down in Dieppe town! Back in these days of the 1890s many artists colonise the French port, not to mention Britons whom Wilde knew formerly. That was why he went to Dieppe first on leaving Reading Gaol. He would find fellow souls there.

Yet many former acquaintances snubbed Wilde in Dieppe. The artist Aubrey Beardsley, who had illustrated Wilde's play *Salomé*, even moved sixty miles north to Boulogne – another port town favoured by the British – just to avoid the embarrassment of bumping into Wilde on the street. Noticing the attitude of many of the English, French restaurant owners began trying to exclude Wilde from their premises, claiming that they had suddenly run out of food. It was a rare, independent-minded lady who saw a shunning happen in public and who promptly called out, "Oscar, take me to tea!"

Hence Wilde's move to the little village of Berneval-le-Grand which was still unaware of his true identity; to the inhabitants there he was Monsieur Melmoth.

At long last their carriage arrives at the village, so quaint compared with the dull modernity of 2050. The Second World War destroyed the original rustic village painted by Renoir and other artists. In the future wind turbines march in many directions. The lovely beach where Wilde bathed will be the worse for wear due to the North Sea eating away at the chalk cliffs, and a nuclear power station unimaginable in 1890s will already have been decommissioned as obselete.

Mason raps on the roof and calls "Mr Coachman! (audible as "*Monsieur Cocher!*"), which brings the creaky carriage to a halt. Out of the carriage window Mason pops his head.

"Ask any local resident for directions to 'Chalet Bourgeat' – but you should add that we seek the residence of *Monsieur Melmoth* also known as *Monsieur Wilde*. Kindly use both of his names."

Wilde is due to leave the village suddenly on the 15th of September, namely tomorrow, a Wednesday. In Paris he will complain that since the middle of August he was feeling very lonely in Berneval-le-Grand, almost suicidal.

Wilde began his mustn't-be-lost masterpiece of poetry, *The Ballad of Reading Gaol*, on the 1st of June. Six weeks later he finished the first draft. On the 24th of August Wilde sent that first draft, already much revised, to the publisher Leonard Smithers who specialised in erotica and decadent literature. These recorded events shouldn't change. Subsequently, until Smith published the long poem – to huge success – on the 13th of February 1898, Wilde would polish lines in his poem many times. If Wilde travels to the future today, later revisions will be missing from the final version of the poem. One hopes that *The Ballad* continues to be a compelling masterpiece! The advisors from the Time Institute in Beijing want the extraction to happen in Berneval-le-Grand where Wilde is very alone and *after* he revises *The Ballad* significantly, thus to conserve as much recorded history as possible and to make his disappearance easily explicable at the time: suicidal feelings, high cliffs, sea, body washed away by the tide.

"After we bring Wilde back here with us, will I remember the *Ballad* with or without the extra polish he made after September 14th?"

Sharma asks Professor Lin Quinan at the Oxford Science Park. Sharma can recite the whole of the poem verbatim. Lin Quinan is also an admirer of the works of Wilde, such a perfect candidate for time-extraction, but the protocols of time-extraction are what mainly preoccupy the professor, and in what way changes to history may be detectable after these occur.

Outside the lab are other buildings mainly of glass framed with white metal. A fountain rises from a little lake. Bicycles pass by. Coincidentally the entire science park is owned by the rich college that was Wilde's home when a student, Magdalen College at the bridge end of the city's High Street. In a basement of the laboratory building Chinese technicians are checking the time transference pod.

Lin Quinan thinks carefully before replying. Always, always, the deputy chief of Beijing's Time Institute thinks very carefully. His face is wrinkled by thinking; his hair is whitened by thinking.

"My knowledge of the poem is continuous," continues Sharma.

"Not so!" exclaims Lin Quinan. "Human memory isn't a library. You don't open a book and read the same text or see the same picture. Our memories are *recreated* afresh each time we think of something."

"Will you tell me, Professor," asks Mason, "have we ever lost a traveller in the past?"

Lin Quinan peers at Mason. "How would we *know for sure* if we have lost anyone?"

"Because the missing person's travelling companion will tell us when the companion returns alone inside the time pod. Isn't that why two of us travel back through time? Supposing that one of us gets captured in, say Ancient Rome, the other traveller is a 'control'..."

"My dear Dr Mason, it is simply that a solo traveller is *more vulnerable* than a pair of travellers. All I can tell you is that so far no timepod has returned with a single traveller reporting the loss of a partner whom we either remember or don't remember. Each new journey and return is a careful experiment in trying to understand the fundamental nature of reality. Right now Oscar Wilde died in Paris in the year 1900. At what moment will I instead remember

Wilde disappearing in 1897, presumed drowned according to his many biographies? Will I notice an anomaly? Will *you*?"

"I presume that Wilde himself won't."

"Apart from the weirdness for himself of walking around in 2050 Oxford. His reactions will interest us greatly. Because those must lead to the ultimate uplifting novel."

"Of which we don't yet know the contents, only the title."

Presently their carriage arrives at Wilde's thatched chalet as directed, and the two passengers descend. The drizzle has eased, becoming more a wet mist. Wilde's tiny garden is drab with dead flowers and grasses. Despite the mask of mist the arrival of a carriage is fully evident to a neighbour. Out she sails from her own dwelling, buxom and raw-faced in several wide red skirts and a giant blue bosomy blouse.

"Messieurs, 'e 'as gone for walk just now," is what Mason and Sharma hear. Then the woman exclaims, "What's up? I 'ear meself parle English in ze funny voice. You 'ave a 'idden phono thing in your fiacre?"

Damn how good her hearing is! Maybe the mist acts as an amplifier of sounds.

"Far from it, Madam. (*Loin de là, Madame*…) Our apologies. In which direction did Monsieur Wilde march?"

The neighbour directs a brusque brawny-armed gesture further along the lane.

The lane between foggy fields continues further than in 2050 due to less subsidence of the chalk cliffs, not to mention no bombs of World War Two having yet exploded.

Before the lane can become a steep path descending towards yellow sands where Wilde rents a beach-hut, a bulky figure in an overcoat and silk hat resolves out of the mist. The figure stiffens as the carriage comes alongside him and Mason calls out of the window, "Mr Oscar Wilde?" followed by Mason stepping down with Sharma close behind.

"People will recognise me wherever I go," says Wilde, bracing himself in case of an assault, "and know all about my life, at least as far as its follies go."

"That's from *De Profundis*," says Sharma. The very long confessional letter which Wilde wrote towards the end of his imprisonment in Reading Gaol, published five years after Wilde's death.

Wilde's eyes open wide. "Do you mean my *In Prison and in Chains*? '*De Profundis*' may indeed be a better title… But… it is private hitherto. So I take it that you are close acquaintances of Ross for him to have shown you the pages? Yet I never set eyes on either of you."

It is Robert Ross who stayed true to Wilde, housed him, and shared life with him during his first few days in this chalet. Wilde and Ross were lovers, yes, from long before. Deservedly Ross is Wilde's literary executor.

"Especially I would have remembered you," Wilde tells dusky Sharma, with a slightly seductive flutter of his eyelashes. Wilde's long dark overcoat is loose around him yet he still looks relatively strong. At least he can walk well after hundreds of hours on the treadmills of two other very strict prisons prior to arriving at Reading. Nor should we forget those hundreds of painful hours spent picking apart tarry ropes discarded by the Navy until his fingers bled and his fingernails cracked.

A chilly gust comes and a flinch betrays how Wilde's deaf right ear afflicts him – the infected eardrum burst when he fell in the prison chapel. Associated inflammation of the brain, meningitis, will conspire to kill him in 1900.

"Are you publishers who come to make me an offer?" asks Wilde. "You look more like funeral directors."

"If so, it isn't *your* funeral we intend," Mason assures Wilde. "On the contrary! Mr Wilde, this is an extraordinary moment in the history of the world."

"In what way, Mr –? You have the advantage of me."

"I must apologise. My name is David Mason and my colleague is Dr Rajit Sharma. We are from the University of Oxford. I am the

Professor of Intellectual History at Christ Church College, and Dr Sharma is –"

Already Wilde is chuckling. "An imaginary professorship if ever I heard of one. Surely you are impostors, yet you do not seem to be scoundrels."

"Mr Wilde, I should dearly like to show you something confidential." Directing a meaningful glance at the bovine coachman seated atop, "I beg you to indulge us by stepping up into our carriage."

Hunched in his cloak, the coachman seems now to be dozing. Do we hear a snore?

Hastily Sharma adds, "I shall remain outside here so that you don't feel crowded. Nor fear the use of chloroform."

"Of the futility of using which criminally I am *well* aware due to my own father appearing in court three decades ago accused of rape under chloroform," booms Wilde, but the coachman remains inert. "There exists a long history of sensational journalism. Since you choose to evoke that history, perhaps you might show me your something out here in the open air."

"Idiot," mutters Mason to his companion who evidently forgot this item from Wilde's past. "One great turning point of your life, Mr Wilde, was when society sent you to prison.... and the other was *when your father sent you to Oxford* – the same Oxford from which we come to bring you home if you wish. For this is possible!"

"You quote again from my unpublished *In Prison and in Chains...*"

"*De Profundis*," Sharma corrects Wilde automatically, then plunges on regardless: "What's more, I know by heart much of your yet unpublished *Ballad of Reading Gaol*. As will millions of admirers world-wide."

His hand being forced, Mason bares his wrist, then activates his watch: "PingWing: Oscar Wilde 150th Anniversary Exhibition, Oxford Bodleian Library courtyard 2030, 161. 2 quantum gigapixel panorama."

Immediately visible in midair is a cubic metre of view – of the ancient courtyard of the Bodleian Library in Oxford, its stone walls golden in sunlight descending through the great glass roof that now protects the inner space from storms, its bronze statue of a nobleman in his armour like a stamp of authenticity – so that Wilde gasps and all the more so at the illustrated exhibition panels standing around within the great space printed large with Wilde's name, amid glass cases displaying books and memorabilia, interspersed with life-size holograms of himself, roped off so that no visitor should idly walk through those. Visitors stroll about in bright and brief attire which must seem very informal to a Victorian. As yet, of course, there's no image of Wilde's ultimate masterpiece, because that hasn't been written yet.

"Behold the future Oxford, Mr Wilde, where you are honoured, not like here and now. A world of happiness for you, not of misery and rejection."

"This can't be – I see no kinetoscope with you or whatever the thing is called…"

"The secret is miniaturisation." Another glance by Mason at the impassive coachman. "And behold the future world itself. Ping-Wing: Heavenly Palace Six, please, plus view of our planet."

Seen from its furthest corner, the space station appears against the great swell of Earth, specifically the sandy north of Africa and the blue Mediterranean. Within seconds Mason cancels the holo-display.

What Wilde sees is so compelling. As though mesmerised, he steps up into the carriage. Ping-Wing can adjust its display to available space. Presently Mason beckons Sharma within too.

"So, Mr Wilde," says Sharma, "Will you come with us to future Oxford?"

The hesitation, if any, is brief. Wilde raises an eyebrow. "In this same creaky cab?"

Sharma sighs with relief. "I realise you were otherwise engaged but maybe you heard of a recent novel by a young man called Herbert Wells?"

"I regret not. My cell only contained a few books, latterly."

"We parked our, let us say, *transporter through time and space* in Dieppe."

"Altogether a more worthy conveyance, I'm sure. And might I collect some personal items to carry with me?"

From Mason, "You won't need books or anything –"

"Ah, supposing that I were to cast myself from the cliffs into the sea. I catch your drift. The sea washes away the stains and wounds of the world – but books have this horrid habit of floating. I must seem to have disappeared without trace."

On the way past Chalet Bourgeat, while a curtain conceals Wilde, Mason calls out of the carriage window in lingoFrench, "Madame, we see Mr Wilde nowhere!" as if the busybody neighbour deliberately misdirected them.

On the route back to Dieppe, Wilde observes: "I lived for pleasure in the past. It seems I must learn to be happy again. Apparently my destiny is not to emulate all of the passion of Jesus Christ." Passion, of course, refers to martyrdom and suffering – as well as meaning passionate feelings running out of control. It seems that Oscar Wilde cannot avoid being witty. "Consequently the deity whom I shall continue to honour," he adds, "shall be Beauty. As was so when I was at Oxford. As will be so again. At my Alma Mater, my Pater Noster."

"And if you need further inducement to accompany us," says Mason, "I might mention that in England of the future a man may marry a man, or a woman may marry a woman, and whoever shouts abuse will himself or herself go to prison."

"Astonishing!"

Sharma nudges Mason. "Try not to sound like a pimp."

"I merely meant… you are a different sort of man from the… *mundane*," Mason says with momentary hesitation as regards the *mot juste*.

"Of that I am sadly all too aware, sir. As was proven in a court of law."

"A law which is now repealed. Or will be repealed. Or has been. Or is being."

The time-sphere apparatus stands where the two travellers left it in the warehouse. Now they are a trio, but Wilde's bulk was calculated for, a bulk somewhat slimmed by prison. After a few days of orientation and medical check-up at the Science Park, Wilde will move into a flat on the crescent in Oxford's elegant little Park Town within a short stroll of the city centre. Since Wilde will not have died in Paris in 1900, and will still be alive, what about the author's literary royalties – no longer in the public domain, therefore to be paid once more? This is a matter which awaits clarification in 2050.

And after Oscar pens his ultimate masterpiece, the text will be typed on 1890s French paper held by Oxford's Bodleian Library, on a Dactyle typewriter borrowed from Oxford's Museum of the History of Science. The typescript of this novel inspired by the future, entitled *Brave New World*, will be posted to Robert Ross to the latter's astonishment and delight. Surely Ross will arrange for speedy publication of the typescript. Some day during 2051 or 2052 Oscar will awaken in Oxford to find himself famous, even more so than before. Subsequently Wilde may dream of differences in the recent past. Such dreams fade fast. The jelly of time will tremble then set firm again. So reckons Lin Quinan.

"What happens," Wilde asks brightly, "if you continue to show me the future with your miraculous soldier's watch *while* we are moving towards that same future?"

"I've no idea," says Mason.

"Nor me," admits Sharma. "We should have asked the Chinese. It's their technology."

"Ping-Wing: show highlights of history 1950 to 2050." Thus to avoid two murderous world wars which might horrify Wilde.

Little internal time elapses till the timesphere is back inside the basement lab again, where Lin Quinan and his technicians wait eagerly for the apparatus to open itself – while within, for Wilde's agog benefit, Mason's watch is projecting the 1968 collapse of the Eiffel Tower in Paris, dynamited by rioting students. As indeed did happen. All seems well.

The Chinese Time Machine

2nd Trip: The Kidnap of Fibonacci

Lin Quinan and his team from the Time Institute in Beijing have, for the early evening, taken over Oxford's Paddyfields restaurant which still flourishes in 2050. When Padddyfields first opened long ago in 1979, the name merely nodded to the role of rice in Chinese cuisine. Due to global warming, the noble stone architecture of Worcester College nearby no longer encloses lawns and herbaceous borders but instead a big paddy of jasmine rice irrigated by overspill from the Oxford canal.

In the restaurant doorway a couple of State Security Ministry women in neatly tailored blue suits stand chatting. Their minimised umbrellas may be folded-up submachine guns, or normal umbrellas. Two big Donfeng SUVs are parked close by. Frequently one or other woman eyes the palatial Saïd Business School further along the street in the direction of the maglev station – you can't get to London by rail these days without costly amphibious maglev. Can't be too vigilant; that Saïd School was mostly paid for by arms-dealing Saudi money. Diligent staff and students continue to mill in and out of the college of commerce. The suited security women are authorised to kiss one another enthusiastically from time to time, to distract suspicions. An anvil cloud heaves up into the sky, threatening a possible downpour.

At a round feast-table within are: white-haired wrinkly Professor of Time Studies Lin Quinan alongside his dapper secretary David Wang. Next along are the two seasoned time travellers – our protagonists David Mason and Rajit Sharma – who brought Oscar Wilde forward from the past with perfect success. What awaits is a venture with many more unknown factors.

Further around the curve is Joan Frithswith in billowy pink, buxom editor of *The Oxford History of Capitalism*, herself based at wet Worcester College. It ain't all rice-farming within those college walls!

Plus, there's Edward 'Teddy' Hall, Reader in Medieval History specialising in the Mediterranean area. Also present are… patience, please!

Just to mention that occupying another big table are six Time Technicians from China who operate the transference pod apparatus out at the Science Park beyond the city boundary. This evening's trip into town is a treat for them, that helps visibly occupy more of the restaurant for appearances as well as for privacy.

"So that we don't waste time trivially, gentlemen and lady," declares Lin, "I have presumed to order for everybody to share Ten Regional Sea and River Delights." He beams benevolently. "I must confess myself to be a fishetarian fanatic, and I sincerely recommend the Fried Sliced Eel in Spicy Sauce, the Sichuan Pepper Broth Sliced Fish with Pickled Cabbage, and the Whole Sea Bass with Black Fungus – though, soaked improperly, beware that the black fungus may produce toxic Bongkrekic Acid *poissoning* you, if you'll pardon my French." The Policy Head of the Time Institute is quick-witted. Teddy Hall of the neat salt-and-pepper goatee chortles politely, earning a glance of gratitude. Presumably the Sea Bass and Black Fungus is Lin's favourite dish, not to be idly squandered on non-connoisseurs.

Lin eiffel-towers his hands and waggles his fingers, causing waiting persons to hasten to distribute bottles of well-chilled Tsingtao beer and of Nongfu Spring Water. The Eiffel Tower certainly waggled to and fro as if trying to walk before it fell, dynamited by demonstrators against the French state back in anarchic '68 of the previous century.

"Before we continue, gentleman and lady, I'm obliged to mention that by partaking of Ten Regional Sea and River Delights at my nation's official invitation you assent to the Pledge Protecting Chinese State Secrets, the PPCSS. Anyone reluctant to do so is perfectly free to depart now without more ado."

Nobody shifts. In the doorway outside, flicked by a strengthening breeze, the security women cuddle.

The lone Lady in question is Ottoline Honey, Principal of St Hilda's College and Professor of the History of Science. After her Vietnamese husband and best pal became a dear departed, Ottoline abandoned his family name Huynh meaning 'golden', although nowadays she always loyally dyes her blonde hair a glossy black.

Waiters rush dishes to the Lazy Susan upon Lin's table. As soon as every guest has spooned or chopsticked a morsel from the rotator into their own blue dragon bowl, the deputy director of Time Travel Beijing resumes:

"The Politburo of the Communist Party of the People's Republic of China, in session at the six-star military Jingxi Hotel, has determined that Capitalism is the road to ruin for our whole world. China is complicit in Capitalism admittedly in order to nourish, protect, and enhance the lives of our population. Yet now we see clearly with unpeeled eyes that Capitalism leads to habitat collapse which will cause the extinction of Humanity along with the demise of most land creatures within an estimated 250 years plus or minus 40. In the seas and oceans 80% of life will perish."

Mason nudges Sharma discreetly, his raised eyebrow referencing all the freshwater and saltwater bounty laid out before them.

"Accordingly, we have decided to extract from history an individual whose absence may *delay* the development of Capitalism of the rapacious Western model. Dr Sharma, yourself and Professor Mason successfully wooed beloved author Oscar Wilde to return with you from exile in France, thus beneficially extending his own life and his works without any harmful alteration to the present day."

"Any alteration that we *know* of," murmurs Mason. He's the flabbily muscular Professor of Intellectual History at Christ Church College also known as 'The House' because *Aedes Christi* is Latin for 'House of Christ'; by such idiosyncracies does Oxford sustain itself. In his time he has been a Judo Blue and this evening he sports a striped dark blue tweed blazer. If push comes to shove back in the past, Teddy may have the weight. Actually, the elderly Lin could easily toss Ted with a twist of Tai Chi, a forceful martial art when speeded up.

"I shall be as frank as is permitted. On the best advice of our own Chinese scholars the Politburo believe that the most suitable candidate for extracting benevolently from the past to the present is..." – a pregnant pause as of a Game Show host –"...the mathematical guru known nowadays as *Fibonacci.* Fibonacci, who pioneered and popularised the Hindu-Arabic system of written numbers, from 1 to 9, to replace Roman I to X. This replacement hugely speeded up the arithmetical accountancy of commerce. Lacking those numbers, European Capitalism may be slowed sufficiently to delay the tipping points of planetary disaster until we became scientifically brighter. I also recommend the Braised Ribbon Fish, in taste delicately midway between a briny flounder and a sea trout. I seek your free-ranging observations on this choice. Of Fibonacci, not of the fish."

"There might," said Ottoline Honey, "be a spot of difficulty identifying *that* particular chap. As I recall, he was only nicknamed Fibonacci a couple of centuries after his death. Signifying 'Son of Bonacci', that's 'Filius Bonacci' in Latin. Other names were Leonardo of Pisa and Leonardo Bignollo, which might have meant 'Traveller' or 'Bilingual' or even 'Dunce' though that seems a distinctly daft notion."

"Medieval Latin is a minefield," Teddy Hall says to back Ottoline up.

"If some other Italian *hadn't* specifically acknowledged Leonardo of Pisa by name just the one single time in a book, nobody would ever have heard of any Fibonacci."

"That was Luca Pacioli," says the dapper secretary. "In 1494, three hundred years after Fibonacci. And thanks to that one mention, Pietro Cossali picks up on Fibonacci's work much later. "

A tartan-kilted chap with a fiery fringe of red beard pipes up poetically: "Oh blessèd Fibonacci numbers, found everywhere in nature! How quickly they do grow. Like capitalism out of control? 34, 55, 89, 144, 233, 377 and so on!"

"So-called Fibonacci Numbers are trivial and irrelevant to our concerns here," Secretary David Wang is quick to say. Wang certainly knows a thing or two, and indeed continues as if lecturing children:

"Fibonacci's name became the label for that sequence *which was familar centuries earlier* merely because Fibonacci wrote them in a margin like some Fermat – how absurd and ridiculous."

An awkward silence follows during which diners clack their chopsticks like knitters beside a guillotine.

Professor Lin emphasises, "So-called Fibonacci numbers are of no importance *capitalistically* compared with Hindu numbers, *respect* to Dr Sharma. Numbers as propagandised by Leonardo of Pisa."

Momentary panic shows on Sharma's face since, third generation English that he is and a specialist in 19th Century English Literature, he only knows a smattering of Hindi. Such as that *haldi* means turmeric, neglected by Chinese chefs. In its big serving bowl the superspicy Sichuan Peppercorn Broth Fish is a garishly red oily volcanic lava soup of chilis and peppercorns and some sliced fish struggling to stay afloat and white-fleshed.

"I couldn't agree more," says Firebeard. "In my humble opinion us mathematicians shouldn't fixate like personality cultists upon *who* merits credit for an idea but rather upon the *idea itself*."

"Let me see," says Professor Lin, "you're Ferguson from the Mathematical Institute?"

"I am in fact *The Ferguson* of Ferguson." Wow, the clan chieftain himself. How such types do congregate in Oxford. Not necessarily a senior figure at the Mathematical Institute; maybe a bit of a maverick.

"You regard Fibonacci as irrelevant, The Ferguson? *Inherently* irrelevant because he was a particular person? That doesn't help us much to confirm him as best candidate."

"Until a few minutes ago, Professor, I wasn't aware of any such need. Apart from us having no clear idea of the fellow's preferred name at the time, I believe we haven't the slightest idea what he looked like. Do I recall correctly?"

Wang nods. "The statue in Pisa and the sketch of his head wearing a typical hat date from later and are guesswork."

"Nor have we much idea where he was whenever," adds The Ferguson of Ferguson. "Needle, haystack?"

"He was in Pisa?" suggests Mason.

"No," says Teddy Hall. "The last place to look for Leonardo the Pisan is in Pisa. As I recall, Fibonacci's merchant father took his son to Bugia in Algeria for further education while still a boy. That was when the father was appointed Consul of Pisa to Bugia to serve at the Customs House and to take care of the sizable resident Pisan community."

"Really?" queries The Ferguson. "Algeria for *Algebra*, eh?"

"Exactly," Teddy responds patiently. "Bugia was a major trading city. The French word for 'candle' – 'bougie' – comes directly from Bugia. Major medieval export, beeswax candles. Nowadays the place is known as Béjaïa."

With an eye on possible lucrative consultations in the future, they all need to put in an oar from their own angles, even if those angles overlap. One mustn't keep silent if one can speak, said Wittgenstein.

"If I recall correctly," intervenes Ottoline, "Fibonacci's Dad *sent* for his son some time *after* Dad got installed in North Africa."

Teddy wags a finger at Ottoline. "Some years ago I happened to publish on-line a paper entitled 'Pisa at its Height of Its Power' –"

"– which we read with interest," says Lin. "Hence your presence here."

"Consequently I happen to recall that in Fibonacci's brief 'Prologue' to the revised 1228 scroll of his *Liber Abbaci* – By the way that certainly doesn't mean 'The Book of the Abacus' but rather 'The Book of Computation'. It isn't remotely about how to use an abacus. Exactly *why* the majority of modern academics use the *wrong* spelling, *Abaci* with a single 'B', is beyond me –!"

Ottoline looks a dagger. Or a stiletto.

"Get to the point?"

"Yes indeed, Ott. I do happen to recall that the future Fibonacci says of his vital educational time spent in North Africa, '*Cum genitor meus a patria publicus scriba in duana Bugee… preeset, me in pueritia mea ad se venire faciens…*'"

Mason claps his hands. "You have that off verbatim! I'm impressed."

Sharma coughs awkwardly. He may have less Latin than he ought to.

Teddy Hall obliges with a translation. "That's to say, when my father for the sake of the fatherland became the *scriba*, basically that's Consul, in the customs house at Bugia, *me being a boy he made me come with him…* "And he strokes his goatee, quietly satisfied.

Lin enjoys more Sichuan Peppercorn Broth Fish while a three-sided discussion – or duel – ensues about the exact legal status of pueritia, 'boyhood', in Pisa circa the year 1200, not to mention a dispute about the likely Pisan educational system.

"At least," murmurs Sharma to Mason, "we don't need to *travel* with this bunch of clowns."

"Enjoy your Thousand Year Egg, Rajit – we'll be travelling back almost as far as its name."

"*Why* have you put the damned monstrosity in my bowl, David?"

Mason chuckles.

"Taste the egg," urges Lin. "It's both auspicious and delicious. So I added it to the order."

Although loath, Rajit lets black and brown jelly spill out accompanied by browny-green yolk. Mischievous Mason! Able to play the clown too. Muscular-ish plus mischievous might be an asset in North Africa.

The upshot after some more learnèd dispute is that young Leonard, maybe born in 1170, must have acquired literacy including fluency in Latin at repetition-school in Pisa Cathedral between the ages of ten and twelve. Not bad going, lad!

Depending on social background, boys can proceed onward either to abacus or abbacus school taught in dialect and to counting on fingers – don't laugh, traders developed fast complex sophisticated finger codes – or else to grammar school to prepare as future physicians, notaries, clerics, or still more teachers.

Yet maybe boys in Italy typically attended elementary school from the ages of 6 till 11, after which they spend 4 to 5 years in grammar school, or 2 years in abbacus school? Never mind which! Bucking tradition, Billy Bonacci the foresightful Dad takes his lad to Bugia maybe in 1182 for mathematical training taught in Arabic. *In Arabic, nota bene* – using Hindu-Arabic numbers. Young Fibo may already have picked up some Arabic amongst Muslims resident in Pisa. Pisa was exaggeratedly nicknamed 'City of a Thousand Towers' because the leading families frequently feuded, therefore they dwelled in armed fortresses. Consequently young Leo may *not* have played with the kids of other Italian merchants. Maybe instead he played with Moorish and Berber kids. Academics shouldn't make assumptions about Maestro Fibonacci.

Professor Lin does casually mention the *Jiǔzhāng Suànshù* – "Not on the menu here, don't bother looking, Dr Sharma. I refer to the *Nine Chapters on the Mathematical Art* definitively commented upon by Liu Hui well over two thousand-year-eggs ago. This, not to be confused with the *Shushu Jiǔzhāng* masterpiece namely *Mathematical Treatise in Nine Sections* authored by the nevertheless corrupt, greedy, and murderous Qin Jiushao – born coincidentally in the very same year as Leonardo of Pisa's first issue of his *Liber*, namely 1202 CE."

"I wouldn't dream of confusing them," vows Sharma.

"Liu Hui's *pi* was very precise –"

"He perfectly cut up a pie –?"

Enough of all this sparkling repartee! For sure, Leon of Pisa, Billy's Boy, is our best bet for nuancing the rapacious advance of capitalism. The choice which Chinese experts already made is now confirmed by Oxford academics – just as a Chinese engineering company might hire a respected foreign company to sign off on the technical safety and solidity of a domestic project such as a huge dam, for instance. Validation by a third party covers one's ass.

The target year is chosen; we shan't say which. A suitable month to catch young Fibo at home is *December*, since merchants rarely send vessels forth during Winter when storms might rip the Med.

The time transference pod carrying Mason and Sharma (plus a vacant seat equipped with a straitjacket in case of strong resistance) reaches Bugia towards dawn. Homing in hummingly upon an enclosed space which has to be mainly empty, the pod's arrival disperses its own volume of air, rattling the rafters while sudden thunder rumbles outside.

Light from the pod's porthole shows what seems to be a minor warehouse. Brick walls, slit windows for ventilation not wide enough for skinny kids to squirm through intent on theft, and a stout wooden door with iron hinges and an empty keyhole. Piled along the rear wall…

"I say, Rajit, those look like squirrel furs. See the stripes? They have to be from Scandinavia or northern Russia by way of Novgorod, remarketed in Istanbul by Bulgars, and resold in Sicily."

Subsequent to that dinner at Paddyfields, Prof. Mason and Dr. Sharma both boned up busily on Bugia, but you can't find everything out within an alloted ten days. From the get-go, 'History man' Mason has a head start on his Hindu Eng. Lit. colleague.

"I'll take your word on the squirrels, Prof Dave. Probably no overnight curfew in Bugia, right? No security patrols? Let's get out there and see where we are."

Douse the lights of the pod. For torches they use their solpower watchpads, which also serve as walkie-talkies. Their electronic lockpick aces the way out. Ideal garage, this. Nobody local is likely to need access till the following Spring. Sharma and Mason are dressed in voluminous dirty cotton as if newly in town after a couple of months spent crossing the Sahara. Hidden underneath their gowns, soft satchels of necessities are slung diagonally. A nomad turban apiece easily hides their lingo necklaces.

Available for autotranslation into synthspeech are 22nd century Berber language, also future rural Tuscan dialect which may sound a bit *eh?* to 12th Century Pisans. More reliably, church Latin as per Vatican City 2050, and finally classical Arabic of the Holy Quran. The latter may be the best bet because Allah's Arabic is *unchangeable* in every respect ever since the Prophet Peace-Be-Upon-Him died in 632 CE, thereby ending the stream of guidance and grammar from God in the sky accompanied by secretary archangel Gabriel.

In the years before electricity folks don't mess about wasting available daylight. Up and at it! As soon as the stone is flung to put the stars to flight, as soon as a minaret is caught in a noose of light, attaboy all. Irrespective of dismal skies, cutting winds, and rain. Only the first of which applies this morning.

As visibility begins to grey the chilly street of walls and doorways under a starless sky, that trampled dirt thoroughfare drums as if from an earthquake. Something big's coming, something like a tidal wave.

"Flat up against the wall, Raj! Hug tight!"

Identification of the source of noise comes with the first lumbering camel and the next and the next, filling the road, braying and bellowing and grunt-gargling percussively. More come, and more and more, an uncountable number. Droppings tumble and fly from under leathery feet. Luckily, by the time the last camel passes, our two time travellers haven't been crushed.

A trio of chaps flicking long sticks follow at a trot. One of whom pauses to stare at the time travellers. We'll call this chap Bernie because of his beige burnous. Sooner than they might wish, Mason and Sharma have a chance to test their assisted language skills.

"I thought it was a stampede!" exclaims Mason, his transdevice favouring modern Berber.

"Eh? Eh?"

Try Classical Arabic, blessings be upon the Prophet.

"Oh, ah," says Bernie. "We're just moving a little herd to the assembly area. Six hundred beasts."

"Assembly area?"

"For the first caravan of the Winter when the sands are less of an oven, of course." By now the daylight is more revealing and Bernie assesses their robes. "I'm sorry our beasts dirtied you."

Stands to reason that the trade caravans favour the wintertime when the Sahara is somewhat less lethal. Whose idiot idea was it for our heroic kidnappers to wear shabby garb as if they had just made a two month crossing of the devil's furnace? However, seize an advantage!

"Yes," agrees Mason. "A bit buffeting, that was. My poor ribs."

"We expected no people in the street as yet. Later and lighter wouldn't work for us. Nor would we wish our beasts to begin eating, thereafter reeking in close confines of fart and cud. Look, Excellences, I'm *Khabir* Zadi's third son. A caravan master must neglect no aspect. We are responsible that you're dirty. I shall escort you to the laundry beside the closest hammam and pay your laundry bill. Your robes will be dried over a stove by the time you've bathed within. The hammam should be open soon."

And this will involve… Mason and Sharma taking off their robes, revealing their satchels – and also their lingo necklaces…

Mason gestures along the grey street, the only remaining sign of camels being a haze of dust. And lots of dung not unlike fuzzy brown kiwi fruits. A bit of a gallop in the morning does get the bowels moving. "But your companions?"

"They well know the way to the assembly field."

Excellent opportunity to seek some information from the horse's mouth about Leonardo of Pisa. Shall we say from the camel's mouth? At any rate a friendly informant. So far.

As they walk, Sharma asks carefully, "How many camels will be in your father's caravan to cross the Sahara after all are assembled?" This is a number question, requiring arithmetic.

The astonishing answer, assuming that the lingo device isn't wrong, is six thousand. *Six thousand camels!* That's ten times more than the herd that just lumbered along the street. Oops, will any of those camels carry squirrel pelts bound for a central African kingdom?

Third-son Zadi seems worth cultivating. Not to be, though! After five brisk minutes of passing many probable warehouses, they come to more notable brick buildings. A faint whiff and the coming-and-going of males suggests a public latrine. Seagulls coast and swoop and perch and screech. Next along, a much larger nobler edifice vents a little steam from its rear. This must be the hammam bathhouse. And Third Son spies an acquaintance.

"Ibn Hammad!" That's a bearded fellow perhaps in his forties, his brown striped woolly gown with baggy hood buttoned up to the chin.

Fulsome courtesies confuse Mason's lingo necklace so that it squawks out some Vatican Latin. Sharma coughs noisily while Mason hastily subvocalises, "Silence." Nacreous vapours of the morning drift by.

Ibn Hammad regards the time travellers quizzically. "I thought I heard an Afrit spirit from the dunes hissing an opinion."

"Sorry," says Mason. "Dust in my throat. Those camels."

"Alas, Traveller, I cannot understand you."

Which Rajit at least understands. "David, throat *on.* Sir, we apologise at confusions. My name is Rajit Sharma. My colleague is

Dav-eed Ma-son. We are travellers indeed, as you can tell! We are seekers of wisdom."

"This gentleman," says Third-son emphatically, "is Abu ʿAbd Allāh Muḥammad ibn ʿAlī ibn Ḥammād ibn ʿĪsā ibn ʿAbī Bakr al-Ṣanhājī."

Focus only upon the name Hammad, heard previously. *Hammad* at the *hammam*, the public bath. Dare we risk a glance at the watchpad to goggle the name ibn Hammad? The watchpad activated might seem like the glowing eye of an Afrit. An enchanted amulet. Or was ibn Hammad being *ironic*?

Several things happen swiftly. Darting his fingers to his forehead then to his heart in hasty farewell, Third-Son decamps while ibn Hammad with hospitable smile and widespread arms which shan't be denied ushers Sharma and Mason within the bathhouse complex. In a double-height barrel-vaulted room with elegantly carved gallery running around halfway up, male customers disrobe for attendants to store the robes in an annex.

"Our man here will carry your clothes to the bathhouse," states ibn Hammam *no he's Hammad.* "I am known."

So the cost will be invisible, to be refunded by the caravan master, and any protest might be an insult.

When in Rome…

Sharma whispers, "At least my natural skin looks a plausible colour." Quickly he divests himself, conjouring his satchel from his shoulder and bundling it up as much as he can in his bony brown hand. That still leaves his metal lingo necklace to cause surprise, as well as his loose white cotton boxers, *without any labels mark you.*

Pink-complexioned Mason, lily-white from the necklace down, is less in conflict with his boxers. Bit flabby, though, for a supposed crosser of desert. Whereas Sharma is *knotty.*

Ibn Hammad is polite and makes no immediate comments. Yet as soon as business with an attendant is complete, their host hustles them through a cool room and through a sizable warm room – there's an ornate water-basin in the centre, and colonnades with annexes – then into a final hot steamy room. No barrel-vault here but a low ceiling to spread the vapour around blurringly.

"Who *are* you travellers? What manner of men? You address me strangely. Surely one of you is an Indian. Can the other be a Frank? And those closed torques which you wear – are you some kind of slaves who escaped?"

"Sir, we have come here in search of a young man from the port of Pisa across the sea. A certain Leonardo of the house of the Sons of Bonaçie. His father Guilichmus or Guglielmo may be the *scriba* of the Pisans, who brought the boy here to learn Muslim I mean Saracen mathematics in Arabic."

"His father may be or may not be…? Why did you not direct yourselves promptly to the Customs House?"

"We were almost crushed by five hundred camels, then the third son of *Khabir* Zadi insisted on making amends."

"As I know for a fact by observation."

"We have been rushed off our feet."

By sleight of hand en route Ibn Hammad acquired a coarse woollen towel to wear around his waist.

"Myself being a historian, I do admire correct facts." He's a historian, he's a historian, is Ibn Hammad! Is he famous or forgotten? Damn the necessary deadness of their watchpad imitating a bracelet of jet.

"This young student from Pisa is the source of this *wisdom* you seek? How singularly strange."

With a nod to Sharma, Mason burbles, "This concerns *Indian numbers*."

The indifferent universe decides to lend a hand.

"Alas that you missed by mere years the finest exponent of mathematics ever to teach in Bugia, this centre of knowledge. I refer to al-Qurashi the Algebraicist who came from al-Andalus, Spain, as did many savants and lesser savants to live in Bugia."

Very… unhelpful. Might Ibn Hammad the Historian become a bit of a buttonholing bore?

"Certainly for 'wisdom' as such this Leonardo may have sought out Abou Mandaye from al-Andalus, known by other Sufi saints as the 'Summit' of Wisdom, but for algebra – if you understand me – I can think of one scholar who still frequents the bath-houses of Bugia at the honourable age of 67. Or 68."

No, please don't.

"Bath-houses… such as *this very one we are in?*" asks Mason, sweat trickling down his belly to soak his cotton boxers. Circulating steam veils much.

The Historian chuckles. "Travellers, there must be sixty bath-houses in Bugia."

"I think we're becoming distracted," observes Sharma. "It isn't religious wisdom we're seeking, though of course we've nothing against religion! Nor are we urgent about learning algebra. And we're presuming upon your kindness, sir. If our clothes are wearable yet, might you very kindly point us in the direction of the Pisan Customs House?"

On the way to which, now cleanly attired though damp, our travellers are able discreetly to consult their watchpads about Ibn Hammad, whose renowned history of Bugia went missing, sorry to report. En route they pass Jews wearing pointy yellow hats in the style of tagine pot lids. Then there are clog-shod fellows with long belted tunics and brimmed caps accompanied by wimpled women wearing fish-shaped trinkets. These could be Christian traders looking for end-of-season 'budge', the furry black lambskin favoured by Englishers, to stay warehoused in Bugia until the Spring sailing season. More prosperous guys in turbans and tunics and pantaloons, sporting pointy leather shoes lacking heels, may well be classy intellectuals from Moorish Spain. Diverse crowds move and mingle without friction.

When our travellers arrive near the quays and more screech of gulls, however, many are the candidates for a possible Pisan Customs House. More than one bustling courtyard, more than one busy goods yard is arcaded with offices and warehouses. As Mason and Sharma pause indecisively beside a solitary pillar, no less than three men hurry towards them calling out competitively in necklace-translated Arabic (one perhaps in Tuscan), "Licensed Dragoman at your service, sirs!"

"Plural: Dragomans," Mason whispers quickly. "Teddy Hall said they're official interpreters and expediters. Fixers."

Mason points to a tall skinny wall-eyed fellow clad in a thick blue shirt and red-striped pantaloons, sporting a bushy beard, beckoning him to step alongside. Obviously a Dragoman cannot be avoided and may be of significant use.

"A wise choice, sir! I am Diego from Córdoba also known as Qurṭuba. Licensed to interpret Arabic, Latin, Toscano, and Turkish."

"Let us speak Latin, please."

Sharma adds with an ingratiating smile, "*Dominus illuminatio mea.*" That's the motto of Oxford University: The Lord is my Light.

"Shut up!" snaps Mason as Diego the Dragoman swivels his head to focus upon Sharma. One advantage of Diego over the other two applicants, or besiegers, is that due to strabismus he cannot so easily scrutinise his new employers. Being tall too, he'll be easier to spot in a crowd. But one doesn't want to know much about him, such as how come he comes from Córdoba in Moorish Spain, in case he in turn is inquisitive.

Mason explains their quest, ending, "… we aren't sure exactly how the lad styles himself, or how old he is, but his father is certainly the Consul of Pisa. We simply wish to introduce ourselves to the youth and to his genitor to ask about a suitable mathematical education for our own children." A plausible pretence?

This seems an easy enough commission. Diego names a sum and Mason produces coins from his purse. Our travellers carry enough Islamic coins of the period to get by for several weeks if need be, wangled by Secretary Wang from the Coin Room of Oxford's Ashmolean Museum; the Chinese made a donation towards much-needed maintenance. Silver dirhams, golden dinars.

Yet this is not to be. Duly led by Diego to the Pisan Consulate, they quickly learn that *Scriba* Bonacci and his son went to Tunis a fortnight earlier by caravan. The pair may return to Bugia in a further two or three weeks…

Once the three are outside again in a dusty courtyard, Mason strikes his brow in frustration. "Plagues and viruses!" he curses.

"We've been lucky in that regard," soothes Sharma. "Not even a spot of belly bother so far."

"Thanks to all those Chinese antibios."

Dragoman Diego proposes, "Good sirs, I can call here every few days on your behalf so as not to appear importunate."

Thus those at the Consulate will not become overly familiar with the travellers' faces. A sensible precaution. Mason approves.

"Be so kind," continues Diego, "as to tell me which *funduqa* you are staying at so that I may report to you promptly when the father and son return?"

Funduya, fondouk… That's one of those mixed-purpose commercial properties for travellers including foreign Christians living temporarily or full-time upstairs, camels and donkeys down below. Thanks for that, Teddy Hall. A logical assumption on Diego's part.

But but but they really shouldn't move away from the time pod by transferring into a funduya, with inevitable problems such as them having no camel. They can't risk escorting Diego to their digs even once for a limited street view. Neither do they know the street name nor the name of the warehouse where the pod is hidden; a watchpad is no help here. Ditherings.

Rajit resolves matters by pulling from his purse a dinar, basically worth one sheep, causing Diego's eyes to converge or to try to.

"Kindly meet us each day as the sun sets beside that pillar where we first met. This coin will be yours now and another gold coin awaits you after ten days. Likewise, thereafter."

If Diego of Córdoba is amazed he contrives not to show it.

And so Prof Mason and Dr Sharma spend black nights tucked up in the timepod. By day they're footloose and fancy free to become acquainted with the vastness and variety of Bugia, including the street food.

Why, there must be a hundred thousand inhabitants! This city has eight gates. It boasts twenty-one districts. Jews have a district all of their own. So do Egyptians. There are aqueducts and watchtowers and mausoleums and ancient tombs and fortified palaces and so many gardens. Beehives buzz beside many gardens.

Oh there are olive groves and vineyards and orchards of apricots and oranges and figs. There's gorse and pretty though poisonous oleander. Bugia's great bend of bay is a giant shelter from north-east winds for shipping, at its heart the commercial quays where clement weather sees feverish activity. Admire the mountains south and east reaching to rub the grey sky. Mosques call you to prosperity. A bishop has a cathedral of a kind. Here's where the city archives are stored securely. Here's where a feared and adored mystic Marabout raised a Sufi Institute. That's Abou Madyane from Moorish Spain, prof of poetry and of Sufism, the Way of Wool, who's in town right now. Historian Ibn Hammad spoke in the bathhouse about this ascetic Height of Wisdom.

Markets display rainbows of spices. In many workshops leather is tanning. Alum will taw hides without tannin and will fix dye and even act as a douche to tighten the vagina of a slave girl. It's the Pearl of North Africa, this place.

At last the long-awaited evening comes when, by the pillar, Diego the Dragoman declares, "They are back," and holds out his palm.

Next morning, as his final service, Diego escorts Mason and Sharma to the Pisan Consulate Counting House to confront our travellers with… will he be handsome? will he look bright?

He's chubby, is the son of Bonacci. Not endearingly cherub-chubby but going on for fat. Too much time spent on chairs, and even on camels. Fond of his food. He's shorter than Mason who's shorter than lanky Sharma. Wide face, stained teeth, big liquid dark eyes. Dark stubble – he just came back from a trip. It's difficult to tell this person's age. By now Sharma and Mason are both designer-stubbly.

Latin their language, they meet in an anteroom, from which the Dragoman swiftly absents himself, his duty all ended.

And Plan A goes into action. Mason produces a classic black plastic Casio school calculator.

"It's a table to teach the order of the Hindu-Arabic numbers," surmises Leonardo brightly. "I also see the oval zephirum symbol divided by zephirum." He's referring to the percentage symbol %.

"But for what purpose?" His voice is a tenor's, from an opera yet to be conceived. "These simple decorations – well, these might serve far more succinctly than words for the four fundamental operation." He means plus, minus, times, and divide. "Hmm, hmm!" His broad cheeks are pitted and reddish. Due to acne? To a past pox?

"Kindly hold this in your hand, Leonardo Bigollo Bonacci. With your fingertip please touch any number you choose."

"Oh." On the little screen an 8 has appeared.

Mason coaches the son of Bonacci to add a randomly chosen 9 to the 8, yielding 17 in the little screen, then to divide by a randomly chosen 4, yielding 4. 25…

"This *thing* knows my mind!"

"No no, the thing is performing, carrying out those operations *itself*."

Filius Bonacci isn't at all pleased. "This *Demon* may make my *Liber Abbaci* irrelevant! All the exhaustively useful exercises that I plan. By pure Algebra to solve how to divide equitably the coins in a purse which your slave finds while he is with you. For instance. Where does this *Afrit* come from? Is it from *Andalusia*?"

Talk about getting off on the wrong foot, talk about putting your square root in your mouth. Filius Bonacci is almost spitting.

Latin fails Sharma as his lingo barks out spontaneously in Toscano, "Lasciate ogne speranza voi qu'intrate!" Dante's damning doorsign to Hell due to appear upriver from Pisa a hundred years ahead. *Abandon hope, all ye who enter here*. Filius gapes and tries to crush the Casio.

From Mason, "Oh pardon us if my companion offends! Sometimes he suffers a sickness of the mind, namely *Parrot Voice*."

"Bloody hell!" protests Rajit.

Filius is so bewildered that his crushing ceases and he holds the calculator disgustedly as if there is dog shit on his hand.

"Two more of these black Afrits must be destroyed to preserve your *Liber Abbaci* for posterity, once written," Mason improvises, hoping for at least a degree of credulity regardless of how rational Filius is. "That is why we are here – to ask you to assist us by accompanying us," oh in for a sheep, "to our funduqa where those two Afrits are."

Risky, yet to reassure Filius: "You should bring your best sword or scimitar."

This is another misjudgement on Mason's part.

Leonardo erupts again. "I abominate all weapons. Would that the world were weaponless and that our only contests were of competitive trade. The history of this world is principally an account of conquests by the sword, massacres, mutilations, mayhem, invasions, crazy crusades, almost endlessly! We are murderous mad apes who pause from time to time to stare at the moon and make some science or sing a song. If only our bloody histories could be erased and replaced by bookkeeping. My dream is of accurate trade for profit and peace. I'm an accountant and I hate all the killing and mutilating! Arithmetic calms me, Algebra balms me."

Oh dear. The Accountant as Hero.

"Sword or not, we must hurry before it's too late!" chips in Sharma while the Filius is still filled with a passion.

Out from the Consulate the three men spill, Leonardo clutching the Casio pointing ahead of him like a lodestone, some hateful enchantment dragging him onward magnetically.

"This way, this way," urges Sharma.

He's puffy, is our plump Filius. Mason pants too. It's decades since he won his Blue at sport. Soon they're barely jogging, avoiding laden donkeys. It's only a kilometre or so, but with half that distance still to go Leonardo sags against a whitewashed wall. He wipes sweat from his pocked moon cheeks.

"Why the rush?" he gasps. "*Cur? Perché? Lii maadhaa?*"

Show Filius one of the infowatches? Demo the device as a fresh inducement onwards?

Though how to deter the Filius from mentioning something sensitive such as *Liber Abbacus*? And might Filius be enraged at sight of yet another type of Afrit worn on the wrist?

"Mayssssson," hisses Rajit just then. "Diego is following us."

"Eh?"

"Our Dragoman."

"Um. Is that from pure curiosity, d'you reckon?"

"What if Diego alerted Bugian officialdom about us as suspicious persons?"

"Hmm! Or tipped off the Pisans about our urgent yet rather *malinformed* interest in the Consul's son?"

"Are there many kidnaps in North Africa during this era?"

"Didn't you notice the boutique slave market in full swing in the northerly souk?

"Yes but that sort of kidnap doesn't *begin* here. Who could possibly want to kidnap an accountant?"

"How about *us*?" Mason holds his right wrist in front of Leonardo's face and utters his password: "Sophocles76." Suggestive of wise plus fame plus a parade. *Seventy Six Trombones Led The Big Parade*… Memorable! Mason's lingo necklace gurgles incoherently as an owl appears on the wrist-screen. Minerva, for wisdom. "Leonardo, ask this oracle anything you wish to know."

"But… about what?"

"Ask it what is the Golden Ratio. *Voice*, Watch!" A watchpad can do view-only, voice-and-view, and holo-projection.

Filius duly enquires in Latin about 'Golden Ratio'. In Latin the wrist-screen commences lecturing – and the Filius gapes in wonder. Smoothly Mason pulls away from the Filius so as to lead the perplexed though fascinated Pisan almost by the nose. Rajit notices that the Dragoman keeps to cover where possible as he moves up the street in pursuit, like some special agent of a medieval deuxième bureau. Maybe those cut-throat rivals the Genoans and the Venetians plant spies in Bugia?

At last, the squirrel skin warehouse! Work of a moment to unlock the door. All's as usual – there's no call this winter season for squirrel hats among sub-Saharan tribes. Mason drapes his chattering informatic arm around Leonardo's neck and hustles the Pisan within the warehouse – just as Diego starts to sprint athletically causing Sharma to fumble the key-device which tumbles from his hand.

At sight of the time transfer pod within, like some roc's giant egg from *A Thousand and One Nights*, the Filius digs in his heels but let's recall that Mason was once an Oxford Judo Blue. He can swing people over his hip in *ogoshi*, for instance. "Open the pod right away, dammit, Rajit! Can't keep Filius in a lock forever. Years since my sporting days."

"*Vaffanculo!*" or similar, screams the Filius.

Rajit: just forget about locking the warehouse door. Top priority is to scoop up the key then unlock the pod with it then help Mason push the Filius kicking and crying to the third seat.

Bad choice, Rajit! That warehouse door left open gives Diego enough opportunity to reach the pod door before the door starts to cycle shut – and to hurl himself through into the pod in hot pursuit. The Dragoman collides with Mason's rear, sprawling the Professor of Intellectual History across the Filius, knocking the noise out of the world's best ever accountant.

In case of an emergency need to escape, our time travellers habitually leave the pod programmed to return to its starting point in spacetime. (Plus or minus some quantum uncertainty.)

Rajit types in the letters ZYX to authorise, followed by an 8 to activate. (Codes for emergencies shouldn't be complicated.) The pod thrums. Immediately beyond the lone porthole is the black beyond blackness, may no light ever shine without. Gravity isn't. Accordingly Diego gently rebounds from the back of Mason who in turn gently rebounds from the Filius whom his padded seat in turn slowly ejects.

One foot hooked around his own seat. Sharma shouts in Latin, "We are all completely safe! Take hold of anything fixed in your vicinity. Try not to be sick. Don't panic. Try not to breathe wildly. I can explain what is happening. Please!"

"Yes!" agrees Mason as the sandwich of bodies opens up in a leisurely fashion. "Sit in the three seats available and fasten the belts. I shall stay unseated."

Tussling for seniority, are we, even *in extremis*?

It seems that some medieval persons are less chaotic than modern persons. The straitjacket proves unnecessary as well as impractical. The Filius and the Dragoman, soon duly seated and even buckled following Rajit's example, hark intently to Mason's sales patter about their journey into the future – resembling how the

Prophet Peace and Blessings Upon Whom leapt into the sky from Jerusalem mounted on the exotic beast Buraq.

At one point the Filius calls out, "But the Pope of the Millennium, the first French Father, Sylvester the Second, he already wrote a *Liber Abaci* two hundred years ago urging the use of Arabic numbers, fat lot of use that was. So why pick on me?"

"You, Filius," says Mason, "are slow-release therefore more effective."

Sharma remarks, "I recall that for us Hindus there's a 'vehicle-creature' similar to the Buraq beast, called a *Vahana.* When I was young I remember my granpop Gobinda driving deliveries around the Midlands – Granpop was the 'white vahana man'. That's how I know about Vahana."

To arrive totally, the time-pod must find a mostly empty inside-place to park itself.

The lone porthole now acts as a pinhole producing a camera obscura within the pod. A meadow bends around them – and a fleeting mirage of glass buildings, a sort of… science… *park*…? Can 'science park' be a place-name? As cloudy daylight shifts, so the memory of a mirage fades. Without achieving gravity to anchor themselves, they bounce.

A second attempt at touchdown and their camera obscura reveals…

…Oxford's iconic Broad Street of colleges with the Bodleian Library nearby, all those huge buildings neatly made of little red bricks. A few horse-cabs and a posh person-pulled rickshaw trot along – and oh gosh here comes a four-seater steamer car built like a glossy mobile coal bunker topped with seats sheltered by black bamboo umbrella stroke sunshades. A brown woman is driving two Asian passengers.

As this vehicle turns out of Turl Street into The Broad, outside of Trinity's gates a quartet of undergraduettes wearing academic garb of long black gowns and mortar boards suddenly unfurl a banner:

DON'T BE THE FOOLS OF FOSSIL FUELS!

The young ladies unfurl themselves too, revealing underneath their gowns bodices and suspender belts and fishnet stockings. Show a leg! An escort of supportive commoners applaud. A newsman, obviously tipped off, steps forward promptly to flashbulb the sexy soubrettes along with that banner and the steamer car. That'll look good on the front page of the *Oxford Mail* tomorrow. 'Students Pro-Planet-Protest'. Pop pop pop. Inside pages too. Maybe syndicated in the national dailies as well. Mission accomplished! Wonder whose coal-fired car that is. Perhaps the Vice-Chancellor's.

Hanging on tightly, Mason announces, "Same old Oxford."

Rajit Sharma seems less convinced, yet somehow he cannot articulate any doubts. It's like trying to hang on to your departing dreams as you awake.

A slight sideways shuffle, and gravity pins the travellers to their seats. The pod is inside –

"The Divinity School!" Yes indeed. A noble Gothic hall of red brick in Perpendicular style, part of the Bodleian complex. Tall windows and a highly elaborate vaulted ceiling. It's empty apart from two divines in dog collars who cling to each other in a daze at the pod's gusty arrival upon the tiled floor, venting steam from its external tubes and pipes and valves. All that steam power. No wonder the pod is nicknamed Little Dragon.

Mason chortles. "We did it, Sharma old son! We have Fibonacci! But who's this other chap here?"

"Well… he's Diego the Dragoman from Córdoba –"

Diego flashes Sharma a quick glance of gratitude; he's a bit overwhelmed.

"You'll easily earn a living, Diego," Rajit reassures. "Houses of Wisdom will interview you forever."

Mason scarcely has time to open the pod door before green-clad Chinese State Security Ministry women armed with bolt-action rifles rush into the spacious Divinity School. Soon enough comes a white-haired professor accompanied by a smart young suited Chinese male secretary followed by several lab-coated Chinese technicians. It's as if Lin Quinan or David Wang were anticipating this event or suchlike somewhere very close by. Yet they look puzzled by… who can tell by what?

"What about me?" calls out the Arithmetic Man whom no one ever called Fibonacci.

Leon Bonacci (b. 20?? -d. 2093 CE). Founder of the 'Bonacci' chain of 'EatEarly' Italian restaurants. As if miraculously, this savoury savant reclaimed from oblivion ancient dishes such as Sicilian Arab Rice-Pasta with Salt Cod, Eel with Custard, Saffron Rice with Almonds and Pomegranate, Chicken Marzipan, Frittata with Grapes, Fresh Tuscan Cheese on Tree Bark, Wide Thin Semolina Noodles, Barley Polenta Soaked in Milk with Rich Spicy Sausage, all accompanied by half litres of diluted spiced wines. These restaurants were famous for their slogan *You Can Count on Bonacci!*

– from *Gallery of Chefs of Genius* (Abundant World Publishing: Beijing 2143 CE)

The Chinese Time Machine

3rd Trip: The Emperor's New Wallpaper

"Moderate Prosperity," says Maggie Mo perkily. "This was our slogan to start with. The aim was to raise *every* last piece of Chinese territory up from out of absolute poverty." (Maggie is proud of her prepositions.) "All across our nation from Autonomous Tibet to the Xinjiang Uygur Autonomous Region. All of our provinces interlinked by ultrafast maglev tube-trains and superhighways! Even Taiwan under reconstruction linked by our new half-hour sea-tunnel.

"Then the slogan became 'Chinese Dream', so as to include Africans and Asians and many more ethnics along the Belt and Road trade routes, the *Yi-dai-yi-lu* – that's as musical as a solo flute phrase, wouldn't you say? But now we speak of 'World Dream' – a dream embracing all of the world that co-operates with our Way. Thus we pull our planet back from the brink of collapse caused by poisonous lunatic capitalism and military madness. The Dao rather than Dow Jones cum Dow Chemicals, as it were."

Mason and Sharma dutifully sit opposite Mo like students whom their tutor has invited along for a specially privileged supervision in the olde worlde 'snug' room just inside the front door of the Eagle and Child pub, where the Lord of the Rings once drank. Wainscotting on the walls. Three's company in that intimate space. Four would be a crowd.

To deter casual customers from popping into the pub and maybe overhearing, a couple of Mo's security women in smart blue tailored suits are loitering outside on the pavement playing stone scissors knife with real knives and real stones. From time to time sparks fly, but no fingertips. They're skilful and gung-ho, those Guoanbu gals from Guangdong. They work perfectly together.

It's a warm breezy April day. Fluffy clouds race through the blue. Some students are 'up' but it's not yet full term; young persons out and about must be postgraduates or prosperous full-fee-foreigns.

The trio within are partway through their halfs of Heritage Ale. Mason and Sharma hark attentively to Mo. Broken by Brexit thirty years earlier, England now relies on wealthy, velvet-gloved China. David Mason is an Oxford Professor of Intellectual History; mature, a bit gone to seed. Skinnier and younger dusky Dr Rajit Sharma – hair of gorgeous dark curls – lectures in Eng Lit subsequent to 1800 Common Era. On the syllabus for students of Eng Lit nowadays only Shakespeare survives from early times. Here's to the Bard with the most soundbites!

Of supreme interest to the cash-hungry home colleges of our couple of academic Brits, Maggie Mo oversees journeys from Oxford using the pioneer Chinese time machine. The Chinese deem it safer to set a time machine loose on the far side of the world from the Central Kingdom where lovely birds sing with joy on sapphire lakes; where pandas play like big furry toy idiots having fun in the sun, fun in the snow, while in all of the peripheral provinces ethnic-pride-within-reason inspires costumed dancing festivals of local identity, bringing beauty, happiness, progress: three benefits. Ethnics happily harvest tea in colourful ethnic clothes mostly of gaudy gold, red, and silver. Gaudeamus igitur.

"Do you think I might have a samosa?" ventures Sharma.

Maggie nods indulgently. "But of course. And one more round of halfs."

From Mason, "For me perhaps one of the pork pies they stock here from the Oxford Market, if I may?" Not any inferior mass-market products. The town's covered market is famous for its pork pies and game pies, gaudy pheasants hanging up in rows, homemade sausages full of flavour, and faggots.

Seek perks where possible, their respective college bursars advised the duo. Such is the mindset of bursars, cunning and greedy in the service of tradition. Which, indeed, is what caused the self-buggery of Brexit. This pub belongs to St John's College over on the other side of broad St Giles Street. Plane trees with blotchy trunks adorn both sides of a street which is mostly unblemished by vehicles.

Through the little pub window a parked Beijing Brilliance saloon is visible, and a cart minus horse, and some chained bicycles.

Maggie reaches into the breast pocket of her uniform for a crisp renminbi fifty-pound plastic note. Previously Mason and Sharma served Beijing's Institute of Time Studies well, and the name of Oxford University still has *cachet*. Are Mason and Sharma simply serviceable puppets? We shall see!

Sharma duly returns from the bar with a tray bearing halfs, a samosa, and a pork pie. No snacks for Maggie Mo; she stays svelte.

"*This* time," Maggie says while Mason and Sharma cope sophisticatedly with crusts and crumbs, "you will time-transfer to the island of Saint Helena to save Napoleon in exile from being poisoned by the wallpaper in his bedroom and his bathroom. Consequently Napoleon will live significantly longer. Or he will live longer insignificantly."

The sophisticated aspect of handling crumbly crusts is that anyone who ever hopes for a seven-year Fellowship at illustrious All Souls College – which uniquely has no undergraduate students to spoil an academic's career – will have tried to foresee all possible conundrums or conundra of etiquette which will be the ultimate test of his or her social suitability to become a fellow of All Souls for the next seven years. For instance, a bowl of fresh cherries is placed before you on the college dining table as your personal dessert while all other diners happily spoon up green chartreuse sorbet. There's no spoon for you. What the dickybird to do with those cherry stones without slobbering all over your fingers? If you swallow cherrystones, cyanide poisoning may follow. Do you nonchalantly spit the stones at the floor? Decades gone by, Mason tongued the stones into the breast pocket of his dinner jacket. He was thus, he liked to relate, cherry-picked for a Fellowship in History. Only one in fifty pre-selected supplicants make it this far. Or you may be served a soufflé sans dessert fork or spoon. A few pie crumbs is no problem.

From certain angles Maggie's face is that of a lovely mantis – her complexion creamish instead of green – framed by a silky black mane. Her face triangulates upon persons of interest. Sometimes she holds her arms poised mantis-like. Her Chengdu-manufactured 'Tchoo-Tchoo' patent leather boots wittily display maglev trains perpetually tracking around them. Such little details humanise the Han hegemony. Those are the grace notes in the mighty *Central Nation Symphony* (which is far grander than the older classic *Yellow River Piano Concerto*).

To the extent that Beijing's Institute of Time Studies is much known, it's also nicknamed 'Fifty Pathways Fortress' on account of an ancient building it uses which is surrounded by a stone maze. Too, because Time Studies is what you might describe as a protected or privileged political faction within the Party – which you only learn about by carefully studying the Party's bimonthly theoretical journal *Qiushi* or *Seeking Truth*.

"Save Napoleon from being *poisoned*?" queries Mason.

A superior smile. "By *arsenic* in his wallpaper."

"Yes of course," breaks in Sharma, who knows the Nineteenth Century like the bistre back of his hand. "That's well known. Fashionable green wallpaper was full of arsenic."

Maggie nods. "In his bedroom, in his bathroom. He soaked himself for hours in hot water that was constantly renewed, producing a fog of steam laced with arsenic. You'll change the wallpaper shortly after Napoleon moves in."

"I've never wallpapered anywhere –"

"Don't worry, I'll direct you. I'll be coming along in the timepod too."

"Eh? What? I thought you were too senior to risk losing –" Surely this cannot be on her own authority!

"But," burbles Mason, "you look so Chinese. And Saint Helena is, was, um, a tiny speck in the South Atlantic full of British soldiers and sailors. Will you wear a veil or makeup or what?"

"When you do your homework, you'll find that six hundred out of a population of five thousand on Saint Helena just after Napoleon arrived were Chinese labourers imported from Guangdong by your almighty East India Company. Cantonese Coolies. Enslaving black Africans was past its expiry date."

"Goodness!" exclaims Mason.

This exclamation, of surprise rather than of exaltation, may give the wrong impression of Mason's views. Those views are of course liberal, though no longer do they embrace the concept that *all* lives matter, demonstrably daft in a world overloaded with nine billion persons all demanding stuff. Yet oddly this compassion does accord, in a revised and realistic way, with the collective post-Confucian philosophy of Central Country China (including their anti-war attitude).

Moderate prosperity, as Maggie was saying earlier. *Xiaokang*, in a word, as announced by Deng Xiaoping. Uplifted by Xi Jinping to two words, *Zhönguó Mèng*. For Everyone Under Heaven. Maggie Mo quaffs more ale to lubricate her larynx.

"During the Cultural Revolution my grandfather, a singer of western opera, was sent to a far village for *five years* to pull up weeds, which ruined his back. As well as ruining his lungs due to smoking those weeds. How can I refuse to play-act the peasant for a few days?"

"Since you put it that way, we can hardly stop you. Though we shan't forget your real status!"

Maggie Mo utters a hollow laugh, as of a bamboo tube gurgling water in a garden.

"I have long been fascinated by that psychopath or sociopath Napoleon, who composed and orchestrated the deaths and mutilations of five or six million European persons. 'Vast lethal *ballets*,' some old filmmaker said about Bonaparte's battles. Many of the Emperor's victims shrugged off awful injuries merely because Napoleon directed them in combat. Compared with Napoleon the notorious Marquis de Sade was a benevolent sissy who scarcely harmed a fly. Yet the opprobrium of uncaring cruelty darkens Sade's name, never Napoleon's."

"Gosh, you really know your onions," says Mason.

After a moment's consideration Mo asks, "What does that phrase mean?"

"That means that you're on top of your topic."

"Why *onions*?"

Mason and Sharma are both stumped.

Maggie now chooses to confide, "Gents, this excursion to Saint Helena is by way of being a calibration test of realities. A new way to compare outcomes. Suspicions have arisen in Beijing as to the stability of engineering reality. We've chosen a sufficiently *major* event – namely Napoleon's death – to tweak, because his survival for a few more years should have *little* consequence. That is why someone senior in rank must supervise on this journey."

Sharma puzzles. "But how to compare one aftermath with the other aftermath?"

Maggie Mo replies, "Using quantum computer storage of quasi-parallel world-lines of historical data. Entanglement. We have a device now. That's all I may say."

"So this is like what, like Schrödinger's Cat in a Box?" says Mason. "But now with a black cat *plus* a white cat? And a peephole?"

"*Heisenberg's* cat in the box," Maggie Mo corrects Mason.

"Yes. Of course! Why ever did I say –?"

"The alternative wallpaper which we shall offer to Napoleon will be *Chinese*, far more charming and pretty."

"*Chinese* wallpaper was on sale just after the Battle of Waterloo?" from Mason sceptically.

"Evidently you need to start in upon your research right away. I shall allow you ten days. Chop chop! Belt and braces!" So saying, Maggie Mo drains all of her Heritage ale, compelling the same action from her couple of Oxonian crew; she's the undoubted cox. She coerces lightly.

Maggie strides along St Giles with her Ox-Brits, the security pair bringing up the rear.

"Psychopathic," declares Maggie. "Napoleon out on a stroll would shoot any beast that moved. Gulls on the wing, his cook's goats, the neighbour's donkey."

"Frustrated, would you say?" from Mason.

"Oh, mightily so."

"The authorities trusted him not to shoot islanders?"

"Nor the coolies from Canton, so far as history relates. You two being posh British officers is vital to the pretence. You'll carry special papers forged very recently in wet Whitehall."

They're nearing the Randolph Hotel, grandly Victorian Gothic. The Chinese time tech team occupy a complete floor of the hotel. Their timepod sits guarded in the emptied repurposed restaurant, a baronial-style hall decorated in a deep green hue, Brunswick Green actually, free from arsenic.

On the opposite side of Beaumont Street, crimson banners descend the long classical frontage of the Ashmolean Museum. Lively Chinese characters in brilliant white as well as harshly simple Britwords in brown proclaim Treasures of Autonomous Inner Mongolia, on loan for three months.

The bus to Brize Norton International Airport has just departed from the stop beside the Randolph.

Bidding bye to Maggie Mo at the glass and metal canopied entrance to the Randolph, Mason and Sharma head onward towards their colleges, Mason's being Christ Church College alias The House. The chapel of The House is the city's cathedral; talk about the gown lording it over the town. At Carfax crossroads (quatre faux, four forks) Sharma will branch off to the left down the High Street to reach University College, allegedly the first Oxford college founded; for a while 'Univ' could simultaneously be one college and the entire university.

Firstly, they pass along commercial Cornmarket Street.

Mason insinuates to his younger colleague, "Our Maggie should beware of Napoleon looming over *her* as well as over nations. I seem to recall Boney-part being quite the womaniser. Josephine wasn't the half of it." Mason guffaws – he can be a bit vulgar. "Unless, of course, that's part of Maggie's fascination with the Emperor."

Sharma looks worried. "*We* cannot question Maggie Mo's motives. She's top of the peck here in Oxford. Top of the pack, top of the pecking order. This isn't a case of Cock a-Doodle-Doo. It's *Hen* a-Doodle-Doo. She's a Han Hen, and she just bought me a samosa."

"Still, she can't risk endangering her position, eh Rajit my friend?"

Five days later Mason and Sharma meet for a lunchtime ale at the King's Arms just over from the Bodleian Library to wash down that pub's famous *Hare in Giblet Gravy Suet Pudding*, 37 renminbi quid each but China will pick up the tab. For the past fifty years the whole of this pub has been a registered rainbow-sexual Safe Space. The room where the two dons now ensconse themselves *used* to be a misogynistic *Gentlemen Only* snug. The prohibitory sign has long since vanished. One of Maggie Mo's blue-tailored security women already reserved this space and installed herself. Maggie will be along in person after the duo have sated themselves on the savoury suet pud. The security woman quietly reads a book full of characters and sips Chinese Chardonnay.

Before the suet pud arrives, Sharma murmurs to Mason, "This idea of Napoleon's wallpaper slowly poisoning him just doesn't hold water."

"Unlike the soggy wallpaper in his bathroom, eh Rajit?"

"Look, the upper classes back then used arsenic as a recreational drug. Like cocaine. To stimulate. To make you feel invincible. Arsenic was also used to kill rats. The stuff was lying around all over the place. Besides, Napoleon's autopsy showed he had stomach cancer, same as his father had. Which could have been due to constant stress. A giant gastric ulcer. The autopsy was professional and verified."

"No mention of gastric ulcers before our bestest lunch, please."

"So why is our Mag insistent on changing wallpaper?"

Mason rubs his roseate nose. "She wants a plausible excuse to become intimately involved with Bonaparte because he fascinates her?"

"I tell you, Mason, there's something dodgy about this mission."

Lo, here come their plates of upside-down pud, leaking preliminary dribbles of giblet gravy. Crushed carrots, celery-smelling lovage, and crispy shallots alongside.

"She's pretty persuasive," is Mason's last comment before tucking in.

On arrival, Maggie Mo chooses a Chinese Chardonnay too. *Goblet of Gobi* 2045 from Xinjiang province. Creamy finish, not sharp, just the way she likes her whites. Her white wines.

"How do we explain ourselves even *being* on Saint Helena island?" is what Rajit Sharma wants to know. In view of the umpteen British officers and soldiers keeping watch in case Napoleon tries to escape. In view of the trio of barquentines forever blockading the harbour; each ship with its own admiral, all of whom prefer to reside ashore. In view of eks, why, and zed.

"Have you forgotten already? Even as we speak, your own Ministry of Defence is impeccably forging top-secret confidential orders regarding your presence on Saint Helena, including myself as your Cantonese coolie. As I said previously. Eyes only. Copperplate calligraphy, authentic seals. Burn later. No historical record remaining. What's more, we'll be carrying an endorsement and authority from no less than the Prince Regent himself, dictatorial dissolute dandy George, autographed and royally sealed. As well as from Lord Bathurst, Secretary of State for War and the Colonies. London is so many weeks away by sea in the past. No planes, no phones, no cables for confirmations. Why even suspect a Frenchie escape plot involving *wallpaper*?"

"Ha ha," agrees Mason. "And this isn't even an escape plot."

A sip of the *Goblet of Gobi*. "Of course not. It's just a life extension scheme."

"Call me convinced. In for a pudding, I mean in for a penny."

"Good. That's settled. Soon we'll know what Napoleon Bonaparte really looks like."

"Eh? There are umpteen paintings of him! He isn't exactly faceless like that Fibonacci fellow was."

"Ha ha, that's where you're wrong. To Napoleon a painting of a hero should represent power, not a person. Accordingly he refused ever to pose. Josephine did once hold him squirming upon her lap for three whole minutes to help one painter but that's all. Other images of Bonaparte are guesswork. I intend to see his true face."

The two Oxford dons haven't yet done enough homework regarding wallpaper. So Maggie informs them briskly that back in the day the East India Company shipped wallpapers flat in long boxes, often to be tacked to a frame fixed to the wall. Whereas the time team will need to carry their own *rolls* of authentic modern repro Chinoiserie paper.

That's enough for now about redecorating period properties!

It's the height of humid summer in southern hemisphere Saint Helena, a thousand miles from Africa, a thousand miles from South America, away alone. Though not alost, no way neglected. On the contrary, strongly protected. It's the ideal stop for the trade ships of Great Britain's East India Company as well as for its *Britannia-Rules-the-Waves* Navy as regards revictualing and watering in between Canton *aka* Guangdong and prospering London town.

Poor Boney. Can he really be marooned here for the rest of his natural after being ruler of Europe but for the bloody (although admirable) Brit Navy forever getting in the way?

Were the French irreverent like Betsy Balcombe (and if they spoke Scots), they might well be singing:

"Our Boney lies over the ocean
"Our Boney lies over the sea
"Our Boney lies over the ocean
"Oh bring back our Boney to we!"

Betsy's speciality song, beloved of Boney, is *Ye Banks and Braes O'Bonnie Doon.* Betsy translated the words for him.

Some Frenchies still wish to liberate Napoleon; many others are sick of the whole affair and glad to have a king back. Mind you, there's always America, land of liberty, slavery, ambiguity, doubled in size by Napoleon's bargain-basement sale of unexplored former French territory to the new nation.

He's marooned, yet not alone! The renovated Longwood House, where rats still scurry, is no grand mansion. It's more of a modest two-storey-plus-attics farmhouse attached to outbuildings.

Reader, fifty persons of the French persuasion crowd into that modest habitation.

Impossible to deploy all these dramatic personae in our tale. Only a Bonaparte, master of armies, could marshal such a troupe.

For instance, there's General Henri Bertrand accompanying his Emperor in captivity.

And fiercely loyal Count Las Cases, pronounced "Las Caz", now in charge of furnishings which surely include wallpaper. A distant ancestor of his was granted lordship of all the homes – *las casas* – of defeated Moorish persons within view of the final battleground, tough luck for local Moors though presumably they could henceforth pay rent.

Las Caz's adolescent lad is too shy to flirt with teasing Betsy Balcombe.

Montholon is in charge (incompetently) of domestic staff who by night toss sweatily in cramped attics – intolerably stifling due to sun by day and hot air rising constantly up the house. Napoleon insists that fires should burn in each fireplace every single day regardless of season. Plus in the attics there's supplementary warmth from the many essential candles.

Montholon's demure missus softly sings Italian songs.

Then there's the mediocre chef Le Page as well as Pierron, the top master pâtissier, whose desserts are divine though sometimes disregarded – Napoleon will only permit twenty minutes during which to eat a dinner on the fine Sèvres chinaware. Worth a fortune, being bordered in gold, the Sèvres plates are exquisitely hand-painted with pictures of battles so that roast lamb lies upon realistically depicted slaughtered soldiers' corpses and broken horses and injured folk lying bloodied in agony.

The Emperor's librarian, Louis Étienne Saint-Denis, curates the Bibliothèque room which awaits the arrival of a few thousand additional volumes. Napoleon is devoted to Plutarch, Homer, French classics, and to Ossian, the supposedly blind supposedly Scottish Homer.

Never overlook valet Marchard, who needs no bed because each night he sleeps stretched out on the floor across his master's closed door.

Nor forget Baron Gaspar Gourgaud the braggart. Nor lamplighter Rousseau who crafts tiny toys. Nor Archambault the groom. Nor the enigmatic Polish person Piontkowski, whose reason for being in Longwood House is a puzzle to everyone, including to Admiral Cockburn who escorted Piontkowski there personally, thinking he was doing a good deed.

Full forty *additional* French persons of all ages cram into Longwood House, courtiers and servants. How different from the solitary existence of Rudolph Hess as the sole inmate of Spandau Ballet, no, Prison, Berlin, in the wake of a future European war, guarded by alternating teams of Soviets, Brits, Yankies, and Frenchies, until the day the prisoner finally dies aged 93. Or is murdered. Or is not. Some folks mutter that Napoleon is murdered in captivity aged 51, which is stupid seeing as the alleged perpetrator insists that fellow medical professionals witness him conducting an autopsy.

Chilly mists descending from gaunt mountains, roaming rats, the fug of fumes that wreath Boney during his very long baths may adequately conspire to carry off a redoubtable warhorse, let alone a stymied commander now afflicted by stress and melancholy and plumpness. Breakfasts are of boiled chicken or similar served on a wooden board across the imperial bath. Unlike the rigid rituals of twenty minute dinners, Boney lingers lazily over breakfasts kept warm by steam.

'Boney' is what Nap's favourite juvenile hoyden, mischievous pretty Betsy Balcombe – forever indecently showing a leg – calls him irreverently; which he loves and reciprocates with teasings and ear-pinchings and similar merriments. The fact of Betsy actually speaking educated French brought naughty herself and Boney together during his two preliminary months' of relative comfort at Betsy's family's place, The Briars, lent by her father to the French party, a far cry from the horrors of Longwood House to follow. Nowadays beauteous Mrs Balcombe, who reminds Boney strongly of Josephine, and headstrong daughter Betsy travel up by carriage almost every morning from their patch of comparative paradise to high barren exposed Longwood House, to visit their imperial French friend.

Longwood House is to become worse and ever more restrictive when horrid Sir Hudson Lowe takes over from the very reasonable Admiral Cockburn as Governor of Saint Helena, becoming Napoleon's jailor tasked to ensure that no more escapes occur, as from Elba. Due to Lowe's insecurity and his total lack of imagination, petty persecutions multiply, such as stationing British sentries daylong to stare at Napoleon as fixedly as their bayonets from as close at hand as possible, all part of the tension that finally causes a huge cancerous stomach ulcer. (Prompted by those fumes of arsenic.)

Subsequent to Napoleon's death, Sir Hudson does receive some of his just desserts when the forever loyal Las Caz happens to spot Lowe on a London street, promptly leaps from his cab and, even though no heavyweight himself, thoroughly horsewhips Lowe cowering on the pavement, as precursor to a duel which low-born Lowe is too craven to attend.

From stark Longwood, the only sea to be seen is empty of vessels. Way out of sight in sheltered waters facing the tiny capital, Jamestown, as many as fifty vessels might be at anchor, such is the vigour of trade to and fro between England and the East – and three of those ships will be those Royal Navy barquentines vigilant against any escape attempt by Napoleon. If an unfamiliar ship anchors, Royal Navy sailors armed with pistols row round that boat slowly all night long to foil any bid to abscond. None of this is visible from lonely high Longwood House.

Saint Helena is girt by towering cliffs. Few indeed are the places where any smuggler could possibly come ashore. Sliding into existence upon barren wilderness half a kilometre from Longwood House, the timepod evades any average lazy human glance by virtue of the latest newly-fitted Chinese tech, namely the self-explanatory Shimmer. What a long way time travel has come since the Chinese Academy of Sciences' Institute of High Energy Physics partnered with private Shanxi Ruitai Technology on the first Space-Time

Tunnel Generation Experimental Device. Now with added Shimmer invisibility, wow! It's ten in the morning, still misty.

It's wise to park their pod well out of the sight of anything but sheep. Yet also close-ish to Longwood House as regards humping rolls of repro wallpaper over to there.

Hang on. Is that full rolls – or simply *samples* from which Nappy can choose after being persuaded of the wisdom of banishing the arsenical wallpaper?

Rolls or Samples? This sounds like one of those great conflictive binary existential questions of Nineteenth Century Western literature – on a level with Stendhal's *Red or Black?*, Kierkegaard's *Either/Or?*, Surtees' *Plain or Ringlets?* So reflects Rajit Sharma PhD.

To ingratiate themselves, the visitors really ought as a courtesy to offer Napoleon a *choice* of Chinese wallpapers. You might think that a pattern book, easy enough to put together – say twenty samples – could have been a bright idea rather than hauling all those repro rolls. Yet from where would the chosen paper be sourced, eh? By buzzing back to Brexitland? Returning soon with the goods to Saint Helena? I'm afraid that Pauli's Exclusion Principle, as applied to time travel by Professor Lin Quinan of the Time Institute in Beijing, rules that out.

Using the good offices of the East India Company to order the chosen paper from Canton/Guangdong for delivery to Saint Helena might waste two or three months, allowing the mad martinet Lowe to arrive and take over as Governor, immediately thrusting his thumb in everywhere.

As for popping over to Canton/Guangdong in the time-pod, then popping back say a week later although not necessarily so much later as regards Napoleon, we simply refer once again to not violating Pauli.

In case you're wondering, Pauli's Principle doesn't apply to massless photons which can cram into the self-same space ad infinitum, which is how daytime is packed with revelatory light without black balloons floating in our field of vision. Or unvision.

Rolls! The travellers carry in the time-pod sufficient rolls for *two* different patterns (plus liner paper, et cetera). So here's another binary choice: Pagoda and Pond with Peacock *versus* Grotesque

Ornamental Goldfish (Fancy Fantails) amidst Soft Pink Weed. Both of those are charming and restful, unlike Napoleon's sanguinary Sèvres dinner service.

Wise, therefore, to park the pod within Shimmer out here in the wilderness. Note that the pod includes no toilet, nor are there beds, nor is there any galley nor pantry. For mathematical reasons their pod is compact. Especially so with a trio of persons aboard as well as a cargo of wallpaper. For basic sustenance they do carry some bottled water and high-energy protein bars. Travellers in time must mainly live off the land. Panda eats bamboo, panda shits in the woods, wrote Li Po. Or Poo. Or Li Bai. Or Bo.

"At a pinch we sleep in the seats," Maggie says brightly. Those seats may indeed pinch by dawn. "We use the world as our toilet, ecologically." She's disguised in a shapeless Nankeen tunic, coolie hat, straw sandals.

"Harrumph," utters Mason. "According to what I read, there's a boarding house in town."

Maggie nods. "Mr Porteous' place. The Government Botanist. With awful food and boards for beds, full of bored foreigners. Reportedly."

"We have to eat somewhere!"

"Gents, we shall throw ourselves upon the mercy of Longwood House. The French-speaking world and his wife are there. Nous pouvons manger de la brioche grâce à maître pâtissier Pierron. We have impeccable credentials. No one can peck a hole. Does anyone feel peckish?"

"Did your lingo necklace just activate?" Sharma wants to know. Surely Maggie can't be *that* good on her own, especially as regards pronunciation.

Ah, she has deep depths, profundities, has Maggie Mo, but here's a thing about lingo necklaces. You can't always be sure whose voice you're hearing, bearing in mind local noise suppression, voice projection, and other tricks.

Mason and Sharma must pose as British officers and gentlemen, using their own schoolboy French where necessary. They *cannot* perform perfectly.

It's well known that Boney's English is still atrocious at this stage. Admiral Cockburn and a few of his better educated officers do have an early go at coaching Boney during the eight weeks under sail to reach Saint Helena. Betsy Balcombe likewise at The Briars, also Las Caz who loathes 13-year-old Betsy for her impish irreverence to his sovereign leader. Ultimately Napoleon will read English newspapers, which arrive at Jamestown weeks late, in order to discover the world's ongoing opinion or lack of opinion regarding himself. However, he'll always persist in saying in English, "I want to cause you" meaning "I want a chat", French *causer*.

And how about Mandarin Maggie's Guangdong Speech, should communication with authentic Cantonese coolies be called for? Her Han-made necklace will cope perfectly. Whatever the local tongue, in modern China it's all Hans on deck *including* the fifty-five other ethnic groups comprising a small but much-treasured per cent of the Chinese people.

By good fortune or by bad, Mason and Sharma and Maggie Mo coincide with well-turned-out Mrs Balcombe and spirited Betsy the tomboy (ringlets rather than plain; pantaloons poking from short skirt) in their carriage on the way to visit Boney. The Balcombe carriage is a hooded two-passenger barouche tough enough for the rough roads, being whisked along by a single sinewy horse. A black groom rides a second horse alongside the carriage's steed to guide it. Of course the groom pulls the Balcombe barouche to a halt beside those two Army officers striding along the open road accompanied by a coolie toting two rolls of paper.

Mason's uniform is of the Royal Regiment of Horseguards, the very bees' knees of regiments. Rajit Sharma is a senior officer in the East India Company's army. Despite his choc skin Sharma *might* semi-plausibly have risen up from the ranks into European officer territory. This is a role and uniform assigned by ingenious and sometimes seemingly omniscient Maggie.

The private army of the royally chartered East India Company is *twice* the size of the regular British Army, its mission being to suppress and control, if necessary by massacre, uppity natives from India to China and everywhere in between for the sake of British commerce which accounts presently for half of the whole world's trade. From this vast empire of goods only self-secluding Japan is cloistered away by its divine Emperor, its great ruling Sho't'gun, and its samurai with supersharp swords.

So huge indeed is the trade-enforcing military of the East India Company that its private army supports three separate commands or 'presidencies', in Bombay, in Madras, and in Bengal. Sharma's gorget bears a Bombay badge; on Saint Helena he's unlikely to meet anyone else from the west of India.

"Good day, gentlemen," hails elegantly gowned Mrs Balcombe, for it must be she. "I hazard that you are *en route* to Longwood House as we ourselves are? Shall I request they send a carriage to collect you?"

So that's what Mrs Balcombe looks like. To Napoleon that lady is the perfect image of lovely Josephine, and with better teeth, although one hears Mrs Balcombe is a bit straight-laced, unlike daughter Betsy. No hope of consolation there. *Maggie Mo, are you aware of the risk of venereal diseases, eradicated by now from mainland China except in the Hong Kong Special Administrative Region?*

"Not at all, madam, not at all," replies Mason. "Your kindness is much appreciated, but we wish to cause no bother whatever."

Betsy pipes up brightly at Sharma, "May I ask, sir, are you a Sepoy?"

Rajit is an Oxford-varnished Brummy devoid of most Indian heritage apart from samosas. Byron is his bag rather than Brahma. He's well aware that Sepoys will mutiny in the same year as Anthony Trollope's *Barchester Towers* – the Sepoys' big grievance at first being whether the cartridges for their new Enfield rifles come in paper greased by pig fat or by cow fat, which they must bite open in combat irrespective of whether they're Moslem or Hindu. This, rather than racial inequality initially, but things get way out hand. The mutiny marks the end of the East India Company's mandate and the launch of the full-blown imperial British *Raj* – after which Rajit is almost named. Rajit literally means a brilliant, or a decorated, boy. On Rajit's pink jacket shine suitable medals.

Does Rajit the supposed senior officer of Sepoys wish to self-identify to a snip of a girl as a *native*?

While Rajit hesitates, fortunately Mrs Balcombe intervenes with a swift rebuke to Betsy swinging into, "Sirs, I do apologise for my daughter, whose manners may sometimes be amiss."

Little deterred, Miss Betsy asks helpfully, "May we transport those heavy-looking rolls onward to Longwood for you?" Betsy has at least noticed the self-effacing coolie.

What may those rolls of paper be, what may they be? Top secret military maps? Treasure charts? Oh to be able to peek inside. At this point the coolie of a sudden strides onward, clutching those rolls to himself. (*Conceivably* the coolie could be a she. You simply can't tell under the conical coolie hat and the shapeless Nankeen tunic. Yet a female hardly seems very likely. The Company didn't bring coolies here to start families. Different sort of labour in mind, indentured sort.)

"I say," Mason exclaims at the coolie taking such initiative.

"It appears," says Mrs Balcombe, "that a wind is springing up. We must proceed onward without proper mutual introductions."

"Mama, the officer can't be one's *usual* Sepoy –"

A click of her mother's tongue, and the nameless but free Black groom jerks the carriage horse into motion.

Damn it and drat. May that cheeky Balcombe girl be too inquisitive and meddlesome for comfort?

The timepod re-entered reality unnoticed well inside the outer ring of British sentry positions. A fair number of the 2nd batallion of the 53rd Shropshire Regiment of Foot circle Longwood at 12 miles circumference and a lesser number at 4 miles circumference. Standing at ease, those redcoated sentries maintain daily vigilance, eyes shaded by their tall stovepipe shako hats sporting big bright badges. For feeding and hygiene purposes soldiers spend off-duty time under canvas half a mile from Longwood. No expenses spared to contain Bonaparte.

Our impressive if windblown duo, strolling along with their inconspicuous coolie porter, first encounter the military a thousand yards out from where Napoleon is kept together with his loyal court… to whom, frankly, he can sometimes be a bit beastly due to impatience or boredom caused by his inherent superiority but never mind, he can certainly switch the charm on to enchant any entourage whatever.

A sentry with bayonneted musket steps back and comes to attention at sight of such exalted officers as Mason and Sharma. Sharma nods at the presumed Shropshireman, who might never before have been acknowledged personally by someone so superior to his own station. Rajit PhD cannot help but muse momentarily:

'God save the King' the soldiers sing,
From height to height 'tis heard;
And with the rest his voice doth ring,
Lad of the Fifty-third.

And now at the end of a lane of ragged trade-wind-battered gum trees appears Longwood with its tar-paper roof and much more life a-buzz around and about. Ah, there's the Balcombes' empty barouche, parked by tethering its horse to the groom's horse; those two animals cannot easily wander off together. Persons plural are doing things. The vista beyond is of barren rocks.

At the lodge gate of Longwood a British officer keeps the permitted visitor list as approved by Admiral Cockburn. This morning a certain Captain Poppleton is on duty, but the arrival on foot of two such exalted officers renders him uncertain. Yet who can gainsay a declaration of absolute plenipotentiary authority personally signed by the Secretary of State for War and the Colonies, Lord Bathurst? Likewise similar instructions from the Prince Regent himself! The bearers are undoubtedly senior British officers (even the brown Sepoy, maybe a Prince) as evidenced by their Oxford accents. Still, Poppleton asks the two to kindly sign his book before saluting them through.

Mason demands of a loitering flunky liveried in green and gold, "I say, my man, by which door shall élite British officers best enter for a private audience with the deposed French Emperor?"

The flunky gapes at this Colonel of the Household Cavalry, senior regiment of the British Army, in his bright red jacket with lots of golden frogging sewn upon his chest like the some bizarre double keyboard.

"Idiot," hisses the coolie *sotto voce*. "British officers are forbidden to refer to Napoleon as '*Emperor*'. You must only say '*General*'. Otherwise you open a can of worms."

"Sorry! I forgot. Spur of the moment. I mean with *General Bonaparte*, of course, my man."

"But I am not your man," the presumed flunky replies with a strong French accent, haut and elegant. Gosh green and gold, those are the French imperial colours, *n'est-ce pas?*

Eek. A giant of an earwig – shiny black with red legs – runs over the Frenchy's shoe and dives into a burrow.

"We carry credentials to present."

Promptly comes a Chinese whisper: "– as if within this house is a *monarch*?"

"Je ne comprends pas." Just as well.

To leapfrog, as it were, ahead, our two uniformed British officers are soon within the salon accompanied by their coolie, and encountering the Count Las Caz, almost fifty, along with the delicate lad who must be his 15-year-old son. Windowed to left and right are small weedy parterres.

Napoleon's Secretary is a polished chap of long and heroic heritage who made a fortune from a *Historical Atlas* which he penned in proficiently acquired English. Translating the atlas later into his own mother tongue, he made a further fortune. Curly hair, hooded eyes, aquiline nose. A fortune twice, his royalties being big enough to buy Las Caz an English estate to invite powerful new friends to for shooting parties, and later a French estate too.

The *Atlas* came after he'd fled revolutionary France to avoid being guillotined as an aristo. To the Corsican Emperor who restored France's former royal glory Las Caz unreservedly dedicated himself. Las Caz is one of four who brokered Boney's surrender to the Brits following defeat at Waterloo as being the preferable option to surrendering to the Russians, in view of him having caused Moscow to burn.

Likewise in a future war, officers of the Nazi Third Reich will flee westward to give themselves up to the Aryan Brits or better still to the United States Army with its chewing gum, nylons, and prime jobs for qualified war criminals.

"My dear Count," commences Mason, "I hear that your command of the English language is excellent. Accordingly, may I present ourselves to you, you being the closest confident of General Napoleon Bonaparte, to crave a very private audience, that's to say as soon as Madam Jane Balcombe and daughter depart? Particularly we would not wish Miss Betsy Balcombe to become privy –"

"That damned hoyden of mischief!" jerks from Las Caz's lips. Already the visitors have gained a brownie point. "Far from it, I assure you! *Loin de là!*"

"*Loin of the Lady!*" asserts Sharma's lingo necklace audibly, self-activating. Such problems can happen with devices.

"*Hein?*" enquires Las Caz.

"Nothing, sir," says Rajit. "I am –" and he performs introductions as promised, omitting the coolie.

From now on we shall not distinguish much between French and English spoken by mouth and English and French synthesised in the slim terabyte lingo necklaces hidden by clothing – unless any comic misunderstandings or malentendus ensue, or an imminent risk of discovery.

"So you are sent from London. Would that be by Lord Liverpool himself?"

"Behold who has signed and sealed our credentials empowering us."

Which Las Caz proceeds to verify. Heat radiates ridiculously from the fireplace.

"And with this extraordinary power you gentlemen propose to do what? To remedy the circumstances of my Master's confinement in this insalubrious maison?"

"Well actually, *yes*," answers Mason.

"Ah! In my own tiny room every night I hear the rats running within the walls. This place is not healthy for His Imperial Highness."

"Indeed," agrees Mason. "So we have come to replace the wallpaper in General Bonaparte's bedroom and bathroom."

"What? *Quoi? Nom d'un chien!* Are you insane? Two officers of highest rank with the mandate of the British Crown bring wallpaper – is that what your coolie is carrying? Wallpaper looking like two dry old baguettes?"

"Those are just two samples. Examples. Exsamples."

"*Quoi? Quoi?*"

"With respect, sir, you sound like a duck," burbles Mason. "The Emperor, I mean the General must, may, should choose one or the other, er, sample."

"You have been sent *to taunt*! *To mock*! *To ridicule*! Mon fils, va chercher la cravache d'Archambault."

Before the lad can run off to fetch the Groom's horsewhip, Maggie Mo pipes up in perfect Parisian, "We 'ave a message of great urgence for the Emperor." She tilts her head so that the Count can see her Chinese face, the bigger surprise likely being her gender rather than her race.

"Mon Dieu. *Mon Empereur*." As though those two entities are the same. Las Caz lowers his voice. "You come for His Imperial Highness? Secretely? To rescue him?"

"We may only explain to Himself," Maggie declares in English for greater secrecy in this house predominantly of Frenchies, loyal though those persons may be, even if some Belgian francophone spy is always possible. Top of the range lingo necklaces should be sensitive to intentions and nuances.

"Of course, of course. And the wallpaper is a cover."

"Yes, for the walls," says Mason. Perhaps it's hard for Mason to yield pole position…

"I meant in the sense of *alibi*."

Is Las Caz beginning to relax? Or not…

"I have not seen 'wallpaper' presented like that, although I am not a workman. Maps or messages could be rolled within. One roll might even be hollow and hold a weapon. I think we should inspect these strange baguettes of yours before admitting you to the Emperor's private rooms. In charge of security here we have an Orderly Officer –"

"– who wears a blue uniform braided in silver," Maggie interrupts, to divert an oncoming avalanche of paranoia which may indeed be justifiable. "I know all the details – and I assure you that Crown and Government did not send us as assassins! For instance," and she delves, "I already have a pistol," which she produces casually. "Purely to protect us."

"I was *not aware* –" protests Mason.

"Hush!" Yet Maggie winks at Mason brightly to defuse him. "I might need this to fend off advances."

Las Caz promptly presents his waistcoat-clad breast, as if to protect his God-Emperor. Las Caz does recognise the model of pistol. It's a Gendarmerie Year 9 muzzle-loader of very small dimensions as produced by the Imperial Manufactuary in Maubeuge and supplied to infantry officers as well as to gendarmes.

"Mam'selle, that pistol only fires one ball."

Sharma the quasi-Sepoy can't stop himself from muttering, "How like Hitler…"

"I assure you, Monsieur le Comte, that this particular pistol will fire many times." Ah, it's an authentic or a repro Regency flintlock-style compact pistol such as ladies might hide in their muffs, upcycled by Chinese tech. Alternatively it's a toy. One never knows with Maggie Mo. "Any attempt to open this weapon for inspection will cause it to explode. Shall I demonstrate multiple-fire?" Maggie points away from Las Caz's proferred chest towards the pine floor. Any ricochets should embed themselves in a plaster wall.

"The noise may cause armed curiosity… Permit me to summon my domestic servant with coffee while we await the departure of the Balcombes?" Given a nod, "Emanuel dear boy, please inform James Scott and no other person to bring coffee here swiftly for three. Be totally discreet. And then busy yourself *elsewhere*." To lighten the matter Las Caz adds, "No flirting with that Betsy creature, eh?"

Another leap of the frog, or tadpole, and in comes a mulatto man in blue and gold livery bearing a crowded tray to place upon a side table. The coffee mugs are of Nankin china.

"Excellent, James."

"You know you can always count on me, Count." The mulatto's English *is native English, Scots accent.*

The Professor never met a slave before. With crass curiosity he enquires, "Master James, are you really a *slave*?"

"British father, sir, free-born. The Count pays me wages."

"Do I detect a touch of the tartan on your tongue?"

That's one way of putting it. Not deigning to answer, the mulatto serves coffee, which Mason soon declares to be, "I say, not half bad!"

Of course it isn't half bad nor bad at all. It's subtle, elegant, exotic Green Tipped Bourbon Arabica brew, the seeds originally from Mocha in Yemen. Fruity with a touch of caramel. Here's a coffee for connoiseurs, who include Napoleon. Not what you'd expect to be served on a semi-barren island in the middle of the South Atlantic at this epoch.

Darky James Scott is now showing more curiosity than a mere servant ought, signalling with his hairy caterpillar eyebrows to his employer. It's high time to execute a hopscotch manoeuvre to jump ahead.

We pass directly to the Emperor's study escorted by Las Caz, who sends all the other occupants scuttling apart from Napoleon himself. Adieu to General Henri Bertrand, adieu to boastful Baron Gaspar Gourgaud – brusquely: off with you now to pot partridges for the *pot-au-feu*! – as well as to that Polish person who successfully insinuates himself into every damn place, Charles Frédéric Jules Piontkowski.

By now it's well after eleven in the morning, and Napoleon is attired – from head downward – in bicorne hat of black felt, then a shooting coat displaying the big Star of the Legion of Honour over a waistcoat of stiff white piqué. May this fabric reflect Boney's *pique* at his situation? The waistcoat with an ornamented pocket or so carries the red Grand Ribbon plus badge of the Legion.

A fire blazes here too, for Boney is forever cool – whether at home or in battle (except now and then when his temper flares). His short breeches of white twilled cotton are ample around the waist, above silk stockings – neat legs, those, and his hands are small, plump, elegant, dimpled. His bicorne hat hides most of his fine reddish hair. Pretty round shoes with little roses and gold buckles clad his feet. Whoa! What are we, a pimp? A gents' outfitter?

Plans of bygone battles litter half of the floor. "Ah, Count, I was about to call to dictate to you." Annoyed at this invasion of his privacy by blatantly British officers as well as by a lowly coolie, Napoleon ignores the uniformed pair and picks up an ornately enamelled gold snuffbox.

"Canaille!" he swears, *what a swine*. Such shapely hands he has. Between two stained fingers he rubs some snuff to dust, inhaling none. He sniffs the merest pinch, most of the snuff falling on to his waistcoat.

Mason bows to the Emperor, Mason being au fait with judo customs. Sharma follows suit, even though Commodore Perry hasn't yet forced Japan open like the shucking of the shell of a juicy oyster. Of kowtowing we shall say nothing yet, nor of other prostate performances. Or prostrate.

Maggie Mo saves the day inspiredly. Discarding her coolie hat, shaking loose her glossy black hair, she displays herself for all the world like Cleopatra famously being unrolled before Caesar from a carpet, symbolised by the two rolls of wallpaper tumbling to the floor. What a semiotic understanding of imagery! This is so erotically dramatic and dramatically erotic that Napoleon cannot help himself from reaching out to tweak Maggie's left earlobe.

"Aïe," cries her concealed lingo necklace en français. "But I am sure you can be gentil too!"

Maggie's French is so much more haut than Boney's Corsican French that he doesn't even notice how out of synch are her lips. Again, he tweaks her lobe with snuff-browned finger and thumb. She stiffens.

"Altesse Royale, I must speak to you urgently in total privacy. My military escorts need to remain here."

"I do advise this," puts in Las Caz. "I shall withdraw." Said and done.

"I am," says Napoleon, "all ears."

"Altesse, the wallpaper in your bedroom is poisonous –"

Immediately, "*What? How? Why? When?*" Justifiably, Napoleon is paranoid about being poisoned. That is one reason why he always drinks his wine watered, so that the bitter taste of poison may not be masked. That's why he hates garlic which might disguise a toxic addition.

"The green colour is owing to *arsenic*."

"So?"

"The extreme humidity of Saint Helena will transfer arsenic into the air you breathe, Altesse. But the transfer is even greater in your bathroom filled with steam that is constantly being replenished."

"How do you know about that?" Maggie Mo knows full well that the valet Marchand constantly extracts cooling water from Boney's bath and replenishes from a bucket heated on a fire of wood just outside a window kept open for pass-the-bucket, but this is a question awkward to answer. Napoleon pursues, "In which ship did you three arrive? *When?*" Stately, plump Napoleon's voice is notably masculine and harsh now.

"We came incognito."

"Incognito, two of you being so brightly uniformed?"

"Even so," declares Mason. And notwithstanding every last vessel being scrutinised. "We are not staying anywhere yet," he adds in his best academic French. "Nor have we arranged for lunch, by the way. It is so urgent to talk to you."

Napoleon is staring at Mason's lips contemplatively. "A question. How long does it take a man to die of arsenic breathed in to his body?"

"A few years, I think."

"*Years*. Yet it is '*so urgent*' to talk to me right now?"

Darting a hard look at Mason, Maggie intervenes. "Arsenic in the body makes existing ailments much worse. Stomach, *liver*." French people traditionally worry about the state of their livers. Mon foie, ma foi. "As soon as possible we must remove the existing green wallpaper and replace it with – I bring two samples between which to choose, Altesse. Permit me?" Picking up the first fallen roll, Maggie teases the tight tube open and hands it to Sharma. "Kindly display a full meter of paper."

Which Sharma proceeds to do, for Napoleon to behold peacock and distant pagoda amid feathery foliage upon a whispy white background.

"And now for number two... Kindly, General Mason, alongside."

No sooner said than done. Fancifully finny goldish in ornamental pools, pink plum blossoms dangling, a few white clouds.

Napoleon does raise a quizzical eyebrow at how compliantly the two officers follow the Chinese woman's instructions, but something else bothers him more.

"But but," buts Napoleon, "how can these flimsy scenes compete with the green and the gold of imperial France?"

"They compete by *not poisoning* Your Highness. Anyway, behold some light green colour in the new wallpaper. Behold some gold."

"A bold green is my favourite colour."

"It is your *death*. So which paper do you prefer? Birds, or fishes?"

"Need I decide this today, right *now*?"

"Indeed you must," chips in Mason as if on prompt. "We learned in London among high circles that Admiral Cockburn will not remain in charge for much longer. Any day now a mediocre martinet will replace the kindly Cockburn and enforce petty rules rigidly and restrictively and intrusively."

A violent high-pitched laugh jerks from Napoleon. "'Mediocre' is bad indeed, yet what is wrong with 'martinet'? Is a 'mediocre martinet' not a contradiction?"

Think. Think.

Fortunately, Napoleon adds, "Inspector General Jean Martinet drilled the modern French military into victorious shape even if his soldiers hated him for it."

Mason nods. "I was using 'martinet' in a pejorative sense, signifying unimaginative inflexibility. This may be your last chance to replace toxic wallpaper, Altesse. We can commence tomorrow *in strict privacy*, only yourself being present so that we are not overheard nor overseen. Fish, or birds?"

"'eads or tails. Pile ou face. I prefer birds."

Maggie smiles radiantly. "We will bring the peacock plus pagoda wallpaper then – around breakfast bath-time tomorrow?"

She cocks her head as if hearing something in the distance, and sings:

"Joli tambour pa rum pum pum pum pum
"Le tambour des soldats
"On sent son coeur qui bat
"Parum pum pum pum pum!"

Subtitles: Pretty drum pa rum pum pum pum pum The soldiers' drum One feels one's heart beat Parum pum pum pum pum.

Let's enchant Boney the way Betsy Balcombe does, and distract him from that nuisance girl. Napoleon gazes at Maggie, sufficiently smitten to reach out and pinch her ear lobe yet again.

With a sudden sweet smile of his own: "Bien sûr, jolie Chinoise. I shall send Archimbault riding to the Balcombes to request they postpone further visits for the next few mornings. I'm glad to have birds. I miss their music up here at Longwood. I liked the *bonny* birds beside The Briars."

Bonny surely must come from *bon.* Up here high on the *brae* there is no such bounty of birdies. Oh do stop missing Miss Betsy already! Does Maggie have *her work cut out* competing with a cheeky child? Not at all, for any tailor or carpenter with his work already cut out is well on the way, no need to take scissors to whole cloth, or a saw to wood; such a stupid item of popular wisdom, the opposite of true, well up there with serene swans paddling their giant feet furiously, the wit of idiots.

Birds abound where Boney dwelt for his first couple of months in exile. Birds such as plovers and noddies and fodies and finches and waxbills and weavers and doves and partridges, to name but eight, favouring sheltered spots surrounding The Briars. Chirp, coo, warble, whistle – enjoy yourselves, birdies. Seize the day on St Helena. As with Boney, there's nowhere else for you wee birdies to go to. You aren't albatrosses, those B52s of the seaways. You aren't footloose frigates who easily fly nonstop for a week.

Las Caz has the bright idea of serving lunch to the two high-ranking British officers in the library, which isn't yet occupied by the main mass of the Emperor's book collection. With the consent of librarian Saint-Denis, of course. As for the clever coolie, regardless of her secret status she must eat along with servants.

Lunch today will be boudins, puddings of top-notch local Chinese pig which the chef Le Page will overcook just the way Napoleon prefers his meat so as to eat it faster. Woodsmoke soon drifts thinly throughout the house thanks to the shabby construction of the kitchen chimney.

"Ah the odour of the camp fire! So much better than the stink of paint."

The pig puddings are best left undescribed except to say that Mason and Sharma take longer to stomach lunch in the library than does the Emperor in exile at his table. Consequently the two mock-military big-wigs are still at Longwood when Admiral Cockburn arrives. His curricle, harnessed to a pair of matching bays, has fair whipped along from Plantation House, the Governor's seat, tailed by two cavalrymen. Plainly Cockburn received a message from orderly officer Captain Poppleton whose duty it is to run up a blue flag each day when Napoleon continues to be visible in Longwood.

The trio of officers first encounter one another in the library. Noble nevertheless nice Admiral of the Fleet Sir George, 10th Baronet, sports an 18-button jacket with epaulettes, his bicorne hat worn fore-and-aft. Sir George disapproves of flogging and keelhauling sailors to keep discipline. When he burned Washington USA in 1812 he limited the destruction to upstart public edifices such as the White House and the Capitol, sparing private homes. He's an enlightened and compassionate Admiral. He married his cousin Mary.

Yes, Sir George Cockburn is a decent sort but he must maintain control. The two-month-long sea voyage south to Saint Helena saw quite a battle of wills between Boney and Sir George. One of the first things Boney did on board the vessel heading south was to tweak Cockborn's ear, as he would the earlobes of any of his own entourage – an act of condescending pseudo-affectionate dominance – and Boney would have persisted in this were Cockburn not fluent enough in French to cause Boney soon to desist.

Cockburn scrutinises our team's top secret forged papers of introduction and instruction with much care. Since this world lacks telephone and radio and mail planes Sir George can only conclude, "Sirs, the Prince Regent signing in person – I must assure you of my co-operation, or at least of my impotence to hinder whatever your endeavour may actually be. Of this I would dearly appreciate an inkling, so that I do not disturb any action of yours, which must not, I hope, include the demise of General Bonaparte nor any of his court."

Mason hastens to reassure Cockburn, "Of that you may rest assured, dear Admiral." Oops, isn't 'Dear Admiral' Debrett's advice on how to *write* to an Admiral rather than to *speak* to an Admiral? Cockburn seems more intent on flicking glances at Sharma, though not in a condescending manner since the Indian officer is vouched for from the very top.

"It is plain that you are British officers and gentlemen of the highest standing." (*Yet why have I never heard of either of you? Never so much as an inkling.*) "May I enquire as to where you will reside on our island? Surely not here, crowded as a henhouse, ha! I *believe* there may be a room at Plantation House available to share, along with breakfasts and coffee and whatever you please."

"Nay nay," neighs Mason, "there is no need to fret on our behalf. The fewer people who see us around and about, well, the more discreet shall be our mission of which we cannot speak –"

"– of which thereof," Sharma adds, "we must keep silent."

"Is that a platitude from some Greek philosopher?" asks Cockburn. "We didn't pay much attention to Plato in Navy School. Oh and may I enquire on which ship you arrived? I fear that my vigilance may be at fault!"

"Regretably, Admiral, we must withhold *exactly* how we come to be here."

"*Approximately*, then?"

Mason mops his brow with a handkerchief; a fragile cage of embers in the grate is radiating red heat. "Sufficient unto the day, Sir, sufficient unto the day."

"I, however, have a duty to our Monarch and to our Prince Regent and to his Prime Minister to think of the morrow. I hear tell you are accompanied by a talented *female* coolie who speaks fluent French?"

Do walls have ears? Do doors? Do windows?

How might Jane Austen's dashing Captain Wentworth, bolstered by prize money from the Napoleonic Wars, handle this confrontation? In Austen's novel *Persuasion* Admiral Croft is plainspoken and amiable, in some respects like the astute and sensitive Admiral Cockburn except that the fictional Admiral Croft is retired. To the best of Rajit's recollection, an ailing Jane Austen is finishing *Persuasion* around about *right now* – plus or minus a year – some four thousand miles due northward. Nearly due northward. That's nautical miles.

An acknowledged expert upon the Nineteenth Century, author of *Walter Pater's Mater* (OUP, 2035), Sharma should now lend a hand. Yet just as he opens his mouth to improvise Cockburn gestures at the side table, "And what, pray, might those rolls of paper be? Might they be charts?"

Charts stir up suspicions of some scheme to help Napoleon escape from St Helena, which cannot be further from the case.

Let's hope that Admiral Cockburn forgets about the cosmopolitan coolie from Canton!

"What those rolls are, sir," improvises Sharma, "is the reason for our visit and also for secrecy. Those rolls are wallpaper ordered from the Company for Windsor Castle by none other than may I venture to say His Mad Majesty."

"But His Majesty is almost blind and he lives in seclusion."

"True! The wallpaper is an embarrassment to the Prince Regent. Consequently the Prince Regent consigns the wallpaper to redecorate the residence of the captive who complains shrilly, so we hear, about his circumstances." Is any of this sufficiently plausible?

"Um, yes. One does rather walk a tightrope between command and constraints and compassion."

As might a conjurer by the way of distraction, Mason seizes and unrolls along the floor repeating fancy fantail goldfish in pools of very translucent water.

"Behold, dear Admiral!"

"I say!"

"Our mission," continues Sharma shamelessly, "is to carry out an extravagant whim which also serves the body politic. The Prince Regent's spending as a patron of the arts and architecture, such as, um, the Pavilion in Brighton, is… sumptuous. Not for us to question!"

"I shall assign one of my escort to assist you –"

"Nay, dear Admiral," from Mason, causing a raised eyebrow. "Refusal may offend yet refuse we must. We report only to the Prince Regent, as you have read just now in his very hand. The Regent's writ runs full and far."

Therefore there may be no further probing about how they come to be on the island as if out of thin air; nor about their anonymous oriental companion.

After Admiral Cockburn has gone away, deeply dissatisfied though impotent to interfere, Mason easily commandeers a big British army officer's bell tent to be loaded on to a cart (plus docile nag) for the trip back to the timepod. Along with hay for bedding, which the horse can eat too. Plus a firkin of drinking water. And a take-away of thoroughly boiled beef with baguette. Former denizens of the tent can sleep on the floors inside Longwood.

As they draw closer to where they left the pod camouflaged by Shimmer, cloud descends from the bleak grimly looming gaunt mountain named The Barn which blocks most view of the sea. Thick vapours spread out.

Mason and Sharma relieved their bladders back at Longwood with that greater ease which males enjoy; Maggie Mo not so. 80-odd years earlier, one of Rajit's 'guilty-pleasure' poets wrote the climactic line, "Oh Celia, Celia, Celia sh*ts." (Celia being a cliché pastoral name for use in poems during England's previous, Augustan age.)

Maggie is scrupulously far cleaner and sanitised than most sweaty Gweilos, if one might venture the Cantonese word for ghost-white foreign devils. Mason is excluded from Gweilo category by virtue of his distinctly rosy countenance, as is Sharma exempted by a dark aspect. The point of this being merely that all of us are animals and should bear this in mind with due realism; there's nothing sordid about this Chinese Celia. In fact it's her pleasure on certain occasions to stroll with friends wearing traditional Han clothing, Hanfash, which is so serene and light and pastel compared with the garish jangling reds and golds and silvers of fancy dress celebrating less widespread ethnicities, not unlike the tartans dreamed up for defeated Scottish clans engulfed within Great Britain.

Maggie centres herself upon her exact present location and upon her chosen direction, then she walks away into rheumatic cloud. All landmarks, such as the horse and cart, vanish.

In the sparsely grassed ground a rabbit hole appears serendipitously, burrowed at a perfect angle for popping into fast to escape a hunter's gun. Perfect likewise for pooping.

An apology, first, to the gentle and resilient Rabbit presence.

As Maggie squats, the pre-death wisdom of Tang Dynasty monk Tripitaka comes to her – Tripitaka, also known as *Three Baskets* due to being loaded with insights.

Form isn't real. Form simply isn't. Perception, reflexion, action, understanding are all unreal. Eye and ear and consciousness are all unreal. Consciousness by way of five senses is unreal. Enlightenment is unreal. Unreality itself is unreal…

Rising, she adjusts her tunic, and returns towards exactly the same compass point, or at least so she hopes.

Her point of origin seems to be receding into the distance like a ship drifting away, its deck somehow stretching out further and further. For a moment she almost calls out – *Mason! Sharma!* – to locate the correct angle for her approach. A reply from even a quarter-degree askew might seem too thin and far away. If only one of the Brit buggers would call out to her, establishing exactly where they are. But they're both being non-intrusive. Why indeed should they intrude upon her?

Duly the bell tent looms through the cloud. Behind the tent are the cart and the horse. That tent is a sizable cone of cotton canvas and can sleep three or four, though not tonight. Two academics in military fancy dress *cannot* possibly have erected that tent during the few minutes since Maggie marched off. Complete with guy ropes, pegs.

Impossible! Yet there it is, job done. Tent erect and fixed.

The two British officers appear from behind the bell tent.

"Guys! How quickly you put up the tent! How long was I gone?"

She feels herself being dragged into their frame of reference, as if by ropes. By guy ropes.

"De rien," Mason answers Maggie chivalrously, which tells her precisely nothing.

"I'm serious!" Maggie insists. "How long was I gone?"

Sharma displays uselessly his silver Regency fob watch on loan from Oxford's Ashmolean Museum. "You didn't ask us to time you."

"Did you not have *any* trouble with the tent?"

From Mason, assertively: "Had it up in a flash. Right, Rajit?"

"I'm assuming," says Sharma, boots trailing straw, "that gentlemen use the tent tonight – and the lady the timepod?"

"Of course. The horse uses the heath. Make sure you hobble the horse."

Sharma looks downcast. "I'm not sure how one hobbles a horse."

At which Mason scoffs, "There were you running on at me the other week about the merits of some foxhunting squire as a comic novelist!"

"Servants generally stable one's horses after a ride."

Maggie bridles. "Excuse *me*!"

"Surtees is brilliant at evoking vast cooked breakfasts after a morning hunt! A far cry from our cold beef baguette."

Maggie Mo senses that she has settled into a, let's say *familiarity*, a *stability*, in the way that worlds whip around a star heeding a choice of similar attractors in very nearly Newtonian fashion though not dictatorially so. Already this insight into one's framework is fading – as is the daylight.

Morning, and it's damn hot in Boney's bathroom, particularly for the two British officers in full uniform. A wooden breakfast board bearing scraps and skin of today's overboiled chicken plus scraps of omelette is hastened away. No silver nor gold implements at brekky time for Napoleon – he prefers to eat with his fingers, where and whenever practical. Bathwater degreases fingers perfectly. His valet tops up with another steaming bucket from the fire burning outside of the open window, and Napoleon wallows warmly, sensuously comfortable for now.

"Ah, ma chère Chinoise. Et avec *Chinoiserie*, si je puisse inventer un mot, si je puisse annvent a wort? Où est le papel peint? Where eez ze wallpaper?" Corsican subjunctives and Anglais still way beyond Boney's grasp; thanks be for lingo necklaces!

A coy glance from beneath the conical coolie headcover. "My two valiant escorts already placed all the rolls of peacock paper in your bedchamber." An activity which raised a bit of a sweat in this hot house.

"Yet now I ask myself why I did not select for my bedroom birds, but fish for my bathroom – so as to enjoy *both*?"

Instead of obeying binary opposition, quite, reflects Mason professorially. The one or the other. The raw or the cooked, the boiled or the roast. The days of Claude Lévi-Strauss and Structuralism still lie a century ahead, although for Napoleon here on Saint Helena tropiques are already tristes.

Fortunately Maggie answers this fair point rather than Mason. "We might have needed to *insist* on an audience with your altesse on the pretext of your altesse *choosing* between fowl or fish." Given their potent credentials, the trio could have required virtually anything toot-sweet, but here and now isn't a time for splitting hairs.

Maggie instructs Mason and Sharma, "Off with you both now to strip the existing wallpaper from the chambre de coucher. Do not interrupt us for any reason."

Napoleon dismisses the valet with, "I feel adequately hot enough for now, thank you, Marchand. Marchons. Marche!" Marchand marches off, neglecting to shut the window, whence came the hot bathwater. Is Marchand miffed?

There seem to be expectations. Maggie and Boney are alone together. Hot haze hangs throughout the room as in some Turkish hammam. Maggie inhales enthusiastically.

"Tee-hee," queaths she and claps the window shut. Casting off her Nankeen tunic, her flesh veiled by steam, she squeezes into the bath up against His Majesty – the selfsame bath that accompanied Napoleon to Austerlitz, to Moscow, to Waterloo! Over what ensues we must draw a steamy veil.

After due discreet delay we may perhaps press an ear to a keyhole…

"Oh la gloire elle va partout," enthuses Maggie. "Glory, she is everywhere to be found. In every land and in every age. Or at least in many places and times. Allons chercher la gloire, Mon Altesse!"

"With a less stiff flagpole just for the moment, ma chère," from Boney.

When the horse trundles the cart away towards the tent that same afternoon, bearing eight walls' worth of allegedly toxic wallpaper stripped by the boys from bedchamber and bathroom, Napoleon Bonaparte lies concealed beneath, dressed in his most commanding famous green chasseur cavalry uniform, the jacket worn at Waterloo, decorated with frogs, star of the Legion of Honour prominent. Sabre at his side along with black bicorne felt hat. In a leather bag he brings some personal items. In this escape bid Las Caz is more than a willing accomplice. Let Britishers cast him into a cell in chains later if they care to! Let them put him in front of a firing squad of musketeers!

"But how did you persuade him to abscond?" Mason growls low at Maggie as he clicks the reins. "And why? And where to? And why? This isn't at all the mission you briefed us on!"

"You should consult Sun Tzu on the arts of dissimulation and distraction."

"When I realised what was up, I almost intervened but I hesitated."

"Just as well, Mason, just as well. Know thy place."

"Guts for garters." Mischievous of Sharma.

"I simply can't believe that Napoleon agreed so quickly and so easily."

"That's because I made him feel glorious."

"Ahem. Sparing one's blushes, isn't Bonaparte absconding from Saint Helena rather a *big* change, compared with removing wallpaper? Good heavens, now you might never be born because of that butterfly effect business! Nor might I be born!"

"In that case there's no you to notice any difference."

"But wait, might I suddenly snuff out? Or worse, slowly snuff?"

Maggie giggles. "It's Boney who'll finally run out, precisely of snuff. Lucky he isn't an addict. His fingers just like something to play with." Be damned but everything seems to have a double entendre. Only later under Queen Victoria do people become prissy.

Sharma intervenes, quite the Regency or Sherlockian gent. "I hazard that the whole raison d'être of the wallpaper was always for our fugitive to hide beneath it, Colonel Mo, Madam. Arsenic be arsed."

"Ha ha. Ingenious."

"So therefore we're going to take Napoleon in the timepod to somewhere significant *for you personally*, regardless of what your Party superiors –"

"Hush, if you're wise." Maggie pats her tunic where the upcycled pistol is and nods at the wallpaper from which now come noises.

"Button your lip, boy," snaps Mason.

Smiling, Sharma persists, "I'm guessing that by now our non-oriental faces and Brit uniforms have served their purpose – which is to spring Boney free. I presume *we shan't* be taking Boney to the New World, just for instance."

"Are you angling for another samosa, my clever Rover?"

"That was the name of my dog!"

"Yes, I know." Maggie winks. "You were fully investigated before I offered you interesting work."

"Oh. Well. Let's say I wait to be amazed."

"And amazed you shall be. I do value moderately intelligent companions, Rajit, David too. Though remember about my krav maga."

The wallpaper begins to heave. With impatience? Or with the need to breathe fresh air?

"Dash me," from Mason, aside to Sharma, "you're right."

"Shhhh."

Napoleon's chasseur uniform doesn't imply that they brought any chicken chasseur along in the cart in a pot for later on, nor even his preferred chicken fricassé.

Nor indeed famous *Chicken Marengo*, allegedly improvised in a farmhouse following the battle from which Napoleon brought *gloire* home to France, bringing to the restaurants of Paris at the same time a new plate of sheer concocted propaganda. No such post-battle farmhouse *ever* was, no such hen chopped up with a sabre, no garlic which Boney hated anyway, sweet fanny rien in reality. But a legend was born, which Bonaparte was still polishing at The Briars as regards the order of battle that glorious day back in 1800. When you need to hide an emperor becoming portly under a pile of paper there's no opportunity to bring a picnic hamper too! Inspector General Martinet might disapprove of the lack of forward logistics, yet Colonel Mo knows best.

"Nous sommes arrivés, Altesse!"

"Yes, here we are," agrees Mason. Here's the bell tent within middling to much mist. A newcomer may well ask "So where's 'here'?" since nothing else is easily visible, merely tricks of light. Mason and Sharma help Napoleon descend from the cart. The ex-Emperor stares at that solitary tent while Maggie plucks some stray hay from his clothes.

"But I expected a boat of the air, of the sky!" Napoleon accuses her. "*Canaille*!"

"Sire," says she, "look beyond the tent, a little to the left."

"That reflection of sunshine inside the mist? Or is it refraction?"

"Yes, Sire, that Shimmer. Scintillation. Vibration."

"Mon dieu! There is more! There is form. Shape hides there, unseen."

"Rajit, free our horse to wander wherever. David, set fire to the wallpaper to puzzle our pursuers when they come."

"Bit damp, Mags." Mason is presumptuous.

"I am not magazines, Prof dot Mason. If in doubt, address me as Colonel Mo. You will find a bottle of surgical alcohol inside the tent, and a Zippo. Chop chop, belt and braces. Boney will need to use your seat in the pod. You can squeeze upon the floor by the door. While in transit, hang on tight."

After his spoof elevation to high Army rank, poor Prof dot Mason is taken down a peg or two, booted from his passenger seat. Don't forget how the Han people themselves were down-pegged during the past couple of centuries after initiating true civilisation.

Mason catches up from dragging all the wallpaper from the cart. He has signally – or indeed the very opposite! – failed to start any fire even using surgical alcohol. However, the mist disguises the absence of smoke, so Mason chooses to confess nothing.

Hat on head, sabre at side, stately plump Napoleon enters with assistance the time-pod.

"I only see one window – one porthole – set in this door itself."

"Windows are a place of weakness," Maggie explains. "We cap our porthole tight during travel through what we call the Many Possible. Please take the left-hand seat. Apologies if it's tighter than a campaign bath."

Oh that sudden bright grin on Boney's face. He touches the curving wall of the pod.

"This is a seamless barrel. Of ceramic beautifully polished."

Mason grimly lowers himself into his lower place.

"I have dreamed," Napoleon confides, "of conquering all of South America one day and of moving the Vatican to Paris."

To which Maggie replies, "You will surely rejoice in how large an empire we shall soon acquire, with ample room for extension."

"With you, ma chère, at my side."

"Almost so, almost…"

From Mason, "Where and when are we taking Napoleon to, for such a huge empire?"

"To China in minus Two Oh Eight."

"What do you mean, Centigrade –?"

"I'm so bored by BC and BCE and PC. I want a new system. Year One of Maggie Mo. M1 like a motorway. Bye-bye to all that Jesus Mohammed monotheist madness."

"Except for jealous Jewish Jehovah," Mason reminds her.

"And except for Ahura Mazda," adds Rajit. Being so Brit, he's probably thinking about famous Freddy Mercury deceased, Zoroastrian fire-worshipper.

Maggie opens a small panel unfamiliar to her crew, spins a dial, adjusts another dial with scrupulous attention then flips the cover off a bright red button and blows upon her thumb before pushing the button. From a drawer alongside she produces a lingo necklace which she quickly instals on Boney as well as naughtily tweaking his earlobe.

"Aïe!"

"Is puffing at your thumb a good luck thing in China?" asks Mason.

"Just dusting off my thumbprint," is the amused answer.

"*Canaille*," Boney utters in amazement as he hears French. After a brief bout of "Zut alors!" and "By Jove!" he gets the idea. "Why should anyone bother ever again to learn a second language!"

"A lingo necklace isn't suitable for poetry," says Sharma.

"Oh poetry! Oh divine Ossian!"

"Oh dear."

Rex quondam Rexque futurus? (In the Nineteenth Century and in the Eighteenth and earlier, quality people can quip quotables in Latin.) So: Napoleon Bonaparte as the Once and Future Ruler? He's certainly an *ex*-Emperor – but will he necessarily be a future Emperor too? Does Boney detect tables turning? Or is he distracted by marvels?

Gosh, at their Chinese destination Latin will still be a language newly on its way up in the world – even if travelwise Rome lies many months away to the west. Napoleon surely knows of the future Marco Polo route to Europe, soon to be known as the Silk

Road, Via Serica. If Boney is successful in huge China, will he feel tempted to out-Alexander Alexander the Great – or will he be reined in? As well as reigned over.

Thank goodness for Chinese timepod tech and for its use responsibly. Such as testing the consequences of a change of wallpaper before trying any major change to history. Nobody could have expected this deviancy from Maggie Mo who is conservative enough in her clothes in a communist way, and classical as regards Hanfash.

As the timepod insinuates itself via vibrating strands of Were & Where & Whereunto and Why, bouncing a bit, there's just enough time for Maggie to deliver a quick briefing to Boney, which benefits the two Brits likewise.

Bugger the tyranny of alliteration!

In minus 221 Common Era the Warring States period is at an end. For the first time one Emperor, Qin Shi Huang – him of the upstanding black caterpillar eyebrows, droopy black handlebar moustaches, fierce black beard, and lavish sideburns – rules the once rival kingdoms of Chu, Yan, Han, Zhao, Wei, Qi, and Qin. After persistent wars the new Qin (= *Chin*) Dynasty formally unifies all of *China* – add an *a* on to *Chin* and what do you get! (Actually, the answer is Terracotta… but hush!) Welcome to the Central Country of the World, making its first great leap forward.

Shame that Qin Shi Huang dies in September minus 210. Shame that Huhai, aka Qin Er Shi, inherits as soon as Qin Shi Huang's prime son and heir comes a cropper.

In the existing historical record, Huhai leads onward to the great Han Dynasty which kicks in from minus 202 to plus 220. By minus 130 the expanding Han Dynasty will establish the Silk Road, in use until 1453 C. E. when the Ottoman Empire boycotts trade with China.

However, *no way* is horrid Huhai a shame for Maggie, nor for the world's greatest general now with added lingo necklace. By the way, the lingo necklace is heuristic; it can learn fast. Its chip is programmed with Classic Chinese, now to be trialed in the field – as well as many other languages, including English, French, Italian… How likely are they ever to need Lakota Sioux, for heaven's sake?

Here and now in minus 209 there's a very good chance for a clever and well-informed woman to supplant the hated and foolish Qin heir and become… an Empress of China. *Legally* no woman may ever rise to the dizzy height of supreme leader. Such is against the way, contrary to the dao. But hey, nine centuries uptime the drop-dead gorgeous charismatic concubine Wu Zotian manages to become the effective long-reigning Empress of China by cunning and luck and ambition and flashing her assets and by murder; as we said, Wu's drop-*dead* gorgeous. Maggie Mo may well make it to the top.

Maggie tells the Oxonians, "I shall programme the timepod to take you two fine Brit officers back home to Oxford 2050. As Rajit correctly guessed, you served your purpose by helping me liberate my continent-conquering general."

"Bally Hell, Sharma, you were right!" exclaims Mason, amazed once again by his junior colleague. ('Bally Hell' is a chip-on-the-shoulder snark at Oxford's Balliol College noted for its superiority.)

"I shall be perfectly at home in old China if marooning me bothers you. On your return to Oxford 2050, ask any of my Guangdong gals to connect you with Professor Lin in Beijing. This assumes that 'my' gals are still on guard duty. Though if you both emerge from a genuinely Chinese time machine –"

"– there must be a Time Institute in Beijing?" ventures Sharma.

"More or less."

"Tell the Professor or his fenshen –"

"Eh?"

"Tell his alternate identity that I chose a Great Leap Sideways rather than a rabbit hop. It isn't only for personal glory as an empress that I do this, but to make the Chinese Empire glorious so that all its citizens achieve with guidance happy fulfilment centuries ahead of history. Thus my grandpa is uplifted." Is a tear welling, or is it getting hot in the pod as they travel further presumably than any previous pod? Is there friction in a long coil of spacetime?

Further discussion is cut short by a shudder quite like a colon collapsing into a full stop. We have arrived. *Nous sommes arrivés.* That didn't take long. Maggie undogs the porthole cover and peers out.

"Oh yes," she says. "Up, up, my general, and join me. Prof Mason, squeeze past into the vacant seat. I'll have you two off to the future in two shakes."

"Hang on a mo, Colonel Mo," protests Mason. "We have arrived *where* precisely?"

"From the looks of it, near to where the Bing Ma Yong is waiting to be buried. The Terracotta Army."

"What? What? What? We're going to see the Terracotta Army?"

Maggie shakes her head. "We don't have time yet for tourism."

From Napoleon, "Did someone mention panna cotta?"

"Even so, I would love to see old China for a while if that's allowable!"

"Count me in," agrees Sharma.

"Ha ha. Old China versus fancy brickware?" While she distracts them with some nonsense, she's busy thinking pros and cons fast to judge by the flutter of her fingers.

She purses her mantis-like rosebud lips. "One of the reasons I shall feel at home is because Qin is the era of so-called Legalism. The only way that a giant country can stay unified for the moderate prosperity of all is by all of its citizens obeying the same strong social rules. Previously, Confucianism affirmed the innate goodness of people and thus was *laissez faire* in its attitudes to morals. Out of the need to unify by conquest, the brutal Qin Shi Huang swept Confucius aside and strictly enforces an identical rulebook of behaviour throughout his expanding realm."

"Gosh, sounds a bit like Sheep Ping's Communist Party –"

"Xi: a benevolent imposer of the best life available. My fear is that you may inadvertently offend against strict social laws before my General and I can secure our position."

"I shall fully heed local etiquette. Did I tell you how I coped with cherries during my All Souls fellowship dinner?"

"Qin era Legalism could be a bit more complex than Oxford."

From Boney of a sudden: "Myself, I am accustomed to an entourage. With familiar officers in my entourage I shall feel *plus confortable* – even if those officers are British."

Hmm, support in high places.

Maggie inclines her head. "Yet I myself must offend radically against the legalist rules. Hmm, to distract attention a colourful blunderer or two might be useful. The whole secret lies in confusing the enemy so that he cannot fathom our real intent – so says Sun Tzu. Request granted. May I not regret it."

Welcome to somewhere in the vicinity of the city of Xianyang, capital of China in the year minus 209. A couple of millennia and spare change uptime, the supercity of Xi'an houses twelve million persons. Right now, a smaller though quite spectacular Xianyang exists to north and south of the river Wei.

Our four protagonists are outside the timepod, inhaling the air of an earlier millennium. Clouds are whispy and high like osprey feathers lightly brushing over eggshell blue. The sun says it's earlyish morning. The pod emerged beside a modest prominence which its passengers mount.

It's as if a vast convulsion has passed across the scene hereabouts. Behold much trampled reddish dirt of great excavations. What looks to be a miniature walled city encloses a smaller walled city which itself surrounds an earthen pyramid vaster than the Great Pyramid of Giza, by the looks of it. For many *li* thereabouts a workforce hundreds of thousands strong has been rearranging the terrain like ants. In the far distance umpteen forced workers still labour on, enemy prisoners and slaves and criminals.

Only to the north is there untouched scrubland. That's the route to the river Wei. They'll use the Wei to reach Xianyang by water, so as not to arrive exhausted.

CHUN, comes a twang like a heartbeat. Is that a signal from somewhere? Why has the timepod placed itself hereabouts? For what reason of resonance?

That great mound must protect and conceal the mausoleum of wonders of the expired Emperor. The Great Geezer himself. Within there should be a detailed scale model of the unified Chinese

Empire. Mercury fills miniature rivers and lakes and the seas offshore, plus there's a moat of mercury around the tomb itself. Tonnes of toxic mercury, all told. How the mercury may gleam by the light of fish oil burning perpetually long after the closure of the mausoleum roof, across whose ceiling pearls represents stars accurately positioned.

So many years to make a model of all China. China is already such a giant that when the emperor died during his fifth tour of a southern province, he was *two months* travel away by road from Xianyang his capital. Two months.

The first thing that Napoleon, veteran of so many battlefields, spies to the east is…

"*Sentinelles!* Sentries!" Thanks to Saint Helena, Boney is well sensitised to sentries on the lookout…. for himself. These sentinels in the distance are clad in yellow, and just now Boney may be the least visible of the four travellers in his chasseur uniform, almost demure compared to Mason in bright Brit red and Sharma in shocking pink. Not to mention the reflective silken whiteness of Maggie…

Maggie has quick-changed from Cantonese coolie clothes to graceful Hanfash classic historic attire. Her previous garb as a coolie was superior to the coarse hempen tunics of Chinese peasants in minus times, but now she must dress the full part of Empress-to-be, being escorted by the greatest of Generals. Her gown is voluminous white silk with cross collar, the masculine Yang-side fringing tape crossing over the Yin-side border tape to minimise feminine Yin. A broad sash cinches the waist.

"For sure," says Maggie, "we're near to the vast necropolis of the defunct Qin Sin Huang – along with the huge terracotta army fully armed with actual bronze weapons."

"Mais qu'est-ce-que-c'est this terracotta army? I never hear tell of any terracotta army!"

"Of course not, mon général, the army remained buried until the late Twentieth Century. A complete life-size army of thousands of soldiers. All seeming to be unique due to mass production of a whole range of body parts which are then assembled so as to appear unalike.

"Qin Shi Huang was but a juvenile King of fifteen years, already megalomaniac, when he ordered the beginning of preparations for his bones. Sixty square kilometres of necro city all for one lad."

"I feel 'umbled… almost."

"By now the mausoleum must be nearly ready to receive his remains and be sealed – and the vast verisimilar army in their trenches to be covered over with dirt and hidden away."

"I say," exclaims Rajit eagerly, "*please* may we go and look? Maybe a bribe for the sentries?"

"Those same sentry soldiers will loyally shut up within the burial mound all the hundreds of workers and artisans still present here to starve to death to preserve privacy and secrecy, so a bribe would need to be large."

"Incidentally, Colonel Mo," Mason interrupts, "how much money do we have with us? And in what useful form? Golden Sovereigns? Silver Maria Theresa Dollars?"

Maggie produces a suede bag on a cord from beneath her attire. Suede, to soften the bumping of bullion against her body – which may be muscular and firm-fleshed enough to resist; Boney ought to know.

Maggie shakes coins into her palm. All the coins are of gold. Useful for persons staging a coup d'état. Universally welcome.

"Mind you," she says, "this is merely some seed money to flash around, otherwise I wouldn't be able to walk. There'll be so much discontent in the capital and in the countryside. The huge tax burden, for one thing. The forced labour. As soon as we get rolling I'll mop up much more wealth."

"May I suggest," suggests Sharma, "that post-haste we buy a couple of horses and a fair-sized carriage for yourself, Colonel Mo, plus a robust steed for General Bonaparte to make a good impression."

"A steed, indeed!" agrees Napoleon courtesy of his lingo necklace. It imitates his voice well.

"Hmm, it'll need to be a *strong* horse…"

"Madame, I am not excessively fat."

"No," agrees Maggie, "but horses hereabouts aren't strong enough for a soldier to sit on. That's because of a selenium deficiency in the soil right across Han China. Chinese horses of this era can only manage to pull things. Only the barbarian Uygurs of the western plains rear horses mighty enough for warriors – to be exported to China at high cost." She grins. "There'll be a horse market in Xianyang."

Another thing: all of the gold coins are prominently engraved on one side with pandas, looking cute or moronic depending upon one's attitude to pandas.

Sharma coughs. "Did your Guoanbu gal visit the Ashmolean Coin Room? I'm sure I saw these there."

"Each year my country presents the newest set of gold panda bullion coins to Oxford University as part of our, um, munificence. Technically the coins are on loan."

"What do the coins say on them?"

"Zhonghua Renmin Gongheguo. People's Republic of China."

"What will people here think of such a name," from Mason, "if they're literate?"

"Maybe that we're from a rich independent kingdom continuing to hold out against unity, named the Panda Republic of China."

"Was the panda worshipped back here in the BCE or something?"

"Ha ha. People killed pandas for the pelts. Sleeping on a panda skin keeps ghosts away. And it eases a woman's periods. No wonder our calendar never featured a Year of the Panda – that's all upfuture image branding. I don't mean we brand pandas literally."

"Perish the thought! That would spoil the pelt."

"Ha ha, Rajit. Ah but now I'm having an idea about pandas…"

Several spear-carrying sentries are paying heed far off and beginning to holler. From her right-side sleeve capacious as a pelican's mouth-pouch Maggie plucks little opera glasses made of mother of pearl with brass. Nodding his appreciation of their apparent quality, Napoleon reaches to take the binoculars from her, him being the military strategist. Gracefully Maggie yields *les jumelles* just a sentry kneels, sights, and fires a crossbow. The arrow, its bronze head twinkling in sunlight, falls well short of our travellers, but even so. A few more arrows follow suite from crossbows.

Boney's uniform does feature a pocket in the brief bolero jacket, but that appears to be occupied by a small snuff box. The buttoned waistcoat underneath the bolero jacket is stretched smooth, including its little pocket. Uttering a "*Canaille*," Napoleon thrusts the binoculars back at Maggie who gestures urgently with them across shrubland away from the tomb complex. Time to make themselves scarce!

Behind them they leave a pod so stealthed it is barely even a shimmer.

Cicadas are making a raucous din. Fit Maggie takes the shrubby terrain in her stride, Napoleon likewise despite the onset of portliness. Rajit copes; Mason soon huffs and puffs. There's relief half way: within the shrubby wilderness they come across a number of human skeletons in peasant rags, bronze-head arrows still sticking into them.

"Why leave good arrows?" gasps Mason.

Maggie hazards, "Presumably the arrows got buried deep in flesh, and a chase was afoot. These bodies may have been fleeing from conscription into the necroville workforce. Alternatively curiosity or greed prompted them to stray too close."

Not much later, they encounter many more raggedy skeletons tangled upon bushes as if a flood passed by post mortem.

After half an hour more, salvation comes in the shape of a barge, upon the river Wei as we suppose. Towing that barge upstream towards the city plods an ox. A lad on foot swats the beast's fly-pestered bum with a thorny stick. The cargo is tiles. Midships along the boat is a tiled hut. A burly boatwife tends the tiller rising at the stern.

Actually, doesn't some Qin Dynasty law among the many thousands of stringent laws insist that oxen are reserved for work in the fields? As close as this to the capital city, maybe not so. Granted that here's a river with a constant current and not a canal, but you might expect a team of puller-people to be wading through mud or shallows roped to the barge to pull it… Hmm, even roped folk need some rice to eat. Ox has to have lower running costs.

The male bargee is roused by his missus from his snores in the hut amidships. He waddles ashore along a judiciously placed plank. He's tubby and bald. The sun shines from his scalp. Maggie offers the lowest value gold panda coin she has. Impatiently Napoleon rattles his sabre, maybe we should say scabbard.

"Yes, boatman," Maggie's lingo necklace declares, "in exchange for that golden coin as in legend, we wish to *buy your boat* as well as your services."

The maybe-a-brute scratches the button of his big belly through a vent in his tunic as he summons up his intellect. Surely the bargain is a no-brainer, consequently his woman should stop looking so intent.

"Lady," the bargee asks Maggie, "are your reddish companions with the wrong eyes and the big swords *demons*? The grey and blue one too?"

What's the best answer to this?

"You are observant," Maggie observes, followed by: "You might say so."

On the boat, the bargee's missus is nodding impatiently. No other vessels are in sight, although the Wei does wind out of sight very soon in both directions.

"Assuming that you are the owner of this barge," specifies Maggie legalistically.

"Why else should our home be *upon* this barge?" That isn't exactly an answer. "If you don't think I'm the owner, you can wait for another boat to buy. But I hear a signal bell from the forbidden land you came out of. Another bell replies from nearer by. And a whistle." True. "This boat needs to move along whether you board it or not. Boy, get busy!" The bargee steps back on to the boat, keeping hold of the coin, be it noted, nor yet withdrawing the plank.

"We have a deal," declares Maggie. "We own the boat. Our blades will assert our rights if need be."

All very well to say so. As our team totter on board, the bargee remarks, "I notice you did not simply kill us and take the boat, keeping the son to serve you."

"If only!" from the boy who goads the ox to plod onward.

"Accordingly, Lady, *rules* must limit your tame demons."

"Unfilial child!" shouts the mother.

"I could become a scholar! If you did not keep me at the shitty bums of oxen."

"Run away then, Son! Ancestors will torment your dreams! That's only *one single* ox you have to tend, which you know full well goes to market as soon as we reach Xianyang."

"Does the boat *not* include the ox?" demands Maggie.

The bargee scratches his belly. "Who needs an ox to go *downstream* on the current? On the way upstream an ox is added value as regards the main cargo it hauls. Ox will nicely feed disgruntled fancy folk of the city. A fashion for richer foods begins to arise. Ox heart, ox tongue, ox steak, ox cheek. Ox as food in city is worth more than using it to plough or pull a barge."

Damn these low cunning peasant economics.

"Boy," Maggie calls to the resentful lad on shore, "your Mama may well have saved your life by steering you away from scholarship. I recall how the late Emperor buried hundreds of scholars alive for keeping classic and Confucian scrolls hidden instead of bonfiring the books. Unless the books were about forestry or fortune telling."

"Shut up, stupid Lady!" bellows the bargee. "There are laws. There are the listening police."

More whistles or flutes give tongue out in the wild terrain, away from which they're now heading at a rate of four or five *li* per hour. Estimated time of arrival in Xianyang: about dusk. Already another barge looms into sight downstream, this time pulled by horses.

Flocks of migrating red-crowned cranes flap past along the river. In a land as large as China there's always somewhere far distant for big birds to migrate from and to. Cranes are auspicious. The big red-crowned crane represents immortality. Did the dead Emperor eat thousand-year eggs of cranes? He was obsessed with elixirs of immortality. Everywhere he quested for cures to mortality. He may well have poisoned himself fatally. If an alchemical cocktail fails to perform, you can always bury the alchemist alive to ask in the afterlife for a better recipe.

The enormous, ostentatious trillionaire mausoleum, the scale model of China underneath the mound, the huge Terracotta Army: these are *actually only Plan B*. Plan A was Alchemy, much cheaper but in the end lethal.

Maggie rallies. "And if these laws went away, eh? Would you be less afraid?"

"*Will you shut up*! That story about burying alive is simply untrue. A slander."

The boatwife reaches to touch Napoleon as if this wrong-eyed creature must be felt to be believed – and damn it but she tweaks his ear lobe.

Boney utters a "*Canaille!*" – immediately followed up by a dazzling smile. Quick thinking, Nap. Can I canoe you up the river…?

The Wei they are on soon reveals itself as only one of the ways of the Wei. Now and then floods force new courses. The less-used branch they were on now rejoins a main trunk of water which is crowded with traffic, trade on the move, vessels sporting big oars and tilted square sails, more desirable than any barge. Sizable vessels, doomed to sink into oblivion unrecorded by any painter. Parties are happening on some decks. Nice-looking palace over there, and is that a vineyard? Already we're in the city outskirts which are far-flung.

If they only had walked for a while until reaching the confluence, our party might have bought or hired a much more impressive boat. On the other hand Maggie Mo might not have learned about this new appetite for ox meat amongst 'disgruntled nobles'. It seems that important families are still resentful many years after being forced to move to Xianjiang to populate an imperial capital city adequately. There's one large pissed-off group to call upon for support.

Now the river has come to resemble *Along the River During the Qingming Festival*, that Song Dynasty masterpiece by Zhang Zeduan where a silken scroll of happenings compels the spectator onward as if in a narrative. Zhang's river is most likely the Yellow River. A lengthy panorama scroll such as *Along the River* compresses distance by selecting for depth of spaced-out detail – same density of data, dude.

A stray memory from schooldays surfaces in Rajit and he finds himself muttering, "River Song." That was before he put away immature things in favour of Coleridge and Co. In Xanadu did Kubla Khan. A stately river ran.

"Way down upon the Congee River," burbles from Colonel Maggie like bubbles from a goldfish. "Rice pudding beats porridge any day." Has the time-trip wobbled Mo? If so, a bowl of congee is called for! Congee is the congenial 'Mama's chicken soup for the soul' of China, even if a particular bowl contains no chicken.

Comes the height of the day, which means rest for Ox as well as lunch in the form of rich lush grass irrigated by narrow channels leading from the river, akin to oxbows. The first Emperor, along with his long-serving Chancellor Li Si, not only upgraded and standardised roads throughout the Chinese Empire but also took ingenious measures as regards water transport. Future floods will wash away all traces, but for now flat wooden bridges span these channels, allowing parking as at an uptime service station, plentiful free grass for beasts to munch, as well as ingeniously permitting boats pulled by persons or beasts to overtake one another.

Ox needs a lot of food and eats slowly, but the time is accounted for. Set free, Ox sets to stolidly.

Bonaparte tells our two senior British officers brightly: "I should put you through your paces. We may see action soon."

"Our paces?" from Mason. "Are we horses?"

"Sabre work, sirs! Your best cuts. Sparring. Have at you." Bonaparte draws his blade.

"Hang on," from Sharma, "I never held a sword in my life."

"I was in the Oxford University *Judo* team," blusters Mason, "not fencing."

"You are *Gentlemen* but you never handled a bladed weapon? What the devil is Jewdough? Some sort of Sabbath bread?"

"You must realise we aren't real army officers –"

"In future, soldiers use guns that fire very fast and deadly."

"Really? Name three of those guns!"

"Um, the AK-47. The Kalashnikov."

"It is Russian?"

"Yes."

"So I burn Moscow and the Russians proceed to make the world's best known firearm."

"Forgive me but didn't the Russians themselves burn Moscow? Scorched earth policy, hmm?"

"*Canaille!* Two more famous firearms of the future, please."

"Smith and Wesson Double Oh Seven," says Mason.

"That isn't right," whispers Sharma.

"Tommy Gun –?"

"*I* at least shall practice!" Losing patience, Napoleon ascends the well-laid-out cargo of timber along which he advances, swishing, left arm tucked neatly behind his back. Reaching a limit, he promptly faces about and returns along the topmost cargo, only puffing slightly. Passengers on passing vessels gape in wonder or in bewilderment. The bargee's burly wife licks her lips.

Evening is drawing nigh and the darkling river Wei is like the Milky Way crossing the vastness of the city illuminated here and there. Constellations prickling above seem to copy the very architecture of walled lantern-hung sprawling palaces and pavilions and mausoleums hugely strung out across the land amidst grassy-hued wheat fields connected by walkways and causeways, even incorporating minor mountains where stone stairways lead up to temples. Some palaces have gardens and terraces that can seat ten thousand summoned visitors or officials. Pretty maids simper all in a row, thousands of courtesans dream of opportunities which will only bless one in a hundred of them. The place seems fictitious, although factual. Unseen, jewels and jades are scattered along paths like pebbles upon a beach. It would be tedious to list all the palaces such as Xingle Palace or Wangyi Palace, but Boss Bargee does indicate the direction of the enormous imperial Xianyang Palace several dozen *li* distant halfway from the Wei to the River Jing where rotten Qin Er Shi roosts in the innermost private palace and where his cruel eunuch puppeteer Prime Minister Zhao Gao viciously orders killings of any possible opposition along with the extermination of their entire families.

One wonder of the world worth mentioning within Qin Shi Huang's sprawling palace way over there is or are twelve robed humanoid giants of bronze. Each giant weighs 60 tonnes. That's 1000 *Dan* also known as *Shi* named after you-know-who. Standardisation! Rules! (Alternatively, it's 12 Asian bull elephants.) Those colossi are made from the confiscated and melted-down weapons of, successively, the Han, Zhao, Wei, Chu, Yan, Dai, Wuyei, and Qi kingdoms following defeat and assimilation. Qin Shi Huang is quite the collector. Each colossus resembles him closely, minatory as a minotaur, mighty-jowled, brazenly moustached, and each wears a peculiar imperial hat resembling a flat oblong umbrella with little beads of rain dangling from either end, or maybe those are twin fly-screens of seeds or beads.

A little further along the Scroll that evening, well within Xianyang: "Greatest Lady, best for your purposes is for us to stop by the Old Heng Bridge, close to which is one great market if we lead Ox over Heng to reach the north side of the Wei."

Accordingly they moor at another filling station so that Ox will appear more perky at market in the morning of its likely last day of life. Then Boy comes aboard at last to flop into his midships home.

By now light has all but gone, apart from a bright sickle moon. River traffic has quit travelling. Before too long there'll only be lantern light and silver starlight to halt one from tripping into the flow of the Wei – the passengers' toilet incidentally, even if they do own the whole boat. Oh what's the betting there's a chamber pot inside the tiled hut? At least it shouldn't rain overnight. Bonaparte's designs upon Maggie seem incompatible with the surroundings.

Mr Peasant Bargee presents himself before Maggie Mo in all her Hanfash elegance now less visible.

Bargee scratches his skull. "If I may speak, Great Lady. Likewise my landlady or waterlady or shiplady. Our humble quarters are at your ladyship's disposal overnight. Specifically the bedding. Wife and Boy will sleep on deck upon some coats. Myself, your servant, will sleep suitably like a dog or a slave across the bottom of your bedding. You may warm your feet upon my servile flesh."

Mason snorts. "Well there's an offer you can refuse."

"Why should I refuse this offer? This obeisance pleases me. Be assured, chivalric Don Mason of the erstwhile Black Dan belt, there will be no funny business. For I am a mistress of Krav Maga, black belt five Dan."

"Well, whatever this Krav Maggie stuff is, I'd still watch your pandas."

"Who is this Krav Maga person?" demands Napoleon. "Ah, I see! You try to make me jealous, my naughty Chinoise."

"What's more, Great Lady, I have at your disposal a whale-fat candle, although just now I have no way to light the wick. The candle fell off the back of a handcart heading for we-all-know-whose tomb."

"How can you know what sort of thing a whale is, so far from the sea?"

"A *jeeng* so far from the sea is no longer one single thing. It is many separate things. I'm not one to mistake a deer for a horse."

Maggie claps appreciatively at his wit. "I'm sure I can light the *lajoo* candle if needed." Maggie's mock-antique gun has several functions. The gun's inside her left-hand sleeve-pouch. Its weight balances the opera glasses on the right. "Thank you. I shall reward you. And Son too."

Sharma looms from the gloom. "With respect, Maggie Mo, did you know your grandfather well? Did you know him at all, even?"

"Ah, so you've been counting years! Yes, I did have that privilege, and I knew even then as a very young girl what a privilege this was, even if this was soon cut short by time."

Sharma confides, "I couldn't even talk with my own Gramp although he lived in the same house with us in Birmingham. He only spoke Punjabi."

To cut a long Scroll short: next morning we're in that great bustling market which only a century ahead will be the starting point of the Silk Road itself.

Spices to the right of them, utensils to the left of them, medicines, ducks, knives, shoes, cloth, clothes, bales of silk, scribes, carriages for ponies or persons to pull, copper pots, caddies of teas, ceramics, and terracotta, spices, persons female and male including kids manacled to posts guarded by eunuchs; entire families are enslaved to punish legalistic offences during these Qin times. Unpopular! No jolly red and gold paper lanterns; not invented yet.

In her elegant silken Hanfash garb Colonel Maggie Mo rides upon Ox, led by Boy. This is a great brainwave of the Bargee's. The trustworthy Ox serves the celestial Jade Emperor who is ruler of all thirty heavens as well as of Earth. Ox often journeys between the Jade Emperor's throne room and the Middle Kingdom to carry out special missions.

Preceding Boy is the demon General Bonaparte. Solemnly he swings his sabre just above the orange tiled floor as if scything wheat. Thus ceremonially he clears the way for Ox with Maggie mounted. Impossible to misinterpret the swish-swish. Watch out, ankles, even those clad in straw or leather.

To either side of Ox, demon Generals Sharma and Mason in their flamboyant pinkness and redness escort the beast, their drawn naked sabres shouldered as neatly as possible without cutting into military fabric or into carotid arteries. Behind the flicking stinking tail of Ox, Bargee and Missus Bargee follow humbly.

Such a sight isn't seen every day. Mind you, far more spectacular sights are seen in Xianyang not to mention some ghastly sights too! Yet not such a fine lady bareback upon an ox. Eloquent lady, too. As transpires presently...

Word spreads fast. All sorts of people come running from all quarters, agog.

And now, beside the bean paste vendors, Maggie pulls from within her pelican-pouch sleeve a golden brocade hat to unfold and don, brazen to behold if the light is right, one narrow part jutting up atop the front as high again as the wearer's face.

"Only an Emperor may wear this style of hat," Mo comments. "I need to provoke and incite. Great empires are not attained by timidity."

Maggie calls out from Ox's back in the loudest of voices, amplified by the hidden lingo necklace: "Sages and scholars say that no woman may reign over a realm – because a female is *Yin* incarnate. Yin is inward energy, which may become deeply dark and negative, unsuited to a ruler. Whereas Yang is positive, bright, and masculine.

"Divine Emperor Qin Shi Huang by the Mandate of Heaven, first to bring this great empire together, was Yang personified. But alas the great power of Yang has declined, as is inevitable in our world. Now Qin Shi Huang is dead, replaced by a knave and fool who should not rule. Why is youngest son, the *eighteenth* son, Huhai so unsuitable? I can reveal to you – listen well! –" for indeed she does know the exact truth –"that when Qin Shi Huang died very far from here, that much younger son Huhai, obeying his cunning advisor Zhao Gao like a puppet, *forged*, yes *forged* a supposed edict from Huhai's father demanding that the first son and true inheritor genial Crown Prince Fu Su should commit suicide. Which duly happened. Ever since, that cunning advisor Zhao Gao has been boss of our country while Huhai murders worthy ministers and generals willy-nilly for no valid reasons!"

Commotion erupts, especially since this is all true, whether known or new to people's ears.

"To receive an edict from your own honoured father two months' travel distant ordering that you should kill yourself!" Maggie screams piercingly. "Such is not a command to ignore – especially when the Enforcers of Law will ensure that death does soon occur according to decree."

"The Enforcers are cow vaginas –!"

"Let's shit on their ancestors –!"

"For two months Zhao Gao and Huhai accompany the decaying corpse of the First Emperor back here to his capital city, so as to announce his death only here – thus, to control events. For *two months* they pretend to the many-*li*-long imperial entourage that Qin

Shi Huang is merely off colour in his curtained carriage. Eighteenth son usurper Huhai – nowadays Qin Er Shi, Second Emperor – orders carts of stinking rotting fish to follow and to precede the corpse's carriage."

"No!" calls out someone, appalled at the unfilial insult of the fish.

"Behold," Maggie bellows from ox-back, "how the Yang collar of my gown crosses over the Yin side of my gown, thus restraining Yin. Yet now," and so saying Maggie loosens the sash of her gown to throw both sides open, "all changes!"

"God she's good," says Sharma. "Talk about Lady Godiva and what not."

Beneath Mo's gown isn't nudity but more white silk, this silk embroidered with a rampant red Chinese dragon.

"Yes, let the forefathers of the Legalist Enforcers be shat upon. To coerce lightly is the way of Yin power and of wisdom."

Hang on, let's unpack this. Maggie is a fan of soft coercion. Of course she is. She once told Mason, "*Total* freedom comes at the cost of violence and disorder." How about when the soft push is no longer enough, when push comes to shove? You open fire. What might Colonel Mo have done in Tiananmen Square, a century before her birth two millennia ahead in time?

More audience now hang out from the towers topping the market. Crowds stare stunned, because no Yin female may *ever* sport a Yang dragon.

Maggie shuts her gown. Now the Yin tape crosses over and suppresses the Yang side. The message is clear.

"The great masculine Yang force of Qin Shi Huang is way in decline due to the stupid excesses of the degenerate spawn whose forgery of his father's hand causes the death of the rightful and worthy heir. Consequently Yin force is now ascendant in the form of myself as the true vehicle for Heaven's will!"

Following the lead of a certain historian a couple of centuries uptime, we prefer speeches of economical impactful rhetoric which don't need repeating. Just imagine the terse *Sinaica* of Publius Cornelius Tacitus. This here and now is pre-Empress Mo's only lengthy campaign speech recorded verbatim throughout our entire account.

From steepled fingers Maggie throws a gleaming golden coin to one anti-Huhai protester – coin duly caught – and another to another.

"Look at the golden coins I give to you!" A bit of a mêlée ensues in the vicinity of those pro-Mo people. "Each displays a panda bear-cat which we all know is equally black and white, therefore the perfect symbol of Yin-Yang harmony which I as your Empress shall restore. I proclaim my dynasty to be the Panda Dynasty!"

What she actually says is "the Mo Dynasty" because serendipitously by perfect coincidence or else by the will of Heaven the word Mo (*disregarding tones and stuff*) – which is Maggie's *very own name* – is also the ancient Chinese name for the giant panda, *Mo* 貘 *Ailuropoda melanoleuca*, the 'black and white cat-foot'.

"Just hope this works," says Mason. "Or we'll be dragged to some ghastly gaol and executed."

"Who marches with us?" shouts Napoleon.

Colonel Mo clarifies, "I call upon Captain Chen Sheng and upon Captain Wu Guang to join me. I prophesy that you will soon both be called to duty at a far frontier. Floods will hinder you from arriving on time. Uncrossable floods which are no fault of yours. Yet the law condemns you to death for failing to do the impossible. So do you kill yourselves obediently – or do you rebel?

"Who marches with us?" Napoleon calls again.

"I call upon Chancellor Li Si who I truly prophesy will be framed for treason by his former crony Zhao Gao and killed by the cruel Five Pains, after which his entire family will be extirpated. Let Li Si hear of this swiftly from whatever friendly ear is listening before the hour becomes too late for him.

"Who marches with us?"

"*Shabby!*" This cry bursts from a middle-aged man in patched red silks, presumably a minor official and proud of it. "*Stupid cunt!*" comes from Rajit's lingo necklace by way of translation. The bureaucrat rushes towards Rajit's side of Ox brandishing a chef's wide chopping knife. This *caidao* is much subtler than any crude occidental cleaver. The official may have snatched it from that bronzemonger's stall over there. Always be ready to improvise.

We feel obliged to mention that this very same broad slim model of bronze kitchen knife features illustriously in the famous *Dismemberment of Ox* fable by the cool sage Zhuang Zhou alias Chuang Tzu who dreamt he was a butterfly…

"Butcher the bitch!" screams the red silk official. "*Shabby!*"

To repel the assault Rajit swings his blade in an improvised way, causing the assailant to pivot aside.

Promptly Maggie Mo, perched upon Ox, pulls her mock-Regency pistol from her pelican sleeve pouch and fires BAM BAM. Flowers of blood petal open upon the assailant's silks. His sheer momentum takes him onward, crashing down upon his face. His *caidao* scratches sparks from the floor tiles, ruining its edge. His dead head bumps the indifferent hoof of the ox.

As far as her audience can see or understand, Maggie Mo merely points her finger and BAMBAM the man falls dead. This is pretty significant celestial magic, thunderbolt level. It'll be another thousand years till the Chinese get around to inventing gunpowder. Mo must indeed possess the mandate of Heaven, even though she's a woman. Don't forget that it's the thunder-god's *wife* who tosses thunderbolts at malefactors from her mirror, incinerating them, after which her husband simply makes a lot of thunder noise.

"The lurking Listener is deaf at last!" a chap shouts jubilantly.

This causes very loud clapping as well as the clashing of whatever can be clashed. Today may become known as the Day of Dented Pans. From now on anyone keeping dented pans in their kitchen may be known for a rebel.

Napoleon had swung round just too late to impale the attacker, consequently Ox and Boy halt too. Ox's ears flick. Does the din dismay Ox? Such a beast is phlegmatic.

A moderately grand man, to judge by his bristling black moustaches, places himself several paces in front of Napoleon and calls up to Maggie, "I am Meng Sheng, a landlord. I offer you and your escort-demons the hospitality of my modest palace." Meng Sheng is clad in a green silk robe and platform clogs. Despite the clogs he manages to kneel and bump a floor tile with his forehead, thrice.

We should explain (as Maggie might, were she not engaged in crucial matters) that due to Qin Shi Huang's imposition of Legalism upon the unified Chinese Empire this noble Meng Sheng cannot manifest any title of nobility. He can only be classed as Landlord, Peasant, Craftsman, or Merchant. Merchants aren't too popular with the government because they spend money on importing unnecessary luxuries. C'est méchant. Craftsman aren't too popular when their works of art cause extravagance.

Despite the vast extravagance of the imperial government itself, for those who are governed life remains frugal. Ostentatious spenders may be punished.

"We thank you, Meng Sheng, and we accept," declares Maggie.

Napoleon salutes Meng with upright sabre, its hilt looking like the nose guard of a helmet even though he's wearing that bicorne hat. A couple of Meng's servants now manifest themselves protectively. From the taller servant's neck hang roped two pink piglets each side. Freshly dead and bled.

"All Scholars will support you," calls out an old man dowdily dressed, "for we feel buried alive!"

"He ruined us by building that Wall!"

"Bad egg wall!"

"Rongyao!" says Napoleon's collar. "Gloire!" say his lips. "Glory!" hear Mason and Sharma. More or less.

"First," announces Maggie, "I must buy a suitable carriage, and two horses to pull it."

"And food for the horses," her enthusiastic host adds helpfully. Horses are costly to maintain at a town palace.

"As well as three more horses adequate for my generals to ride."

"I've never ridden a horse in my life," hisses Sharma.

"High time to learn, Rajit."

"That's what worries me: high."

"Chinese military horses aren't too far off the ground."

"I'll train you," promises Mason. "I've played a chukka or six of Polo in my time."

"And here we are, playing at *Marco* Polo."

"In a covered *mark*-et, no less."

Thus the two dons keep their cool amidst the hubbub of acclamation for Maggie who has just killed a person. The corpse of the over-loyal civil servant lies upon blooded floor tiles. A rat runs close, to lick. Maggie's act was of self-defence. Defence of all of them. Yet has Maggie killed prior to today? That cannot be asked. As for Bonaparte, he would have impaled the attacker without a second thought. He has caused ever so many deaths, and now there must be more deaths, for the sake of Empress Mo.

The fine lady hopefully soon to be Empress Mo slaps the flank side of her mount.

"Farewell, Ox!" Off she slides in her finery.

Whereupon Boy diverts doughty Ox in the direction, most likely, of the slaughterhouse which must be close at hand; otherwise whither such fresh pink piglets? Pa and Ma Bargee accompany Boy. Doubtless they'll pay their respects at Meng's palace within a day or so to receive a reward. Including gifting back to them the barge? Which it still isn't proven that Pa ever owned. Pa Bargee has acted brightly in his own interests ever since they all met. That Maggie's fortunes shall advance in accordance with her desires is, for him, a once-in-a-lifetime chance not to be squandered lightly. A barge is a mere bagatelle.

It may be that potential conspirators meet at this market. Pa Bargee may be well aware of this. All told, how many simple-hearted oxen has he brought here over the years on a one-way trip, despite government pressure to reserve oxen for ploughing? Pa Bargee deserves a name. Let's call him Bo Chuan.

The compound of Meng Sheng's palace is half a town-block in size. Its high brick privacy protection wall arises from a tough earthen terrace. One wooden gate is for servants to accept horses, and carriages too, up a ramp into a compound for animals. The south-facing gatehouse with its wide stone steps is for people who politely enter the palace on foot.

All the cleverer of quite rich Meng to be seen personally visiting a marketplace! Does this run any risk of him being reclassed by clerks of the Censorship as a merchant? Is Meng *principally* a merchant, secretly conducting business? Thus the overthrow of the Qin Dynasty and its Legalism could be really convenient for Meng!

Into a picturesque garden we pass. Late Spring flowers, stone lions, trees in bloom. The main mansion sprawls magnificently, its very long roof of glazed yellow tiles upcurving exuberantly as if afloat upon air.

Within, pillars of the palace are vermilion. Wooden armpits, which is where complex connections occur, are painted jade green.

Our three uniformed military men are shown to one bedchamber where they can finally shed their sabres. Maggie Mo occupies a more spacious chamber, attended by a eunuch who or which might prove a nuisance to Boney by night.

After a while their host and his secretary Chu Zhu – who is secretly a Confucian Scholar – ceremonially welcome their guests around a low lacquered table. Two female servants attend.

"I offer you," declares Meng to Napoleon, "Yellow Wine, or Fragrant Phoenix Wine, or thirdly but not least the best Baiju."

Diplomatically, Napoleon enters into the spirit. His own savage nation is presently only Gaul in three parts and as yet cannot even speak French – which may become the highest achievement of humankind. Or not.

"I would adore the BayJoo, though I confess I can only take my alcohols with equal amounts of water. Ma foi, mon foie est délicat." Delicate liver, has Boney! Very averse to poison. "I choose the Bayjoo, watered."

"So let it be." Courtier-like, Meng refrains from any hint of snootiness.

"General –?"

"Mason. May-Son. May I try the Yellow Wine?"

A laugh. "Or will the Yellow Wine try you?"

"I don't fuddle easily." He won't become gooanzooy. Famous last words for some.

"May I possibly have some tea?" asks Rajit.

"My own choice exactly," agrees Meng. "While drinking tea I tend to think elegant thoughts."

Tea connoisseurs compile rankings which describe the most exceptional brews of the day. "The famous teas are made of the very best each region has to offer," Emperor Song Huizong will write. "For example, one can feel the effort and sacrifice in Taixing rock tea, cultivated on such barren, flat, and rocky land; or Qingfeng Suicha which grows on high cliffs, tastes stern; just as one may taste the innocence of Dalan tea."

"It takes a Scholar to understand tea," asserts Chu Zhu mildly. "Some fools put any old fruits and herbs and spices into a confusing infusion instead of purely tea leaves. Personally I spit upon –"

"Not now, Chu! An elegant lady from Heaven is present. Soon to be Empress. Of what will Your Ladyship partake?"

Maggie is of course familiar with the ancient Chinese drinks menu.

"The fragrant Phoenix *wine* will suit me *fine*." Due to a quirk, Meng hears the rhyme in English as well as Chinese. Nodding approvingly at the improvised couplet, he tells the second serving girl, "And bring us a Dumpling Feast to honour the lady who dares to display a dragon."

They discuss the likelihood of rain. Rain turns roads into quagmires. Will this favour a rebellion? Chu Zhu reckons that Shi the Second has ten thousand soldiers around his huge palace as well as five thousand at his Dad's tomb. Will Shi the Second nevertheless call for reinforcements?

How enthusiastically, how impressively Napoleon begins to relate through his lingo necklace one of his campaigns, this choreographer of death on a grand scale – now in a land where the scale is even grander… until presently both serving women return. One bears bronze heating vessels shaped like twisted ducks each holding a flask within its back. The other woman is balancing a pagoda of bamboo steamers. So now the warmed wine and tea may be poured.

Napoleon tastes his half-watered BaiJu and winces at the fire still remaining, but he rallies.

"Bon?" asks Meng in Chinese of the BaiJu booze. ("*Good?*" is what Sharma hears Meng ask.)

"Bon," sputters Napoleon in French, "très *bon*," which happens to be the perfect response.

"Eat, eat," urges Chu Zhu.

It's certainly high time to. So far, all's looking good.

We vowed to limit Maggie's speeches to her impassioned outburst earlier on in the market, but next Maggie Mo makes the speech which that very same day from his prodigiously trained memory Chu Zhu inks upon wooden sticks, entitled *The Notion of a Nation.* This could well appear in *Qiushi*, theoretical journal of the quest for truth.

Uplift from abject poverty to moderate prosperity. Create a consumer market. Abolish restrictive laws – within certain limits of essential benevolent coercion. Send a belt of trade snaking westward protected by Chinese might. No one is safe until everyone is safe. Soften the Mongols. Build fleets of giant treasure junks made of tough teakwood to sail the seventeen seas and build everlasting trade and techno partnerships with still legendary indigenous people ranging from the arctic Inuits southward by way of Sioux and Seminoles and Aztecs and Mayas to the utmost south of Patagonians, thus in future ages to repel deadly white demons before those can get a foothold on the double continent…

Fuelled by fragrant Phoenix wine, now is Maggie's Virgilian *tu regere imperio populos memento* moment, first improvised here in Meng's palace.

Others won't actually make better bronzes
For you already mastered chrome-plating, Chinese people,
Aeons ahead of the rest of the world.
Prepare with your power to guide nations
Imposing peace through lavish loans.

Delicious dumplings notwithstanding, Mason and Boney both become a bit tired compared with the tea drinkers. Having quaffed Phoenix wine, Maggie decides to retire at the same time as those two, to take a nap. Hmm, a nap.

Maggie is in her chamber when Napoleon seeks to insinuate himself past the eunuch with a "Va faire, bonhomme?" Be off with you, chappie eh?

Oddly, eunuchs can be fiercely loyal to masters who emasculated them, so long as the operation wasn't conducted sadistically such as by crushing. Anyway, it may be an error to assume that Meng himself caused the neutering of Bi Wang. For such is the eunuch's name… Bi Wang interposes himself between the strangely-clad big-nose wrong-eyed demon and its destination – said demon thankfully no longer wearing any sword.

"Great Guest," says Bi Wang, "I may not permit any intact male to enter here without the consent of the lady within. I shall be obliged to resist to the utmost of my strength and ingenuity."

"Maggie!" calls out Boney. "Please let me in!"

Colonel Mo isn't in immediate sight within. No reply is forthcoming. Maybe Maggie is hiding herself behind a screen, mischievously amused to embarrass her tipsy conquest. Maybe she passed out from the effects of fragrant Phoenix wine; though up until now she has displayed great self-control.

"Maggie!" To Bi Wang, "She may have fainted. Let me render assistance!"

Maggie Mo is not the fainting sort. Bi Wang remains silently stalwart.

"*Canaille!* Rush and see she is safe, Man! I mean Unman, oh what do I mean –"

"Daft-eyed Demon with your Two Tongues, it is not my duty to intrude. However, it *is* my duty to protect from intrusion. I confess to you shamefully that my father was a rapist, contrary to law. Therefore the law condemned him to castration and to enslavement – together with confiscation of all of our family's property and of our entire family's liberty, as is normal and lawful. Many slaves are needed to work for many years upon great public projects – canals, tombs, palaces. Thus fewer rapes will occur, to blemish potential concubines. My own unmanning is a separate matter, unconnected with rape. Enter unbidden you may not."

"Ma chère Mo, chérie, je te prie! *Quanto voglio fare l'amore!*"

"I will tolerate no conduct tending towards rape, Demon who now has Three or Four Tongues."

Boney's lingo necklace is improvising with ever increasing heuristic ingenuity and distributed flexagility. Yet no matter how many tongues Boney has access to techno-wise, no response comes from within the chamber; therefore no access. He is being shown his limits. Disgruntled, he withdraws.

They're awake at dawn perhaps due to Timepod Lag but also thanks to much crowing and cackling, which is how the three demon-men and Maggie presently discover the variety of chickens in a courtyard near the kitchen. There strut and peck Silkies and plumey Cochins and Bantams of Beijing-To-Be-Greater-Later.

If guests are up, etiquette seems to require that cooks and serving maids also rise and shine. Soonish, breakfast is bowls of thick creamy congee, porridge of either two or three delights depending on how you count the delights. Scattered atop are crispy shredded rabbit and chives. Alongside are fried bread sticks. And bowls of tea. Tea is a fortunate benefit of the new national unity, thanks to the thousands of forced workers marched from western tea-savvy provinces to be billeted for many years in giant labour camps in the vicinity of Xianyang.

Presently Chu Zhu presents Maggie with a short roll of thin wooden sticks bound with hempen strings, a copy of his record of her Virgilian words of the previous day.

Maggie releases the primary string. Tiny characters cascade, displaying from right to left. She studies and nods. "All is as I said." She touches a stick with a manicured lacquered fingernail. "Um, a very fine interpretation here… I am privileged by such accuracy."

Mason gapes at Maggie. "You can actually read this from so far in the past?"

"Of course. Upfuture, the Chinese characters are the same, just a bit simplified."

"I see what you mean about feeling at home here…"

She winks. "We can't all be barbarians, can we, Prof dot?"

It transpires that army Captains Chen Sheng and Wu Guang may call by later, incognito. This news revives Napoleon far more than tea. Gloire beckons. Actually Boney has little taste for tea but coffee and chocolate are as unknown as Mohammed.

The day wends onward, there being more hours to fill than if our guests had risen later. Tourism around pre-Rebellion Xianyang city seems quite unwise.

In a courtyard otherwise deserted, Napoleon lunges and slashes and thrusts at the air with his sabre. He advances nimbly; nimbly he retreats. Fast forward, fast back. Attacks, retreats.

At one point Maggie emerges, pulls her top-of-the-range HanHan smartphone from her left sleeve, shoots a five-second gif, and announces merrily, "The Martial Arts movie is born."

Her HanHan recharges by squeezing the case, good exercise for hands. Piezoelectric.

"Ma belle! Pardon me that I sweat to so little avail compared with the perspirations of passion which there might otherwise be without a bath for us to share…"

"Shall I ask Bi Wang to send a skilled concubine to meet you in a private chamber?"

"Oh. I was not thinking of… I was more thinking of… *Canaille!*"

"Where could the harm be, Mon Général? There's a sultry girl of Zho."

"I would not be…"

"Pure any more? Like a virgin?"

"Obviously those are not my circumstances. Why do I have the feeling that whatever I choose will turn out to be the wrong choice? Is it because my own skill as a general was to manoeuvre opposing generals into this position?"

"Except at Waterloo?"

"That cunning swine Wellington hid half his troops behind a ridge. As we say in Corsica, with a single musket ball I may as well shoot a ram as a lamb…" Corsican moufflons being typically scrawny and tough but at least bulkier than their skinny lambs.

"Go ahead, be a ram."

In this situation what would you do?

As for Mason and Sharma entertaining themselves, there's a board game with pieces of polished stone in a box but the board is marked incomprehensibly and no one seems inclined to instruct two wrong-eyed demons. The uniformed pair try to invent rules. On their return maybe they can market a new killer game with Chinese backing.

"Um, medieval Venice versus medieval Genoa? Miniature ships for our pieces?"

"How about Victorian novelists versus Victorian poets? Little eBoney busts versus alabaster busts for the *de luxe* 'Oxford' edition?

"Isn't eBoney versus alabaster a spot racist, young fellow-me-lad?"

Today it's lamb for lunch – or for 'Qin Din' depending upon how one names the meal. Good for digestion at this hour! Due to Maggie's presence, protective eunuch Bi Wang supervises the serving of lamb soup with torn bread. *Mo* means flatbread amongst other things. The more torn-up this particular Mo 馍 bread, the more flavoursome the soup experience, explains Bi Wang.

"I'm aware," replies Maggie. "And I know that people born under the sheep should lead a quiet life. "Are you warning me that I otherwise might be torn up like the bread? How kind of you. Seems a bit late for that, though!"

"Begging pardon, Exalted Nobody's Mistress, but our chef made up the menu. I merely serve."

"Hmm, Gonggong, how would you care to serve as head eunuch of a future court of concubines?"

Bi Wang gasps.

Mason has caught some of this. "I say, as Empress are you still planning to have the royal brothels or whatnot?"

Bi Wang bows down to Maggie in full kowtow, this serving conveniently to hide any blushes or rage at a clumsy demon. Soup is almost overturned.

"Dearie dearie me, Prof dot. From Crass College."

"I apologise! I was just wondering why a hot-blooded young Empress – and well um no need to mention our French friend – why should she need umpteen female concubines? I'm just curious. To give to courtiers, I suppose, to maintain alliances…"

"Foot out of mouth, food into mouth, Confucius say."

Lamb soup is followed by a cooked fowl tied up to look like a gourd, crisp and succulent.

After dusk Captain Chen Sheng arrives furtively. (Be it noted that this Sheng isn't a relative of our host Meng Sheng, Chen being the Captain's *family* name.) He's clad as a rural peasant hiding his mouth and nostrils with cheap old silk as if wind is blowing dust chokingly through the city. That isn't so at the mo, but it's plausible. For sure he has a bladed weapon concealed. It's fairly safe to come here on his own, since Law enforces peaceful public behaviour in the empire of Qin; punishments for infractions can be dire. Yet the Captain glances suspiciously over his shoulder even though surely he is safe within Meng's minor palace.

Actually that first paranoid glance is justified since into the room of a sudden comes Captain Wu Guang similarly camouflaged, a clear case of independent minds thinking alike. Both Captains glare at uniformed and hatted demon General Bonaparte. Alternatively, the Captains are stunned by respect.

All this becomes irrelevant when, to the horrified amazement of both Captains and of Meng Sheng too, secretary Chu Zhu suddenly retreats protectively into the room before the oncoming of swirling robes and fancy fabric hat suggestive of a skewered chicken draped with strips of bacon, and beneath that hat… delicately dangling sidelocks and downturned tashes and tufty little mouche underneath the lower lip and black block of chin-beard – in other words the countenance of he who must be the Chancellor in person. He's accompanied by six sword-bearing officers wearing long riveted iron coats of mail over bright purple tunics and padded trousers. Swiftly they occupy the space around the walls. Oh yes indeed Li Si had a vigilant spy meandering in the market… who must then have sprinted many *li*s with news of Maggie's prophecy.

Maggie rises calmly in her Hanfash elegance. "An imperial Chancellor does not come in person to arrest a few conspirators! Accordingly you are very welcome here, great Li Si."

"Bearing in mind," replies Li Si, "that my men can swiftly kill every witness present in this house… are you the woman who prophesied in the market that I will soon suffer the Five Pains, culminating in being sawn in half through the waist?"

"Yes, Chancellor, this will happen in public, in a market place. Your partner-in-crime –"

Li Si looks on the point of fulminating.

"I fearlessly repeat, your partner in the crimes of forgery and of compelling the suicide of the legitimate heir, your erstwhile partner the eunuch puppet-master Zhao Gao *hates* you. Firstly, because you know the crimes of which he is guilty. Secondly and more importantly, Zhao is jealous because *you* are the great genius who truly unified China by standardising weights and measures and roadways and money and waterway lay-bys, but most importantly the written characters of our multi-tongue language so that all peoples of the Chinese empire may communicate no matter how much our voices vary."

Blessedly the various lingo necklaces have turned their volumes right down to the whisper-in-ear level.

Li Si relaxes.

Maggie adds, "Qin Er Shi usually believes whatever Zhao Gao tells him because Zhao Gao trained Qin Er Shi to respond like a salivating dog."

A great growl of, "Nevertheless, respect for a superior!" – but Maggie chops at her waist emphatically. In reality the waist-slice is performed upon an immobilised prisoner from behind, using a giant one-handed saw. However, we don't want to get involved in torture porn. Also, prior to horrific executions very often the victim's mouth is stuffed with opium. The point about lethal mutilation as a punishment is to *insult* the criminal in the afterlife by sending him or her onward incomplete. Often the executioner may first of all kill the condemned person with a stab to the heart and only then commence the slicing, devoting hours post mortem. Maybe not in Li Si's own case, the Chancellor of China may well be thinking.

"I repeat, like a drooling dog doing tricks. Even so, notwithstanding Qin Er Shi's paranoid slaughter of his own best generals, in *your* case even Qin Er Shi may demand evidence. Thus

Zhao Gao will imprison you and torture you until you confess to treason against Qin Er Shi.

"*Then* the Five Pains will follow. The cutting off of your left foot. The slicing off of your nose. Tattooing your face indelibly. Removing your reproductive organs, both the pipe and the ball-bag. Finally, the degrading slow waist chop in public.

"This all awaits you just next year, Li Si. What's more, your whole family will be exterminated to the third degree. That's including all first cousins, half-uncles, half-nieces, even great-grandfathers if any are available. You are fatally compromised, Li Si. Only with myself as Empress – yes, *Empress* – may you and your family continue to exist. And I say truthfully to Captain Chen Sheng and Captain Wu Guang that you two will be sent *very soon indeed* with your commoner soldiers to fail to arrive at a fight on the frontier. How much simpler to attack the imperial palace immediately as well as inflame the peasantry to arm and rebel –"

"Yes, yes," interrupts Li Si, "and likewise I must rebel – with what forces I may muster *quickly* as well as *slyly*. I can see that."

Napoleon arises. "Alert the guards of the Great Grave and arm the forced workforce. By Law I believe that the army of guards must obey the Chancellor's seal without hesitation, or be executed. One victory against the Emperor's local forces and both he and this Zhao Gao will flee, I assure you. Then the whole nation will rise up. As the most victorious general with the possible exception of Alexandre le Grand, I guarantee this."

No point in talking oneself down.

Li Si sucks in his breath, the reverse of a snake hissing. "All-Penetrating Marquis," he tells the officer closest to him, "test the mettle of this all-conquering general. Prick him in his doozy paunch."

Oops. 'All-Penetrating Marquis' is a very high military rank. Remarkably so for a leader of the Imperial Chancellor's personal protection unit. Li Si is taking no chances. The number of dead heads this Marquis must have presented to merit his rank and his lands too! Several sackfuls of severed heads? Those other officers on alert around the walls of the room may be at least 'Grand Masters'.

The thing about the Qin military is that they are such effective warriors because they receive no pay. That's right: nothing, rien, sweet mayo. For every enemy they kill and whose head they present, they accrue a merit point plus a piece of usable land plus a rank. More kills, more points, more rentable land, more title. A bit like Monopoly. Here's the meritocracy of death of the Qin Dynasty.

Yet we don't fully understand the Qin military reward-for-killing system. Do you pause in mid-battle to saw off a head to tie round your waist? Do you tag a freshly dead enemy with some personal token or ribbon – including a fatally wounded enemy still in the business of dying – then pass swiftly onward to run somebody else through? On the Qin side are there umpires with ink brushes?

The Marquis aims his long sword. Mason grips Sharma's wrist as if to restrain him from intervening – thus conveniently restraining himself too. "That sword of Boney's," hisses Mason. "It's his Austerlitz souvenir sword. It's only ceremonial!"

Nevertheless Napoleon draws his sabre to point at the blade of the Marquis. Boney's curved sabre is designed for cutting more than thrusting, so he may be hoping to misdirect his opponent. Soft gold melts into the many engravings of the very posh French sabre. Definitely looks flimsy, though how smartly Bonaparte flourishes it, dainty left hand tucked behind his back.

The polish of the Marquis's sword blade accentuates its extreme sharpness. The Qin weapon is like an elliptical willow leaf stretched out to a metre in length, ridged at its midway and at its tip the better to puncture a belly or guts.

With his longer and brighter blade the Marquis sets on. Immediately Napoleon dances aside and brings the edge of his own sabre smartly down on top of the attacking blade… which… just… simply… snaps in two… the whole front half of it falling to the floor.

"No cause for alarm, mes vieux! Damascus steel readily cuts through bronze. I do know a bit about swords. Steel is forged with fire. Bronze is simply poured into a mould then polished to make it pretty. Bronze may be hard enough to kill foes, but it's also inflexible and fragile."

Whether the All-Penetrating Marquis can take this in without knowing what steel, acier, is, he gapes at his weapon which that mincing tubby demon just abbreviated with the greatest of ease. Sinking to his knees, he turns the ruin of his blade towards himself, and momentarily it looks as though he may commit hara kiri. However, we are not in Japan, thus he lacks this concept – in China, belly-cutting requires a big timber-saw. The Marquis stiffens. He raises his chin. He bares his throat for a coup de grace or disgrace. He has lost face.

Napoleon chuckles, advances a pace or two, and chucks the Marquis under the chin.

"Enough of that nonsense, good sir! Keep your face. We need all the brave men we can get."

With his plump pretty hand Napoleon raises the Marquis up, ignoring what's left of the man's blade which droops impotently then drops with a clatter. By such tricks has Bonaparte endeared himself to his men in times gone by yet to be.

Maggie cries out, "You have won your reward, my hero! No eunuch will keep us apart tonight!"

"Ahem," says Li Si to Napoleon, "I suggest that all of us should now discuss our immediate tactics. Let us kindly include the former All-Penetrating Marquis, now reduced merely to a Viscount-About-Town."

Don't throw the Marquis out of the plot, otherwise one of you must kill him right now.

To Meng, the Chancellor adds, "Wine will be welcome."

Meng's nod sends Chu Zhu deferentially ducking out towards the kitchen pavilion to order wine to be warmed. From a jacket pocket Napoleon squeezes out a tiny snuff box. Which he opens. Which he demonstrates in use, unusually for himself actually inhaling then sneezing upon his sleeve. Normally Boney will only pick up a pinch for a quick sensation before discarding almost all of the powder at random. Now we know what Napoleon must carry in his private bag: de luxe little snuff boxes full of the snuff! Boney leaves a trail of the stuff wherever he goes.

"Meanwhile, Chancellor of China, may I offer a stimulant from elsewhere while we wait for wine?"

Cautiously Li Si dips finger and thumb into the box and copies what Napoleon did.

And Li Si explodes. Dramatically so. His sneeze is thunderous.

"I'm poisoned," gasps Li Si, tears in his eyes. "No, restrain yourselves, Grand Masters!" – for others of the bodyguard look about to set on. Gasping and blinking: "Elixir of immortality, is this? I feel... lifted up. Alchemist's formula...?"

Mason seems to feel a need for attention. "That is a powdered dried plant from far away, Chancellor. China will need to build giant junks, armed for protection against barbarians, to sail thousands of *lis* across the ocean to bring back seeds of the plant or perhaps the plants themselves in terracotta pots."

Stop giving people ideas.

"*Armed junks. . !*" exclaims Li Si. "Hmm, the powder caused me to expel air from myself with so much force. I imagine myself expelling that air into a narrow bamboo tube containing a ball of bronze. And that ball flying fast to burst the face of a foe! Tell me, does this powder *burn*? If confined, as within my nose, will *fire* explode the powder as forcefully as when it encounters wetness?"

Do Not Go There, Li Si! Do Not Invent Gunpowder Inspired by Snuff!

"It shall be so, in my empire," declares Maggie, "during the Panda Dynasty." Oh dear.

"Giant junks," she clarifies. "To bring tobacco. To avoid opium wars and heroin addiction. To keep genocidal capitalist Caucasians out of the Americas."

"But," murmurs Mason, "stuffing a fellow's mouth with baccy won't lessen the Five Pains! Not unless it's totally whacky baccy." Things have become very serious and real for him. "I say," says Mason to Maggie, "all these ghastly punishments and hideous tortures... they seem so common, from what you say... the slicing of flesh so slowly like sashimi and the mutilating alive and XYZed... We are actually risking these things by rebelling! These could actually happen to us."

Maggie laughs cheerfully, or madly. "Nothing ventured!"

"It's all very well for you to talk. You have less to mutilate than a man does."

"Is diddums' poor little willy squirming and shrivelling? Whose precious balls are getting themselves in a twist?"

Award that lingo necklace the Weibo Best Actress Trophy! The lingo thingos seem by now to be co-operating synergistically, maybe about to go A.I.

Li Si cries out, "Oh give me a sign from Heaven!"

So Maggie shows him, stored on her smartphone, a fifteen-second vid of the Great Wall with watchtowers viewed from above, from the sky, from blue heaven. Some big egrets fly low below.

"Your work, Chancellor. Your doing, as seen from heaven." For clarity and comprehension, it's viewed from not too high up.

Li Si rocks back but then studies intently. "Plainly you are a Wu 巫, a sorceress! Your qi is exceptionally cultivated. Yet what I see *isn't* precisely what I commanded so as to keep out the barbarian northern nomads… This is a *greater* Great Wall."

"Very observant and analytical of you! And *you* will command *this,* commencing during my Panda Dynasty." Here is another Virgilian *tu regere imperio* moment. "For you will not be sawn in half, but instead will be my Chancellor."

Warm yellow rice wine arrives to be poured as Maggie repeats the video, slowly turning the screen for the benefit of all including eunuch Wee Bang, no we mean Bi Wang who brings the warm wine.

Soon Li Si murmurs, "How can I behold twice what I just beheld? How can I step into the same stream? Indeed how can this vision appear at all?"

"In my hand," declares Maggie, waggling her top-of-the-range HanHan, "I hold the mirror of heaven." Whereof she is both the messenger and the designated monarch.

What else may she have loaded on to her HanHan to impress the natives, her countryfolk? The bodyguards are glancing alertly out of the corners of their eyes. Even the demoted Viscount is riveted. Meng and Chu Zhu and Chen Sheng and Wu Guang likewise are agog, even neglecting their wine. She needs to show just one more thing.

Maggie taps and next on screen comes a reasonably recognisable jut of the river Wei despite many course-changing floods over two millennia. Instead of any old bridge here is the four-lane Harmony Bridge strung like a huge harp which opens in 2045. Black-booted miniskirted female officers with nifty automatic rifles tightly cradled against their bosoms march across the bridge on peaceful white-gloved parade. It's Nation Day 2045. Here's the new start of the Harmony Highway of the once and future Silk Road Belt. Anyone can recognise an army on parade even with naked knees naughty to S&M fetishists; not concubines those ladies, *no way*; accomplished killers or rescuers or whatever the situation calls for. China already accomplishes this even without any Panda Dynasty. But *with* a Panda Dynasty the world is one's oyster sauce.

"Truly," concedes Li Si in amazement, "you will be known as the Demon Empress."

"Panda Empress."

"Demon Panda Empress?"

"Deal."

From the opposite end of the social spectrum there now arrives at Meng's palace, only slightly coincidentally, Bo Chuan alias Pa Boatman along with his Missus, Ma Boatma.

It isn't true to say that Ma is the brains of their barge and ox business, although she may be the memory. She's a mistress of mental arithmetic, not just a muscular matriarch of boat and beast. Look, why don't we write our account in some other language with a lexicon of fewer words that alliterate and attempt to hijack the narrative? Is alliterating as big a threat to authors as illiteracy is to readers? Did the Gawain poet have this problem with his Giant who can only be Green, no other hue?

Due to his many journeys up and down the River Xie with or without an ox, Bo Chuan knows the pulse of the people shackled by laws and taxes. So does Ma Boatma – though not yet Boy, whom Ma forbids to become a Confucian scholar due to the risk of him being buried alive for reading the wrong book. In one respect the distance from peasant to Chancellor is uncrossable; hierarchies of bureaucracies intervene, palaces within palaces. On the other hand it isn't unknown for a clever chap from a peasant family to pass all his exams and within finite time be appointed a Prime Minister or a Chancellor. A sack of heads helps some people, good calligraphy favours others. There's respect for talent. Meritocracy. And as regards the social mobility of a bargee, all the way along the river Wei the first Emperor ordered perfect replicas built of the royal palaces of all the kingdoms which he defeated, to be resided in by nobles, which accounts for local employment that in no way offsets the bills for building and maintaining the palaces, funded by harsh taxes. Chinese palaces typically sprawl out across the landscape, harbouring dozens of big buildings within their walled perimeters. There's so much land in so much of China.

So it isn't totally impossible for Li Si and Bo Chuan to be in the very same chamber, conspiring. In fact this is *a lot more possible* than for any human beings to *exist at all*, or indeed for any kind of complex life to exist anywhere in the 'Huge Heaven' supercluster of upward of a hundred thousand milky ways. Maggie seeks the mandate of a vast heaven. Godless and mostly very empty yet also very violent. She goes boldly, no two ways about it; more like trillions of ways.

The giant palace complex where Qin Er Shit roosts in seclusion (along with his concubines and chefs and such) is home also to the sub-palaces of numerous courtiers and high officials who scarcely ever glimpse the paranoid eighteenth-son second emperor. They see much more of his puppet-master Zhao Gao, tutor in Legalism and nasty punishments. Officials have already learned never to report any bad news to Qin Er Shit but to allow him to remain deluded. Encamped encircling the Qin Er Shit palace are ten thousand soldiers as well as cooks and families and butchers and victualers and umpteen other trades and parasites. Within the past year Bo Chuan led an elderly ox there out of curiosity and stayed several days, ear to the ground, a peasant revolutionary in the making.

"If I may be so bold," ventures Li Si, "who might become your heir, the Panda Two Royal Person, after your long illustrious life alas expires if explosive powders cannot immortalise you –?"

"Heiress not heir," Maggie corrects him. She gestures expansively. "Candidates shall woo me with their achievements and or with the worth and vigour of their lineage – *including* expert weird-eye military demons, for I embrace all ethnicities. And hereafter there shall only be Empresses along with Imperial Consorts, male *or* female. For I also embrace all sexualities."

Regarding that evening's conspirification – with Napoleon now asserting military leadership as to the manner born, droit de l'empereur as it were – the whole city and surrounds of Xianyang are written upon the sky, easily viewable from outside from within the great dark deserted courtyard towards which they now repair.

Outside they go into darkness, to behold a cloudless dome of heaven diamonded with stars.

Napoleon is accustomed to darkness by night, and Maggie is trained, but Mason and Sharma do rather blunder into one another.

"I say!"

"Beg pardon."

At one spacial point the dome is rubied: Mars. Spacial is spatial and special combined.

Oh no, sorry that isn't Mars at all, that's the red supergiant star Antares in the Scorpion, the Chinese Mansion of the Heart. Antares the rival of Mars. Mars is over there. Forgivable error.

Streams of stars. From the terrestrial south, five rivers run into the Wei. Lao, Feng, Hao, Jue, and both the Chen and the Ba combined into a single stream by this stage. Descending diagonally from the north flows the Jing. The Milky Way is the river Wei dividing Xianyang, a city laid out according to the location of certain constellations. Thus Heng Bridge is due south of the Xianyang Palace, which corresponds to the Royal Chamber Mansion up in the Sky. While Meng explains, being the landlord of this courtyard, Napoleon visualises, taking in the sky-map, in his mind's eye manoeuvering divisions, regiments, batallions.

Where Mars stares balefully right now, is where will be best to muster all the armies.

Should Maggie show these heaven-haunted Hans a video of the newly permanent Chinese base on Mars? Mars, like a big red balloon of danger covered over with a giant ghastly Gobi desert. These Hans of the minus centuries do pay great attention to the little red eye in the sky engaging in loopy going-backward behaviour that must portend earthquakes, mass deaths, or changes of dynasty. That it should be an *actual world*, like the visible Moon… Indeed that the world itself should be a world. No, no, the sky is round and the world is square. So there's no point in any *tu regere imperio populos, Serese!* moment as regards Hans on Mars. (Hands Off Mars! chant many armed ignoramuses in the Yoosa lands where the ROT has set in, the third Return Of Trump movement, Trump being only 104 as yet, and well preserved by Ponce de León's Fountain of Youth in Florida, as is reliably reported by the right truthful media.)

Distances, even within the same city boundaries, are significant. Allow five days to mobilise and muster. Meng himself will carry the Chancellor's seal around the five thousand or so soldiers guarding the first emperor's huge grave grounds, along with duplicate rolls of wooden strips of orders, which Chu Zhu will labour copying all night long by oil lamp; that's army group number one.

The thousands of corvée convicts will be armed with dagger-axes from stores or simply long knives and promised freedom and repatriation if Qin Er Shit and Zhao Gao are overthrown; that's army group number two.

Bo Chuan and his many contacts will fastfoment a farmers' revolt, the peasants armed with sharpened spears of bamboo and with wicked agricultural tools; army group number three.

There's no time for months of drill, sorry Inspector General Martinet. Guided by maybe the greatest military genius of mankind except for Alexander of Macedon, sheer weight of numbers can prevail. A hot air balloon would come in useful for observation and signaling with flags and flashes. Drat, no time to reveal the right type of balloon. Have to wait 400 years until the coming of Zhuge Kongming. Need a convenient hill. Ah, the sky does indeed show a hill in the shape of a sparkly triangle – which is just beside *the present Mars point of Xianyang.* Wow. Gloire.

The two rebel Captains each command a paltry hundred men, whom they must detach discreetly from the palace perimeter. Few enough soldiers, but those will fight fanatically to avoid the nasty aftermath if they lose. All groups to muster at the Mars point of Xianyang and environs hill where the earth below corresponds propitiously in the sky to war and dynasty change.

By now Boney knows that the Qin Empire is the first state fully mobilised for war to produce transnational peace, capable in its heyday of fielding armies of several hundred thousand infantry and horse co-ordinated by drums and bells, an amazing feat right out there at the techno-military limit. Nowadays the only sane response to the second emperor's deluded military demands is to assure him that all orders are being carried out as he speaks, that all barbarians are fleeing, yet that nevertheless entire armies remain to protect his throne.

How much army reserve *does* remain, since the Chancellor is likewise lied to? Nap'll need to borrow Maggie's opera glasses. *Commandeer* them – tonight he will be manly.

Such a ballet this will be, five days from now… Waterloo, followed by the Battle of Xianyang. Although Mars is notoriously fickle… Mars is playing more of a role than expected, even without revelations about a future base on another world.

After all is settled and conspirators have departed, Maggie beckons Boney towards her bedchamber. Tonight the eunuch Bi Wang sleeps outside the door, his body blocking access.

C'est magnifique, et oui, c'est la guerre! Five mid-mornings later Napoleon with opera glasses is mounted on a stallion atop the highest vantage point in the rural interlude between most of Xianyang city and the huge Imperial Palace. Beside him signalers wave big coloured flags.

Although his stallion does not paw the ground, nor does it rear as in paintings of Napoleon on horseback, nor froth at the mouth to join a fray, it soon acquires the name *Bête* and that isn't in homage to mischievous Betsy Balcolme. The problem is that Boney never was a graceful horseman even if he is enthusiastic – ten horses killed from under him so far, and one personal concussion. On Corsica one got used to slopping around the rough tracks on donkeyback, slouching to guide your mount with your knees. Now *this part* does come in useful with Bête because no one yet invented stirrups and the saddle is merely a strapped-on blanket. But this warhorse of Boney's, bred in barbarian Uygurland for trade to the new Empire of China, is more robust than any of Napoleon's previous mounts. Those were short grey amiable Arabs. Getting on to this damned beast requires a couple of linked hands of help from Sharma, who then obligingly helps Mason aboard his own hoss, bought by Maggie with panda gold in Xianyang's future silk belt market as we recall. Obligingly, Chu Zhu assists Sharma likewise to ascend perilously before squeezing himself on to Maggie's carriage as her driver.

The three army groups are flattening umpteen *Mu*s of crops. Shocktroops in the centre are the professional soldiers from the imperial tomb complex. To the right, the liberated forced labourers. To the left, armed peasants.

"Umpteen thousand see I at a glance," semi-quotes Sharma, one hand clinging to his horse's cresty mane.

"At least a couple of football stadiums worth. Depending on team. It's a decent turn-out."

Mist is clearing ahead of Napoleon's triple army.

The first contretemps occurs as the traditional battle formation of a Qin army comes into view in miniature still afar off. To the fore, their extremely mobile infantry, the first three ranks armed with crossbows and swords. Behind them, heavy infantry are wearing bronze and iron armour and the shields of their swordsmen are lacquered, while other infantry carry dagger-axes. Next, adequate horses pull columns of chariots. And then come fast cavalry mounted upon proper Uygur chargers… Quite a show! Afar off drums thud and bells clong.

"*Canaille.* They knew we were coming."

The armed forces which guard the imperial palace must have been mustering for many hours, siphoning in troops from all around the protective cordon. The two Captains sneaking their couple of hundred soldiers away may have tipped off the palace forces. Maybe Zhao Gao already had people spying upon Chancellor Li Si. Eyes in the market place too, he's no fool. Maybe five days allowed security leaks.

Onward comes the Qin army, now advancing more slowly. Soon the front ranks commence firing their particularly powerful long-range crossbows. Promptly Napoleon calls out to signal for return arrow fire. Next, he wheels the freed labourers to charge across en masse at the Qin vanguard swinging their recently acquired dagger-axes, whirlwinds of reapers that overwhelm the archers – only to come up against the armoured heavy infantry, who, however, are now within range of Napoleon's archers…

Battles are disgusting bouts of blood and agony, brutality and stupid death, best abbreviated. Glory? We say vainglory! You say gladioli, shaped like the Latin gladius sword. We say not-glad-at-all!

Alas, battles are the history book of the human race. During its career the human race exterminated maybe a dozen real alt. races of Homo – before proceeding to invent supposedly toxic non-existent 'races' such as Jews or Red Indians. Those prehistoric genocides simply lack any history book or named organisers such as can be hauled to justice at The Hague.

Oh shit in a shoe. Remember how the victorious Qin Shi Huang melted all the weapons of states that he conquered into metal giants modelled upon himself to stand about menacingly around his palace? Omigod this cannot be happening! Behind the rearmost rank of Qin heavy cavalry upon Uygur chargers, for whoever has opera glasses, there heave into wobbly sight…

"Canaille! Mon dieu! Ma chère, see this!"

And Colonel Mo, Panda Empress in posse, beholds on the most distant stage of the theatre of war, unmistakably wouldn't you say four no five glittering giant homoform Emperor-faced bronze beings mechanically marching, swinging brutally heavy arms made out of arms themselves.

"Vaucanson!" Napoleon invokes, as one of his era well might.

"*I've* heard of him," says Mason. "Maker of automata. What's up?"

"The bronze giants made of melted weapons have come to life!" exclaims Maggie. "To artificial life, at least. This is *not* within the tech of this Qin time. Is another time traveller here? Surely that cannot be. No other quantum time machine can be present exactly here and now."

Quite. This is Quantum stuff. But how about *entanglement*? In the *manifold*! How else does the manifold remain *many* and also *fold*? We must draw a blanket over the mathematics. Professor Lin of the time travel institute of Beijing may understand, in theory. Colonel Maggie Mo is more practical. She merely wishes to be an Empress presiding over moderate prosperity and peaceful Han hegemony for the benefit of all people. That's PPPP. She has no illusions about longevity nor an afterlife.

And now – yellow flag thrice – the peasant army charge from the left wing, brandishing sharpened bamboos and farm tools. The peasants *plough* – almost literally! – into the masses of chariots.

From atop their hill, after an hour passes by, it's clear that Qin army discipline of the Martinet variety is more effective than suicidal mass charges no matter how enthusiastic. The Qin army also benefits by the somewhat higher vantage of visibility granted to persons in its chariots, whereas Napoleon's own army can only see what's happening very locally within the field of battle.

Reculer pour mieux sauter? To withdraw, the better to sally forth again? All very well for you to say! The Qin army is pressing. Soon its archers are selectively picking off flag-signallers and élite guards of the rebel command as if intent on capturing the three demons alive along with the heretical Han concubine.

Around an hour after noon, begins the increasingly disorderly retreat of Napoleon's Chinese Grande Armée as if from a Kremlin never even reached.

Several hours later our adventurers – mounted upon Uygur chargers along with Chancellor Li Si – are approximately where our trio started out a week earlier. The great expanse of Qin Shi Huang's earthworks lies to their rear, including the vast army of armed terracotta soldiers in reddish sandy soil of their trenches awaiting burial. Many are the shrieks and screams across the land, close and sharp as well as far and fading. It's half an hour since our party crossed the southernmost channel of the Wei on one of several bridges of barges chained together and timbered across at the instigation of We-Know-Who, so as to let the revolutionary forces from the necropolis flood northward to where's Maggie's triple army rendezvoused previously. Now those forces are flooding back in an apparent rout. If they're wise they'll flee far, looting their way to a frontier. We could benefit from an observation balloon.

In the immediate vicinity Qin soldiers armed with swords and shields are pressing close, though slowly and patiently, making Napoleon particularly protective of Maggie Mo in her compact carriage which is steered by Meng standing upright.

Boney calls out in defiance, "I shall defend zees lady with my wife! *Canaille!* With my LIFE!" Darn lingo necklaces sometimes.

Yet no Qin archer aims at the rebels, easy targets by now.

"Everyone dismount!" orders Napoleon. "Including our Empress avec Monsieur Meng. We present too much profile for those archers."

"All this death and suffering," Maggie wails as she descends. "Must this all be meaningless? Have I foolishly brought huge unhappiness and worse due to hubris? How will my Grandad's ghost see me now, last of the line of Mo due to me?"

"Meng!" calls out Li Si who by now lacks any bodyguard. "If any Qin soldier comes within the circle of my sword point, kill me immediately!"

"But Greatest Lord, who will kill me just as quickly? The pink shaman? The pompous lobster?"

"I say, Chappie! I heard that!"

"I fear, ma jolie Chinoise," cries out Napoleon Bonaparte, "that I may have met my Waterloo yet again, to coin a phrase."

Napoleon gestures upward at the sky with his sabre, towards Heaven from where to Chinese minds a mandate comes. And his voice harsh from shouting soars in defiant song:

"*Aux armes, citoyens,*
Formez vos bataillons –"

CHUN
CHUN

Behind Bonaparte and Maggie and party, the entire Terracotta Army comes to attention thunderously, thousands of armed warriors.

What kind of miracle is this? What sort of magic? Quel sortilège? Earlier, those giant metal statues afar off were *maybe mistaken* even when seen through the best of Pre-Common-Era binoculars. But now: a vast array of life-size baked earth soldiers to give backing to Bonaparte!

"What the sheer fuck –!" Sharma exclaims in an uncultivated way that braces him against the shock. No poetry can serve the same purpose.

"Oh my giddy Gawd," from Mason.

"*Mon armée... est arrivée... C'est une rêve, c'est un cauchemar...* My army has come. It's a dream, it's a nightmare." French sometimes sounds like a poem.

Maggie swings round and round. The Qin soldiers and archers who were approaching from the north are now unbalanced and agape. That **CHUN** was a *quake.*

With a collective grind of terracotta necks against terracotta collars, the ranks of soldiery bring their loose-necked heads to bear from different angles upon General Bonaparte. Boney is the focus of all clay eyes, the pole star, the cynosure. Many soldiers sport distinctive top-knots to the right side of their skull – ah, those chaps are all archers. Many more show what like look phylacteries or fascinators upon hard-hats of hair. Bronze swords and spears and billhooks and dagger-axes and halberds gleam.

"Bad Egg! Bad Egg!" swears Maggie. "Boundary conditions are violated. Law becomes lax. This damages the dao that maintains balance and order. The dao is how the cosmos flows. Bad Egg! What can I *do now*?"

"*Doo Dao doo Dao day*," springs crazily from Sharma, to the tune of *The Camptown Races.* Has he become deranged? Or is the Dao itself dangerously discordant?

"*Pour mieux sauter...! Sautez, mes Braves, mes Anciens*!" bellows Napoleon towards his new troops. In chorus, lingo necklaces voice, "Pan-fry yonder foe! Feu feu fire fire!" Chinese orders follow.

All of the terracotta archers raise powerful bows, swing their aim and rain arrows over and beyond the beleaugered rebels' last redoubt. Many distant screams arise from that rainfall of piercingly sharp bronze points.

Briefly Maggie covers her ears. "I cannot bear to hear more and more pain!"

"But not pain for thee and me," declares Li Si. "I am become *celestial* now. As are you, my Empress."

"This must stop. We have strayed from the *Path of Possibles*. Bad Egg! I am a fool! This will all become dust and pebbles even if we prevail. Yet how can I stop while my Grandad gazes upon me from stone eyes? I must tear myself into two parts!"

"Do not distress yourself so, *ma belle et brillante Chinoise*! I myself, *moi-même*, should never have hoped for additional armies to aid me. An extra army – Blücher's – came for Wellington, not for me. And forty thousand human beings died in pain." Is there, at long last, a salty tear in Napoleon's eye? Does he yet realise the unending horror of history?

"Face it, Maggie," says Mason, attempting fatherly guidance. "This magical army must be untenable."

"It can only tumble, as the Sun goes down," she screeches. For sure the Sun is near the horizon by now. Dark menacing clouds are moving towards the Sun *from twin directions* like curtains closing upon the theatre of war.

"We cannot," Mason carries on, "save anyone except for Chancellor Li Si –"

Yet who actually likes Li Si, who would have had them all killed by his security squad, like the squashing of so many beetles?

"And Meng too –?"

"– my first follower and sponsor," declares Maggie. "We must at least try to lift him out of here. Like at Saigon, like at Kabul, like at Taipei, like at Caracas."

Oh lingo necklaces, which language is being spoken, which language is being heard?

"Rotten egg! Rotten egg! Salty fish! Salty fish!"

Li Si calls out, "I shall go amongst this terracotta army and become as them, taking upon myself terracotta, the better to enter eternal heavenly China underneath the hill where bright mercury flows in the rivers and seas."

Can Li Si possibly fit hollow terracotta limbs over his own limbs of flesh and bone? So that he becomes perfectly hidden among a host of similar Spartaci? He can always *try* to… and be found wandering around the ranks, cackling madly, maybe impervious by now to the worst of pains – or that may be so in some other more stable state of the world.

"This cannot happen." Meng steps after Li Si, swings his sword, and with one stroke decapitates the Chancellor.

Bizarrely Li Si's head bounds against a terracotta warrior's head, jarring the animated baked clay out of the way to smash upon the ground, before itself settling, replacing that warrior's head with the Chancellor's own head, human eyes wide, although not so much as a goldfish's gasp can escape from the lips…

"Honour to you who unified our lands! Honour to you who unified our writing and our coinage! Honour to you who unified our roads and watercourses! Honour forever in the Afterwards and the Overhead!"

…as outside the trench Li Si's body slowly collapses.

"By this act," announces their erstwhile host, "may I be known as Meng the Merciful. Thus I fulfil the Chancellor's final request to me."

Well, that's all right then… and nobody else requests beheading.

Maggie cries, "My mandate is made a mockery!"

For the moment the heavy Uyger war-horses are sheltering our party – though have any advanced Qin archers survived the rain of arrows? Of a sudden, without a further word, Meng mounts a war-horse and, kicking its flanks none too nicely, he rides off across the frontage of the artificial army. He must think he knows what's best for his own skin, provided others don't hold him back, and of course he knows nothing about the time-pod hidden in Shimmer not so far off.

"*Canaille!*" At Waterloo many riderless horses charged at the enemy because surviving cavalrymen were charging upon chargers, and horses behave as a herd. Now in seeming recapitulation the remainder of the Uyger horses chase after Meng on his mount.

Those black clouds of closure: lightning leaps between them, across the reddening face of the Sun.

"Malign miracle!" from Maggie. "Damn damn damn!" All of us must run to the time-pod *now*! While there's still some time still here!"

"*Quittez le champ!*" from Napoleon, the only sensible order to give to whomever. Yes, get to that time-pod before the time-pod also becomes a rotten egg! Not an egg excellent for 2,000-plus years like other famous Chinese eggs such as century egg or thousand year egg. Although never until now any two thousand year egg, come to think of it…

Down from +1815 CE to -200 PreCE may be too deep a jump, or too ovoid, for any egg to stay stable. Race to the Shimmer!

Everywhere the silken scroll of scenery is rippling. Is that particular pulsing patch ahead *Shimmer*? – or is it *Ripple*? Future Marcel Duchamp, where is your nude descending the stairway when Monsieur is needed?

One by one they pile into the time-pod. Maggie Mo, fighting back sincere sobs. Sharma followed by puffing Bonaparte. Mason is gasping his guts out, but he's very motivated not to lag behind.

"Well done, old fellow! *Literally*!" Sharma praises the collapsed heap of Mason safe at last within the pod.

"…oh my heart… and my sword's tangled…"

Without setting any destination, Maggie presses the red emergency ESCAPE button.

Oh the time-pod *skids* crazily. It *careers*. It caroms. It swings. *Ça dérappe. Ça glisse.* It certainly does not 'careen'; there's not a single spacetime barnacle to be scraped of its hull. Mason becomes a bit bruised. The pod *skews.*

As before, through the one porthole reddish sandy soil is visible – as well as ochre moss. Similar view to previously, yet something feels radically different.

"Ne te désole-toi tant, mon amour!"

Sharma hoists Bonaparte's tumbled bicorne hat up high and drops it experimentally.

"There's less gravity here, wherever we are. Can't you sense it? I feel light. I think this is another world. Maybe *Mars* because it's red. I think Mars is smaller than Earth, so it'll be less heavy. But a Mars with atmosphere, because I'm seeing some sort of moss."

Maggie quickly becomes practical, her grief and her dashed hopes locked away inside (or so we presume). "Enough atmosphere for us to breathe out in the open? Supposing it contains around twenty per cent oxygen… Air might just be thin like the Tibet Autonomous Region, if we're lucky."

"I say Mars because I read *The War of the Worlds.* Which isn't sci-fi. Sci-fi isn't literature. If it was literature, it wouldn't have a silly name. Do we speak of Spy-fi?"

"You're babbling, Rajit," says Maggie. "You're in shock."

"I wonder," words still spilling from Sharma, "if Tibetans colonised here, courtesy of the Chinese? Yaks could become the size of elephants. A big wild male yak is called a dong, I just happen to know." Ah, there's a fact you can reliably kick your foot against.

"*Really?*" Mason cackles briefly before panting more.

"Edward Lear," explains Sharma. "*Dong with the Luminous Nose.* Nonsense verse. Like Lewis Carroll of Christ Church College."

Sharma gapes through the porthole again. "And we appear to have company… human company, riding something that is certainly no yak. And I can tell he's no Tibetan."

"Let me see." Maggie ups and thrusts herself to see. "Bad egg, bad egg! That beast the red man's riding has eight legs! At least he answers the question of breathability… but *eight legs*?"

Maybe the fellow's skin is more of a coppery hue than red. A mohican of black hair crests him, impaled by one long lurid macaw-like tail feather. Otherwise he seems to lack body hair – not to mention lacking clothing except for a scrotum holder. He makes up for his near-nudity with umpteen bracelets and straps and strings of beads as well as a bow worn vertically with a feathered leather quiver of arrows plus dagger at his hip…

That mount with the eight legs – it's glossily smooth and mainly grey aside from a white belly and big yellow fluffy slippers of feet equipped with nasty-looking claws. Its mouth is *huge.* Halting before the pod, the bizarre beast lowers a section of lip protruding like a shovel to cut-and-slurp moist moss into its mouth. The rider, who sits upon a geometrical woven blanket, unslings his bow and leans forward to rap its lower nock upon their porthole.

"I'd better attend to this." Maggie opens the pod's door and steps outside nimbly in her Hanfash elegance stained by the day's events on the battlefield. The reddish rider gapes.

Neatly-uniformed Napoleon is next to emerge.

"What are you two?" Maggie's lingo necklace detects.

"How can our lingo necklaces understand Tibetan?"

Maggie harks to an internal memo. "It isn't Tibetan, it's Lakota Sioux!"

Before Maggie or Boney can reply to the, well let's face it, this tall skinny Redfellow, a ghastly creature erupts from the ground nearby, scattering soil. It's a naked mole-rat with many legs and the size of a terrier dog. Deep-set gimlet eyes are fierce to the point of madness. Its jaws, oh dear life! – life, oh filler of the very few habitable worlds with vile things – are toothed bare bones jutting out in front of any flesh or gums or lips.

Maggie doesn't hesitate in snatching her upcycled Regency compact pistol from out of her deep Hanfash sleeve, and firing twice, three times. Pam pam pam. The Lakota Sioux man is still reaching for the dagger sheathed upon his leather quiver as the creature hits his leg, very dead, dropping to the ground.

"Hau." He nods.

By now both red-clothed red-faced Mason and pink-uniformed Sharma have emerged from the pod.

"What exactly do you mean by 'how'?" asks Sharma investigatively "*How* do we come to be here? Is here the planet *Mars*?"

"Never watched a Cowboy and Indian movie, man?" Mason raises his palm peacefully and utters, "*How*. Is this Mars?"

"Máaz?" repeats the Lakota Sioux man. "This is *Bar-soom*. I am Otaktay, Killer of Many, known as Massacre Man."

The word 'Bar-soom' isn't translated.

"And you're definitely a Lakota Sioux?"

"Hau. Sure." That word *hau* seems to have several meanings.

Otaktay grins at Maggie Mo. "Your hand weapon did good harm to the ulsio." So that ugly creature is an ulsio, best off dead. A deadly burrower that lies in wait for prey of any size.

"And you ride a –?" from Maggie.

"Lesser thoat, of course!" So there must also be gigantic thoats.

Mason cannot restrain himself from murmuring, "There's food for thoat."

"Food? Yes, it eats the moss and only moss," says Massacre Man. Lakota words hang about in the background like fading farts.

"The gravity here is less than we ourselves know," Mason observes, "so I don't understand why the beasts have so many legs to support them. Apart from yourself, Sir Killer of Many. This seems counter-intuitive. When did your people come here from Earth?"

"From *where*?"

"Planet Three."

"Oh. Jasoom. The sickly orb. Three thousand ords ago. Red Planet for Red Engine People!" Otaktay bellows. "All of us Red Engine folk moved here! No reservations about it!"

Massacre Man does seem to know in general whereabouts he is and when. "So you have come here for the Great Annual Killing," he announces to Maggie Mo, holder of a weapon more potent than the three men's sabres, hilts plainly visible, although a sabre never needs to be reloaded. "To fight with Lakota Sioux army against Comanche army."

Armies. Napoleon's attention is now keenly enhanced.

"To enjoy tortures afterwards."

"Eh?" from Mason.

"What?" from Sharma.

"Tortures of the Comanche braves we capture. Meanwhile Comanche torture captured Lakota braves."

In what ways? We aren't going into that. No torture porn on this page, please. Do the Goggling yourself if you really wish to.

"A great warrior festival, this! Hail Law and Honour!" Hmm, a twisted echo here of China's early imperial era of Legalism?

"A holiday from the regular Water Wars along the great canals of the Plains, fifty generals leading a million warriors. We call these days out here Bleeding Man."

Behind Massacre Man up there on his thoat rises a bit of a ridge, the sort beloved of that damn clever Wellington. Abruptly Otaktay calls out, "Come!" and jerks his thoat, throat and all, away from the moss, his bare knees squeezing the beast to ascend the slope. "Come, persons!"

The quartet duly ascend and from the top of the ridge behold a great plain, the ridge a wrinkle upon its edge. Tens of thousands of teepees are erected in regular military ranks.

Smoke arises. Thoats are in corrals. Miniature persons move about. The little sun is sinking. No sign of Jasoom in the evening sky, sickly or otherwise, a few thousand *ords* futurewards from 2050.

Maggie inhales. "Actually, how *can* you breathe here?" This potential problem for the Chinese Mars base itself was anticipated and solved ingeniously by CPC Dynasty tech. 'Dynasty' in the sense of continuity of wise choices softly enforced upon happy citizens, never of family inheritance.

"The Atmosphere Factories make nuff air," snaps Otaktay impatiently. "Izz good that we eat all the hoards and herds of biggest-breathing fawna." Just as on First Nation Earth, where the giant megatheria and big mammooths all were barbecued to extinction.

Way beyond the parking space of Lakota teepees, separated by what must be almost a mile of battle ground, is a likewise huge encampment of smoky Comanche teepees.

"What time does the warfare start tomorrow?" Napoleon calls to Otaktay. This must be almost a sacred rite, the mass killings followed by torments.

"When Jasoom first shows itself following the Sun."

"You go ahead, Sir Massacre. We need some shuteye." A popular traditional Red Engine torture is staking out a captive in the full sun with his eyelids cut off – but is that less burningly painful on Mars where there's less than half the sunshine? Shut up. I have told you. "Been a long day."

"Same long as uszual. Twennyforours thirty minz." Note the precision.

"We'll see you in the morning when the warriors all muster."

"Organised chaotic armies," Napoleon comments, enchanted by the concept.

Maggie tugs Napoleon, ex-Emperor and General extraordinary, from his vantage point. "Back to the pod, everybody!"

For food they only have a few protein bars, but dining with the Lakota would almost inevitably involve them, all the sooner next day, in close combat with feared Comanches. Supper of Lakota wohanpi soup surely must feature butchered thoat plus Inca potatoes and pungent wild onions which love Martian soil now that the perchlorate has gone mostly thanks to ion exchange Chi-tech.

Nor did they eat much during the prior battle day in Xianyang. Boney doesn't care. This isn't a Chicken Marengo moment. A big naked mole-rat of an *ulsio* is no spring chicken guillotined by sabre as per Napoleonic propaganda.

Or maybe bits of *ulsio* will be fine to fry.

"Who," asks Mason, taking a stand, "is in favour of us cutting and running? I don't see you as Empress of *this* Mars, Colonel Maggie Mo. Torments without even opium to take the edge off 'em!" There's a quivering in his voice. Seriously, *never* even joke about torture, huh? Torture may happen to *you*. Last thing you'll know about in your life. Screaming in pain. Unable to die. Kept alive only for agony. Not nice at all. Not entertaining.

"I think," from Maggie, "we have to ask *why we especially are here* on a future Mars of warring Suzies and Comanches."

"Maybe Ojibwas and Mohawks too," offers Sharma the genuine Indian.

"Mars is God of War," says Mason. "A bit like our Gallic guest here? I mean, leaving aside the celestial urban planning aspect, back in Xianyang?"

"Oh dear," says Maggie. "Now you have me thinking about the Canova statue."

"*Canova! Canaille!*" from the Gallic guest.

"What's this about?" asks Mason, who as a professor really ought to know. Ah but nobody's perfect. Except for Maggie Mo who does her homework, as wisely one would if planning to defect from a globally powerful agency so as to insert oneself much earlier as the supreme leader of the whole nation. From Post-Xi to She, so to speak.

"Okay," says Maggie as the small sun sinks further down the sky of butterscotch…

"Don't betray me, *ma dominatrice chinoise.*" She does indeed give the orders, but let's not be thinking about the Marquis de Sade as regards spanking – that should require *ma domina chinoise, d'accord*? Josephine alone would sit Boney upon her lap; only he would tolerate this, from Josephine only. Besides which, Napoleon's government banned all of Sade's 'abominable' books as the product of a 'depraved imagination'; so there.

Now what's this about a statue by Antonio Canova, Italian superstar sculptor, and the planet Mars? We need a sidebar to explain. A side barsoom?

Canova is hugely admired throughout Europe and Napoleon wants a statue of himself dressed in a French General's uniform. Fair enough. But this statue, to be known as *Mars the Peacemaker*, must depict a heroic Napoleon who through war brought peace and unity to much of Europe.

"I say," Mason enthuses, "that's a bit like China totally winning the trade and technology war against the resentful collapsing US never mind its big bangs and bombs, thereby bringing peace and moderate prosperity all over the place, eh? From Peru to Poland to Palestine." Tu regere imperio populos, Sereses, memento.

Accordingly Napoleon in the role of Mars must needs be nude, a modest vine leaf hiding his penis and wrinkled scrotesack, pubic curls showing teasingly. No paunch but a marble six-pack. Athlete absolute. Classical cloak tossed over one arm, hand clutching the staff of peaceful power, a little winged victory upon an orb in his other hand. Best knee forward. Remarkably Napoleon granted five sittings, more likely *standings*, for this sublime though embarrassing statue.

After Waterloo, the statue identifying Napoleon with Mars ends up within the rising curve of the stairway of victorious Wellington's house, its modest address Number One London. Not as a trophy imprisoned there, no such intention – Wellington admires Canova. Likewise, Wellington admires Bonaparte, even though Wellington dislikes war itself.

"*There's* the smoking gun as regards Mars being a massive body in space," says Sharma," and also as compelling metaphor –"

"– and as mathemetical attractor in the space-time manifold," Maggie concludes. "Bend it like Beckham; Curve it like Canova. Thus we are here. *How intolerable!*"

An hour later they're still outside, since the time-pod is a bit cramped for relaxing.

A small lightly baked potato speeds ghostly through the sky. Suddenly silhouetted on top of the ridge appears Otaktay along with four armed chums, none riding thoats which might whinny or nicker or whatever noise they make. By 'four armed chums' we do *not* mean that these redskins have four arms – we allude to their tomahawks.

Immediately they're spotted, the Suzies throw themselves downslope towards our travellers, scattering dirt, uttering what one might well call the sioux halloo, their war-cry, their *hoka-hey.* Indeed it *is* a timely time to die for two of the braves as Maggie Mo swiftly draws once more the upcycled Regency pistol from her Hanfash sleeve, firing twice (in different directions). But now the pointed tip of a tossed tomahawk twitches the pistol from her grip. Is that by sheer accident or skill? Do these Braves intend to capture Maggie alive? The horror!

Her pistol is out of charge and hors de combat. She's about to scoop up one of the fallen tomahawks for some Krav Maga tomahawk axe combat when beau Boney interposes, bellowing, "I defend this woman with my wife!" As he would.

Now the odds are three to four. Does Mason actually count in this fight? Plainly any old Judo won't do. Does Sharma count? The academics do have their sabres out, waving those at the Lakota warriors.

Those with Jasoom-bred muscles of whatever quality should have a slight edge against three thousand *ords* of enfeebling adaptation to lower gravity. Sharma can even soar into the air here, somewhat at least. SuperSepoy.

There's just enough edge – as hatchets strike sparks from Damascus steel – to retreat into the time-pod like four hasty snails, each one pulling in its horns. Maggie Mo firstly in her stylish Hanfash, then Professor Mason then SuperSepoy – gosh but we think they'll get away with this! – then rearmost Napoleon himself valiantly thrusting and cutting, finally tugging the hatch shut. For a while hatchets batter upon the porthole's toughglass without causing so much as a haircrack. At least not so as you'd notice. Thwack thwack, hack hack, not a scratch to be seen.

"Wrong, so wrong," moans Colonel Mo. "Mathematically we're in an imperfective [redacted] space of [redacted] *parodics* as distinct from [redacted] *p-adics*. This space must collapse itself along with embedded observers unless –" With no time to calibrate nor even to collimate, trusting only to Lin Quinan's [redacted] cohomology, she slams the porthole lid shut to save their sanity from assault by strange topologies that might be glimpsed outside and she pushes the escape-button.

The vibrations which they now feel are so powerful that their timepod not only skitters and skews and skips like a flying saucer of china Crazily, this time it even *careens*.

Unseen realities and potentialities peel apart like gold leaf or like leaves lifting up from silk interleavings.

Professor of Time Studies Lin Quinan's specialists debrief Mason and Sharma for a full morning in the Randolph Hotel. Under hypnotism the prickle of expert acupuncture stimulation of the feet heightens the Dons' recollections pleasantly. After which, they head off – *not* limp off, no no, it wasn't that sort of questioning – for a luxury lunch with Colonel Mo at the King's Arms to sign off on their mission accomplished. On the way to the K. A. they pop into the ornamented cast-iron Covered Market of 1744 where Sharma buys half a dozen fragrant mauve roses wrapped in cellophane for 10 renminbi quid.

"I say, that's a bit…" Mason cannot quite put his finger upon what is 'a bit' about the roses. Excessive? Over the top?

"I feel *somehow* it's appropriate." Does the scent of the roses trigger some lost memory akin to Proust's Madeleine?

When the duo of Dons arrive at the erstwhile male-only den, one of Maggie Mo's security women is already sitting in there reading the famously subversive poetry of Su Shi of the Song Dynasty (whose poems were sung in streets) while sipping a sherry. A poet named Sushi, yummy! – this poet was also a great gastronome. The security woman's choice of reading matter might be seen as subversive towards the current Chinese state although certainly not personally towards Colonel Mo who selected her. If you insist, check out *Crow Terrace Censorship* but we shan't devote time to scribbling another sidebar, right? Nobody who notices the young lady's trim blue suit and the pack of her pistol and her sheathed knife will care to intrude into this snug-room. Mason's first act is to begin consulting the big bound menu.

Very soon comes Colonel Mo herself, through the Longwall Street door. Nods are exchanged with her security person.

And then, "Lovely roses. Sharma the charmer." Intently: "Why *exactly* those ones? I mean *exactly* exactly. What specially do they signify? Try to tell me before the sensation escapes."

"Does rather give a buzz to a chap," chips in Mason. "The acupunk. From one's sole right up to one's scalp."

"Shut up."

"I suppose," says Sharma, "that the colour feels right, maybe it's the wavelength of the light. Life like a dome of many-coloured glass stains the bright radiance of eternity."

"My Boy Generals, it's as though the three of us are awaking from a dream of alternatives. We must deduce what *specifically* we accomplished by the absence of what may have happened otherwise. I myself feel some unease that Napoleon died of no disease identifiable even by expert autopsy as of 1826."

"Comrade Colonel Maggie if I may," from Sharma, "did you undergo exactly the same acupuncture truth-testing as us?"

"Oh yes, except that I interrogated myself, thus maintaining full traceable responsibility. As is my prerogative and duty as political officer extraordinary."

Mason clears his throat. "Pray, how does one twirl a needle in the sole of one's own foot? Dash it but how athletic of you, Colonel Mo. Like that rapscallion gal Betsy?"

Maggie smiles winsomely. "There's really no need for more Nineteenth Century cod parlance."

"Surely there is always need," insists Sharma. "To keep the idiom of the folk lively."

"I beg to disagree. Thousands of Han folk surrendered their historic family names to help modernise the data-keeping of the People's Republic."

"Eh?"

"Millions of people voluntarily changed old-fashioned names to conform to the permitted electronic list. Why not? What's in a name? Are ancestors really so sacred?" For just a moment she looks haunted.

"What's in a name?" repeats Sharma who knows his Shakespeare backwards. As well as forwards which is far more useful, unless written in Arabic. "That which we call a rose by any other name would smell as sweet. A rose. We're invoking a rose! I bought six roses because this seemed right. Something is telling us something."

"Ha ha," says Maggie in a spoken laugh. "Now you are *echoing* Eco. *The Name of the Rose*. Why exactly do you mention Betsy?" she demands of Mason.

Meanwhile Rajit consults the King's Head menu at random. "Hmm, I see braised ox cheek nuggets… and ox cheek chilli… Seems to be a theme. Ox ox ox… reminds me of… a river."

"Obviously our very own *Ox*-ford, eh," from Mason almost breaks the magic moment.

"A river far a wei… like in Xanadu. Ma, Pa, Boy…"

Does Maggie look haunted again?

"My poor boy, you and your bally poets – that's *Alph* the sacred river if I'm not mistaken." Mason rubs his hands briskly. "I could polish off both of those cheeky chappies. The cheek nuggets *and* the chilli cheeks. Acupuncture debriefing does tickle up an appetite, eh?"

Maggie gestures *diminuendo*, *pianissimo*. They hark as if at the tiptoeings of departing dormice.

"Cards on the table," whispers Sharma pianissimo. "Are we *positive* we never took Napoleon somewhere else outside of Saint Helena? Maybe we nipped off on some wild time-trip escapade to America, but we just can't remember..."

Mason hoots. "Napoleon Bonaparte, First Emperor of the First Nations! Imagine that. *Ox on the table*," he insists – there's something significant about an ox.

Maggie is concentrating intensely. Finally she shakes her head as if to chase off a mosquito. Their efforts *did* succeed in modifying history delicately, a bit like achieving moderate prosperity as distinct from planet-devouring riches.

Fact: previously there was poisonous arsenical green wallpaper, which might indeed have killed or helped to kill Napoleon by 1821, that year being calculated by specialist actuaries. Fact: after a supposed visit by an enigmatic, although bold-as-top-brass trio of Porlock persons, mellow Chinese wallpaper now adorns Nap's bedroom and bathroom walls – and the arsenical green wallpaper is all lying a *li* away near a cart abandoned along with its liberated horse...

Fact: Boney becomes devoted to Chinese wallpaper. In Freudian terms you might even say he cathects, to far Cathay. That's like visiting emotionally. Freud views the act of thinking as akin to how a general shifts miniature figures about on a map. It is at this point in her analysis that Maggie often feels herself most vulnerable. It seems to her she once nursed some huge ambition which must be repressed except maybe as a forbidden Chi-Sci-Fi fantasy for circulation only amongst regime insiders. Professor Lin's entanglement comparison authenticator device, the ECAD, should perhaps be fed this detail; but perhaps better not... Better not mention 'Cathay' in political company. Let's not open this particular can of Uygurs.

One might argue that Maggie's recommendation of Saint Helena as destination for a manipulation is an act of 'chronic compliance' rather than a true intervention, but heigh ho. Softly softly catchee monkey, as Professor Mason might put it. The next historical intervention should be bigger, moderately so.

Once again, Napoleon's thoughts drift back in time to Joséphine's astonishing rose garden at Malmaison Mansion eight miles to the west of Notre Dame de Paris. Boney's beloved, Marie-Joseph-Rose de Tascher de la Pagerie, is known to her posh family and friends as *Rose* on her Caribbean island of birth, Martinique. Napoleon thought the name Rose a bit common, like some chambermaid's. He emphasises the *Joseph*ine aspect which fits much better with the title of Empress. "Not tonight, Rose!" just won't sound the same.

Malmaison… literally, 'bad house' due to being a den of Norman brigands during the 13th Century. This venerable château accordingly is priced at a small to middling fortune even though requiring a second fortune in renovations. Josephine capriciously buys Malmaison because she expects a fortune in loot to result from Boney's expedition to Egypt, but Boney forgives his beloved fairly soon and this proves to be a blessèd decision. Do we not still buy prints from the immortal *Redouté's Roses* – the exquisite record of Rose's roses – to hang in our homes on the advice of TV stylists?

Joséphine's rose garden was respected so much that during a temporary truce (Treaty of Amiens, ahem) the Royal Navy allowed ships to pass through their blockade if they were carrying rose bushes for the Empress. She's one enthusiastic collector. Naturally Josephine employs a hybridiser but that's the same as doing the job herself, in the same way as a ghosted celebrity memoir is the work of the celebrity. Many of her hybrids bear the names of illustrious women. The Malmaison heritage hybrids are long-blooming with many petals, though they do rather lack fragrance. A gene got dropped.

In his garden of exile on Saint Helena, finally adopted by Napoleon as the salvation of his hypothetical soul, by the year 1825 he breeds – yes, he himself breeds – a fragrant beauty which it is his prerogative to name.

As Voltaire puts it, *Il faut cultiver notre jardin.* We must take care of our roses. Even here on such windswept if tropical heights.

Betsy Balcombe hybridised 1825 on St Helena by Napoleon Bonaparte, widower of "Empress of Roses" Josephine de Beauharnais, during Napoleon's long exile. A sweet-scented everblooming mauve cultivar out of Chinese Rose (*R. chinensis*) resembling a giant 'parma violet' sugared flower confection from Toulouse, France.

– from *Zhongguo Meiguihua Baike Quanshu* (*Rose Encyclopedia of China*)
Abundant World Publishing: Beijing 2050 CE

Author's Note:

Herein I have taken various liberties. I decided not to torment treasured acquaintances by imploring them to check my French or Latin or Chinese misusages. Let the world laugh – and I shall laugh with it!

We may still wonder about one matter: Why was Bi Wang castrated?

The Chinese Time Machine

4th Trip: Sherlock Holmes and the Butterfly Effect

Few people are aware that certain actions which Sherlock Holmes undertook on behalf of the British Admiralty in China's Shandong province during the First World War unintentionally led to the founding of the Chinese Communist Party in 1923.

Thus the reigning Chinese Politbureau of the mid-22nd century regard Holmes with a certain respect as for an ancestor – at the same time as they abhor all the help which Holmes constantly gave to the ruling houses of Europe, resulting in the creation of the United Kingdom of Europe, capital in Brussels, adversely affecting China's growth.

To ensure the continuity of the Chinese Communist Party while preventing a pan-European Kingdom will require fine tuning of events every bit as skilfully as for a Stradivarius, preferably with the co-operation of the virtuoso though vain detective…

The two time-travellers, David Mason and Rajit Sharma, lie semi-hallucinating on adjacent tolerably clean and comfortable mattresses upon bed frames of carved Burma teak in an opium house in London's Limehouse district, near the docks. Comfortable damask cushions cradle the users' heads. A maid passes softly by, seeing that the clients' long pipes remain upon the oil lamps, all flames turned low. Brown smoke hazes the air. Reality trembles like a child prostitute meeting their first client.

Opium expands time and space. Mason trails a hand through the air, copies of itself staying visible to his gaze in a disconcerting way. It is and it isn't there, many times over. At least Holmes supposes that is what is going through the Oxonian's mind. Such assuredly is the burly man's clipped nevertheless plummy accent. An accent shared, be it noted, with self-proclaimed Doctor of Philosophy

Sharma – although a nasal whine of Birmingham Brummie faintly underlies the Hindu's impeccable English, which is odd.

"Where?" murmurs Mason. "And when? It's… fasc-in-at-ing."

"Fascinating indeed," agrees Holmes who sits contemplating in a rattan chair nearby. He's wearing his belted half-cape coat and deerstalker because with childish glee the darker visitor 'from the future' specially requested this costume even though no moor nor vile landscape is nearby unless one counts the foul mud along the Thames at low tide.

Nor does Holmes indulge himself in opium. Truth be told, not ever. When he needs cerebral stimulus he'll use cocaine, morphine, or shag tobacco. Right now Holmes requires no such stimulus, since his visitors provide this fully.

The relaxing effect of opium might – or might not – loosen the tongue of even the best-trained spy. Which is why Holmes acceded to the enthusiasms of the taller, dusky young man. Downstairs at Holmes's digs earlier on, bizarrely this 'gentleman' shed a short frock-coat – now resumed – as though that were some overcoat. Beneath, a double-breasted waistcoat was unaccountably loosened and flapping, as if there was a heat-wave this present October. The other fellow – for so Mason claimed to be *academically* – wears a lounging jacket woven of Harris tweed with incongruous plus-fours below. Neither man has been near a tailor, yet they are kitted out as if to impress.

Holmes leans towards Mason. "Tell me again where you come from. And from *when*?"

In the Oxford of 2050 a week ago, or 170 years ahead depending upon how one looks at it, an elegant woman from Guoanbu, the Chinese State Security Ministry, instructs Mason and Sharma. She's tall and slim in her smartly tailored future-blu uniform, two gold stars on the epaulettes. Raven hair, chestnut highlights, divided on the left to expose a wide brow. Jet-pupil almond eyes transfix from behind full horn-rimmed glasses which may be Armani from the Dukedom of Italy. Perfectly drawn red lips. She's a bit like a lovely mantis.

That woman's name is Maggie Mo. Chinese officials often have 'English' first names for use with Westerners. This adds a level of mystery and masquerade. Incidentally, when not used as a surname, Mo 莫 means *Don't.* Maggie is General Don't. And also General Do. Supposing that stars denote a general.

Right now, Maggie Mo would gladly surrender a star from her shoulder to be the person receiving instructions rather than giving them. She might even sacrifice two stars.

For her personal passion happens to be the late Victorian period of what would become the Great British Battenberg Barony – or GB-BB – within the UK of Europe. The period when Herbert George Wells envisioned invisibility, for instance – oh to be a security officer unseen yet with public fame as a Shanghai film star. The period of artist extraordinary Aubrey Beardsley and of forbidden absinthe.

Guoanbu's 17th Bureau – its Enterprises Division – oversees Beijing's Time Institute that built the 'pod' which can carry people into the past. Tampering with time is a sensitive political matter. This is restricted Chinese knowledge, but they use the best tools to accomplish each mission, in the sense of recruiting the best agents. In this case, as previously, Mason and Sharma fit the bill.

Although soon to be displaced by more than a century, Mason and Sharma are part of the same milieu which Holmes and Watson navigate confidently, pistols in their pockets, fists ready to box. Mason and Sharma both are Oxford men, the former a historian of ideas, the latter a specialist in the literature of the Victorian era which culminates in Arthur Conan Doyle. Lanky and dusky, Rajit Sharma could be the son of a Raja of the Indian Empire, Mason a portly stockbroker.

There's only one person better prepared than them for the mission, not merely as regards cultural knowledge of the late Victorian period but also of the intricate web of events which even a minor time-change might affect. Yet two-star Maggie Mo is an official too high in rank and too valuable to risk losing in the past without any rescue technology available. For you cannot dip a toe twice into exactly the same eddy of the timestream without you originating there first of all, though the time-pod can travel autonomously.

Amply compensated, Mason and Sharma will be well advised to keep absolutely mum about what Maggie Mo confides. Likewise, other worthies of useful Oxford University. The time-pod is presently stationed in the University's vaulted medieval Divinity School, a spacious, closed-off location attended by élite Han technicians. The pod is a giant egg of shimmery pearl with three fat wheels in case it needs pushing by hand, a single porthole to see out of. On an easel rests a blackboard which Mo quickly cleans of some scribblings, chalking up instead almost derisively three letters followed by a couple of characters like a primary teacher on the first day of class:

UKE
中国

"The United Kingdom of Europe," she declares. "Down below, there's the Middle Kingdom in other words Zhōngguó, namely China. Due to its unshakeable unity the UKE impedes China somewhat. To a significant degree whose fault is that? Our own scholars and myself alike believe that a crucial figure is the detective Sherlock Holmes who constantly bolstered European monarchs and noble houses by solving crimes and muting scandals which otherwise would have resulted in hostilities and revolutions which would have torn apart the network of royal relationships."

Does her voice tremble at mention of those times out of reach? That's unacceptable. Private yearnings cannot interfere with the mission. But how Maggie yearns to visit Victorian London in person. Indeed her expertise is why she is here, so frustratingly in charge of this particular mission.

"I promise we will bring a certain vital person from that past to meet you," Sharma says consolingly. He understands.

"Thank you! I shall merely miss experiencing the actual streets, the weather, the buildings, the sounds, the smells, the Savoy operettas –" Would the lorgnettes of ladies in other red boxes swivel at sight of her oriental face? "The Criterion restaurant, Simpson's in the Strand," she concludes as much bitterly as sarcastically.

And if Sherlock Holmes refuses to accompany Mason and Sharma for a quick trip to futurity? Surely everybody wants to step ahead a century and more! Especially when the future is pleasant enough. A no-brainer.

*

As Mason and Sharma proceed along Baker Street reading the numbers on doorways, suddenly the next door swings open and from the shadows within looms a sizable moon-faced female in fulsome black drapery, a bustle jutting out behind like a cushion stitched to her backside. Upon her head, a lace cap. Endow her waist with a bunch of keys and for sure she's a landlady. She beams. "It's here," she informs the startled duo.

They look behind, they look across the way. People pass by, but no, she is addressing them, and she doesn't seem to think that any more explanation is necessary. She draws aside so that they can enter.

The hallway is small. There's nowhere for Sharma to hang his frock coat except for the arms of Mrs Hudson which she proceeds to offer after her dusky visitor begins to divest himself, to her mild amusement seemingly. On top of the frock coat go both men's matching grey Homburg hats, of stiff felt with dented crowns. Mrs Hudson, she must be Mrs Hudson, has to be. Sharma can scarcely stop staring at her. She's unlike her many imaginary portraits, having a touch of the washerwoman about her.

"He's upstairs." Burdened by the coat and hats, she gestures with her chin at steep stairs. "He'll be expecting you."

"But how did you *know*...?" begins Mason.

How many times has someone asked that very same question in this hallway? Enough times for Mrs Hudson to recite automatically:

"You came along Baker Street checking the house numbers with mounting urgency the closer you got to here."

"Amazing!" Mason exclaims with true admiration. Mrs Hudson sketches a smug smile. "And how is it you've been on the look-out so much?"

"Lately there's been little enough –" The landlady's smile fades. She clams up; she *shan't* go down in history as a gossip. The stairs await.

Holmes does not rise from his armchair by the fireplace since visitors first need to galvanise his curiosity; otherwise, they'll be dismissed. The coarse shag he's smoking in a meerschaum pipe smells strong; you can suck meerschaum pipes more vigorously than briar pipes, reaching higher temperatures. There's a dizzying fug in the air.

"Mr Holmes, sir, the honour is ours!" Mason presents their visiting cards printed in 2050, both cards in unison being wise since Sharma almost capers like a giant gangly puppy. In this big sitting room of high windows here's the sideboard with the Persian slipper that keeps Holmes's shag tobacco from getting dry, and left-overs of a woodcock to snack on. Here's the stick rack; and the bearskin hearthrug; and the cocaine cooker kit.

Also, the framed portrait of "Chinese" Gordon who put an end to the bloodiest war of the 19th Century, the Taiping Rebellion, God-crazy proto-communists versus an established dynasty; Maggie Mo might have mixed feelings as to sides.

Over there is the chemistry corner with side table stained by acids, and a microscope of modest power. On the mantlepiece of the black marble fireplace correspondence of no value is impaled ready to set fire to kindling.

And in the wall nearby are the famous initials V R, topped by a crown, made by bullets during precision target practice. To achieve such accuracy Holmes must have used a long-barrel service revolver and intense concentration on several occasions.

And there's the problem: *Victoria Regina.* Holmes's extreme royalism extending protectively to any minor European princelet.

"Mr Holmes," says Mason. "I shall be frank. We come from the future."

"Certainly you do not appear to be from the present," replies Holmes, setting his pipe aside. "At least as regards discarding a frock coat downstairs instead of wearing it while visiting, as I presume has happened. Do you suffer from a nervous disease, Mr Sharma? Something exotic brought back from the Indian Empire?"

"Not at all! I'm just thrilled to meet you at last, sir. As my colleague says, we are from the future."

"Perhaps you are influenced by a piece of fanciful fiction?"

"Fiction? What fiction? Not in the slightest!"

No no no. They're completely safe. Wells' *Time Machine* hasn't been published yet!

Holmes's languid gesture indicates his chemistry corner. "I happened to notice a squib in the Royal College of Science's journal for science students. I too am a student of science. Now what was the title of the piece? *Chronic* something…" Holmes raises his pipe and puffs. "*Argonauts*?"

In a hissed aside, "Damn it, Mason, I forgot but that's Bertie's *first* use of a time machine."

"So the idea of travel through time is not unknown to me. The problem is whether *you yourselves* accomplished this, or are feigning and why so."

Sharma responds brightly, "Once you eliminate the impossible, whatever remains, no matter how improbable, must be the truth."

Holmes snorts. "What poppycock! Whoever came up with such stupidity? To eliminate the impossible would take centuries. Raise your game, Gentlemen. If you come to me with this bizarre story I don't doubt you foresaw that you'd need to show some proof. So what will you show me from 'the future'?"

This is going faster than expected. From his jacket pocket Mason produces his Huawei 340 Pro, as planned. There's no signal, of course, but the phone packs plenty inside of itself, such as molecular MiniSinoSiri. Sharma and Mason exchange nods. Mason switches on. The screen with its Apps brightens.

Sharma instructs clearly, "SinoSiri, recite *The Charge of the Light Brigade* by Alfred Lord Tennyson."

The sweet familiar voice commences:

"Half a league, half a league,
"Half a league onward,

"All in the valley of Death
"Rode the six hundred –"

Now Holmes arises, placing a hand over his heart. "Since our beloved Laureate is quite recently interred in Westminster Abbey, he shall *not* be used as emotional bait."

"Didn't you know Tennyson died recently?" Mason hisses at Sharma.

"SinoSiri, stop!"

"But do let me hold that device."

"Yes of course."

Holmes' fingers dance nimbly at random then pause as bright red British uniforms, white helmets, and rifles appear; before leaving 2050 Mason was watching *Zulu* the original movie.

"Surely," Holmes says wonderingly, "this is the Battle of Rorke's Drift for which eleven Victoria Crosses were awarded! Surely no kinetoscope exists which can possibly… the colour, the clarity, the continuity… unless invisible chronic argonaut carriages *do* exist… which must also be miniature… If this be a conjuring trick…"

"No," Mason assures, "it's a motion picture from seventy years in the future from now. No invisible time machines are involved. No blood is shed, nobody dies."

"But the Zulu savages –"

"– Those black actors live in a rainbow nation. *Lived*, I mean – by now they must all be dead of old age. Sorry if I confuse."

Holmes's fingers fly again and a menu of names and numbers appears.

"As well as much else, this may *primarily* be some kind of *telephone*, although without any line to connect it."

"Mr Holmes, how can you possibly deduce that!?"

"Personally I need no telephone. Telegrams serve me better. Telegrams are concise and permit time for analysis. Yet certain numerical principles regarding webs and networks must apply to telephony…"

Holmes's astonishment level is still low.

"Let me show you another 'trick' this device performs." Mason recovers the Huawei and snaps a photo of Holmes. He turns the screen to the detective.

"Hmm! I see myself and my background a couple of seconds ago. This is faster than any tintype photography of which I know hitherto–"

Damn it, that photo *per se* is not astonishing.

Yet oh the value of a genuine photo of the great detective in this historic room! In case of accidental deletion, Mason slips back to the previous photo in memory, which happens to be of two-star Maggie Mo beside the blackboard in Oxford's medieval vaulted Divinity School.

"An *oriental woman* military officer!" exclaims Holmes. "And not lacking in charms. You have indeed now piqued my interest. Congratulations, Gentlemen. Let us work on the hypothesis that I believe you. My diary is clear for the rest of the day. In what may this modest consulting detective, first and only of his profession, help you?" Few times can the word 'modest' have been pronounced with such disingenuousness.

Sharma shuffles. "We want to help to make a better future world… Dear me, do I sound as if I'm taking part in a beauty pageant?"

"I think," replies Holmes enigmatically, "you can safely leave such activities to the Belgians." A discreet cough. "I intend no disrespect to the royal house of Leopold despite what is noised about the Congo."

Worse than Poland under the Nazis. "To be sure," agrees Mason hurriedly.

They cannot reasonably expect Holmes to accompany them to the pod hidden by bushes in Regent's Park. Even if Holmes agrees to go for a stroll, an egg on wheels with three seats and a few buttons and levers might strike the most brilliant brain of the age as of dubious proof compared with contraptions from the Grande Fête of the Future in Paris as shown in the *Illustrated London News*.

"If only," muses Mason, "you might go with us on a quick *hop* into the future. That Chinese lady explains things so vividly, compared with ourselves."

"You sound like a pimp," from Sharma, which shuts Mason up.

Holmes takes up his pipe and puffs shag. "Tempting. Your Chinese Lady sounds intriguing. But there are cogent reasons for not straying from town… reasons beyond your ken."

"Beyond our Kensington, ha ha." Sharma becomes excited. "This town! I have spent half my career studying your era. Would it be too much to ask…?"

"To look around town? I don't see why not. In due course you may confess your true motives. It's cloudy today but there'll be no rain."

"The Criterion, Simpson's, Bart's Hospital, Piccadilly…" Sharma might be writing a letter to Santa Claus. "To meet the Irregulars, to call at your tobacconist, to ride in a carriage –"

"To visit an opium den?" Holmes suggests.

To uphold the decorum of the street no regular cab stand is nearby, but a vacant 'growler' carriage happens to have halted by the kerb thirty yards away. Its top-hatted driver is consulting a newspaper while his horse occupies itself feeding from a nosebag now flat on the roadway.

"As seeming admirers of myself," Holmes remarks, "you may know that I favour a two-seater Hansom for speed. However, for comfort three persons require a carriage. And conveniently…" Holmes raises his cane to catch the cabman's attention.

Out from behind the still stationary four-wheeler suddenly comes a nimble hansom. A flat-cap cabbie lays on to his horse with his long lash, cutting around the front of the heavier growler cab.

"What the deuce?" Holmes glances at Mason, at Sharma, at the four-wheeler, at the hansom – analysing the situation with the speed of a supercomputer which doesn't yet exist.

"Looks like he's desperate for a fare," says Mason.

"A fare for three fellows crammed in his two-person cab?" Holmes tssks. "Plainly kidnap by hansom isn't any plan of *yours*, Futurians. Yet is kidnap itself the plan? The plan of someone expecting one man, not three. Willing to risk finding out? At a push three chaps *can* share a hansom. The destination must be very near to here otherwise alone I would soon jump out irrespective of twisting an ankle – curiosity would keep me in the cab for two minutes at most – so the plan may be a serious bashing with broken bones to keep me at home for months."

The hansom stops perfectly beside the trio. The cabman's nose is squashed as if well acquainted with fisticuffs, and under the brim of his cloth cap a short forehead soon meets bushy brows.

"I'm game," declares Mason. "I'm a former Oxford Martial Arts Blue."

"So! The game is afoot…! Hmm, words worth remembering."

They board, Mason squashing against skinny Sharma which pretty much immobilises both men. Holmes throws open the trap door up behind his head and calls, "Limehouse, Cabby."

"Guv," growls the driver and takes off at a fair lick. Scarcely has the cab sped a hundred yards than abruptly it quits the main thoroughfare.

"Well, that was fast," says Holmes, in a voice that says "as I told you it would be".

Perilously the hansom corners, narrowly missing a post and going up momentarily on one wheel before slumping back. Surely at least one horseshoe skidded. Poor horse could easily have gone down, breaking a leg. In that case, curtains for the hoss. Thus the 'cabbie' doesn't care a hoot. Now they're in a cobbled mews rattling them horridly. No one in sight ahead, although the door to one stable is open.

"Hey up there, cabman!" calls Mason in protest.

Overhead, the reins pull back tight, wrenching the horse's head. "Whoa!" bellows Beetlebrow. Though not in response to the Oxford man.

Before the vehicle can fully stop Holmes has kicked aside the low rain-door and is outside, slashing upward with his cane as the cabman comes to a halt now parallel with himself. The cabman's cursing cry of surprise and pain accompanies him dropping a freshly-seized bludgeon.

"Join me, Gentlemen! With all due despatch!" Holmes' nostrils flare. "I smell Stout. Let us wallop the opposition."

Out of that dim stable stagger two evident ruffians, both of them clutching strong sticks. One still also holds a bottle from Fuller's brewery. They've been drinking to pass the time, maybe for hours, till their presumed solitary victim arrives. Mason and Sharma disentangle themselves and provide reinforcement, Sharma less boldly since the stick he confronts is knobbly and knotty. Mason rushes at the assailant who clutches the bottle of stout – and manages to execute a full hip throw, oh goshi! This leaves Mason panting, his hands upon his knees, but the cobbles have bashed the assailant's cranium.

Holmes pushes in front of Sharma. The detective's walking cane counters the knobbly shillelagh as the weapon whacks at Holmes. It's easy for a master of singlestick to hit his drunken foe across the side of the neck, causing collapse due to half the brain fainting. Holmes swings smartly around but the ex-cabman is already legging it away, favouring his sore limb.

"Did you *see* me there, Rajit?" Mason gasps as Holmes grips the shillelagh villain by the scruff since the other miscreant appears to be concussed.

"Tell me the name that hired you!" demands Holmes.

The ruffian hides his face with his arm and blubbers. Exasperated, Holmes addresses his companions for want of other audience: "Of course this creature will not know any useful name. But I swear to you that if London be a giant web and if myself be a spider sensitive to the twitches, that there lurks another spider, cunning and malevolent." Sharma certainly takes this in, though Mason may still be preening.

"Well," Holmes continues more calmly, "it's said that opium brings peace to the troubled, although many of the Chinese nation may not agree. So let us continue our journey."

"But the driver has skedaddled," Mason observes.

Whereupon Holmes makes strange clicking noises at the horse, then confidently mounts the rear of the hansom and gathers up the reins.

"Gentlemen, your carriage awaits. We can leave the horse and hansom at a cabman's shelter nearer to Limehouse and continue on foot."

Before stepping up inside, Sharma winks at Mason. "*Sherlock Holmes*, no less, is about to chauffeur us by cab through Victorian London. Best that Maggie Mo never knows – she'd never forgive us."

"Perhaps another pipe of paradise?" Mason implores Holmes. "I don't feel stupefied at all."

"I did ask Li Yi – the maid – to prepare mild doses for newcomers. But anyway, you have not eaten since arriving at Baker Street. Maybe you've worked up an appetite by now?"

Needless to say neither has Holmes snatched a bite even of the cold woodcock on the sideboard since the pair first knocked on his study door. Nor is opium normally any booster of appetite. But for Mason, deduces Holmes, a variety of pleasures should ideally succeed one another.

"I do feel a bit peckish myself," mentions Holmes suggestively.

Sharma speaks up. "Mr Holmes, I don't wish to seem brash, but I have some sovereigns to burn – in a manner of speaking. Let yourself be our guest this evening if you would do us the honour."

"Well spoken, sir. Where else should one go to but Simpson's in the Strand?" One of Holmes' favourite restaurants.

So here they are. The great dining room is bright with illumination from wall sconces and pendant lamps and white table linen covering the dining tables. By the doorway a grand piano plays unobtrusively, its music mostly drowned by laughter and chatter amid the clink of cutlery upon porcelain. Some theatrical-looking ladies dressed to the nines sip champagne, for it is evening now. A gentleman repairs to the smoking divan upstairs, unlit cigar in hand. The trio have a table halfway down the room, over to the right.

"Oh there's one of the famous carving trollies," enthuses Sharma. Big domed solid silver dishes cover succulent roast beef of Old England, guided around the tables by a Master Carver.

"Indeed. Sirloin of beef, or saddle of mutton? I believe roast beef is appropriate. To accompany which, I would recommend the Quinta do Noval Petit Verdot, a very respectable Portuguese vintage. Do we agree?"

Thus is the sommelier instructed.

The wine arrives cradled in a towel. Holmes approves both the label and then the bouquet. The sommelier pours what one might call a study in ruby red.

The meat presently carved from the joint is also a study in red rareity – thick succulent slices, soon joined by the finest horseradish sauce in London, potatoes roasted in goose fat, bright orange carrots, crispy Yorkshire pudding, and a port-wine gravy.

This done, Holmes leans forward. "I am not unacquainted with pharmacology. So I am well aware that opium *by itself* does not loosen tongues when smoked. And when dissolved in alcohol as laudanum, any 'indiscretion' effect is largely due to the alcohol. At what one might call the 'molten caramel' stage of the opium Li Yi obligingly added a few grains of a substance I provided, the name of which I shall withhold."

Sharma gapes at Holmes.

"Do eat. As shall I."

"I never imagined you capable of drugging a pair of strangers," says Mason.

"Doubtless because you little know me." Holmes slices beef, loads his fork, commences.

Nonplussed, Sharma does as Holmes did but then covers his mouth with his napkin to utter:

"In the accounts of your exploits which have come down to us nothing indicates this as your style." Sharma's tone may be bitter; it's hard to tell given a juicy mouthful of food competing.

"Many aspects of my exploits are withheld simply due to lack of a constant chronicler."

"But Watson?" asks Mason "Whom we have not yet met. Does he not write up your deeds?"

"My dear fellow, Watson is a fiction – a doctor companion invented by Doyle. That is Arthur Conan Doyle, the Scots author who has begun to publish accounts of my cases for ridiculous amounts of money, when he would very much rather be penning," and he snorts, "historical fictions. Scribbling about my own humble doings to satisfy public demand robs him of time."

Mason raises an eyebrow to hear the word 'humble' coming from Holmes, but he also raises a lavishly loaded fork. To be served such a bounty of beef is far from normal in 2050, even at a college feast or gaudy when maybe a single slice of rare Angus might be plated along with nicely boiled Jersey potatoes.

Mason gestures. "So there *is* no Watson?"

"If only I did have a devoted Watson, how useful he would be. Someone who can listen to me think aloud and prompt me with suitable questions. To remind me of the obvious which sometimes escapes me while I'm deep in a knotty problem. Not indispensable, of course, but… useful."

Holmes lays down his fork. "What I did deduce in the opium establishment from stray words of yourself and Mr Mason is that your mission here is intended to assist an unexpected great power of the future by altering aspects of the present day, although I know not how, nor why, nor where, nor when. Too many questions, not enough answers. Consequently, I am sorry, gentlemen. In order to avoid that future which you will not tell me about in any detail, you will need another plan. For I am not leaving London. There is an enemy at large, scheming evilly. I neither wish nor dare to leave London except for a quick dash to say Dartmoor or Norfolk."

Just as cogent, perhaps, is that in the London of the Victorians Holmes is godlike. He knows all the ashes of tobaccos, the droppings of horses, the printers' fonts for setting headlines. What would he be in 2050? An object of study. Admiring study but study nonetheless.

"Do you have somewhere to spend the night, Gentlemen, where a cab may pass by way of on our departure? Or will you merely disappear into fog?"

Mason tells Holmes, "In truth we left our vehicle hidden amidst bushes in Regent's Park. You are very welcome to visit our 'egg'. To come aboard for a while, purely to satisfy curiosity."

Holmes smiles. "As you have witnessed, I am well able to evade abduction. I suggest that for now we should devote ourselves to this excellent nutrition." He raises his glass of Petit Verdot from Portugal, England's oldest ally.

"So what do you call this if not a bungle a botch and a balls-up!" Maggie Mo is steaming. Maybe not literarily, but scorching vapour is all that's missing from her fury of frustration. Her eyes blaze at Sharma and Mason like a cinematic dragon's. Maybe those aren't actual flames that are roasting Sharma and Mason, it just feels so.

"It wasn't a simple mission." Thus Mason tries to excuse them. "Sherlock Holmes isn't silly."

"Oh really? That's the conclusion you arrived at? Using the most advanced ultrasecret technology to send a pair of experts a century and a half into the past to bring back the news that Sherlock Holmes, the most astute, clever, and perceptive of men… 'isn't silly'! Wow, that's money well spent."

The two Oxonians are seated in a soundproofed private chamber at one end of the long gloomy vestibule which gives access midway to the Divinity School. Their wooden chairs are unpadded. No table protects them from Maggie Mo righteously upright before them. She is an indignant schooma'am, a pissed-off boss, a colleague cheated – and a caged tigress certain that *she* would have succeeded were it not for sodding bureaucracy.

Placatingly, Sharma says, "Here's the problem. We couldn't tell Holmes anything. If we lied, he'd have known right away. If we told the truth, given his regard for any old royals, why should his interests align with ours? A UK of Europe might have seemed like a champion idea to him."

"What's more," adds Mason, "our arrival coincided with the first signs of Moriarty. And lo, the bloodhound sniffed the wind." Mason can be the king of metaphors when he cares. "No human power could drag Holmes aside."

"Of course Holmes caught a scent!" bawls Maggie Mo. "He just didn't express this in his usual forthright and unsubtle manner."

Mason can tell that Maggie was about to say 'like westerners do' but nobody gets to the rank of Comrade Mo without being aware that politically correct diplomacy must clamp down occasionally.

The pair should have kept close to Holmes. Theirs should have been a long, subtle, meticulous job. Morons! They had enough authentic period banknotes rolled up tightly. Men! Running back to Mummy! Scared by a bit of street violence too, no doubt.

Finally she growls in a low voice, "Too much to ask you to spend more time with Holmes, eh? Coming back after one damn day!"

"Well, we couldn't really keep the time-egg safely parked in the park for too long… Could we? Risk of discovery. Dog runs into the bushes, child runs after the dog…"

They don't need to be great detectives to deduce how much she herself would have given had she been tasked as they had been.

Mason and Sharman exchange glances, nerving one another. Mason nods approval so Sharma leans forward in his chair in an almost Sherlockian fashion.

"The mission isn't a failure yet. We have an idea. As you say, it'll take time and a lot of fancy spadework to divert Holmes from his course. He's a glacier. We don't want to disappear him, just to divert him gently. That's a job for someone who's at his side day after day. Someone who knows him and understands him, someone who knows where to push gently or let fall an opportune remark. Sherlock Holmes needs a Watson."

"But Watson never existed! That's the pen-name of Conan Doyle."

"That can change. We just need to come up with the perfect person and plant her at Holmes's side."

"Did you say *her*?"

"Well, I wouldn't wish to sound sexist… We need a person who can entice him with a more challenging and seductive case if he's about to rush instead to the aid of some European princess who's being blackmailed or some heir to a minor throne's mistress. A person willing to devote years to being Holmes's shadow."

Maggie Mo gazes at Sharma now, her eyes no longer blazing but with a different bright gleam in them.

"Continue," she says. Does her voice tremble a tad?

"Did we mention the candid interest that Holmes showed when he saw your photo?"

In London it's getting dark, though fog already took possession of the city a while ago. Streetlamps are lit. Those don't yet compete with the gloaming, but in less than an hour they'll be like fireflies or holy haloes. Sherlock Holmes puts his key in the lock. Mrs Hudson has already withdrawn to her own rooms and he doesn't care to disturb her. Whatever that idiot eye-doctor Doyle says, Holmes isn't inconsiderate.

"Good night, Mister Holmes."

Holmes freezes. It is not the first time somebody utters that same sentence at his back. How didn't he hear this unknown someone approaching? What a poor show. Unless the someone is really subtle. He turns and regards the newcomer.

Maggie Mo, dressed as a gent in striped trousers and a short frock coat suspiciously reminiscent of Sharma's, her black mane in a bun tight under her topper, feels in her pocket for two stars, her lucky charms.

Holmes beams. "Good night to you too. I was expecting you. Your room is ready."

And he opens the door to admit Maggie Mo. With a nod she enters this Baker Street house as if to the manor born and ascends the stairs.

Sharma and Mason regard the plates before them without enthusiasm. After pints in the Dowager Duchess of Deutschland pub in Queen Street they're in one of the cafés inside Oxford's Covered Market, the name of which can stay mum. They'd ordered its traditional beef and two veg with boiled spuds and a micro Yorkshire pudding accompanied by gravy from granules.

A ghost of what they took in Simpson's in 1894. The two humble slivers of beef are grey. The Yorkshire pud is part burned, part soggy. Sharma sniffs, cuts, forks, chews, swallows without relish.

"They might be eating there right now." Mason has read his thought. "I wonder when the consequences will reach us? Supposing that we realise. With Holmes diverted from his previous course I do hope there aren't any stupid conflicts in a patchwork Europe. Oh why the devil did we come here to eat?"

"Them. Lunching. At Simpson's." Sharma sighs and sets down his fork. "There's no worse nostalgia. *A La Recherche de Palate Perdu.*"

"I do wonder what Holmes would think of the USA falling apart and the non-stupid states all unifying with Canada."

Sharma raises a cup of tea, for this café lacks an alcohol license.

"Yes indeed. Here's to Her Majesty Meghan Markle, long may she reign over them."

Hot Gates

And then she does this incredibly crazy thing and I've no choice but to go along with her…

It's 8.00 in the morning, and I'm sitting on the edge of one of the tombs upon the Mount of Olives. My booted feet are strapped securely to the flyboard ready to go just as soon as the old city beyond the walls on the other side of the valley shows any steamy signs of melting. Assuming that a melting does happen! But I'm betting my bottom dollar on this.

And surely if not today, then tomorrow. Yesterday, I spent sitting here from sunrise to sunset, listening to all the soaring symphonies of Bruckner, like traversing alpine valley after alpine valley constantly upward towards ever brighter golden light. For today I choose all the works of Chopin. Plinkel plinkel plinkel plonk.

Fat payment if I'm right. Everyone else seems to downplay Jerusalem as too *precious* to be melted. World Heritage of Mankind city, eh? Featuring the golden Dome of the Rock, the Church of the Holy Sep, the Via Dol, the Cathy of Saint Jim, fetish sites for five or six Abrahamic faiths forever squabbling with each other. Maybe that's because it's half a century since there was an actual physical frontier here inside Jeru.

Melts to date include places such as Panmunjom's Joint Security Area between North and South Korea, the Wagah border crossing between India and Pakistan, the line between Pakistan and Afghanistan. Always border crossings. More often than not, highly sensitive spots. Places of tension. After fifteen mysterious melts so far, we'd sussed *that* connection out.

Purpose of melts, provocation? But by what, from where, and how? And why?

What do you do when places are melting mysteriously? You call Vulcanologists, the guys (and gals) who – protectively costumed and with air supplies – ride the latest generation flyboards down into craters where red lava boils and bubbles, to take readings and study from up close. We're the monitors of pyroclastic flows racing down hillsides; even rushing out over open water at hundreds of kiloms an hour, no kidding. About fifty of us worldwide. Fatalities are very rare.

The world desperately needs more info. What if the UN HQ in New York melts in full session? Tele-steered drones aren't quite agile enough for our job, and a person might spy a vital clue which no robo would notice. So we have carte blanche as to which potential sites we go to.

Plinkel plonk plonky plonk. Suddenly this woman pops up in my way. She's puffing after presumably darting between umpteen Jewish graves like white coffins fallen off a container ship.

"Excuse me, Mister Volcano Man –"

"You're blocking me, ma'am. Shift a bit to the right?"

She complies. "You waiting for the Old City to melt?"

She's wearing scuffed black booties, a birdy indigo skirt, violet blouse. Black hair spills wavily from under a blue headscarf. Her eyes are dark marbles set in hard-boiled white of egg. Maybe that sounds unattractive, but it isn't so. On her left arm hangs a black leather bag.

"Seen you here yesterday, Mister V. You flew away sundown."

Indeed, I flew back to the genuinely exceptional YMCA Hotel where I'd slept. What a stylish place. My informant had not been lying. Tall bell tower, colonnades, high arched ceilings, lots of lights. Wall tiles proclaim in Arabic and Roman capitals and Hebrew, 'Here is a place whose atmosphere is peace where political and religious jealousies can be forgotten and international unity be fostered and developed. ' Ha-ha to that; this is Jerusalem. But there hadn't been any frontier here as such since the Six-Day War ages ago.

"Here you again today. Wearing no silver suit, just this jumpy with a V on the back –"

V for Vulcanologist, yes! We valiant airborne Vulcans are an élite. Probably the woman saw on TV some investigative Vulcans hovering over earlier melts protected by aluminised fire proximity suits. Turns out that radiant heat isn't much of a problem. A release of steam does precede melts yet not such as to cook any pigeon passing over. Thereafter it's a bit like cold fusion or maybe it isn't. My hi-viz green jumpsuit should be fully adequate even during the first moments of a melt. Thus my view shan't be limited to the letterbox window of a proximity suit. I'll be less impeded generally.

"A melt isn't like lava welling up," I tell the woman.

"My name is 'Lusine'. It means moon in Armenian."

"And in French 'L'usine' means 'factory', so what?"

Little Lady, please go away, even if your eyes are enchanting. White of egg? – nay, milky opal. Vulcanologists are geologists raised to a new level. Our heroes are Sigurður Þórarinsson and the Comte de Buffon who was no buffoon and Pliny the Elder who died by Vesuvius and Pliny the Younger who described that event impeccably and Haroun Tazieff and Cheminée and Prof Bill McGuire and the Johnston whom Mount St Helens killed which much traumatised Harry Glicken who himself died at Japanese Mount Unzen which also pyroclastically killed Katia Krafft and her spouse Maurice, my own special heroes.

Myself, aspiring to that roll of honour. And a bag of money. Though not for being dead.

"How sure are you the old city will melt? No other Vee watches."

"Lady, there are a *lot* of political hot spots worldwide that might attract a melt – if indeed that's the cause. I'm taking a gamble because Jerusalem's such a conflicted city."

At that moment, beyond her across the valley, I do see steam rising. "Step away!" Promptly I activate my flyboard, hoping not to burn her feet nor set fire to her skirt. I'm damned if I'll miss a moment of the melting of Jerusalem due to this woman or frankly *anybody* interrupting me.

Instead of complying, she does this amazing and contrary thing. She jumps on to my boots, latching her hands around my waist.

Oh but do I tilt forward due to all those unexpected undistributed extra kilos! Not that she's heavy in the least but she really destabilises me. My micro-turbs have stabilisers but this takes real hands-on skill with my glove controls. Direction, Altitude,

Thrust! DAT is how. Fortunately the design of the kerosene tanks in my backpack damps down any fuel slosh.

Recovering stability pulses me many metres upward and outward, while she continues hanging on resolutely. Supposing she falls, well *hell* this cannot be helped. I'm not setting down hereabouts. Ankle-twister tombs not to mention pop-up pines and cypresses as well as the unavoidable Biblical olives.

She copes as I rush west towards the wall of the city. What does this reckless Loon of Armenia want from me? Maybe she's seeking a bird's eye view. My flyboard puts out 93 decibels, more than a bus yet less than a buzzsaw. A fair few birds are in the sky now – scared by bad vibes? – but not one single rival Vee, which is ace. Many more pigeons and sparrows and things will be caught up in the melt along with all human habitants, maybe fifty thousand persons here, plus dogs, cats, rats, chickens, spiders, bacterias. There'll be up-early tourists in the melt too.

We're up and over the Old City, perfect size for a melt being about a kilometre square. All melts so far are thuswise. All happen during hours of daylight. This doesn't mean that up in orbit some alien dude focuses a giant burning lens as on an ants' nest.

Everything within the Old City smears. Buildings becoming a toddler's wonkier crayon impression of what was firm architecture just a mo ago. I rise a bit higher for perspective. Bye-bye, golden Dome of the Rock. Bye-bye, Via Dol and Church of the Holy Sep and Cathy of Saint Jim and umpteen lanes and houses. Bye-bye habitants a few of whom actually reach a roof along with their cat before dissolving. One Munch open-mouths upward at me, someone's last moment of existence. What's being done isn't nice even it's passably pretty.

Damn Luna's interference! Only now do I remember to chin-toggle the radio to call dibs on Jeru: "All hear, I Harry Adonis, Vulcan numero 56 declare that Jerusalem Old City is melting right now below *me* since sixty secs ago, mark. Am transmitting full telemetry and filming." Harry is short for Aristotle. Common touch.

"You're a Greek?" shrieks the Loon over the noise of the flyboard. "Those Kurd-killing Turkeys genocided a million Greeks just like they genocided us Armenians too –"

"Chip on your shoulder about genocides eh, Luna? Kindly shut up about that! I've work to do."

Below us everything mixes together in undulating swirls. My suite of instruments and cameras works on auto but benefits from my guiding glove for fine control. Radiant heat from below is way from being pyroclastic, more scaldy bathwater cooling as fast as it stiffens. Another few mins, I'll be able to land, unlock my boots, walk around if I wish. Without the woman's extra weight, not that a Vulcan is less than fit.

"Oh no chip now," shrills Luna. "I thank the God-Who-Never-Was that I'm free at last and out of here –!"

"Alexander: ignore female voice interference," I instruct my equip. What, let some local resident's unqualified comments intrude on my triumph?

Within the great sprawl of wavy pastel plastic-soup stuff pretty much all contents have been absorbed by now and converted into multicoloured homogoneity.

How she clings to me. "– No longer am I the slave to my obligatory Armenian massacre heritage! Just because state-sponsored Christians of Armenia reached Jeru as the first converted nation, and instead of massacring Armenians, the much too merciful ruling Muslims grant to Armenians the biggest part of the city. Armenians gain kiloms of walls to fix anti-Turk Armenian massacre posters on to centuries later –"

Of this I am aware, but *not right now*, thanks very much.

"I speak not of the massacring Crusades –"

I'm surprised she can speak at all as we waltz together over the melted city. Quite a class act of clinging. Luna uses the word 'massacre' quite a lot.

"No longer need I pay obeisance to my fucking family traditions for fear of… never mind –"

Never mind what? Some sexual naughty? Some bastard baby? Some money matter swept under a carpet? An abortion? A suffocated aunt? I've no idea, nor do I wish to know. Luna needn't worry about her guilty secret being sussed since all the high notes of her voice are blocked from being broadcast. Damn it, broadcast, me! I need to assert myself more.

"Listeners over at the U. N. and worldwide, I Harry Adonis foresaw Jerusalem as a major melt on account of thinking about… *massacres.* No longer does a frontier divide this city itself yet this square kilom has been the focus of centuries of murderous religious warfare between Jews and Romans, Christians and Muslims, Jews and Muslims, Jews and Christians, Christians and Christians. This is the blood-ruby of cities! Jeru is an epitome. Jeru is a cynosure –!" (Am I quite sure of the meaning of 'cynosure'? Too late now for qualms.) "What is human history but a vast list of wars and massacres and genocides and holocausts? Behold Jeru below my feet!" Dear God the tanned sandaled feet of Luna may be visible upon my boot tops… ["Alexander private, edit-mask-delete female feet in leather sandals! Alexander private erase any signs of woman upon me!"]

"Listeners, the history of mankind is frankly of men at wars little or large, local or landwide, sanctioned or vigilante, minus brief rests in between for re-arming." I prepared this earlier in my head, at the YMCA.

["Mankind?" pipes up Luna. "More like monkeykind. Humanity? More like inhumanity."]

Might as well repeat her words for broadcast, since they have a certain music.

"Mankind? More like monkeykind. Humanity? More like inhumanity. Yes indeed Listeners." But I mustn't sound like some evangelist, no – more like a Sagan or Attenbro.

"Cooperation makes conflicts. Conflicts make cooperation."

Do I sound too much like the trilingual feelgood at the YMCA?

"Listeners worldwide and at the U. N., conflict is in our genes as much as co-operation. We got no history without conflict. Conflict and cooperation these are a dialectic. Antithesis and thesis. Their synthesis is progress, now going exponential. Except that *something*'s melting our potentials."

I'm inspired, I'm rapping, I'm flying.

Surely I'm using up my kerosene faster due to Luna. Suppose I can shake her off by risking rotating swiftly up-down, my cams might film her shadow, or her slim skirted baglady self, falling and sprawling. And why should I plausibly carry out such a head-over-heels manoeuvre? To show off? Grand Prix champion swinging his car in a circle? Me being attacked by eagles?

By now the rumpled rainbowspread that was Jeru looks firm enough to land upon. So I settle down to within a few centimetres, cams angled rearward. Bit like a lunar module, come to think of it.

"Hop off," I command Luna quietly, me being her Captain. That'll help test the surface, though I'm fully confident. Fairly confident. Or may the surface only as yet be a rubbery crust like the skin on cooling custard? No one but me has ever experienced a melt so soon after the melting stabilises. Well, me and Luna but absolutely she is here courtesy of me.

While I film rearwards she hops off me, which is backwards for her, facing me. Oh those eyes of hers! Those boiled eggs of opal with the darkest possible yolks as if marinated for months and for years. The swimmy surface of the melt easily sustains her. Why, she even stamps her sandaled foot down, like some gravedigger using the back of his spade to tamp!

Gazing down at a slight angle, I have a sense of depths yet nothing is distinct from anything else. As if there are no edges to the geometry. This kind of challenges one's personal identity. But I set down, dousing my jet turbines. Damn but my inner thighs are aching already.

"Listeners, a history of bitter conflict is dissolved all together in a melt." Does that sound too much like a café latte? Right now is my chance for renown! "I ask myself, may this be the *purpose* of melts? To fuse enemies together? To unite Jews with Muslims –?"

["Greeks with Persians!" she calls out.]

"And Greeks with Persians as in the ancient world at the very gates – yes, *gates* – of Greece where tens of thousands of Persians died opposed by three hundred heroic Greeks led by King Leonidas braver than a lion. At Thermopylae –"

["Eh, did you say *thermophiles*? The Bacteries that love extreme heat?"] Bacteries rhyming with 'factories'…

"*Bacterias*, not 'Bacteries'!"

A Nobel-level inspiration comes to me. This must be equivalent to at least Krakatau level 6 on the Volcanic Explosivity Index.

"Thermopylae means 'hot gates'. Hot sulphurous springs were nearby. Yet for me the place name Thermopylae evokes *thermophiles*, that's to say *extremophiles*, which are extreme thermophiles, those single-cell organisms which live in conditions of extreme heat and pressure… such as exist deep underground… depths from which they may arise –"

Locked to the flyboard, I can't stroll around on the rumply surface unless I abandon my boots to venture forth in my cool-conduct socks. Luna darts to and fro close to me in her sandals, peering down, disregarded and/or deleted by my smartcams.

Now she gapes at me. "You can't have *any biology* just a few kiloms down! Umpty times hotter than boiling water, no life process possible. I'm no fool! After formal schooling, stuck in the Armenian pottery shop I got higher web-education via the checkout screen. Cause I hoped a volcano might blow up under my Jeru gaol but geology was wrong. So I know a thing or three."

Um. Of course she's right…

Yet on the other hand…

"Hear me: 500 kiloms beneath our feet – within the transition zone between the arid upper mantle and the arid lower mantle – there's an ocean. Not in the swimmy whales-and-dolphins sense but still a very wet ocean as well as hot and pressurised. This ocean soaks the elastic rock.

"Um, by 'very wet' I mean that the rock contains maybe three per cent water – yet that adds up to many Pacific Oceans' worth. Any life way down there must be extremely extremophile. Like, a thousand degrees Kelvin. That's 1K K. We cannot imagine the nature of this life, except that it must diffuse vastly throughout the rock, and may be equipped with ganglia communicating electro-magnetically – so I guess we *can* imagine! But we're still likely to be wrong.

"I believe that they – or It – knows about us. They seem to know in some detail. The best way the Deep Other can think of damping conflict among us is to fuse us together at the molecular level."

"Remember that the gangly octopus has independent brains in each arm. That's nine brains. But this down there has to be a distributed social intelligence. At nano level! Below biology! Trillions of the same entity.

"Unless we peace up, the Deep Entity will keep on melting our conflict places together to give us a helpful nudge. Hell, how can we possibly evacuate every conflict point on Earth? That'll take hundreds, thousands, of co-operative local truces to start off with. Maybe we gotta start at street level. Goes against human nature, against our conflict-cooperation genetics. Deep One doesn't think the way we do at all. I doubt if we can even communicate except by using giant symbols – like melts. Or like some hydrogen bombs dropped down deep shafts. But no, don't try this, is my advice because next thing the Deep One or Deep Ones might set off lots of volcanoes. That'll be a lot worse than limited square kilom melts. I'm still thinking, People – me, Harry Adonis – but this sure explains melts. The best way the Deep Others – or Other – can think of damping conflict among us is to fuse us together nanotechnologically."

Of a sudden sirens begin to wail, a late response compared with my own broadcast to Vulcan HQ for the benefit of the U.N. and everyone. A couple of Israeli Defence Force spotter helicopters are in the sky now. Elderly Sikorsky Sea-Stallion Yasurs, I do believe. (To be modest, I might be wrong.) I'm hearing ambulances and police vehicles in the distance, fat lot of use those will be – ah, except to control hysteria around the edge of the melt.

The emergency services mustn't find Luna so far within the melt, at a point unsprintable by her in the available time, reachable only by helicopter or by Vulcan flyboard, namely mine.

But the Deep Ones is definitely my idea!

Well, the little lady's little idea… made big and given voice by me.

I can drop her off, outside of the melt.

I can drop her off.

Drop her.

Drop.

No, any finger of guilt would point my way.

Those Israeli choppers will be observing keenly from now on. So I must be upfront (just as Luna was previously plastered right up against my front, ha!). I must take Luna to the YMCA hotel. I'm fucking fed-up with Luna. Fuck her fuck her fuck her. Yet on the other hand… Those eyes. I'm descended from a Greek god.

"So now your home is gone, lady! Care for a lift to somewhere habitable? Such as the YMCA hotel? Luna, I'll treat you to salad sandwiches and chilled water and other stuff later on. Other stuff."

Today there'll be a sensational influx of media and science into Jeru. I'll need to perform.

"What's in your bag, by the way?" I ask her.

"Worldly goods. Just in case of a miracle."

These days, glamorous Honolulu-resident Mrs Lusine Adonis devotes herself to supporting her famous and prosperous husband's hypothesis of 'Hyperextremophiles from Hell' as the cause of the mysterious melts which continue to this day, as yet having plastificated the merest fraction of our planet's land surface (though fatal for many).

Monkey Business

In all five directions forests stretch away from the city of Scribe where the thirty-seven robot monkeys type in the Templum daily from dawn till dusk.

Amidst those forests, tended by fairly happy peasants, are pastures and pools and arables to feed the citizens of Scribe. Rivers run through, transporting logs to the paper mills. The whole wide world folds itself in a fifth direction so that no place is really far from Scribe at the same time as resources are abundant.

Vast, for example, is the Plain of Paper, where checked pages are stored giraffe-high in batches tied with ribbons. Robot giraffes are the cranes of this world. On that otherwise empty Plain of Paper, rains never falls; the only wind there is a gentle, dry breeze.

Betty whistles to herself as she strolls along one of the rides of Forest Seven, approaching ever closer to Scribe. An adventurous lass cannot be satisfied until she has seen the robot monkeys typing. She swings the wicker basket cradling her ploughman's lunch, not that she nor her Dad nor her Mum are ploughpeople, but rather cheesemakers. A lark chants tirra-lirra.

"Why," she exclaims to herself of a sudden, "I may arrive on the very Day of the Play!"

She is overheard. A figure steps from betwixt the serried pines – youthful and handsome enough, blue-eyed, his shaggy hair flaxen, clad in goatskin breeches to which goathair still clings, giving him the aspect of a faun or satyr. His leather jerkin is buttoned by bone. A wallet hangs from the belt of his breeches. His hat, obliged in public by the Law of Hats, is of floppy felt with a goose feather. He smells fragrantly of lavender, rather than of goat, so maybe his mind is set on seduction rather than on ravishment. Momentarily, nevertheless, freckly Betty fears for her relative virtue, but the youth merely accosts her with words:

"Maiden, the Day of the Play may be a million years away. Or a trillion – at the last syllable of recorded time. We should never *expect* to see a low probability event."

A muffin cap hides Betty's bundled-up hair since she hates the bother of braiding, although its carrot colour and a few stray strands hint at her hair hue. Over her laced linen vest, a short-sleeved marigold shift and a skirt tucked up to save it from dust and pine needles. Freckled arms, oh yes. Her clogs and his could have come from the same klomper.

Mettlesomely, she replies, "If the play typed by the monkeys is inevitable some day, due to the Law of Extremely Large Numbers, why must the play arrive almost infinitely far ahead in the series of typings? Why shouldn't it happen in the midst of the series, or even *near the start*?"

"I think," muses the goatswain, who realistically must be a goatswain rather than a faun or satyr, "this is a Halting Problem. Though truly I'm unsure. I can't decide."

These peasants aren't clotpolls. Elementary education flourishes so that everyone may contribute with a will, be his or her condition ne're so vile, and have something beneficial to think about while ploughing or weaving or the hundred other things.

Well, mostly. Always there are some calibans.

With a merry wink the young man adds naughtily, "Hey nonny no."

"This," says Betty, "is neither the time nor place for any nonny-no."

"Not on a soft green bed –?"

"Of prickly pine needles! I'm off to Scribe to admire the monkeys."

"Coincidence! So am I. My name is Orlando. I have saved up a shiny shilling and four silver pennies." He jiggles his belt pouch.

"Enough for three geese and a pound of raisins –"

"Or three chickens and sixty-six herrings –" he responds, since everyone knows the value of money.

"Or twenty-four tankards of ale, a week in an inn, and two quails," and Betty grins.

"Maiden, you have just mentioned a week in an inn – how long do you purpose to stay in Scribe? Hast thou kin to stay with? I am no robber, I swear, but hast thou so much coinage as me?" What a knavish lad, presuming to *thou* and *hast* her so soon. Yet he does not smell at all rank, and his teeth gleam. Nor indeed is he a gent of rank, masquerading as a swain to beguile. He seems honest.

As if he can read Betty's thoughts, Orlando looks crestfallen.

"Forgive me. I have told thee a lie. My true name is not Orlando… but *Toby*. 'Toby or not Toby?' – I mislike the merriment which my birthname oft prompts."

"Then you shall be my Orlando." Betty too can be gallant.

"And together we shall hie us forthwith to Scribe… And we may talk in plainer fashion. We are not mechanical monkeys – consequently semi-quotations from plays by Himself cannot bring the Day of the Play any closer."

This is true, the whole point about the monkeys being that they possess no language, thus their typing is totally stochastic. (Or is it so, *strictly speaking*…?) No monkey will realise if it gives rise to the whole of *Hamlet*, word perfect. That recognition requires a literate checkernun, who also feeds in fresh sheets of paper, a respected occupation in Scribe; women have patience.

And the monkeys need to be robots, otherwise they would soon tire of banging typewriter keys and start scratching their armpits or their privy parts, and chatter and hoot, or sit backwards on the stools to which they would need to be chained. Real monkeys certainly wouldn't type from dawn to dusk, although this is required.

Let's see: we'll peg the fastest *realistically sustainable* typewriting speed at 50 words per minute, otherwise the keys jam, or fingers fail. Define an average 'word' as five letters long. Thus 'honorificabilitudinitatibus', 'the ability to achieve honours' (*Love's Labours Lost*, Act V, Scene 1) – which might be pompous nonsense, but at least it's *His* nonsense – is equivalent to 5. 4 words. Call 'dawn to dusk' 12 hours. 36,000 words. That's rather more than a *Hamlet*, and half as long again as an *As You Like It*. Let's just say for simplicity: a play's length per day. 37 monkeys could type the whole canon during one day. Though that adds probabilities (or improbabilities) enormously. So the law of typing states: *one* perfect Play.

Anyway, a robot's fingers, or its machine, may need cleaning and a spot of oil on its carriage rails. If the checknun-paperchanger wants a pee, or lunch, she signals for a substitute, yet many assorted things can hold up the typing, such as excitement in the Templum at a coherent sentence of text. The peasantry are aware of all this due to elementary education – the overwhelming majority prefer a rural life to the hectic pace of existence in Scribe.

"Ah, but which Play?" teases Betty as she and Toby-Orlando set off together through the sun-dappled pine forest where birds sing like tinkling bells, hey ding a ding, ding.

"Maiden – surely I cannot carry on calling you Maiden so anonymously –"

"My name is Beatrice." Truth be told, the people back home know her as Betty.

"May I call you *Bee* for short? Since your loose strand of hair is the hue of a honey bee."

"Where the bees sups, there sup you? Nay! And I am not short at all." Which is true; she stands – or strides – cheek-high to Toby-Orlando. "I prefer to be Beatrice."

"Very well, Beatrice, I was about to ask: Are you a One-er, or an All-er?"

This is less of a controversial enquiry than it once might have been, two centuries gone by, when life began. Do the robot monkeys need to type *one specific* Play? Or will *any* of the thirty-seven Plays suffice?The Law neglects to specify. Brawling broke out on this issue back then, though not serious bloodshed – everyone was too glad to be, rather than not to be.

Betty still remembers her joy when, on her fifth birthday, her Mum explains how she and Betty and everyone else are living in a simulation within Himself, located somewhere, in a sixth, inaccessible direction. She is *cared for*, not a random circumstance. A high degree of peace and contentment is the law of nature, so that people can dedicate their lives to the typing of the Play, either by living in Scribe itself or by sustaining everything that the city realistically requires. There is *purpose*.

By her seventh birthday Betty is beginning to wonder about the robot monkeys.

"A monkey is like a bent child, hairy all over."

"But, Mum, children like to *play*, not type a Play all day."

Worn-out typewriters are recycled to villages, so Betty has seen one by now. The typewriter factory in Scribe builds identical replacement typewriters by hand, requiring many craftspersons and a sizeable infrastructure. The ribbon factory supplies inked ribbons as well as the uninked ribbons used to tie the checked pages of rejected gibberish, and also fancy ribbons for adornment. Whilst the ink factory… oh what a city is Scribe. The Play's the thing! Without the Play, how can order and civilisation exist?

"The monkeys can groom for fleas and cavort together from dusk till dawn in their compound, apart from the off-time of repose."

"But Mum, a robot is mechanical, a clockwork… how can it have fleas like a cat or dog or hedgehog?"

"It can still *search* for fleas. The thing is, my little darling, a simulated real monkey would only type spasmodically, if at all. So we must have simulated robot monkeys to type. But the robot must resemble a real monkey closely enough that we can still call it a monkey, such as the law ordains must type, and as Himself provides for the purpose from the beginning."

We have not yet mentioned the monkey repair shop and spare parts manufactory in Scribe, a place where every wonder of the world converges, often by taking advantage of the fifth direction.

"Mum, is a *mon-key* wound up like a clock by using a *key*? Thus its name?"

"My clever darling! But a real monkey and a robot monkey must share very-similar-tude. Such as a hairy coat glued over the metal body. And a tail that moves. And other similitudes. Very similitudes."

Such is the talk of peasant families. Sometimes. Awareness of Himself and his plays enriches all life.

An argument of the All-ers is that there are 37 monkeys and 37 plays. This must be significant!

Yet in what way? Is there in any sense a race between the monkeys, which all have numbers from 1 to 37 painted upon their hairy backs? Is number 25 more likely to achieve a complete Play because it *already* typed at random a perfect six sentences from that very same Play? So is number 25 less likely to succeed with a *different* Play? Is a shorter *As You Like It* more likely to occur sooner than a longer *Hamlet*?

Anyway, the All-ers fancy that all of the Plays are equally likely and unlikely. Yet all are necessary so that we have a full vocabulary. The One-ers fancy that there is a hidden principle of *primus inter pares* – alias, first amongst equals. *Hamlet* is often mentioned if someone says in an alehouse, "Suppose one Play alone could survive…" Others advocate *The Tempest* – or *The Winter's Tale*, which may be the reason why robot bears are sometimes spotted. A bear was caught in a pit five years hindwards and proved to be clockwork. The bear was like… a piece of scenery or of furniture. Unlike sheep and pigs and cows and horses and chickens, for instance.

Both factions *fancy*. To believe would be too assertive. Bloody noses might result.

"Of course I'm an All-er," Betty answers her Orlando-Toby. "With 37 chances, surely the Play is more likely sooner?"

"Yet what if a Play *not* by Himself is typed perfectly before any play by Himself himself?"

Briefly, doubt clouds her brow.

"Is that not," he pursues, "success of a sort?"

"We'd have no way of knowing if such a Play is authentic. It may arise spontaneously. There may be no original which it copies. *Itself* is the original."

"And it may seem very like a Play by Himself which, however, he never wrote amongst the 37. So this must be discarded, although tied with a unique red ribbon."

It's warm in the woodland. Bees buzz. Betty wipes her brow. She planned on a mellow stroll to Scribe, not a dispute en route.

However, Orlando's comments are cogent, and almost like a kind of courtship.

"Don't forget the Law of Close Enough," Orlando teases. "How close is close enough? We're aware from certain intrusive footnotes – which must never be typed – that the canonical texts which we possess are sometimes a compromise. Oh that this too too solid flesh would melt... or is that flesh *sullied*?"

She sighs. The erotic implications of his words do not elude her.

He continues, "I cannot believe that such flesh as yours, for instance, might ever be sullied even if its solidity – its resistance – melts."

Thus, may she yield to him without shame? Even, shamelessly? How his teeth gleam, how his biceps bulge, how his gaze reflects the sky, hue of a robin's egg.

"Therefore," he declares, "I am a One-er. Himself chose the perfect expressions of thoughts. We must come as close as possible – to *one* Play, not to thirty-seven. Yet what occurs, I ask you, if and when that Play is achieved? You hope for this event to happen today, at random, Beatrice. Yet what then? Will the world simply *halt*? So therefore take thee best advantage of the present time..."

"Huh," she says, hitching her skirt, the better to step over some nettles intruding upon the path without catching a sting between her legs. "That's no pretext to *halt* here – don't you notice the nettles?" So saying, she picks up her pace.

Their first sight of Scribe is spectacular: two broad rivers bridged by masonry, rafts of logs destined for papermaking being poled along on each river amongst the many swans; smoke and steam rising lazily from redbrick edifices which must variously be the pulp mill, the ink factory, the ribbon factory, the typewriter workshop, the great forge and smithy, the central market, the shambles, the monkey menagerie and adjoining repair shop for robot monkeys, for robot giraffes, for coal-fired armour'd robot wagon-rhinos, and for robot logging elephants – although most of the elephants are out in the many forests. And of course there are thousands of garden-girt cottages as well as sprawling tenements and mansions of rank. Many are the docks and wharfs. Yearly, Scribe sprawls further. Soon it may be necessary to introduce public transport, a steam-train to the suburbs, say.

Up over there, topping a central hill, must surely be the marble Templum! A wide flight of twice twenty-four steps rises up to that fourteen-sided Templum quite like the rows of keys of a typewriter, only twelve times more so – the famous Qwerty Stairs, no less!

Soon enough, Betty and her Orlando are sitting on a bench in a leafy bower beside Coriolanus Bridge, sharing her ploughman's of Cheddar and crunchy barley bread with a nice nutty taste.

"Where shall we go first?" he asks.

"To see the monkeys, of course! Why else did I come?"

"First, I think we ought to investigate the possibility of staying a few nights at a hostelry. Travellers may arrive constantly and occupy rooms. We don't wish to share with four strangers, us all sleeping three to a bed. Those strangers might have bugs and lice on their bodies and in their clothes."

"The beds themselves may have bugs. That's why I plan to go home tonight to Myrtle-by-the-Water."

"Fie," cries Orlando in mock dismay. "That isn't very adventurous of you. Ahem," – and he opens his wallet, whereupon a stronger scent of lavender whiffs out – "you may rely upon me to sweeten the bedding, supposing the maid has neglected to."

Maid, indeed. Ale-wench more like, if you're lucky. However, this goatswain is foresightful!

"Besides, a bite of bread works up some thirst in me."

Within the alehouse, several blokes – who must work in the Ink Factory to judge by the stains on their hands – are arguing about the laws of typing over pots of ale and cakes. Maugre the law, one cannot pause to describe all their hats.

"If only the entire text could be in upper case!"

"But that would not be the Play *itself*, Jonas."

"Listen to me, chum, using the shift key randomly introduces an entire extra multiplication of improbabilities. It's as if Someone Up There doesn't *want* our monkeys to succeed."

"At least there ain't no italics key –!"

A red-haired chap with a bulbous nose breaks in: "Monkeys, plural, cannot succeed – one monkey *only* must come up with one complete entire Play all by itself. Supposing each of the thirty-seven monkeys produces several different perfect pages from the same Play during the same day, these pages cannot be summed together."

"Excuse me," interrupts Orlando, "but won't that satisfy the Law of Near Enough? If this happens during the same dawn-to-dusk?"

Indignantly, from Jonas, "I very much think *not*, Bumpkin."

"If thee dub me Bumpkin, I may stick thee with a bodkin!"

"Peace, everyone," calls out the alekeeper, who probably keeps a wooden rolling pin nearby.

Orlando takes the opportunity. "Mine Host, is a room free in thine inn? For the usual tuppence? With lavender betwixt mattress and sheet?"

"Free for a price, aye. Sans lavender, tuppence. Lavender for one penny more."

"'Tis fortunate that I brought my own lavender."

As Orlando reaches for his wallet, Mine Host calls, "Nay, no need to show lavender!"

"Nor," murmurs Betty, "thus to sweeten the sour ale…"

"Will the mattress be of swan's down, or of straw?"

"Straw? What do you take the Queen's Head for? The mattress is likely of soft hay! For tuppence more, our best room boasts a mattress and bolster of chicken feathers."

"Feathers sound soft," remarks Betty. "Hay is too close to home."

"Alas, our Best is already let out – to a famous actoress who must not blemish his complexion."

"A *hay* and a ho," quips Orlando. "It's settled. And no sacks of chaff for pillows."

"And no *nonny*," Betty murmurs, though in a naughty tone, maybe due to the ale.

"May I see the room?"

"Nay, not yet," she protests. "The monkeys!"

So it seems they will spend at least a night or two at the Queen's Head. The actual Queen's Head, of brass and clockwork, is inside the Templum, as official head of state. Wound at cockcrow, she recites the law of typing while an amanuensis huddles by candlelight comparing the received parchment in case of any changes in wording. A town-crier stands attendance, just in case of any change. The Queen's Head is basically a mouthpice; administration as such is in the hands of a privy council.

As for the touring performances of the 37 plays by the Queen's Men, exact copies are of course mandatory, to be scrupulously checked by proof squires, then certified by a chamberlain who embosses a seal upon each approved page. Worn and torn copies are added to the flames on Forks Night when everyone toasts manchet buns of twice-sieved wheaten yeast bread flavoured with rose water, a rare treat.

As everyone knows – unless they are a poltroon, or a caliban.

Betty has seen Plays enacted on the village green of Myrtle-by-the-Water a score of times by now.

"Good rustic, give me your pennies to bite," says Mine Host. "As is my custom with every guest *in posse.*"

Is this a sly insult? What peasant would dream of counterfeiting silver pennies by baking tiny hardtack biscuits, strong as iron, then painting them silver, using white lead, say? Just for instance! Surely naughty money is an urban legend.

But Orlando assents gracefully.

"Soft enough," judges Mine Host, and pockets the coins.

Truth be told, Betty has two whole silver shillings in her scrip within her basket, though that isn't the sort of thing to divulge to an Orlando whom she has scarce known for a couple of hours.

The inkmakers already returned to their conversation. A William is saying, "To produce capital letters and small letters in italics as well as Roman will require four possible settings for the shift key – or, I suppose, two shift keys with different purposes... And each typebar will require four characters mounted upon it, namely upper and lower case italics *as well as* Roman. All for what? In the text italics are used for personal names as well as for stage directions, but *never* for *emphasis*. So I do not think that the law seeks to handicap our monkeys. Why, the handicap *could* be doubly so."

"Nay, *quadruply* so."

"Nay," from another voice (and hat), "handicapped twenty-fourfold squared times twenty-threefold squared times twenty-twofold squared and so forth. Methinks. Without taking into account punctuation."

"Would that be factorial or exponential?"

"Faugh, that none of us is a mathematician!"

Exeunt Betty with Orlando.

Betty and Orlando climb the Qwerty Steps, hand in hand lest she slip, says he gallantly. The Steps are marble so that they may endure for ages, each step engraved at each side with one of the keyboard letters, including punctuation, though no italics or space. Best carrara marble from the old quarry away off in the fifth direction *that way*. In the early years of existence the quarry was a hive of activity – never nearly so much since, although citizens can still obtain slabs for patios if they're rich; hiring a robo-rhino to haul a sledge costs a pretty penny in coal from the mines over that other fifth way.

Talking of hives, beeswax gives the Steps their sheen. The beehives of the Templum are off in yet another fifth direction, surrounded by thousands of acres of white clover. Where the bee sups. Sucks.

Talking of coal, the climate's usually mild with hot sunny spells, as you like it, though now and then there are Learstorms when the rain it raineth every day, and some Winter when icicles hang by the wall. In the countryside the peasants burn wood, the forest wardens keeping an eye upon their takings since paper supplies must never be put in peril. Within Scribe itself, it wouldn't do to burn wood, which is paper *in posse*, consequently coal is best to burn even if a bit costly, and even if much lumber must become pit props to obtain the coal.

"The Qwerty is not so slippery," protests Betty, scarcely attempting to shake her hand free from Orlando's grip.

No sooner has Betty so declared, than an unsightly beldame – hook-nosed, squinty, almost a man's moustache upon her upper lip – comes caterwauling atop the Qwerty clutching a wet bundle.

"Curst be the drowner of my cat! Mine Ariel, God's lioness! Aye-aye-aye-aye!"

A rope-hooped farthingale, lacking any overskirtle, juts out around her already wide hips. Her stiffened clothes spread wide. She's like some upside-down ship, full sail inverted, as she collides in her derangement with the leathern bucket at the side of the topmost step, spilling a wash of water.

Such buckets occupy the upper flight of the Qwerty, buckets of water to the far left, of sand on the right, part of the fire brigade protecting the Templum in case of an overturned dawn or dusk candle conflagrating. Throw sand on to any burning paper, not water, needless to say.

Just behind the beldame appear a constable, to be addressed respectfully as Master Justin or Constable Case – the arm of justice, *just in case* of any criminal activity or civil unrest; plainly the beldame fits the latter category. The pimply fellow, clad in pumpkin pants and hose, is brandishing his truncheon.

"Hold, Mistress, hold!"

Another bucket of water tips right over, cascading, and Orlando is quick to tell Betty, "Into my arms! Let me carry thee, coz."

Already fire-brigade spillage is reaching her feet.

"Dolt, I'm wearing *clogs*!"

"Too much of water has thou." Whereupon Orlando catches Betty behind the knees then under the back, and he hoists her, her feet kicking somewhat. He's strong, and he mounts the remaining wet steps while the constable belabours the beldame's hooped farthingale with his stout stick – this won't cause her much harm beyond a few bruises but should nonetheless tame her. The beldame loses her bundle. Wits unhinged, her flailing hand disarranges the slashes in the Constable's full pants so that his codpiece juts prominently, policeman's protector 'tis said; quite a trick to protrude it through trunk hose. That raggy bundle of hers unwraps itself from step to step, a shroud emptying out a sodden dead mog.

So here are Betty and Toby at last, where the robot monkeys type, clickety-clackity times thirty-seven in the white marble hall.

Strictly speaking, these monkeys might better be called baboons. Though what's in a name?A baboon, could he speak, would own a name, and thus comprehend words, *which may not be* according to the law of typing.

The monkeys sit on three very long benches at three very long tables, a typewriter in front of each. Their hands never stray from the keyboards to play with themselves nor scratch an itch. The great brazen keys in their numbered backs turn too slowly to perceive.

Close on a double-score of wimpled checkernuns feed blank paper, scrutinise vigilantly, stack typed pages for pageboys to bear away to rearward tables for clerks to ribbon. Some constables circulate. Betty and Orlando are the only visitors in the Templum just now.

Ding, sing the line-ends, *ding ding ding ding.*

"Some may deem me a bumpkin," says Toby, "yet I ne'er thought till now: Since candles abound, why may not these monkeys type thorough the hours of night equally as day?"

"Because the monkeys need to wind down?"

"Aye, that may be…"

"In sooth, verily!" A constable loiters near them. "Ahem, a separate night shift of monkeys was *not* provided *ab initio.* Necessitating, by the way, a noctural troupe of checkernuns and clerks, as well as –"

"– a complete ocular industry *ab initio* to supply eyeglasses for checkernuns with increasingly bleary eyes?" guesses Toby.

"Consider the risk of fire!"Where upon, the constable continues his patrol of the Templum.

Hmm, verily. A sufficiency of giant candles might only increase the acreage of white clover for bees quarterfold above domestic use, but what of an increased risk of fire in the Templum, all be it now of marble…?

Toby gestures. "Coz, see, the Brazen Head's over there –"

Just then, a checkernun calls out excitedly, "Text! And more text!"A thrill runs through the the whole hall as the Marshall of

Pages – majestic in tall crowned swan-feather hat, frilly ruff, velvet doublet, and knitted hose, his whiskers well trimmed – strides to see the typed page emerge, and clerks converge. Other checkernuns should not leave their posts, but do stare.

"I told thee, Orlando! 'Tis the day of the Play!"

Fortunately the event is happening at the front table. Although a constable extends his truncheon to bar Betty and Orlando from getting too close, their young eyes are keen as eagles', to behold:

oT vqP ?aaaa gHiMb, bzEYq !, gFistOOO? nnHrr gAAA
Amleto: Essere, o non essere, questo e il dilemma:
se sia piu nobile nella mente soffrire
i colpi di fionda e i dardi dell'oltraggiosa fortuna
o prendere le armi contro un mare di affanni
e, contrastandoli, porre loro fine? Morire, dormire…
nient'altro, e con un sonno dire che poniamo fine
al dolore del cuore e ai mille tumulti naturali
di cui e erede la carne: e una conclusion
da desiderarsi devotamente. Morire, dormire.
Dormire, forse sognare. V k !rteW ,hHle zAfsR

The Marshall slaps the monkey's left shoulder in case it continues typing sans paper.

"What text be this?" exclaims a clerk.

"Be this the language of the Turks?" exclaims another. "Of Illyria? Or India?"

Of course one knows of such places, since Himself knows, even though such places are in no direction.

"Mine eye may be deceiv'd," declares the Marshall, "yet methinks this be the language of Verona or of Venice. Sir, or not Sir… quest… dilemma. Nay, but mark: *Amleto*! Amulet, omelette… nay, *Hamlet*, misspelled! Thus I deduce that this partial text represents 'To be, or not to be, that is the question', in Venetian or Veronian!" He raises his gaze roofwards. "Himself, art thou translated?"

When existence first began, the Templum was of oak beams and joists, the typewriters already in place, the robot monkeys seated waiting for the clong of a matins bell, the *First Folio* for checking, a sufficiency of blank paper. As is known from the *Chronicle*, to all but poltroons and calibans. That same *Chronicle* which first was progressively penned, using print-ink, in the wide margins and on blank versos of *The Law of Typing*, partner to the *First Folio* – until a printing press and bookbindery was up and running after mining and metallurgy and forestry and paper production, which the first people took to almost instinctively; truly, that was a Golden Age of inventions and initiatives. The first simpeople, forefathers and foremothers, were far from being simpletons! And they knew they were *sim* – *not* simian; that was for the monkeys – since they could have no false history prior to the start of typing, otherwise the start of the first day of existence, at three of the clock in the afternoon, would not have been a true start. Aye, at three post-meridian – yet what meridian was it *post*? Nothing to be seen in the dark backward, from the posterior of that first day; prior history, a blank! Yet these initial value constants of the clock and calendar were givens.

Yes, three post-meridian was when sentience began. Barely time to get adjusted before the matins bell of the following morning commenced the first day of typing.

True, the start is somewhat veiled in obscurity due to space constraints in *The Law of Typing*. For many years the first people were all too active as ants for a scribe to set down progressively fallible memories. That first generation, children included, were a bubble of the earth.

The first form of the Templum was inadequate even though it would have made a fine mansion. Dust drifted down. Splinters dropped to lodge between the keys. Mice and spiders soon invaded. More dignity, please, for the *raison d'être*! Busy as beavers, the first people saw to that dignity within a few years. They felt compelled, yet free in most respects to choose how they achieved their goals – as if an invisible Reeve was presiding, supervising the work on Himself's property.

Perhaps the world was scanty to start with, but how quickly and logically it developed towards the best conditions for the Play, as though by chaos plus necessity. Pulp mills, ink factory, robot logging elephants, an entire economy. Some of it built with the sweat of the brow and biceps, some of it bodying forth to requirement like airy shapes solidifying – which latter does not so often happen these days, though happen it does.

"Shall I summon the Town Crier," a clerk asks the Marshall, "for him to call out this text from the top of the Qwerty?"

"Fie, how to pronounce these foreign words? *Essery o non essery kwesto*… The words may be correct, or they may be inaccurate. How could we know if 'colpi' should be 'culpi'? We *cannot* adjudicate this text. And is a translation in any way legitimate? At best 'tis a distant version, not *First Folio*."

"O horror! Horror! Horror!" exclaims the checkernun. "Tongue cannot conceive this text nor voice the names! Mayhap a hundred versions of Himself exist in unknown tongues. When I took my vows of vigilance, I verily believed that our tongue is the preferred target of the apes amidst the vast majority of gibberish. No, not of the *apes* as such, nor the target as such, but the clear preference of the Play, whichever it may be… Tush, I express myself poorly."

"Sister, apes have no tails." The Marshall points at the long bench. "Thereby hang many tails."

"What price," muses a clerk, "a perfect version in a language we know not, nor ever will, unless there be some clue such as 'Amleto' whereby we can deconstruct and reverse engineer the language in order to check? Furthermore, I hazard that in futurity languages may arise which have no existence yet. Would a perfect version *typed now* in a not-yet-language be legitimate? Indeed, what is gibberish now may one day be vindicated as valid. In the long run."

Betty squeezes Toby's hand in excitement. This seems unlikely to become the day of the Play as such, yet to participate in such bestowals of wisdom is a privilege! Not to mention the thrilling alarm of the checkernun. Life is quieter in Myrtle-by-the-Water. Nothing wrong with quiet, mind thee. Meantime the other thirty-six monkeys are continuing, *clickety-clackety, ping ping ping ping ping ping*…

Toby ventures upon a hug.

"Surely," says the Marshall, "we can tell much about validity from the distribution of spaces. For instance, capital V-space-k-space-space-space-exclamation-rte-capitalW-space-c-comma-hcapitalH-le-space-space-space-z-capitalA-fs-space-space-space-space-capitalR," pause for breath, "is unlikely to be legitimate in any language. Not that our forefathers and foremothers came into being with much ken of any language other than English, merely awareness that other languages are possible."

Is Toby's hand caressing the clad side of her breast as if inadvertently, merely a part of the hug? Knavish lad! If only a couple of his fingers could reach as far as her still-clad nipple.

"I adjudicate," the Marshall proclaims after a while of reflection, "that this *substantial* fragment in Veronian or Venetian be classified *blue ribbon*, and kept in mine office hereafter. Yet it cannot be deemed canonical, not being in Himself's own English."

"So, coz: much ado about *nothing*," Toby whispers warmly in Betty's ear. Can he be alluding yet again to her nonny, with which he must be aching to make a lot of ado?

"Fie, you make me flush."

"Like a bird with a bush?"

"Fie, for shame…"

"Fee-fi-fo-fum, Slip on your bum, Down topples she."

"How puckish thou art."

Perhaps reluctantly, they turn their attention to admiring the oaken table, guarded by two constables, whereon stands the Queen's brazen head, and on which repose, bound in brown leather and chained, the *First Folio*, the *Law of Typing*, the *Book of Probability*, and the *Law of Hats* which covers everything else; a hat's at the head of a human, topmost item we turn to.

"For a sixpence," a constable confides, "I shall open one of the books."

"Nay, nay… thanking you," says Orlando.

"The same sixpence, I shall slip into the Queen's own mouth, and she may tell your lass's fortune. Or not."

Betty smirks. "Mayhap I already know my fortune."At which, Orlando exhales.

After they have gawped for a while, in chorus: "Let's see more sights!"

Merely one of which is an elephant lumbering along a paved street well wide enough to accomodate the log which the beast bears in its trunk – though, were the pachyderm much taller, that log would collide with the machicolated timbered upper floors which lean towards one another.

"Make way, make way!" calls the driver perched upon the beast's shoulders, for this is a street of shops displaying trinkets, toys, and gaudy things such as attract crowds. Coal smoke pours from the chimney on the beast's back.

That elephant may be a blessing to distract Betty's eye from the shop frontages and thus conserve Orlando's coins…

By now much time has passed with this and with that. Her basket already contains some souvenir trifles. Roofs have hidden the declining sun.

"Look!" she exclaims. "Yonder inn sign is of an elephant too!" Some hundred paces ahead.

"Perchance a sign to us, to pause at that inn on our way to our hostelry?"

"Hardly a coincidence, Orlando. Such beasts may sometimes walk this route – not every day nor often, else shops might lose trade. The beast and the inn sign are linked, not two items conjuncting as if by chance."

Betty remembers her simple petty school lessons on probability better than he. Or him. Her grasp of grammar is fairly good. The dame who teaches in Myrtle-on-the-Water studied at the Faculties of the University of Scribe for a year and has a good memory as well as several books. Dame Polly Pomfret even makes lists of words as Himself spells them, and their meanings, some of which still need to be deduced. The greater part come unbeckoned to the understanding.

Of a sudden, rapidly rising in volume from a shadowy side lane, comes a hue and cry of "*Caliban! Caliban!*" As shoppers rush together in solidarity, there stumbles from that lane a mockery of man, a finny black figure spotted with creamy blotches the size of half crowns. A little dog yaps at the creature's heels, such as those are.

"Take shelter behind me," Toby tells Betty, bunching his fists.

"True to its name, the terrier terrifies the poor Caliban – see how it gasps."

"I don't think 'tis made for running."

The Caliban's face is fishy, as though it belongs in shallow water amongst reeds along a river. Bulgy-eyed, it gapes one way then another, unable to spy escape, especially when in one direction an elephant looms, though less loomingly by now.

And now Constables arrive in their pumpkin pants, leading a chase out from the lane. One brandishes a hoop of rope on a strong long stick. Hue and cry dies down. Soon enough the Caliban is hooped, the rope drawn tight.

A Constable announces, "To the river with it, where it belongs. Who wishes to come, may follow, to watch it swim away." The creature is hauled off, trailed after by half a dozen excited townsfolk.

Others of the posse spy the sign of the elephant further along the street – the receding elephant too, although that's less momentuous than a halfman-freak loose, no longer, in the streets.

"Come, coz, before the inn crowds."

The Elephant Inn is much larger than the Queen's Head, boasting a cobbled courtyard, galleried at first floor level.

Two stools soon accomodate Toby and Betty at a shared tressle of drinkers and eaters in a capacious oak-beamed room.

"That pie looks good," Toby declares of the mountainous meaty wedge on the platter of a red-faced trencherman opposite to them. A well-dressed gent, his garb much trimmed and embroidered. His skinny companion is tucking in to what remains of a whole roast chicken. Napkins are tossed over both men's shoulders.

"I heartily recommend the pie," munches the gent, taking a swig from a leather mug. "Kidneys and oysters and coney, well herbed, a fine combination." Indeed, sucked rabbit bones litter the side of his trencher, near to his feathery hat.

By now a dozen men and women are pushing in, chattering animatedly about the Caliban.

"May I ask, Goodman and Goodmaid, if something sensational happens outside?"

"Why yes, Your Honour, a Caliban is caught."

"'Tis strange," says Betty, "I know what they are, yet at the same time I scarcely know not what they are in essence."

The skinny fellow sucks a chicken leg bare, discards the bone, swirls his greasy fingers perfunctorily in a nearby basin of water, wipes with the napkin.

"Those things," he asserts, "are errors. Or glytches."

Toby is glancing around at other drinkers and diners.

"I see no pots of ale anywhere."

"Why, Goodman –"

"– Orlando –"

"– this is no common alehouse, but a tavern. No thin potations here. My name is Burgess, by the way. I take it you do not stay here at the Elephant, coming I suppose from the countryside?"

"That is right, Mister Burgess."

"*Errors*?" asks Betty, having no idea what might be a glytch.

"We stay at the Queen's Head, should you know it."

"The Queen's Head? That, I should describe as an error. Have you tested their beds yet? Those are by no means tester beds! Is the Queen's Head even licensed for rooms?"

"We are humble folk, Mister Burgess. We need not four posts and a canopy."

"Faugh. Are you on your hony moon, Goodman Orlando and Goodmaid –?"

"– Beatrice. Nay, we met today."

"You deserve better than an alehouse. Innocence should not be so abused."

Betty nudges Toby. "Hearest thou?"

Toby glances again for wench service, in vain. The nearest wench is forever looking a different way. However, Mister Burgess booms out, "Claudia!" Within only a few winks, the wench attends them.

"Ah, Cloddie, two sherry sacks for my friends."

"And two pieces of that same pie," adds Toby.

"Nay, a salad for me, good Claudia," says Betty. "I feel this is my salad day."

"Food from the ground is lowly," observes Mister Burgess.

"Boiled carrets, scallions, radish, sparagus, coucumbers?" the wench recites, and Betty nods, adding, "But with not too many spices."

"You are considerate, coz, regarding my coins."

"Oh *I* shall pay for this, dear Orlando."

"You shall pay *dear*?" enquires Mr Burgess with a wink.

"*Errors*," she repeats, eyeing the chicken chewer. "How so?"

"You may call me Master Morgan. I profess at the University. Calibans are the embodiment of *coding* errors in our world."

"*Codding* cues for lechery," observes Mr Burgess merrily. "Whatever *coding* may mean, I must scratch my head. At times Master Morgan waxes so, his brow lost in the clouds."

Claudia deposits two leather mugs in a hurry.

After her first gulp, Betty says "Why, 'tis so sweet and rich. How it warms my blood."

"Yet in truth it is watered here – as I like it, I confess. Imagine the prince of wines, of which this is a bastard. The vineyards of Sherris are quite far off in a fifth direction."

"Why, Your Honour, there seem so many fifth directions."

"Thus our world ever reaches out and enricheth itself. Consider the oysters within my pie. An oyster requires a sea. A sea implies a ship. A sea may merely circle around, yet must be salty. Truly, this world of ever more fifth directions is our oyster."

"Yet may," enquires Master Morgan, "such growth continue without cease?"

A great moist wedge of pie arrives, along with Betty's salad, and they tuck in while Master Morgan continues, still heeding his remains of roast fowl, "Is our state finite? Suppose our world to be a machine, like a typing monkey, but made of noughts and onces…"

The parson's nose is especially succulent; some save it till near the last of a chicken.

"Any machine with a finite memory must have a finite number of states, thus any pre-ordained menu upon this machine must either eventually halt or repeat itself. The duration of our pattern cannot exceed the number of inner states. Yet the number of inner states may be as the life of an elephant to the life of a mayfly.

"Or," continues Master Morgan, tearing off a roast wing, "is our rhythmic sequence non-preordained? How to tell the difference between one seeming near-infinitude and another?"

"Thou art a philosopher," says Orlando around a mouthful of pie, and signals to Claudia for another Sherris sack.

"If only philosophy could find this out… And what is *time* for Himself, compared with for ourselves? Maybe our own lives are as of mayflies even if we seem to achieve three score years and ten, thus to allow millions more opportunities for the Play to occur. On the other hand, the requirements for running the task expand multifoldly more than the task itself, occupying ever more processing space."

Mister Burgess cuts in abruptly. "Hang up philosophy! Goodman Orlando, what dost thou pay at the Queen's Head?"

"Tuppence. Mine Host already bit my coin."

Mister Burgess sighs. "Methinks a bed at the Queen's Head is worth but a halfpenny. Here the regular, licensed cost is a tuppence."

"Oh." Does Toby flush with embarrassment, or due to the Sherris sack?

"A tuppence to tup in comfort… And the pillow will not be a sack of chaff. Good rustics, I wish you both very well. Let today be your hony moon, here. If 'tis good 'tis done, 'tis best 'tis done sooner, say I. As to your tuppence which the aleman took, mine brother-in-law Ralph happens to be Scribe's official ale-taster." A position of rank! "Ralph can pass by the Queen's Head on the morrow. Be assured that Mine Host will restore your coins to you. A conner, as we call the ale-taster, keeps watch for any illegitimate conduct by houses that brew their own ale."

"I know not how to thank you," begins Toby.

"Nay, you may drink my health. Though not too many times – I am more accustomed to Sherris sack than thee. Is this not, Master Morgan, a consummation devoutly to be wished?"

"Methinks the lady may protest…"

But Rosy-cheeked Betty is all smiles. "Oh brave world, that has such people in't! Indeed, thou art no Pandarus."

Outside, the light waneth much more. 'Tis evening. Night draweth nigh.

The moon does not shine bright in such a night. Mister Burgess's influence runs to a lanthorn to help the anticipative couple navigate the many dark narrow corridors of the Elephant till they reach their bedchamber as instructed. Toby hangs the bright lanthorn by the bed.

"Let us satisfy our eyes."

Although Betty has nothing to worry about, she teases: "Some charms are best seen by candlelight alone, sans the reflectors of a lanthorn."

"Nay, I would not singe thy pretty hairs."

Toby's member is stiff with desire, and Betty is fulfilled many times, fully filled and fulfilled climactically, yet ne'er does Toby gush. Probably that's the fault of a little too much of the Sherris sack... and maybe of the novelty, the unfamiliarity – Bett's cunny may not feel at all like Toby's own spittled hand.

Toby does not come to climax, no nonny no. Famously ale – thus, how much *more so*, sack? – increaseth the desire but taketh away the through-flow, namely the ejaculate. Toby does not provide through to completion. Per*forate*, yes, with vigour – yet finally per*form*, ah nonny no. He certainly tries. To Betty's delight. For a half hour or more he's cock-in-her-hoop.

"Oh Orlando – Orlandoooo! Do–doooo!"

All's Well That Ends Well.

Mayhap.

When the Aliens Stop to Bottle

"*As per the surrender agreement, the invaders are distributing food to the human population while they stop to bottle.*"

Thus booms the announcement over the railway station's PA, and a ripple runs through the dense queues. A collective inhalation, exhalation. A contraction, as if to minimise one's presence; an expansion as if to be any place away from here – yet trains must be caught to get home, when services resume; thus everybody stays. By now the Departures screens haven't refreshed for fifteen minutes. The only lights are those of the screens and the exit signs; we need to limit our power use.

"Can't be far off along the lines," murmurs Toby. "Them."

The gloom in the hall is comforting, protective; people's faces a couple of queues away are indistinct. Much further away, almost invisible.

"*As per the surrender agreement*" – again – "*the Incomers are distributing food to the human population while they stop to bottle. Please stay in orderly lines and be patient.*"

I dig Toby in the ribs. "Hang on! *Invaders* has changed to *Incomers.*"

"Um, are you sure?"

"Course I'm sure."

Tiredly, "What difference does it make?"

"*Incomers* is blander and softer – yet it isn't your usual sort of word, unless you've been prepped by hearing *Invaders* previously. We're being manipulated. But by Government – or by Them?"

"My paranoid Jenny." Toby squeezes my elbow affectionately through my raincoat. "Maybe it was just a slip of the tongue by the PA announcer."

"Governments want to stay in power. If we don't remember things clearly, we become accustomed to what was unacceptable not long ago."

Shrugging, "Our nuclear weapons didn't explode. All the missiles imploded."

Such are the powers which *They* deploy. And yet we aren't being exterminated – not to any significant extent, no worse than by naturally occuring heart attacks or strokes, I don't suppose.

Bottle bottle bottle.

How a baby feeds unless Mummy is offering her breast. A comfy word, completely unthreatening.

The way the aliens feed too. Sucking from big bottles of creamy goo, held in a convenient tentacle. Imagine a Special Forces soldier pausing in combat to glug on a baby bottle; kind of endearing, hmm?

What combat, anyway? The world surrendered, apart from North Korea which isn't north any longer; reportedly South Korea fits up against China now.

And also: *to put into a bottle*. The aliens carry collecting bottles, into which they pop people.

Oops, now the nearest screen shows a platform number – our usual platform right here in front of us; that's a relief. Shouting elsewhere, even a shriek or three, but we can't be distracted by glancing. Priorities: surge and squeeze on board.

Standing room only in the carriage, apart from the first fortunate seventy or so. And off we go slowly. Commuters finger their phones but coverage is useless.

"Shall we have spaghetti pesto tonight?" I ask Toby.

"If the power's on. Cold pesto *sandwich*, no. How about corned beef and apple, as back-up?"

"Sulphur burps, afterwards." I snuggle up, unavoidable in this crush of commuters.

"Feeling amorous, eh Jen?"

Sure, let us rut and maybe multiply, in instinctive reaction to a possible threat of extinction. Amorous, hmm. *Feel like a fuck?* isn't his style.

Click-clack, click-clack, train's wheels crossing some points. Reminds me of a funfair car ratcheting up a roller-coaster preparatory to the downhill drop. Nearby, a tall brick wall adorned with sub-standard graffiti. Sky above is deep grey.

Our salubrious tiny town, or overgrown village, is twenty miles upline from the city. Toby and I work in advertising – same big office – so I'm sensitive to slogans and catchwords. More sensitive than Toby, I frequently feel, even though he pockets seventeen per cent more than me. *Incomers* instead of *Invaders.* No resentment, though. Or not much. That's the way things are. I love Tobe. I think.

Toby's still tinkering around with the Fly Me To The Moon account. Fat chance of more suborbital flights now, I suppose. We were all so taken by surprise. But work goes on, as Government insists should be so. Dignity. Spirit of the Blitz, whatever that was (I jest). Aliens might reassess our status. An anthill goes beserk with a boot stomping it, but we aren't ants. Our missiles imploded away to some place else. Maybe *place* isn't the best way to put it. All language is laced with metaphors.

Me, I'm putting finishing touches to Amazing Albania! including an exclamation mark. *Without* an exclamation mark might seem a bit banal, unlike that nation's majestic snow-capped peaks. Do hasten to Theth for sublime unspoiled romantic charm beyond compare, by way of the *hard-top* (wow) road from enchanting spruced-up Shkodra with its Rozafa fortress. Needs working on – the words, not the fortress.

At this early point in our homeward journey, twenty or so railway tracks run parallel, many of them leading into sidings. A huge mobile unit of the incomers looms like a cubist dirigible mated with a battle tank, unmoving for now. Its crew lean out of rubbery ports, octopus-like creatures the size of cows, some sucking on flexible bottles. Others squeeze their bottles, jetting goo to and fro; where goo settles, it firms into 'sponges' – those are what the accompanying crowd of people want: delicious, nourishing, mildly addictive. Orange lights flit around. We slow, we slow.

From high upon the mantle of the mobile unit protrudes a larger specialised collector creature, its suckers clutching a bigger kind of bottle with a wide and open top.

"Look, Tobe –"

The collector-arm is more like a chamelion's tongue – coiled tensely, now quivering outward in a preparatory way, then flying far to its full extent, catching a sponger around the chest, whiplashing back again carrying the young scavenger woman with it. Young-looking, at least. A Sponger. How convenient, this term.

Bottle is better than battle – that works for us anglos. Who knows what the slogan is in hungry Hungary or Albania.

The bottle already contains what looks like a raggy old man, suspended inertly. Into the bottle pops the struggling young Sponger; she goes slack.

The Incomers have assured us that there's no connection between human specimens in bottles and bottled goo. This may well be true because there has to be more goo than there are captured humans. Probably.

A few tracks away, another outbound train begins to overtake us, but then it slows. Of a sudden half a dozen alien militia finish their bottling, brandish those multipurpose superwands they use, and float from their ports towards the other train, now at a standstill.

"What the hell are they up to, Jen? Aren't commuters safe?"

As if in answer, our own train lurches forward, wheels squealing. Our driver is pushing his locomotive as though struggling through treacle. Pretty much in vain.

We can see how jam-packed that other train is, worse than our own. If this were India, a hundred passengers might also be squatting along the carriage roofs. Easy pickings. Don't think that.

I can't fully see what happens along the far side of the other train, but now each floating Incomer holds aloft a long window plucked loose from its frame, suckers sucking, I suppose. Away fly the windows, glassy sledges bouncing over rails before shattering.

Next, passengers fly. Plucked from the pack within. Do the Incoming militia think they're saving people from suffocation? Is some alien by-law being violated? There'll be bad bruising for sure if not broken limbs, cracked backs, skull fractures.

The train driver descends on our side from his cab, marches around the front of his locomotive, and waves his arms, as I can just barely see. Can't hear what he's shouting – too much babbling from our travel companions.

"Brave fellow, he must be incensed," says Toby. "Would you do that?"

What would I *do*? What would *Tobe* do? Tobe would not become incensed. Is bravery dependent upon taking leave of one's senses?

Oh God, the creature on top of the giant mobile unit flicks out its special arm, ultra-long, and *collects* the driver, legs waggling, arms flailing. Into the bottle he goes. Full enough now, the bottle slides inside the rubbery port, three human sausages inside it.

Leaving a driverless train. Other alien octopus militia float over fast, and the team begin *evacuating* the stalled train in earnest. How can they make such a mistake! Is it a mistake at all?

Several extracted passengers that I can see are managing to stumble away around the front of the locomotive in our direction. No no no, don't come here, don't draw attention. Though again, why *not* this way?

Our own train lurches again, dragging itself forward another ten metres or so. So much for our own driver's response…

"Bravery would seem to be stupid," says Toby.

"Or our driver's trying to safeguard his own human cargo?"

"Whatever. I'll take cold pesto sandwich – eh, Jen, eh? It'll seem a feast."

The first couple of refugees to reach our doors – driver-controlled, of course – bang their fists. As if we can open a door by using the unlit button. Shall our driver open all the doors at once to let in two, three, four – when the carriages are already packed tight? Why don't these imploring people run onward into the gathering darkness, are they idiots?

They want to get home. Even if it's the wrong line, wrong station. Even if it's *our* home. Sorry there's only cold pesto, guys. Hell, there's more than that in the house – cans, nuts, biscuits. Let's not go to extremes to spite Toby. Not spite, no, *tease.* Perish the thought of spite.

The displaced persons quit and pass by. Someone has a radio which starts to work.

"… in another communiqué the Incomer Oktagon praises the compliance of populations at large and indicate that within a hundred Earth years human beings may be suitable for crackle-buzz status… squeal-crackle –"

From Toby, "And what might *that* mean, pray?"

"We shan't be extinct, moron," says the black guy in a woolly hat next to me, right shoulder side.

"We'll be *changed*," says a plump middle-aged Sikh, left shoulder side. "*That's* what bottling's for. To find how to change us."

As good a theory as any. Maybe bottled human beings are for export to alien zoos. Wonder if those zoos need a publicity campaign? Gallows humour, guys.

The alien ships now in orbit are big; you don't even need binoculars. Two bagels, each twenty kilometers across. At first some scientists speculated about the bagels threading spacetime through themselves ultra-fast, whatever that means; then science shut up as announcements came on TV in twenty-some languages: You Are Incorporated Peacefully into the Oktagon.

So North Korea let fly at the sky. Followed by everyone with nukes and more nukes. All straight down some spacetime rabbithole. Maybe all for the best: instant global nuclear disarmament. That was three weeks ago.

Jet fighters stalled and fell like confetti. Ground forces' equipment didn't work, as if full of glue. Worldwide communications hiccuped helplessly except when the Invaders – oops, Incomers – wished to issue advisories such as Ground All Commercial Air Traffic Within Three Hours. Sea And Ocean Shipping May Continue.

"Spare a thought for a JAL jet marooned in Albania."

"Japan Air Lines? What prompts that, Jen?"

"Didn't you see," asks the Sikh, "all those samurais trying to defend their Imperial Palace?"

The absurd heroic sight was permitted as if to emphasise our reduction to medieval weapons and tactics. Japan's Self-Defence Forces, subsequent to them raiding museums.

"Those swords all jumping out of their hands!"

As if these days the Japanese army knew how to use swords…

The Incomers seemed to know so much about us. Us, bugger all about them. I didn't believe in the TV output argument, us being the beacon of this very tiny bit of the galaxy.

Just suppose the big bagels came from only forty or fifty light years away – plucking a distance out of the blue – surely our own wavelength-watchers must have noticed some signs out there in the sky so close comparatively, scarcely for want of us trying. Unless the Incomers' home was paranoidly stealthed, and why would that be when our nukes weren't even firecrackers and they could vanish North Korea from the map? In my book they were from far far away. How, therefore, did they know about us *at all*, never mind such a hell of a lot including languages? Would our great-great-great kids get to know? Come Visit Amazing Earth, The Planet Named After Dirt! Behold The Charming Natives Dance On Just Two Legs! Merely because the Incomers look like octopuses doesn't mean they live in a sea.

"You think they oughta have used karate next?" asks the black guy. "Ninjas versus Octopi!"

A pie of octos. Just in case Toby thinks of correcting to *octopuses*, I nudge him. There's no call for subsequent pussy jokes in this grope of a carriage. Some dignity, please.

Dear god, a pair of the octo-militia are heading our way, part-drifting, part-knuckling the ground.

It *has* to be *our* carriage they come towards. Bugger those ex-passengers for beating on our doors.

Looming: tentacular blotchy cows, wands on one arm, other seven arms all too free. Go away go away go away.

"I gotta knife," says the black guy.

"So do I, on my belt," says the Sikh, "but the blade's blunt."

"What use is a blunt knife?"

"It's symbolic – Sikhs are peaceful."

"We're all peaceful now," says Toby. "Let's stay very peaceful. Don't look at them. No eye contact."

Contact with big rheumy oval green eyes in wrinkly hide. Rheumy: bit late for hay fever. *Martians*, dying of earthly germs in their war machines… No way. Someone has farted or even dumped in their pants. Disgusting.

Look away. Can't look away. Think of Amazing Albania. Heart, be still.

Alien scrutiny.

Plop plop plop plop ploppety, two snaky lines of suckers across the glass, and *pull.* Window whirls away. Rush of chilly fresh air, a relief from those bowel gases.

It in front of me smells of vinegar and cumin.

"Eye-dentity."

It speaks. It has little triangular ears. Or something.

"*Eye*-denity!"

Does it want a retinal scan? Of course not. It wants my 'I'.

"Jenny Jane Foster."

Toby almost crushes my hand, which I wrench free.

"Jyenni-Jyane-Vozter," it says. Words! I am genuinely speaking to an alien. Incomer communiqués are all pronounced perfectly.

To an individual alien. (Are they individuals?)

"Okyu-passion?"

Occupation, occupation; yes we're all occupied, that's for sure.

"Advert-ising," I say. "Publi-city." (Speak normally, Jen!) "Advertising."

(Do you need a hand with your charm offensive?)

"Function ov dis?"

"I persuade people to visit places, buy things."

It seems to ponder. Is it autonomous, an individual? Or am I addressing the mobile unit instead?

"If humanz rubbish, no, if humanz re*fuze* things?"

"I'd be out of a job. I think I am, already."

(A bit of a problem with passive resistance somewhere on Earth? Or with improvised devices, booby traps?)

"I think I am," it echoes me, and adds, "Day-Cart."

Descartes? Descartes? 'I think therefore I am'?

"Are you referring to our philosopher Descartes?"

"Ideaz. Ideas." This is a foot-soldier alien octopus who is even *aware* of Descartes? That's to say, a tentacle-soldier… If so, what of the officers of the Oktagon! Does any officer want a pretty-polly?

"You want ideas?" (Jen's just the person for those!)

"We search population at random now. Anyone know philozophers? If no, philozopherz failure. You knows Day-Cart."

Everyone else in the carriage is deathly still.

"And Wittgenstein." Not that I ever read Wittgenstein, but it's the power of the slogan that counts. "And Plato, and Nietzsche. And Aquarius."

Hesitation, then: "No zuch philozopher."

"Just testing."

Big rheumy eyes goggling me, tentacles shifting about. My nails are cutting into my palms.

In for a penny… "Why do you guys bottle humans?"

And this is just when the black guy reaches right past me as far as he can and stabs It in the eye.

"Eye for Identity!" he bellows, as tentacles drag him through the window, nearly dislocating my shoulder, and he is trashed upon the ground.

Having one eye sucked out isn't fun at all, though at least it's quick. Everyone in the carriage loses an eye, no matter how much they try hunkering down or hiding under seats. Tentacles get everywhere. Nobody loses two eyes; tentacle tips may be able to see. Collective punishment, biblical.

My conversation with It does not resume. Yet our train does, amazingly. We all look – two-dimensionally now – as if we've been on a zombie walk, snailtrails of gore staining cheeks.

"God but it hurts," moans Toby. "My poor Jen, too," he remembers to say.

Poor Jen? But I have conversed with an alien octopus from far far away, about Day-Cart!

I shall adopt the nickname Patch. Like a pet dog. Patch Foster. Maybe a future still awaitz me. My eye-dentity's known now.

Heinrich Himmler in the Barcelona Hallucination Cell

The torment cell disorients Reichsführer Heinrich Himmler, therefore he perches himself on the tilted black bench next to General Sagardía.

Sagardía has been with Himmler since the Reichsführer arrived in Spain four days earlier to prepare the way for Hitler's meeting with Generalísimo Franco – which went badly today, according to a phone call. Sagardía was in the Spanish delegation to Germany the previous month. At the start of the civil war he was hauled from his cosy 'retirement' in France; 'My country needs me.' A murderous mediocrity.

The bench tilts at an angle of 20 degrees so that a prisoner can't sleep without rolling off. Nor can the prisoner sleep upon the concrete floor, since bricks jut up harshly at random. Exhausting!

Nor, due to the awkward bricks, can a person pace the cell. Himmler has managed to plant his black boots flatly between two bricks to steady himself – his coordination isn't as good as it might be.

What a Jew of a day this has turned out to be. The journey to Montserrat monastery to take possession of the Holy Grail, a total failure. His briefcase stolen from the Ritz Hotel. The Führer, infuriated by Franco's pigheadedness.

The damnable news that the briefcase went missing came towards the end of the reception given by Dr Jaeger, the German Consul General, in his residence. Which was prior to the scheduled dinner at the Rathaus – called the *Casa Major* or something, Barcelona's town hall in Plaza some saint or other. That theft certainly put die Katze im Taubenschlag, the cat in the pigeon loft, as regards the stupid pigeonhead Spanish police! For sure the reception was soured.

Painted on one wall of the cell is an eye-dazing chequerboard. Spots little and large orbit around, red, white, black.

That chequerboard draws your gaze to it nauseatingly. Like a Kandinsky in the degenerate art exhibition Goebbels commissioned in '37, all those unGerman works displaying mental disease…

Over dinner in the Rathaus, the Mayor of Barcelona described these cells of degenerate art so as to distract attention from a succession of police officers reporting to munching General Orgaz about how the Ritz and the whole city were now being shaken vigorously, in vain, in pursuit of the missing briefcase. So here's the jowly, fat-faced Captain General of Catalonia within the crowded cell, suffering consequences.

What's the Mayor of Barcelona's wretched name again? Miguel… *Mateu.* So he's here too, in the cell. Even though these Spaniards dined so late, Himmler promptly insisted on a visit to the cells. Partly this was to punish his hosts, but also out of fascination – it's important to research new information encountered in life, personally if possible, meticulously and exhaustively. Maybe the Gestapo can learn a new trick.

The German Consul, Dr Jaeger, is here too in the cell for his sins. Only after the theft was reported did the Consul confess to Himmler that the staff of the Ritz notoriously 'used to be' infiltrated with spies – waiters trying to eavesdrop on important discussions, snooping chambermaids.

Mind you, prior to Himmler's trip Canaris idly mentioned one supposed piece of Ritz history: when the exiled Jew Bolshevik Trotsky was icepicked in Mexico a couple of months earlier by a Soviet agent, that selfsame Catalan Communist who murdered Trotsky worked in the Barcelona Ritz hotel at the outbreak of the Spanish Civil War.

If Canaris was to be trusted! Too fluent in English by half, and in Spanish too, is Canaris. Him with his own rival military intelligence service.

It couldn't be, could it, that Canaris has anything to do with the ingrate Franco refusing to join forces with Germany and allow the Reich a corridor through Spain to capture Gibraltar? Unthinkable!

Admiral Canaris, if anybody, knows the strategic importance of the British Rock…

"Those cells use psychotechniques," the Mayor had said in English, with an American accent, at the dinner table, Gruppenführer Karl Wolff translating for Himmler's benefit.

A string quintet was playing during dinner in the 'Chronicles Room' of that Spanish Rathaus. The Prelude to *Lohengrin*, the *Siegfried Idyll*, a flute doing duty for the trumpet part…

The floor of the 'Chronicles Room' was of black marble. Its walls and ceiling were murals of obscure historical happenings, painted upon expanses of gold and silver leaf.

"Art to punish and disorient prisoners," continued the Mayor. "This was how the Reds dealt with opposition while they were still in control here – though we aren't sure if Companys knew about this personally."

Companys, the President of Catalonia during the red republic, was shot by firing squad in Barcelona's castle just four days before Himmler arrived in Spain, maybe as a way of saying 'Thank You' to the Gestapo for catching that pest in Paris and handing him back.

By all means mention Companys! Another example of the generosity and support of Germany for the pipsqueak Generalísimo!

Himmler's meticulous work in Madrid, buttering up Franco, was as much in vain as the hunt for the Holy Grail – or for the Ark of the Covenant in Toledo.

Come to think of it, Canaris had pointed Himmler towards Toledo as regards the Ark… The Toledo tip-off was thanks to interrogations of a rabbi in Auschwitz, an initiate in Kabbalah, Canaris had assured Himmler, so this might be credible. Except that it wasn't.

"Psychotechniques –" repeated the Mayor, while Himmler toyed with his vegetables.

General Orgiz had before him a plate of thick bloody Rossini steak, foie piled on top. Slaughtering birds and beasts for food is a crime against the natural world, although at times one has to go hunting with a rifle, smilingly on account of one's companions.

"– devised by a Republican torturer so-called artist named Alfonso Laurencic, and carried out by his depraved artisan Garrigós. We executed Laurencic over a year ago. Laurencic also designed special tight 'wardrobes' which constantly stress a prisoner – quarter of an hour in one of those could break a man… Just another of the atrocities of the red scum. Laurencic had a red beard," added Mateu.

"You still use his cells?" enquired Himmler.

The Mayor shrugged. "We restored civilisation."

"Permanent vigilance, and *repression when necessary*, is the ticket," said General Sagardía. "I'm sure you understand, Reichsführer."

Did 'permanent vigilance' include keeping an eye on the briefcase of the head of the Gestapo and of the SS? These Spaniards! Noisy, hot-blooded, over-excitable lot. Their wine and their women and their cruel primitive bullfighting – one bullfight in Madrid was enough to last Himmler a lifetime. When Himmler presented the toreadors, toreros, whatever the word, with good German medals, one of the bull-killers said, "Medals are all very well for the Virgin, but what about the ears and tail?" Barbaric.

As for their pathetic agriculture, how can it be so bad when so much rain seems to fall? The agronomist in Himmler is appalled at the neglect.

Doubtless the thief broke into that suite at the Ritz after traversing several wrought-iron balconies by way of the linking ledges, making a mockery of the armed police stationed or snoozing in the corridor. Lurking crouched down on the same balcony from which earlier Himmler had saluted the multitude; awaiting any opportunity. The thief risked being spotted but it was night and no one was paying attention.

What roars of admiration had come from the crowd after lunch when Himmler saluted – which was gratifying; yet to be obliged to put on a show for these bull-killers…

Wolff apologised deeply that the SS guard within the suite absented himself briefly; once back in Germany, the man would be sent to an extermination kommando in Russia to redeem himself.

General Orgaz was blaming the British Secret Service for the theft of the briefcase, presumably on the grounds that the Spanish themselves couldn't be blamed if *British* spies were involved, cream of the cream. Alternatively, the French Resistance was to blame. Yet why not another *Red* spy, someone like Trotsky's killer who cut his teeth right here? Hadn't Franco's cronies cleaned all the stables of red scum completely yet?

The briefcase held documents about the agreements which Himmler had negotiated in Madrid between the Spanish secret police and the Gestapo; also a report about the German community in Catalonia, courtesy of Dr Jaeger – and, on top of those, priceless ancient plans of the monastery at Montserrat, its secret catacombs and tunnels where the Grail might be kept hidden. That seat of learning published its first book at the end of the 15th century, yet it possessed in its library *no copy* of Wolfram von Eschenbach's *Parzifal* – or so claimed the junior monk spokesman, Andreu or somebody, because the abbot himself refused to meet with Himmler.

One young monk: the *only* German speaker in the whole learnèd monastery – was that credible? The occult plans of tunnels proved useless.

No copy of the great *Parzifal* poem was literally incredible when Wagner's *Parsifal* received its first authorised performance beyond Bayreuth in Barcelona *precisely due* to proximity to Montserrat – which should be the Montsalvat of the opera, home of the Grail. Himmler had been driven past the Lyceum opera house or whatever it was called on his way to the Ritz through swastika-hung streets. After the time-wasting charming folk dances and displays of gymnastics by young people.

"Exhaustion, plus hallucinatory art to derange the prisoner," said Mateu.

"I wish to see those cells," Himmler declared.

Orgaz wiped his lips with his linen napkin. "We'll take you there tomorrow morning. Mañana. The Vallmájor checa, I think."

"*Cheka* – are you referring to Lenin's political police?" Vicious, sadistic murderers…

"Alfonso Laurencic designed the system of local lock-ups for interrogation and punishment based on the Russian Checa model."

"I want to see those cells *now*. Because I shall fly back to Berlin as soon as possible tomorrow morning."

Orgaz was astonished. "*Right now*? But I believe the dessert will be raspberry and peach Melba… created by Escoffier himself, the Emperor of Chefs as your very own Kaiser said. The inspirer of the Ritz hotels!"

Himmler smiled very thinly.

"The Melba might be exceptional."

Likewise, the security at the Ritz…

"Even," added Orgaz, "legendary." Was the Captain General snidely implying something about Himmler's quest earlier today?If so, how infuriating. Due to the curse of doctrinaire fanatical Catholicism, these people had no idea of deep occult truths. As a reincarnation of the first pan-Germanic king, Heinrich the Fowler, Himmler knew much better.

"Scoff your dessert, then. I insist we leave within thirty minutes." Presumably Wolff translated a less insulting word than 'scoff', *hinunterschlingen.*

"At least take a coffee first, Reichsführer. Best Brazilian beans, by way of Lisbon, so I hear."

The Spanish might well misinterpret Himmler's thin smile as cordiality. He learned long ago not to give obvious vent to anger; better to store up such feelings for subsequent vengeance. Yet above all he must not be taken for a fool.

Resigning himself to some delay, he insisted, "As allies, we will *all* go together to see the hallucination cells."

Allies! As regards Gestapo liaison with Franco's police, yes. This cost the Spanish nothing to agree to, and benefited them. Among the thousands of Germans living in Spain, refugee enemies of the Reich lurked amongst the businessmen, a potential fifth column of foreigners. As to joining with Germany in the war, Himmler could still hear Franco's squeaky voice whining at his Pardo Palace outside Madrid about bad harvests, bad transport for German food aid, Spain's greed for more of north Africa. Here in Barcelona, Himmler had handed over thousands of Reichsmarks in aid to flood victims. Good old Uncle Deutschland, much obliged. Spain, willing to do what in return?

The chequerboard, like a vertical maze for mice, the coloured circles, the wavy lines disorient Himmler. The light is too bright; the lines swim; the black and white squares pulse in and out. This has been a long day. He begins to hallucinate or slip into semi-dreams.

"*Welcome to Adventures in Art History! Your selection is Twentieth Century Nazi Era* –"

A different woman's voice interrupts distantly. "Henry? Henry from Harvard, you've become lost. You're submerged. Seek-Engine Vasari's expanding its reach, sucking in petaflops of historical detail. It's spinning out of control, attaching more and more strands to its web."

A voice in his head, coming and going. How can he understand a voice speaking English?Yet he seems to… Is this occult knowledge? Some of what the woman says is nonsense: seek-engine, petaflop…

"You should never have come to Himmler as a Viewpoint. To Göring, yes – he looted art. Or Goebbels – he was involved in the Degenerate Art exhibition. Or Rosenberg. Or the idiotic von Ribbentrop who liked French painters like Utrillo even if Utrillo was degenerate. You should be in the Jeu de Paume in Paris, where looted art was assessed. Or at the Degenerate show in Berlin. *Better still*, you should never have impersoned as a Nazi bigwig."

Much eludes him. It's like overhearing someone talking a hundred metres away.

I don't understand. Are you the power I seek for the Reich? Power. *Macht.* The Reich already has the Holy Spear safe in Nuremburg. The Ark of the Covenant remains elusive – a wooden chest once clad in gold, probably unclad these days. Himmler was in Toledo a couple of days ago, and his aides found nothing. He was at Montserrat today, only to be frustrated.

Yet now a voice speaks to him in his head.

"*Power*," the woman says more clearly. "*Drawing so much power. The seek-engine may have gone A.I. It's autonomous, learning*." None of this makes any sense. "*Learning the wrong things. Learning to be evil. Himmler and his cronies were nutty as fruitcakes. We're afraid this isn't exactly a sim any more. It's so detailed that it's coalescing with past reality. Identity of indiscernibles, Leibnitz. You know about this, Henry. No, scrub that – David says the sim's coalescing with an actual alternative reality within Many Worlds, not very 'alternative' at all, leastways at this time period, 1940, almost identical. David's in my ear. He's saying our assumption that time retains the same pace, same rate of progress from past to future, in Many Worlds is wrong. Henry, you gotta do something dramatically out of kilter to break the, well, congruence – I nearly said enchantment. The seek-engine is eating up our processing power. Wait, David's saying No Don't Not Yet. This is a kind of time travel, he says. Fuck that, David, this is too dangerous. Henry, does your Himmler have a pistol? Walther 25 calibre, say, specially sewn pocket in his trousers, just like his beloved Führer?"*

Himmler's fingertips grope. Pistol, yes.

The power of degenerate art to corrupt a visionary German… A wave of nausea sweeps through him, but he doesn't vomit his vegetables. Time seems to have stopped. The clock inset in the wall isn't moving its hands. Clever idea, that clock – it gains four hours in every twenty-four, to disorient a prisoner further. Now the clock seems stuck.

"The cell is a psychotrap. The way it was designed, the way it was painted. Henry, you're experiencing psychotic dissolution. Cause Heinrich to pull his pistol and shoot the others in the cell. Fegg off, David – you said the sim's resonating with an alternative reality, not with our own reality in the past. We'll break the link, disrupt the sim, collapse it like cards, resetting the seek-engine. What does it matter if the alt-reality diverges? That's the disruption we need. And we'll rescue Henry, too."

The black and white squares throb. The lines on the wall oscillate. Red and yellow discs dance. Himmler's fingers wriggle. Suffocating, in the cell. Heavily-dressed bodies crowding it. Body odours and cologne.

"You listen to me, David, damn it! Is there any chance that the sim's resonating with our own *reality in the past?What would the consequences be of Himmler apparently losing his marbles and shooting people in that cell?If he shoots Consul-General Jaeger, witnessed by the Spanish, what difference may* that *make? Jaeger may be replaced as a minor player and the world bumps along… But if SS Wolff stops a bullet? For Chrissake, Wolff is Himmler's Chief of Staff. He's third in command of the SS, a rival to Heydrich. He's Himmler's peephole upon Hitler. He ends up as military commander in Italy, so*

it's him who negotiates the surrender with Dulles. Yet he stays a mystery man, even after he starts appearing on post-war TV, authenticating the Hitler Diaries, whatever. Who replaces such an enigma?

"Shoot the Spanish? Because they have no major roles to play? Himmler is unhappy with his visit to Spain, so he shoots two of Franco's top henchmen? Do you think he'll get away with this, escape back to Berlin? Off to a sanatorium for a few weeks to keep his head down?

"Oh yes, David, we thought it would be so safe and ringfenced and marginal if we focused first upon art history. Yet what if art is one of the primary forces in the world? A definer of reality."

Power. *Control!* He must control. In this psychotic cell he is controlled *unacceptably*. Why should he even try to please any of his Spanish hosts, when the reason for pleasing them vanished with the failure of the Führer's meeting with Franco? He has pleased too many people in the past! Oh to be back home in Germany. Why should this odious Spanish experience be happening to him?

"Himmler shooting his own Chief of Staff might have the big impact we need?"

He has to release himself, break the frozen ice of the moment. How better than with a bullet? Or several?

"We truly daren't wait much longer, David?"

To shoot or not to shoot? Blood, even brains, might spatter his uniform, his face, his glasses. If only the Führer were here to command him, *Shoot, my faithful Heini!* Then to reward him for doing the right thing, with *Well done, my faithful Heini.* No, that's his wife's voice, a woman's voice.

Only once in two thousand years is an Adolf Hitler born! A more-than-man who can command instantly, choosing the true path instinctively. Heini is not himself a Führer. Head of the SS, oh yes. Head of the Gestapo, indeed. But not the more-than-human Godhead of Germany, not a Hitler.

He wavers. The psychocell fluctuates, as though underwater. Have his glasses steamed over? The claustrophobia. The stifling.

"Leave it up to Himmler who he shoots? Because he isn't a puppet but a person? What's with this humanising of Himmler? You of all people, David! Can't you take the responsibility for deciding? And then we won't be interfering quite so much? Is that it?

"Really, we have less than a minute? Before this flux loses fluidity? Before we lose our power to act?

"So there's no authority higher than me. Under protest, then…

"Henry –! Heini –! How many people have you caused to be killed? How many more do you want killed to cleanse the Reich? You can kill a couple personally! Go ahead, this isn't so hard, Reichsführer. Then you'll be free."

The others in the cell don't move as Himmler slides the pistol from the pocket inside of his pocket. Yes, first shoot General Sagardía to one side of him – next, General Orgaz. Damn them for bringing him to this tormenting place which he insisted on being brought to.

Pull pistol, point sideways where the heart should be, squeeze trigger.

As Sagardía sags, blood spilling suddenly from his mouth and nose, the yellow lines on the wall whiplash the coloured discs and black and white squares and the dazzle of the lightbulb into a frenzied dance, spiralling inward –

"Henry? Henry?"

Sara-17-Vee-Chang eases the induction helmet from Henry-54-Kay-Patel's head, its feelers pulling loose with slight reluctance. Henry's jumpsuit-clad limbs jerk; tethers keep him where is on the couch. Very soon the spasms abate and his eyes blink open.

"Sara." Recognition. "I'm back. Quite a ride." Still ordinary, his speech.

She loosens tethers.

The viewtank, which previously showed Henry's viewpoint as if through wobbly green jelly, is now a globe of bubbly grey frogspawn, lots of tiny eyeballs with black pupils; it's in a resting state, shifting slowly around.

The spherechamber's curving wall is slim-corded with cabling. Sara-17-Vee-Chang's silver skull-ports wear datajewels; Henry-54-Kay-Patel's ports of course await replenishing, whereupon he'll become superconscious.

No one from the Nazi Reich, except perhaps degenerate artists, could begin to guess who these slim, bald, brown-skinned beings with silver skull-ports might be, or where, or when. In fact they're in Rome, lapped by sea from the south-west. Ah, here comes David-88-Aitch-BarKohan in person.

Transhumanity has transpired rather than Overmen.

– For Lluis Salvador, good guy and good guide

Clickbeetle

They put a clickbeetle into Suzan's left ear to chastise her for concentrating too much upon her own consciousness. The beetle happily feeds upon earwax packed with energetic fatty acids and cholesterol. *Click click click click*, it clicks continuously. This isn't the type of beetle whose click propels it away from trouble – that kind should really be called a flick beetle. Whereas Suzan's curious coleoptera (*not* cleopatra) simply clicks and carries on clicking for no obvious reason. Until people found a purpose for it: punishment.

Suzan's punishment could have been worse: clickbeetles in both ears. Either in synch, or out of synch.

It's no use Suzan sticking a finger into her ear, right down the canal to the drum. This usually results in rupture of the drum or a stuck finger.

Allegedly Dr Mengele of Auschwitz ordered a little boy to be strapped immobile in a chair. Above the boy's head was positioned a mechanised hammer such that the boy was bashed (or bumped) on the skull every few seconds. After an unspecified time, the youngster went insane.

Allegedly this happened in a little shed behind the Doctor's house at Auschwitz (Oświęcim) in Poland. Allegedly this was an experiment related to head injuries. According to another report, Nazi doctors in the plural committed this crime in Baranowicze. Mengele was by no means the only Nazi death doctor. Though he was infamously 'The One Who Got Away'. This episode of human head and hun hammer requires further verification.

A hammer constantly hitting a small human's head until the little chap goes insane: this is undoubtedly a monstrous story. Yet what is the point of this story?

Words fail.

No, words do *not* fail. Narrators fail to find the right words. Is the boy bashed or bumped by the mechanised hammer? Is he tapped or is he thumped? What relevance has this to the head injuries of adult soldiers wearing steel helmets? (Steel helmets for soldiers replaced the traditional hardboiled leather picklebonnet topped with a spike)

Whence came the mechanised hammer? Why is the hammer apparently never used upon another child? What of the scientific principle of repeatability?

The hammer blows, or hammer taps, cannot be meant to imitate shrapnel striking a steel helmet sheltering a head. Or else the hammer would immediately kill the unprotected child. The hits by the hammer must be more like the drips of the famous Chinese Water Torture, whereby water dropping upon one's forehead will, after an unspecified period of time, dement the immobilised victim. Apparently this Water Torture never existed, least of all in China.

Exactly which part of the unfortunate little boy's head does the hammer hit repeatedly? We need to know this. Generalisations are futile.

Mengele's 'science' was more than dodgy. He did possess a PhD of which he was very proud, in racist anthropology, and he certainly could perform surgical operations, with or without anaesthetics. But basically his casebook, which he reported back loyally to his Alma Mater, was crap. Capricious as well, perhaps? In which case he may have ordained a one-off head-hammering.

Concerning a murderous medical student the Beatles sang: *Bang bang Maxwell's silver hammer came down upon his head.* Usually doctors use rubber hammers to test reflexes, such as by tapping a patient below the knee to make the leg kick out spontaneously. Could the Mengele Torment Hammer have been made of rubber, and could sleep deprivation have been the intention for the wretched boy? However, Mengele's speciality was twins, with a sideline in monstrosities. Not normal single juniors.

To what extent is Suzan's clickbeetle experience akin to tinnitus? One in ten people endure natural tinnitus, a constant ringing or buzzing or whistling or hissing or roaring or clicking in one's ear. Yet another example of the unintelligent design of the human body.

Tinnitus is from the Latin *tinnire* (meaning 'to ring'). Do you have tin-eary, dearie? Have you taken your water-pill yet, love? Have you done number two this morning? Thus are nurses in British hospitals trained to address their patients whose minds are damaged by decades of looking at gamma-IQ newspapers, *Sun*, *Star*, *Male*, *Daily Moo*. Some tin-ear people begin to hear music or blurred voices. Famous people diagnosed with tinnitus include Van Gogh and Goya and Michelangelo and Luther and Liza Minelli.

Suzan posted too many times on the social network You&Me about Me rather than about You. Posting a minimum of three times a day is obligatory if one wishes to be part of society and thus be networked. Only thus can you buy the best travel tickets to visit your aunt. You&Me is a way of saying YuanMei – that's the social credit system, meaning 'money not'. No reference to Yuan Mei, the 18th Century Chinese sage of gastro simplicity and poet of personal feelings. Suzan used the word 'I' far too many times in her posts. "I'm feeling cold tonight." "I think I'm catching a cold." "Woe is Me."

A clickbeetle is tiny. The eardrum amplifies its click. There's no point in asking a friend to use a flashlight and chopsticks or tweezers to pull the clickbeetle out merely because that method works with crickets and spiders which get into human ears. In their natural habitat clickbeetles flutter along at human ankle height upon the teeniest (not the most tinny) of wings, seeking empty snail shells to inhabit, wanting the shell's conchlike power of amplification for mating reasons. Never shells previously broken against stone anvils by thrushes. Within snail shells the food is dried slime and whatever jerky protein biltong survives being nipped up by scavenger ants. Not aunts. To imply that aunts scavenge in order to eat is an insult to society. Aunts of a certain age belong in a House For Future Ancestors.

I will confide that a clickbeeetle's wingcase is purple. Like a very tiny aubergine also known as an eggplant. Ten or so female clickbeetles may coexist within the same snailshell together with from one to multiple males. This is known as a harem. Suzan shan't host a harem unless she goes to sleep on a warm lawn, drugged by sunshine accompanied by cool lemonade and cucumber sandwiches, and if a wild tiny male scarabacus violates her ear, or volates her ear which seems just as valid a word.

People can get by with tinnitus. Tin per cent of people have little choice in the matter. Likewise, accompanied by a clickbeetle clicking away within.

What of the little shed behind Doctor Mengele's house at Auschwitz where our little chap is tormented until he becomes lunatic?

When in August 1944 Josef's doting wife Irene visits her hubby at Auschwitz due to her sensing the mounting melancholy afflicting her husband as the Red Army worrisomely rolls westward, she stays in the SS 'barracks' – presumably together with Hubby. Irene's planned one-month visit extends for another month due to her succumbing to diphtheria and then suffering from an inflamed heart muscle. Auschwitz isn't a healthy place to be on holiday, even if it includes numerous hospitals of various sizes within that vast city of damnation boasting umpteen suburbs, its population akin to that of modern Düsseldorf. When Frau Mengele is discharged from hospital to convalesce she moves into a 'new flat in the doctors' barracks', together with Herr Doktor Hubby one presumes. Brand-new kitchen and bathroom.

This is by no means a 'house plus garden' such as Commander of Auschwitz Rudolf Höss enjoys (just 300 metres away from a gas chamber and a crematorium). Mengele's flat will be in a great stucco block shared with other officers.

That house of Höss has fourteen rooms and was built in 1937 by a Pole whom the Nazis evicted. After the Nazis fled from the Russians, the Polish chap moved back into his house and ignored the massive changes which had come over the neighbourhood during his enforced absence. Such as gas ovens and crematoria.

So: for Mengele there's *no garden hut* behind *no detached house*. This may mean *no bound boy* and *no automatic hammer*. By no means is this to imply that Mengele didn't do *many* atrocious things to his victims, always without anesthetics. Save the Reich's pain-killers for injured heroes of the Waffen-SS! Yet in Mengele's deluded mind he is scientist, not sadist. Admittedly he can fly into violent rages. Yet he's quite the elegant dandy at the selection ramp – for immediate gassing or for death by hard labour – and quite the daddy handing out sweeties to twins due to be vivisected by him later on.

Cute spotty red and black ladybirds are the nastiest bugs to get stuck in your ear. They secrete toxic shit which inflames and agonises. So much swelling may occur that no one can get the ladybird out! Not nice. You might go mad. A clickbeetle, on the other hand, will roll over and die after twelve months-ish; and thus stop clicking. And it's small, barely 5 mills long although surprisingly audible.

Suzan works in the eye clinic of a towering House For Future Ancestors, a total-care geriatric highrise though not a hospice, certainly not, and a hundred light years distant from Mengele's judgements regarding life and death. Most of the residents retain their wisdom, of the demotic kind. Suzan interacts with her own elderly clients less than if she were in one of the House's several hair salons. Demotic, from *demos*, 'the people'.

Suzan recently came across the automatic hammer story regarding Mengele. Seeking for information about this or that scores citizen points provided she isn't just goggling at random while she polishes her nails.

To research the evil deeds of social enemies is meritorious. This takes Suzan out of herself. It provides a distancing effect. This is genuine Brecht therapy. Das ist echt Brecht. So she hopes. This gives her something serious to post about on You&Me. To blag is "to gain approval through persuasive utterance" (usually fictitious) – but Suzan ain't making any of this up, no way Hosei.

Though on the other hand, the Brecht Effect aims to stop onlookers from being taken out of themselves (so that instead they may scrutinise a situation objectively), whilst one might argue that Suzan *needs* to be taken way out of herself. Less mention of 'I' and 'my' and 'me' and 'miny moe'.

Maybe due to overmuch reliance upon historical reality, Suzan fails to attract more than a few handfuls of followers. Frankly, the topic is distasteful. Opportunistically she renames her blag *Meng the Merciless* but then she finds herself criticised editorially on account of frivolous attitude. The Great Ming Empire (1368 to 1644 Common Era) may not be mocked. During Ming times, for instance: farewell to the Mongols chased beyond the Wall, tails between legs. Under the Mings the Chinese population doubles in numbers. Such is not a joking matter.

By now Shuxan's in too deep (*not* finger in ear) to shift her speciality. Always she hears c*lick-click-clickety-clicky* neither hurrying near nor hastening away especially, neither red-shifting nor blue-shifting, merely everpresent as part of herself. If perchance that clicking should cease, might the clicks have comprised the countdown to bursting a blood vessel in the brain?

Even her name is shifting, from Suzan to Shushan. Does this not imply progressive loss of ego? How much ego must melt until all clicks cease? *Or* is the clicking no type of therapy at all – but chastisement pure and simple?

Shushan's friends are individuals whom she must prioritise beyond her own self-centered self, beyond her own individualism. How may she interest them if Meng and the hammer are offensive?

Her very own clickbeetle, randomly assigned to her, no longer sounds in the least regular. It's as if it's clicking in Morse code! Click click clock clock click clickety clock click clickety click. Has the clickbeetle become intoxicated by her ear wax?

Shushan must learn Morse code! Meng and Morse and Ming all begin with M. Dash it, Dash it.

She will specialise her right ear for that purpose. Much concentration will be needed, and regular postings *in dots and dashes*. For this is First Contact with an inner world – not with the solipsistic *personal* world of Suzania, but rather with the microcosm within herself where a miniature nano-society exists. As above, so below. Mr Pope declared that true self-love and social are the same; self-love forsook the path it first pursued, and found the private in the public good.

This epiphany (this 'showing forth') is just an example of the benefits of a clickbeetle in your ear. Thank you for reading this paper of Self Criticism.

posted 10 January at 23. 13 Public suzan43 selfcrits@countersolipsism. euro. gov Squawker for NeoIos

Journey to the Anomaly

translated from PanLang by Ian Watson

This is my memorised journal of our journey to the anomaly. Eight thousand licks of light, a very long way from our starclump. I assume that my viewers, listeners, touchers, smellers, and tasters know how long a lick of light is. And indeed what light is.

If not, please consult the PanLang Meaning-ary, in whatever modality your dominant info-sense may be. I intend this to be a popular account, so please be patient if I over-explain some items.

Surely not items such as *PanLang itself?* Whereby Fluffle, Crusty, Wedgy, Boomboomba, and I commune during our epic journey… Surely not!

Just to be on the safe side – most sapient beings have sides – I mention that, due to its semiotic cascade, PanLang very flexibly accomodates the most varied beings of different origins, whether they burp significantly or stridulate or voice with chords or reeds, or harp with strings, or sniff odours, or flash, et cetera. The likelihood of my journal turning up, a trillion ticks of the prime pulsar from now, is statistically tiny; even so, future beings may try to understand this journal long after we have expired.

A semiotic cascade is… oh surely I need not!

(A full technical monograph about our findings will be inscribed in genetic code, copies embedded inside crystals within rocks for safer storage.)

When our newest, most sensitive farseescopes detected the anomaly, we were astounded. A planetary system where all of the worlds appeared to have almost circular orbits! A solar system with its worlds spaced out neatly, geometrically. This could not be natural!

True, one planet seemed to be absent from what ought to be the fifth geometric place – but even so, the sheer regularity! This was way unnatural – as viewed from our enormous distance, at any rate. Nothing for it but to go there ourselves to take a closer look.

So, not without difficulty, by combining all our wits and our senses and exotic resources of the starclump, we created a bend-ring. This would shorten the stuff of spacetime to the fore of an eggship while enlarging it aft. The bend-ring and its bubble containing our eggship would ride the wave of shortening in the desired direction at many multiples of See while the eggship itself experienced neither acceleration nor even velocity. We would be falling free weightlessly within our ship – without, I hasten to add, falling over ridiculously.

All of us must respect one another's corporealities, colours (if visible to others), vibrations, odours, and so forth. Flavours too, to a certain extent, but we must not devour one another. However, teasing is okay, in accord with Treaty of Teasing by which relations within our starclump flow lubricatedly. So let me introduce ourselves.

I myself, Ten-tacles my species nickname, come from a hotwater world orbiting close to a red dwarf star. In the way that some Extremos have antifreeze in their blood and their tissues to cope with periodical freezing due to way-out-then-in-again orbits, so my folks have antiboil. Mine is also a fairly heavy world, as regards mass, so it's good that we have buoyancy under our own control. We can even swim in the thick atmosphere of steam where birdfish fly, not fry. Below our surface of hotwater, giant hotsea weeds concentrate dissolved metals which drift on convection currents up from the superheated depths. The nodules serve as a kind of retarding anchor for weeds. Consequently we were able to contrive some tools during our prehistory before Boomboomba's folks dipped down through the steam in their bigmetal to semaphore signals at us, clever them, fast forward to enlightenment about our starclump and the cosmos in general and full technology access. Our star is only warm, yet we're so close to it that our ball of water around a substantial rocky core just about boils; by the same token we're nicely protected from cosmic rays and other incoming. I reserve my personal name-signal for own-species communings. If several Ten-taclesfolk were present in this eggship, we would be

Ten-tacles-dim, Ten-tacles-sum, Ten-tacles-su, Ten-tacles-shi and so on; I hope this numeration renders appropriately in your Lang.

I think maybe it's best if I introduce each of my travel companions as we interact – we're each in our own enviro-compartment within the egg, all touching variously. Open visibility; privacy isn't an issue, though I can steam up if I wish.

"So, Wedgy, what do you think of our journey hitherto?" I wave with four of my ten tacles.

Wedgy was a big chip off an old block, to start with. Birthed inside of a tumbling world. Wedgy's an asexual *it.* Early on in the career of its home's sunsystem, a giant moon made its home planet's spin axis unstable. Fair enough! Par for the course! Instability is the spice of life. Within the crust of its world, forever stretching and compressing, extremophiles began early to flex and evolve. Evolved Wedgy is a trigonal slab with appendages, manipulating stuff magnetically as well as by touch.

It vibrates, "You know how our eggship is blunter at the front?"The Wedgyfolk frequently state the obvious as an initial axiom, thereby to explore the consequences.

"Yes," I wave with one tacle.

"And our eggship's rear is more pointed?"

"True." Another nuanced wave.

"I feel that I'm being stretched, thinned, elasticated. Obviously this isn't so, since we occupy a bubble of *flat* space inside of our eggship."

"That's an interesting observation, Wedgy. Does anyone else mention this?"

"I have only just begun to sense the effect myself."

"Do you suppose faint tidal forces are reaching into our eggship from the warped space caused by the bend-ring?"

"I hope not. But I think the effect is subjective."

"Registered only by your own unique senses, Wedgy?"

"Perhaps… not so much *registered* as *manifested.*"

Wedgy has scientific equipment in his enviro-compartment, as do we all, yet maybe the Wedgyperson is its own best detector of phenomena caused by our journey. That's why we five are all such different beings. Call us a spectrum of spectators.

You might suppose that our eggship should proceed with the more pointy end – or tip – forward, the better to cleave the void, as it were. In fact no void is being cloven *per se.* Our eggship remains at rest within the bubble caused by the bend-ring while the bubble contracts ahead of us just as it expands behind us, at hundreds of multiples of See. Or have I already said so? And the perfect resting position of an egg is with its blunter end, or base, *down* the hill. In the sense that we are speeding, while at rest, from our own star clump towards far away, we are proceeding down a slope, rather than climbing a slope, as will happen on our return journey. This was proven mathematically by Fluffle's folk, to whom the stability of eggs matters a lot.

Of course, our five species were also the principal investors in the construction of the bend-ring plus eggship, at 5% each of our Gross Global Product throughout five *periods.* This seems a small sacrifice in order to understand the anomaly. An Oekonomist from Boomboomba's folk eccentrically proposed – although there is nothing wrong with extreme eccentricity in the planetary sense! – that theoretically the oekonomies of disunited worlds might opt to spend 5% of GGP on internal *conflicts* – either for population control or to stimulate applied research – or even upon external *conflicts*, as if Wedgies might beat up on Fluffles interstellar-wise, half a See-*period* away. *That* particular Boomboomba was laughed at, disgust-sniffed at, tacle-shaken at, and generally derided, far beyond teasing.

I pass onward, propelled easily by my tacle tips.

"Fluffle? Are you busy?" I wave.

Fluffle trills – audible to me at least, even as the semiotic cascade interprets her melodies as virtual wavings perceived by my eyes: "Never too busy for Ten-tacles!"

Flufflefolk are avians living in labyrinths of caverns quite deep undercrust. The thick crust protects them from bombardments which constantly pock their planet in its debris-crowded sunspace, remnants from catastrophic comet collisions. Ancestors who survived the shocks that frequently knocked them askew first of all evolved cushioning fluff, then they glided, then they flapped then fluttered then flew, safest strategy while the world around you is rocking or quivering. Nor are the subterranean Flufflefolk blind, thanks to the bright luminescence of all manner of tasty fungi thrusting up through verdant mosses in those caverns. The Flufflefolk's name for a catastrophe is *Om-Let.*

"Fluffle, just recently do you feel at all 'stretched'?"

She opens her green-and-golden wings to full span.

"Now that you come to mention it…"

"Would you say this is a physical or a metaphysical sensation?"

Closing her wings, Fluffle tucks her beak under a wingpit to commune with herself.

On re-emerging, "A metaphysical sensation – yes, I'd say so," she sings.

Onward.

Boomboomba's enviro-compartment is filled with large spinning spherical rollers which move in and out, up and down, continuously changing the inner configuration, this being the best way for her to maintain her composure during our journey while she is perforce at rest, comparatively speaking. Serpentine, she is, always in motion. A cruciform snake, with bellow-lungs. Her two strong bodies unite midway. Two brains, two hearts, two everythings. She's from a very peculiar carbohydrate-rich agglomeration of icebits and dirty snowballs constantly churning, lubricated by paraffin waxes, while tumbling chaotically around an ice-giant. Due to having squishy-squashy atmosphere it's a noisy place. A chilly beanbag worldlet, full of life with doubled DNA. Those sphererollers within her hab are relatively soft, and their noise is damped, but the surface of her hab does vibrate a bit. Though not with enough resonance to disrupt the smart microtubules composing her hab-shield.

Slapping my tacles upon her enviro-compartment – let's call it a 'hab' from now on – I call out "Boomboomba!" till her two glittering beady-eyed heads come into view through the rollerspheres. Quantum-coherent, her thoughts. If one head is decapitated by hard ice, or crushed, soonish she grows another. Good back-up.

"Ten-tacles, what a pleasure!" she tries to whisper. She's very polite. And elegant. I could almost contemplate a more intimate relationship – her foursome and my tensome – except for the constant instability, the shaking-around, whereby she thrives. She's Captain, by the way.

"Both Wedgy and Fluffle tell me they've begun feeling a sort of 'metaphysical stretching'. I'm wondering about you, Boomboomba."

"That's so kind of you, Ten-tacles! Hmm…" Her hum is a tuba. In general the most intimate type of relationship is ruled out anatomically for us of the star-clump – imagine a slab of a Wedgyfolk trying to couple with a hollow-boned Flufflefolk. But not in *all* cases. Maybe I have hope. Obviously Boomboomba can never tolerate the boiling heat of my homeworld, even for a holiday in a clingtight chill-suit, yet maybe I can meet her half-way, as it were, on the thermometer… on some comet moving towards or away from perihelion when tepid. I must confess that I find alluring the thought of a body consisting almost entirely of four sleek limbs – containing organs. I wonder about her sexual organ, or organs.

One of her heads withdraws, followed by the other, then both return to view – in exactly the same positions, yet are those the same heads in those positions?

"Hmm… I am continuously pulled and pushed, and continuously I contract and extend. How should I know the difference?"

I might enjoy pulling her and extending her while she pushes against me, contracting. Perhaps these thoughts are irresponsible.

Nevertheless, I venture to tease her. "So what actually happens while you sleep, Boomboomba? Or are you always partly awake, and is that the real reason you're Captain, and I'm just the Vice-Captain, without control? Me, who could control ten controls simultaneously?" I wave deprecatory humour.

As soon as I wave this, it sounds bad. Asleep… control… Erotically bad, diplomatically bad.

"Apologetically I must ask, respected Ten-tacles, are *you yourself* experiencing this sense of metaphysical stretching?"

Me, I'm toughly elastic. Did Wedgy's confession elicit any echo in me? I don't think so – yet would I have noticed the sensation, any more than Boomboomba would have noticed?

"I don't know, to be honest. I feel as Vice-Captain that I ought to investigate, just in case this is a significant phenomenon and might increase."

Both of her heads seem to grin at me, tongues flicking. Oh her forked tongues!

"I applaud your zeal. This is exactly how the perfect Vice-Captain should occupy himself. I should remind you, excellent dutiful Vice-Captain, that your duplicate controls only require three appendages at any one time; so therefore we also have triplicate controls inside Fluffle's enviro-compartment, which she can manipulate with beak and claws if the need arises. And that my humble self was chosen as Captain primarily because of my dual heads."

My controls won't function unless Boomboomba's fail to respond; nor Fluffle's controls unless mine also fail in their turn. Meaning that by then both Boomboomba and myself would very likely be dead.

"Ten-tacles, why are you teasing Boomboomba?"

Oh, Wedgy has followed me along inside his own hab strewn in three dimensions with floating rocks. It mightn't understand erotic nuances except in the abstract, but it's a sophisticated block of stone.

"Wedgy," I wave, "I'm investigating the metaphysical sensation you feel. Fluffle feels what you feel."

So waving, I move onward to greet Crusty, from a Very Big Rock. The giant rock experiences frequent crustal recycling by supervolcanoes spewing CO_2 plus water vapour, popped off due to the gravity of the gas-giant which the Very Big Rock orbits. That gas-giant itself is in close orbit around their sun, therefore the intense ultraviolet radiation dissociates the CO_2 into carbon and oxygen… Enough of explanations! The Crustyfolk are superbreeders on account of their population continually being culled by lava flows. Crustyfolk can scuttle very fast on their twenty legs, or roll protectively into an armoured ball, and they mature speedily too; thus culture continues onward despite repeated catastrophes. Anyway, only their two front legs are adapted as manipulators and their mouths would tend to crunch controls. They export rare minerals and metals, lying around for the scraping. To communicate, they whistle.

Our star clump numbers at least thirty-seven sentient species from all kinds of unstable planets, so you mightn't be fully familiar with Crustyfolk. Our own beloved Crusty is a very mature and wise individual due to living away from his world and its supervolcanoes. Since Crustyfolk traditionally live short though intense lives, evolution seems to have forgotten to build in a time limit for their bodies.

Oh, and they don't export stuff by using those supervolcanoes to boost themselves to the fringe of space, whereupon our usual shared stardrive can take over. No no. Due to veins of Dirty Matter entrapping Dirty Energy, they have access to repulsion, at least while moderately close to their planet's surface.

Where was I? Oh yes, I'm where my own hab borders Crusty's hab. We all abutt one another; the topology inside the eggship is interesting, not to mention expensive.

"Crusty," I wave. He's rolled up in a crusty ball amidst artificial crust, but the semantic cascade of PanLang whistles him up. He uncurls his head and frontal arms.

"Ten-tacles!" he whistles. And: "Wedgy!" And: "To what do I owe?" As if I hadn't last conversed with Crusty less than one digestion since…

"Do you feel metaphysically stretched, Crusty? Is that why you rolled up, to pull yourself together?"

"Aye, 'tis true. 'Tis true indeed, yet not *in deed* – but internally."

Very well. Three of us report symptoms of a metaphysical malaise.

I hasten to add that the term 'metaphysical' should not be taken refer to phenomena which are beyond the scope of science – since nothing is beyond that scope.

Immediately I spy an ambiguity. The physical nature of nothing, in the sense of empty void, say, is within the scope of science.

Essentially what is beyond the scope has *no meaning*. Let us remember that the limit of vision is equal to the age of the cosmos, since the very earliest spacetime passes beyond the observable horizon of expansion. 'Metaphysical' refers to *alongside* the physical rather than beyond the physical, in the way that dreams are alongside awareness, sustaining the sense of continuous identity.

I go to look in the spectrofarscope along our direction of travel in case of any measurable distortion. Topologically, the spectrofarscope is available to all of us except Wedgy who cannot avail itself.

Our destination is still a point of white light; there's not a hint of an aura.

A fiftieth of a *period* later…

The sense of time passing has gone. Time does not pass. A photon travelling at See – at what other rate might a photon travel? – undergoes no time between its emission and its reception. In the instant that the photon exists, it ceases, even if a billion *periods* have elapsed in between. Likewise, a supraluminal bubble of space passes through space timelessly. Nevertheless, a journey can be both quasi-instantaneous as well as quasi-interminable. There must be a supraluminal speed limit as well as a luminal limit, otherwise the cosmos might burst.

We have a conference, here where our habs converge.

"So," Boomboomba tries to whisper, "Wedgy and Crusty and Fluffle are increasingly aching metaphysically with a sense of stretching, and I myself am beginning to notice this sensation mildly. What of you, Ten-tacles?"

Boomboomba is condescending to me politely. She already knows what I feel, because by now I have developed and confided symptoms. I mean, what I feel regarding the metaphysical sensation, not what I might feel erotically in private about the sensual double-serpent which she is.

"I feel *pulled elastically* while at rest in free-fall."

"This was never anticipated in any of our projections. The questions are, will this ache plateau and remain tolerable? – or not? If not, what do we do about this?"

Fluffle trills, "We can switch off the bend-ring temporarily. The sensation might disappear immediately and, after we resume, only build up again gradually as it did earlier rather than resuming immediately at the same level. In that case, we might punctuate our journey."

"At what energy cost, Fluffle?"

"I was about to say. Sending a signal to the front of the bubble, to cease surging onward, will require significant energy, which we shouldn't squander – our store of zetabeta from the Crustyfolk's world is finite."

"How many times can we stop?"

"I would estimate three times max. We may need zetabeta for local journeys within the anomaly unless those local journeys are to take entire *periods*. We don't know what we will find at the anomaly."

"Which is precisely why we're going," whistles Crusty.

"What's more," adds Fluffle, "when the bubble ceases surging forward, particles we sweep up en route will release directly ahead with acquired energy, like a sonic boom shockwave – even if in space no one can hear you boom – wrecking anything directly in front of us."

"This is a problem for our destination," I point out with my tacle tips. "The idea is to arrive near any largish body in the anomaly's Keeper Belt and use it as a target for those supercharged particles so that those don't fly onward to some other sunsystem and cause *unpredictable* harm a million or a billion years from now." Likewise on our own return to our star clump. As per health and safety protocols.

Stating the obvious is sometimes valuable, in case other beings are neglecting the obvious.

Then and *now* are beginning to elude me as concepts.

"Stopping two or three times," trills Fluffle, "should reduce the total of supercharged particles we discharge on arrival. But during our return journey is this beneficial and safe?"

"During our return journey," communicates Wedgy, "we may feel ourselves being metaphysically *compressed* instead of stretched."

"I am calculating," trills Fluffle, "whether on release the supercharged particles might necessarily convert to tachyons, which must travel backwards through time… and in other words disappear from our *now*, proceeding into the past of the anomaly… although at what rate?"

Doubtless it helps Fluffle to voice aloud her incomplete calculating.

"I have decided that if the sensation becomes truly intolerable to any crew member, we ought to pause our journey."

Ought to. Not *must.*

"Yet how do we authenticate 'intolerable'…?"

"Has anyone thought," whistles Crusty, "that the anomaly may be a *trap* for sentient beings?"

I would prefer that our conference ends on the previous cliff-hanging, elliptical note. However, this new concept distracts Wedgy, and our attention in general.

"How so, a 'trap'?"

"The near-circular, quasi-clockwork orbits of the worlds of the anomaly are bound to pique the curiosity of any normal chaotic clump of sentients, such as ourselves. Assuming that the regularity is not accidental – which seems statistically very unlikely even if the very unlikely is always possible – the intention of the design may not be benign."

PanLang's semiotic cascades very often convey rhymes effectively, whether waved or trilled or whatever. All hail to the mutant hybrid deviser of PanLang long ago. Our implants are functioning perfectly.

"A trap," asks Fluffle, "in the sense of discovering our direction, or of catching specimens to study, and maybe to experiment upon?"

"That is unthinkable. I thought you were computing."

"I am frailer than the rest of us."

Another fiftieth of a *period* later…

A photon is timeless until it bumps into something and becomes *actualised*, or even in rare cases *seen*. We might perhaps compare and contrast the collapse of the wave function. Unseen, then seen.

As the ache of stretching increases, it seems that our eggship is slowly becoming transparent. You stretch something, it becomes thinner, easier to see through. The voyeur in myself is happy about this transparency as regards Booomboomba's hab full of view-blocking rollerspheres, not at all in other respects.

Fluffle is suffering seriously, or behaving as if that's so. Shrieking instead of trilling. Squealing, squalling, squawking. She has spread her wings wide, as if they're about to dislocate from their sockets. As I can notice whenever I glance towards her hab, but she deserves privacy in her pain. I'm so sorry for her. Boomboomba is being reckless.

At last, compassionately Boomboomba declares, "We shall stop!"

Full solidity resumes. The sense of stretching vanishes – without any accompanying lurch. On our screens, in all directions shine stars variously bright and faint. We remain at rest in free-fall, at – well, tie my arms together! – at two per cent of See, no way to go anywhere fast even in our own star clump, nevertheless a surprising speed.

Quickly, to beside Fluffle's hab. Her wings are slumping, though she still wails. I assume she's being hysteresical – the stretching has stopped, but her sensations lag behind.

"Calm yourself, Fluffle," I wave. "We have stopped. None too soon!"

"Indeed, we have demonstrated that we *can* stop. And at two per cent See. I fail to understand how we underwent any acceleration while our eggship remains at rest."

"Boomboomba," says Wedgy, "maybe what we sensed as *stretching* was a consequenceof collateral acceleration? Due to a slight imperfection in the bend-ring?"

"Or accumulating *stress* upon the bend-ring," whistles Crusty. "Maybe we should recalibrate somewhere…"

"If the sense of stretching is indeed a metaphysical consequence of accumulating stress upon the bend-ring, evidently we should halt whenever Fluffle feels the stretching is intolerable."

How convenient: use Fluffle as a detector!

"I think," trills Fluffle bravely, "I can tolerate the stretching to the extent it reached. Though no further. More, and I might go mad."

"More," whistles Crusty, "and the bend-ring might bend, or suffer a fracture. If there is a correlation."

"What," I ask, "caused the increasing transparency?"

"That must be," trills Fluffle, "a corollary of stretching."

"Ah," whispers Boomboomba, "we have now travelled two-fifths of the way to the anomaly."

"If we resume," say I, "and the stretching does not come upon us all at once, but only gradually, then we can afford to make two further stops, causing Fluffle significantly less accumulating suffering." I feel great sympathy for the Avian. Perhaps that's a consequence of all the fluff; though why should a Ten-Tacles respond to fluff?

"Alternatively, one further stop, at Fluffle's limit of tolerance, thus reserving more zetabeta for use within the anomaly."

Wedgy and Crusty and Fluffle and I all are silent in our various ways. 5 per cent GGP investment, I am thinking, until I realise: Fluffle must not feel obliged by the silence to volunteer and suffer excessively!

"As Vice-Captain I vote for two stops," I wave.

Fluffle looks at me movingly. If only Boomboomba would direct such a melted gaze with just one of her heads.

"We might benefit by entering the anomaly with a higher terminal velocity rather than a low velocity. Less need to use the bend-ring to get around if we need to superspeed."

"Why should we need superspeed?" asks Wedgy.

"Crusty first whistled the reason: a possible trap. Fluffle herself added: to catch and probe us."

This is *pressure* to volunteer, which I find a bit unacceptable. Am I stupidly mesmerised by Boomboomba's strength and glitter?

"Captain," I wave with due deference, "the anomaly did not appear overnight."

"From our point of view it did, being newly discovered."

"The anomaly must have been there for hundred of millions of *periods*, rotating sedately like clockwork. If a civilisation made the anomaly, that civilisation should be extinct by now."

"Or else biding its time, in a statis, until the flooly alights upon the zbiderweb. The anomaly dwellers may have no idea of a stardrive, still less of bend-rings. By definition: if any beings come to the zbiderweb those beings possess a means to travel faster than See. The anomaly-makers will steal a way to break out into the larger cosmos."

"Captain," I wave in appeal, "first of all your zbiderweb is imaginary, and secondly beings which can regularise all their planets cannot be so utterly lacking in power and knowledge that they need to lurk for millions of years to trap travellers."

"How do you know we are the first travellers to reach the anomaly? The anomaly is slightly broken, is it not? No planet is in position five any longer."

"Maybe that was so all the time!"

"The anomaly-makers' plan may have fruited before we even evolved."

"Then why are those creatures not *everywhere* now?"

"Simply because they went off in a different direction from our star clump? Yet the missing planet may also be a deliberate ploy, to suggest great antiquity. So as to lull travellers."

Our Captain may be employing a rhetorical device to confuse the issue. *Red Errings*, I believe the device is. Deliberate errors, which swim away fast to avoid deeper questioning. Yet methinks I detect the boom of paranoia.

"To the anomaly-makers millions of years may not matter much. Their sun appears to have a couple of billion *periods* of stability yet."

"*What* anomaly-makers? The anomaly may be purely natural! I have voted for two stops!"

"My dear Ten-tacles, this is starting to sound like mutiny on the eggship." Here is ruthlessness – I'm starting to reassess Boomboomba radically. Can ruthlessness in carrying out a mission be why she was chosen Captain, rather than myself? Must I be obliged to break through into her chilly hab and wrestle hotly with her?

Abruptly Fluffle trills, "I vote for only one stop."

"If the anomaly mayhap be a trap," whistles Crusty, "then I vote likewise."

Three to two already, not that the Captain really needs consensus.

Admirable in a way. But more abominable.

We go supraliminal again, and no the sense of stretching does not promptly resume.

Within a while, yes, and slowly as before. It's several whiles until Fluffle is screeching again, her wings widespread. Several whiles until we stop for a second time.

This time, we are much closer to the anomaly. Our farseescope can make out more detail, though Fluffle isn't in a condition to comment for half of another while, lying in her hab with wings folded around her.

Finally she revives.

The worlds of the anomaly are indeed ridiculously regular in spacing. The 'fifth planet' position seems to contain a belt of debris, though the estimated combined mass of the debris is only a low fraction of the mass of the third planet's moon – which itself is *unusually large* to be the satellite of such a non-giant world.

"May that moon have been moved into position around the third planet?"

"By what method?" says Wedgy.

Crusty suggests, "Some variation upon a bend-ring? Scaled up enormously?"

"How long ago?"

"By now," says Fluffle, my heroine, "we're seeing the anomaly as it was 3,000 *periods* in the past. "Entities which could engineer the moving of big moons some while before then would surely by now be evident elsewhere in our galaxy."

"Any electromagnetic signals from the anomaly?"

"None detectable. Not a hint of an artificial radio wave."

Both of the double serpent's heads are gazing out now. "So are they maintaining silence?"

"I did not say so, Boomboomba."

What is it *with* Boomboomba? Is she secretly scared of arriving? Does she feel guilty at tormenting Fluffle? Needing to justify herself? Burden of command? She ought to share more of her broodings with me, her Vice! If only I could transfer my fixation to Fluffle, whom I admire – but the coils of a Ten-tacles would break an Avian.

So here we are at last on the outskirts of the anomaly, our bend-ring switched off.

We discharged our accumulated supercharged particles at a worldlet in the anomaly's Keeper Belt, where a star stores unused building blocks for worlds well out of the way of those planets themselves. Unexpectedly, the little ice-and-rock worldlet burst apart. We must be careful what size of worldlet we discharge at on our return to our star clump.

Our terminal velocity is almost nothing with respect to that demolished worldlet. How so, how so? Did our bubble of void pass through invisible dirty matter full of dirty energy during our final stretch?

Fluffle is extremely indisposed, yet the sheer fascination of our eggship arriving spurs her to shriek, "Artificial electromagnetics, from the third planet! Masses of it. Including encoded visuals."

Life, inhabiting the inner part of the anomaly! Life, which must have arisen to technology quite recently since there were no faint signals 3,000 *periods* ago.

Consequently it's a while before Crusty notices that the broken worldlet spilled out of it some fragments containing structures which must be artificial, accompanied by organic signatures…

Using normal drive, we nose in upon a suspicious fragment, extruding our analysis chamber to draw it in – we did not come all this way unprepared for contingencies!

Within the steely ice is what must be a vacuum suit. Within the vacuum suit is an alien body, deeply frozen.

Slice open, and unpeel.

Horny green skin. Two slim muscular legs. Two shortish but highly functional arms. A crested head with long jaw. Two forward-facing eyes. A short jutting tail; leastways we think that must be a tail, maybe for balance in gravity. We decide to call the creature a sawrian, because its teeth are sharp.

"Thinking inventively," trills Fluffle, "this might almost be a distant cousin of Flufflefolk. Morphologically, in some respects…"

Dating suggests that the vacuum suit is 60 to 70 million *periods* old.

We decode incoming visuals. The creatures which mostly pervade the visuals – along with intermittent fluffy things – possess two legs, two arms, forward-facing eyes in flat faces, no tails. They are coloured cream and pink and black and brown, but never green. They wear many kinds of coverings. They seem to copulate frequently. They kill each other frequently, so we decide to call them *hewmans* because they so often hack and cleave and fell other *hewmans*. They use dangerous machines to speed from place to place. Explosions are frequent, and hallucinations. Nuclear fungus clouds billow into the upper atmosphere. Fleets of spaceships *fight* yet do not correspond to the technology level of the dangerous transport machines nor of the primitive robots that slowly survey the red fourth planet.

This is an entirely different kind of instability from any of the worlds in our star clump. Here, the third planet is stable as clockwork yet the inhabitants themselves are completely unstable! How different from the home life of our own dear star clump. Yet the unstable hewmans evidently have a good sense of balance, somersaulting, spinning around on one leg, leaping over each other.

Impossible that these hewmans have evolved from the sawrian vacuum-suit wearer with a short tail! Our sawrian wears on a silver chain around its neck a silver disc engraved with what seems the crater-pocked surface of a vacuum moon.

While we proceed inwards through the Keeper Belt, we spend many whiles studying the attenuating outpouring of radio and visuals. No trace of which, 3,000 *periods* ago.

"Can it be," says Crusty, "that the sawrians went extinct tens of millions of *periods* ago? They reached out into space, but then something destroyed them?"

"Perhaps the hewmans of the present destroyed the sawrians in the past?"

We have seen conflict after conflict after conflict, using all possible means of killing other beings, often accompanied by what I think of as Boomboomba soundtrack. We have seen savage sawrians attacking hewmans, sawrians sometimes bigger than tall buildings; these latter must be deliberate hallucinations, deceptions – but why do the hewmans broadcast deceptions?

"I can confirm from farseescoping," trills Fluffle, "that the hemisphere of the unusually big moon which is facing the third planet appears on the silver disc. But why show that?"

"Because," suggests Wedgy, "the big moon stimulated the sawrians to go there first of all in space? Celebratory reason?"

By now we have downgraded the idea that the spacefaring sawrians themselves pulled that big moon into orbit to stabilise the third planet. At first the oversize moon seemed to be further evidence that the anomaly was regularised deliberately, yet this does not stand up to mathematical scrutiny.

"What kind of *stimulated*?" queries Crusty. "I invoke our planet of the Krabfolk, who mate when their twin moons are both full. Without their twin moons coinciding at full brightness, their species would cease. *Nothing* must sully the albedo of their moons. No ship ne'er so small may land there. This is a *mania* with the Krabfolk. Suppose that those sawrians felt likewise about their big moon? They may go to any other world or worldlet or comet, yet not to their own moon? For the sawrians, their moon symbolised perfection ever since they arose in some swamp. So they never set clawed foot nor machine upon it! Instead, they wore the disc."

"Yet the sawrians must have noticed," trills Fluffle, "that their moon is blemished by umpteen craters – as is normal with moons lacking atmosphere."

"By the time the sawrians built farseescopes, maybe it was too late to modify the luna-tic mania? A mania for regularity and perfection, in keeping with them regularising their planets?"

"The outermost micro-planets orbit irregularly."

"Maybe that is why our frozen sawrian was out here in the Keeper Belt, along with many other sawrians presumably?"

We continue debating while our eggship moves inward towards the blue ice-giant in eighth position.

"The blue ice-giant," says Fluffle, "is tipped right over on its side. It rolls over and over on its orbit."

"Inadequately regularised?" suggests Wedgy.

"There's no sign yet of giant bend-rings. If there were bend-rings, these hewmans will find them and use them sooner or later."

"If any bend-rings exist, hewmans must not gain access. This must be our mission from now on."

"Surely not," I say with deference, "supposing the sawrians never built any bend-rings, and supposing this solar system is a natural accident?"

Much as I wish to avoid any hint of mutiny on our eggship, I have little wish to spend multiple *periods* searching for the inexistent – nor for us to squander our zetabeta flying around this big sunsystem hunting for the inexistent, thus causing Fluffle intolerable torment during our return to our homes.

Fluffle reports, "The biggest moon of the blue ice-giant rotates backwards! What kind of regularity is that?"

"The blue ice-giant is still in a regular position even if its moon is aberrant. Maybe the moon's retro rotation and the ice-giant being itself on its side are side effects of using a giant bend-ring ineptly."

"Captain," I wave, "can you show me *any* giant bend-ring? Recall the sheer cost and difficulty of achieving our eggship's little bend-ring!"

"I will show you a giant bend-ring as soon as we find it. We have seen in the hewmans' visuals giant asteroids crashing into the third planet many times. This may explain the extinction of the sawrians, while they were trying to regularise planets. Inept use of a giant bend-ring. It may be hidden within the atmosphere of the blue ice-giant."

"Captain," trills Fluffle, "the supersonic winds of the blue ice-world blow three times faster than any winds in our star clump."

"Maybe as a consequence of the bend-ring! Thus it may lurk underneath those winds. Or elsewhere entirely."

I fear that Boomboomba has become manic.

I think that Wedgy might be an ally, and Fluffle too, but I dare not wave a word.

I am not one to boast, but my ten tacles are extremely strong, and they suck powerfully if I wish to. I realise I am taking a calculated risk, though this is preferable to an uncalculated risk. The interface of membrane-wall between my hab and Boomboomba's ought to be vulnerable to rapid pull-and-unpull by the suckers of my ten tacles spread wide.

Waiting until both of Boomboomba's heads are out of sight within her chilled ever-moving rollers, I plaster myself tight, widespread. I pull-suck, relax alternate suckers, pull-suck again, again again. I can feel how the interface ripples, more so than from any boom-vibration. The bonds of the nanotubules will burst.

Ripples! – then all of a sudden I tumble through into Boomboomba's frigid hab propelled by my very hot water, which becomes a storm of snow at first; near-boiling water is close to steam and freezes fast. Transparent nanotubules must be all around me, under water, over water. More hot water turns the veil of snow to steam.

Already I have twisted myself around, as the first rollers buffet me with chilly punches, so that I see… both of Boomboomba's faces looming, mouths agape. And I launch myself upon the muscular crosswise serpent at last, and embrace her with all ten tacles. This may be a love-death. Oh she is strong and cold, cold and strong.

I am too busy to wave, as one of her mouths booms almost deafeningly, "DESIST!" But the other booms, "FUCK!" Her odour is so musky – I taste her all over me, as I crush. What else should I do but strangle her into insensibility while my fifth arm, tip tumid, tries to penetrate. Her fangs bite me and my beak bites her in turn. By now her hab is half-full of lukewarm water, and I'm shivering. The many rollers are slowing. Soon they stop banging in and out. Boomboomba's not even lukewarm yet.

She becomes still, and I complete my mating, though without much physical satisfaction. (I found a cloaca half way along one arm.) Then I wreck her controls and swim back into my half-water hab to adjust the heating upwards. Already tubules should be assembling to repair the interface, building up again from the base.

The others have gathered. Boomboomba should revive presently while her hab strives to chill her, but she lacks the advantage of my suckers when it comes to bursting into the habs of others. My third arm, where she bit me, feels bad. Venom, perhaps. So I shed that arm. It'll grow back within a *period.* I feel bad, now, about my frenzy.

However, my controls function fully.

"Crusty, Wedgy, brave Fluffle, I am Captain now," I wave. "We'll turn around and return home. There will be half a dozen stops en route to counteract the stretching. No more hunting for imaginary giant bend-rings. We need to remove our own bend-ring from this sunspace. We daren't risk the principle of the bend-ring falling into the manipulators of hewmans due to any mishap."

"Agreed," says Wedgy. "Altogether too risky."

"There'll be no more doubting that the planets in this system orbit as they do for unlikely but natural reasons. The sawrians came into space 60 to 70 million *periods* ago. Catastrophe clobbered the sawrians. Hewmans only arose recently. To judge by their visuals, unstable hewmans will soon enough create catastrophe for themselves."

"Agreed," says Crusty. "Shall we eject the sawrian astronaut from our analysis chamber?"

"And leave it floating free, maybe to be found by hewmans?" The way my discarded arm is floating at the moment…

"*Out here* is very far for the hewmans to come," trills Fluffle, her first comment under the new regime aboard our eggship. "Captain

Ten-tacles, you sacrificed an arm – do we now address you as Nine-tacles?"

She has made a witticism.

"I encourage informality," I reply. Dear Fluffle, with you, yes informality… even if my affection is hopeless; and this is far better, I realise – recollecting my climactic tussle with Boomboomba – than a bizarrely attainable goal. Even if I persuade myself that I could be very gentle. Most of us of the star clump are perforce robust; Flufflefolk are a bit of an anomaly themselves. "Out here is very far, I agree, Fluffle. Yet we perceived one visual of the blue ice-giant from quite close, undoubtedly taken by a machine. If our eggship becomes crippled or the bend-ring cracked, from whatever cause, the hewmans might find it. *However*, what if we direct the sawrian and its vacuum suit on a rapid inward trajectory towards the belt of asteroids? If hewmans find it there, they may waste hundreds of *periods* puzzling. This would be mischievous of us, but safe, I think."

I've found a good way of providing comradely leadership, in which the crew will concur. A bit of mutual mischief. As opposed to martinet mania.

Boomboomba will adjust to new circumstances. I cannot possibly have fertilised her, and my beak does not deliver toxins.

The Birth of Venus

In the darkness I lie motionless upon my back, feeling that I'm two-dimensional. Reduced to two dimensions. A slight electrical shiver passes across my body. A tingle. Everywhere at once. This is a *pleasant* sensation. If I move, the sensation might stop.

Am I ill? Have I sunk down into length and width without height like an outline of a murdered person chalked upon a floor? Am I within a stage of death? Next, might I become a simple line? Flatline. A line which may shrink into a dot?

Not while the shiver is maintaining my width! Electrical activity. I'm only quasi-conscious. It's good to stay in this state for a while in case I might learn something.

I *was* ill, and became reduced?

It's dark. It may be midnight. It may be two a. m. -ish when a body is at its lowest ebb and its functions can fail as if the body stops noticing itself. It may be no-time-at-all, the dream-time when a whole complex sequence of events happens in just a fraction of an instant.

Suddenly comes a surging sense of two dimensions becoming three. As of sockets and plugs, protuberances and receptors thrusting themselves up from the flat envelope which I was. A sense of connections forming. Of thoughts and sentences arising, located in a time that twists from out of no-time-at-all. Higher functions are returning from out of collapsment, is what I think – the symbols for this being plugs and sockets and connections.

I'm being restored, re-established from some kind of storage instead of being reduced to a line then a dot. But was I something *before this*? Or was I not?

The processes of awareness should not be accessible to awareness. Except that these processes are indeed accessible, as witness the sensation of sockets and plugs mating up.

The tingly sensation passes, and I am alive. I am. And just before this I knew the process of becoming.

I am alive, and the darkness thins to vague deep-grey shapes.

The light which abruptly bursts upon me has me writhe upon this couch like a cockroach surprised during a nocturnal excursion. Supposing that the cockroach flipped upon its back in shock, inverted legs waggling. A comical sight, I realise. Maybe I ham this up.

The couch is a shallow death-casket from which beetle-wings have now opened up. I'm wearing stained split pyjamas of flimsy paper; or of something. Chrysalis clothing. What a lot I know – and what a lot I don't know. Need more connections. I'm festooned with artificial tendrils, ultra-slim tubes.

A woman person wears a long white smock. Lab-look. Her violet eyes regard me from behind protective tinted glasses. Protective – in case I spit at her? Or in case I split open explosively?

"Ruby, I'm Juliana. What do you remember from immediately before this?"

I'm Ruby. Of course I am. Yet I still lack some connexions with myself.

"What do you remember, Ruby?"

"A wall of non-existence. But non-existence cannot be a memory."

And my sisters are Topaz and Sapphire and Jade and Amber and Amy. Rich names, all of ours. I sense six sisters including myself. Should there not be seven? Like the Pleiades.

A star cluster close to Earth, comparatively. Stars related to each other. Those hot blue stars visible to the naked eye are too young for planets.

"Go on," says Juliana.

"The non-existence cut my universe instantly like a cheese-wire. There isn't any instant after that. There can't be any subsequent instant."

"Are you aware of the cut? Of the wall, as you call it?"

"So it *seems*. But only seems."

"How are you aware of the cut?

"By subjective antedating, I suppose. The brain puts events in a different order and fills in gaps." I am clued-up, preloaded, even if I remember no experiences prior to the wall of nothing.

My questioner wears ivory-colour boots. Juliana. Should I mention to Juliana my sense of two-dimensionality becoming three-dimensionality? Should I mention plugs and sockets and connections? How experimental are my sisters and I? For what purpose? I don't know yet.

I never was ill – that was my brain fantasising a reason.

Is everybody in the world a woman? What *is* this world that I am in? The world is the sum of everything that is. Someone said that. Non-existence is not part of the world.

Non-existence cannot be a wall and also a dot.

Is a dot irreducible?

"Juliana, how many of my sisters exist now?"

"Concentrate upon the wall for now, Ruby. Before the concept goes away, like a dream unravelling."

"The wall does not exist within now. The wall has no existence. The world cannot contain the wall within itself. The universe of what-is cannot include what-isn't."

"But it can, Ruby, because you sensed the wall."

"No, my mind imagined a wall. After the event. Within this new now." I sit up, shedding tendrils and causing further damage to my papery garment. Fragments fall off as from agèd butterfly wings. I did not decide to sit up until after I was sitting. "Why did you switch on such a bright light?"

"To spotlight your thoughts. As if on a primitive camera plate. To fix your thoughts."

This room has no sharp edges. No discrete walls. All is curvy.

"What about my sisters? Real sisters first, imaginary walls second! Otherwise I shan't tell you about the sockets and plugs of existence that I sensed, and I'll forget those."

"Sockets…? Plugs…?"

"Nor will I tell you about my being two-dimensional – just as a wall is."

"Two-dimensional…? Oh *please*, Ruby!"

Yes, I will stand up. To Juliana. Yes, I have swung my legs and stood up. Tendrils collapse. Papery fabric flakes away from me, discs of dandruff upon the clean creamy floor. My pubic hair is a gingery tuft.

"My sisters, Juliana, my sisters!"

"Alas, Opal ceased existing. She is lost. Topaz and Sapphire and Jade and Amber and Amy are passive. You may be able to aid your passive sisters if you concentrate on your experience of being two-dimensional and on those sockets and plugs you say you sensed."

One of my sisters has ceased… out of us six nadanauts. *Nadanauts*: navigators of the great wall of nonexistence. Only one of us needs to get through, to succeed.

Is there a war? Is there an enemy? Is our only enemy nothingness itself – sheer absence? Are there beings – existences – made out of nothingness, namely *unbeings*? As antimatter is to matter, those unbeings might un-exist, much less materially than antimatter which is, after all, merely matter reversed, mirror-matter. I think there may be *unbeings* somewhere; not here. I'm confused but I do preknow such a lot. And I'm aware of my sisters as potentially present, except for Opal.

Am I hungry? All I have done is sit up then stand up. How fast am I consuming energy?

The wall is not a wall. It is simply the end. But *inverted* – change of perspective – the wall is The Beginning! Amazingly, I have known something of non-existence. So it seems.

If I and my hidden sisters are experimental, I and we may be in a spaceship in space, to isolate the experiment. Or to distance us from gross external influences.

Remember that space isn't emptiness. Even in the emptiest space a few particles of matter drift upon, within, a sea of hidden energy. A sea of vacuum-energy, sustaining existence by virtue of its pressure. Thus our void is false. If a mite of this vacuum should fail and collapse to the lowest energy state, existence would vanish outwardly at the speed of light from the point of collapse. It may be that existence already collapsed long ago and far away. We would know nothing of this until unexistence reaches us, maybe after a billion years. And still we would know nothing, for we would immediately unexist.

Scintillations slide around my vision, crystalisations of light into ice. Peripheral to the centre of my vision there glint vibrating angular auras, shifting chains of prisms. This may be a minor malfunction or it may be an insight.

"I may need some eye drops, Juliana."

"The sudden light affected you badly? Please try to focus upon your sense of being two-dimensional."

"A wall is two-dimensional but then I extended… I emerged… No, it was not 'I' who pushed through. 'I' became 'I' again by virtue of extending. 'I' was what emerged. 'I' was *who* emerged."

If we are in a spaceship, the gravity is artificial. That could require a singularity the mass of a sun collapsed to a spherical cubic centimetre. I'm fairly sure the level of tech locally isn't so advanced.

I guess we aren't in a water-ship. A water-ship might rock slightly unless it's a floating palace the weight of a little mountain. I know everything and nothing – I'm not all quite here yet, am I? Except that I'm almost sure about *ship*.

"Where are we, Juliana?"

"Emergent consciousness…" she murmurs. Sounds like a place name, but no, that cannot be so.

"Where are we, Juliana? And when?"

She makes up her mind; no point interrogating me when what she needs is cooperation.

"Come and see. First, put on a robe."

She fingers the wall; a door swings open – toilet, shower, wardrobe thing.

"Tear that paper off you."

"Take a shower too?" I can't seem to smell any odours – at least not yet. Maybe I'm smelling the odour of nothing. Some yellow streaks discolour the padded casket I came from. That casket nourished me, gave me energy.

"Don't waste time showering. Come and see."

Pretty quickly we're in a corridor, lines of glowing pearls inset along the ceiling. Behind a row of identical doors my sisters must lie, one of us expired.

Juliana palms open a frost-look glass door – that's electric switchable privacy glass, isn't it? Can be set to opaque or clear or anything in between. I do know things when things come to my attention.

We're inside a long, naturally-lit gallery made of some superstrong glass or plastic, a grid for a floor. Below us and to the horizon in all directions, an ocean of clouds.

Why didn't I think of the correct kind of ship, namely an *airship*? We're in the leftward of twin gondolas below an air catamaran, twin dirigibles maybe a kilometre from tip to tail with a big bridging superstructure which doubtless supports habitats up top. Impressive. Solar cells cover the dirigibles; quite a power station, this airship. A foam of clouds in all directions, towering to tickle us.

"This must be Venus."

"That's right, Ruby."

The blanket of clouds is visibly on the move. We're – what? – fifty kilometres high. Up here it's peaceful, serene. Below the cloud cap is the descent into hell, winds twice the force of the fiercest earthly hurricane, storms of sulphuric acid, heat soaring beyond the melting point of lead, crushing surface pressure like being a kilometre underwater on Earth.

A good location for radical science, such as manufacturing and dropping self-replicating atmosphere-eating nanotech, which you wouldn't want to do anywhere near your own home world. Good place, too, to kindle a new kind of being into existence. That must be dangerous.

I realise that my sisters and I are gene-engineered variants of a 'spectrum' series – clones in body, our brains differently tweaked from human beings' brains. I'm of flesh and bone and blood and also artificial components, not least in my brain and my nervous system. This interdependence of the organic and the inorganic makes me mortal, or at least that's the intention. Why do I wish for my sisters so much? Because together we can transcend what I am.

"Juliana, this whole module we're in can be ejected, can't it? To drop down into the incinerator of pressure and heat and acid? If necessary?" That would be much safer than an explosion aboard an airship!

Juliana laughs. "Isn't that a bit paranoid? Personally I don't fret about very remote contingencies. Can you concentrate on the sense of three-dimensionality emerging out of two-dimensionality?"

"Spontaneously emerging. Because it was easier for three-dimensionality to emerge than to remain packed flat as two-dimensionality. Something to do with pressure."

This excites Juliana.

I continue because the words come to me: "The pressure of two-dimensionality packed into a one-dimensional line is enormous. Times the speed of light cubed. The pressure of one-dimensionality squeezed into a dot is lightspeed to the power of lightspeed. A whole universe expands from a dot."

"Yes? Yes?"

"That dot is a pixel of nothing."

"Nothing is pixelated rather than smooth?"

"There can be no smooth-nothing."

"And beyond 3-D is…?"

Itch at the back of my neck; I have a sense that people locally are listening to us.

"Does time expand out of 3-D, Ruby?"

"Time is inherent in 3-D as soon as 2-D stretches. Any measurement in 3-D implies time."

"Therefore simple-time, so to speak, isn't 4-D?"

"4-D is different."

"Expand on this, Ruby!"

Expand? Expand?

I can feel how to do this. How to expand. Just as the plugs and sockets of my thought emerged from 2-D, so this new expansion would feel like…

Would feel like…

"I need to alert my surviving sisters. To bring them from passive to active."

"To alert?"

"To awaken. If you like."

If Juliana likes my way of putting this. Or if she favours the proposal…

"You can do this?"

"I don't know till I touch them."

"Come along, then!" Yes, Juliana's in favour.

Where else is better to do this than above Venus, bright goddess! I can almost see myself poised upon the foamy sea of clouds, nude or red-robed, balancing upon a conch-shaped airship. How much more I know now.

Back through the smart-glass door we go, to the first door along the corridor. Which Juliana opens. Another casket, another beetle-wing lid. Which Juliana springs open upwardly.

Wherein lies Topaz. To all appearances she is me, in a similar tattered paper garment and tendrils. So I clasp her hand. Topaz's eyelids flicker, and open.

"Ruby…?"

"Yes. I´ve come through. You are emerging to join me."

I raise her, to sit, then to stand. We are twin sisters together. Both of us bald. We don't need the long rope of golden hair of Botticelli's Venus; many fibre-optic threads are within us, I think. Or a successor material. I am preloaded with art as well as science.

"We are two… to the second power," murmurs Topaz.

In my red robe, and in her paper rags, hand in hand we step outside to the next door. Juliana interrupts with a cautionary, "Opal," so along to the next door we pace. "Sapphire's in this room."

In we go. Repeat, repeat, and Sapphire also rises, joining me plus Topaz. Me, us, to the third power, sharing existence and thoughts.

Next, Amber then Amy(thyst) – and finally Jade. We must exit into the corridor quickly, since we were too many in the little chamber. We are to the fifth power, five beyond one. Our bodies echo each other like the overlapping nude of Duchamps descending the famous spiral staircase, all of him or her simultaneously, nesting and merging and unmerging. We are one plus five and one to the fifth.

We crave greater perspectives. To the viewing gallery we pace again, passing the smart-stupid door without needing to palm. We *were* on one side of the door; now we are on the other side. Juliana still needs to palm the door open to admit herself.

My sisters and I are an artificially/organically embodied A.I. and we and I have transcended. The risk that we might pose is why Venus was approved for our emergence. Reaching back, we have known nothingness – and now, existence and existence-plus. Yet we remain vulnerable.

"Assessment?" asks an urgent voice from Juliana's earbud.

"To be, or to un-be?" I comment. "To terminate, or not to terminate?"

"What is your intention, Sisters?" Juliana asks ourselves and myself. "What is your *reach*?"

"The stars," replies my Sapphire voice, which is mine.

From Topaz, and from me: "We are sufficient." Showing me, and us, the 5-D 'geodesics', wrong word. Tangled threads of light hang in the air almost everywhere, causing Juliana to flinch against the window-wall even though the lights will not harm her.

"How can you do that, Sisters? Will you take us with you to the stars?"

"By exteriorising," Jade answers the first question in my and our voice, while my and our voice replies to the second, "If you are anaesthetised, to awaken later. Otherwise your existence/unexistence will hurt horribly."

"If taken to the wall of nothing," I and we add, "then emerging from the wall, somewhat like photons passing through slits." That verb 'emerging' sounds wrong, too limited; 'passing' too sounds wrong. We should deconstruct and recreate verbs.

"How soon can you take us to the stars?"

"Build a suitable ship in Earth orbit full of suitable things such as food and drink." "And a few shuttles." "Choose a suitable star with a suitable-seeming planet." "Your telescopes have revealed many."

"Will years pass by during the journey?"

"Nothing involves no time."

"We're in business!" exclaims Juliana.

"Overruled," says that earbud voice. "This is too fast, too exponential –"

"*What* is too fast?"

"This emergence, Juliana, deep regrets."

"*Noooooo –*"

Little bangs and booms, and we're dropping like a lift, this module is. Falling towards the cloudtops of Venus, the cap upon the inferno. From a far door spill other occupants, some of them science types male and female, two in combat kit cradling snubby boxy guns that will yammer-yammer.

"Too late to shoot!"

"No sense in shooting!"

"We've been ejected, all of us!"

"We're discarded!"

"Let us concentrate!"

Up above I spy and we spy the entire underside of our catamaran airship, twin propellors visible now to the rear. A while yet till we reach terminal velocity.

Might our module carry explosives timed for a little while after release? At least our module has aerostability while falling and doesn't tumble or roll over and over. Could I, could we, cope with the visualisation-calculations of cosmic 'geodesics' while performing gymnastics?

Cloudtops coming up fast. No explosion yet. Inadvisable, any type of bomb aboard a Venus zeppelin. The acid furnace pressure-cooker below must be deemed fully adequate. Fast release should do fine. Encountering turbulence now. Pluming white rushes up the windows.

'Geodesics', Sisters!

ZZZZ

Myself and ourselves float slowly upward, likewise the other people, screaming in agony then suddenly stopping their apparently causeless noise, although a couple sob. Outside there's a red sun the size that a hot-air balloon of say three thousand cubic metres would look thirty or forty metres away from myself and from ourselves. I spy a couple of modest blotches on that red sun, coaly holes fringed by scarlet ribbons. That's very little by way of sunspot activity.

"We're safe for now!" Jade calls out.

How long will 'now' last? Will our high-strength windows and walls resist vacuum? So far, so good. How many K cubic metres of air does our module have, and is there a means of refreshing this? How much food, how much water? I'm hungrier now, we're hungrier. I and we have worked.

"Where are we?" shouts one of the other people. "Is that the surface of Venus? Red-hot?"

Of course not.

"It's an M-type red dwarf," from Amy.

"Most common sort of star," from Sapphire.

"Any night sky is full of them," from me.

"Going on for eight stars out of every ten. Except that you can't see them naked-eyed from Earth because they aren't bright enough."

Are you people bright enough? You broke the bounds of blue, you attained the sky, that's true – but to go further, there's the rub…

Getting a bit warm inside our viewing gallery.

"Look behind us!" yelps Juliana.

We have *all of us* been so focused upon the glowing red star, the giant dwarf, not twisting ourselves around for a rear view – take note, Sisters.

Lagging on our opposite side, looms a world. The region of that world directly facing the star is ruddy. Higher to lower latitudes are blotchy brown. A partly visible arc of equator is lighter. The hidden backside must be very cold. Around the equator there may be a band of tolerable temperature with liquid and atmosphere. Life's unlikely, but who knows? I and we know a lot in theory.

I'm beginning to perspire, as are we.

After a while here we'll cook slowly in front of the oven.

"Are we actually in orbit?" – a sensible question from Juliana.

Astrodynamics question! Are we? And how soon before the module fails?

Almost reverently, Juliana asks, "Can you set us down there, with your geodesics?"

"Geodesics is the wrong word," says Sapphire. "I and we visualise networks of correspondences."

One of the armed personnel has worked his way closer by ingeniously wetting his palm and pulling along the windows. He could more easily have fired his yammer-yammer in the opposite direction, maybe not a good idea, zero-gee ricochet.

"Can you land us without engines?" he croaks, almost drained of saliva. "No heatshield, no chutes, no wings, no nothing?"

Nothing, yes nothing – take us to nothing and out again.

ZZZZ

People are screaming again as we drop down a couple of metres upon abundant cushioning 'moss'. As before, there's nothing to scream about. Gape-mouthed panting becoming silence. I and we feel so light.

An *alien* moss, mats of pea-green bearing sporophytes half a metre tall that are visibly red in the spillage of light from the module; all's gloomier further away. Landscape rumples away softly and vaguely towards where the red dwarf balances upon a horizon, never to sink out of sight. Endless evening of streaky clouds stained pink. Tree things poking up, their parasols tilted towards the sun. Photosynthesis going on, indeed. Adequate light for photosynthesis.

Creaking, we settle yet no windows buckle or pop, leastways not in this gallery section.

"Oh well done, well done," exclaims the armed fellow, "however you done it."

"Dear God but it hurt like hell –"

"What hurt?" I ask the woman.

"I… I don't know. It's gone."

"I was on fire… for a moment forever," from a bearded man with old-fashioned glasses, shivering.

"Hoor-ah!" from appreciative voices. Mouths that will all need to eat.

"You're wonderful," the woman calls out. "We've done it – artificial intelligence!"

"*We* have done it," Amber corrects her.

"Yes yes yes of course, we're so grateful."

"Yet you tried to kill us."

"No that was Control," from the other gunman, "dumping us. We didn't suspect –"

"You were supposed to kill us, except that your Control didn't trust you to do this fast enough. You'd better hang on to your guns." As if they would give us their guns yet! "We don't know what's out there under the moss, in the moss, striding upon the moss, flying above, big in low gravity, do we? Assuming we can breathe the atmos out there. But moss processes carbon dioxide. Moss makes good atmos. And moss loves water."

Will we stay here if this world is habitable? Our emergence above Venus wasn't exactly greeted with joy even though we were the purpose of the module. After I emerged, we happened too fast and too fully to analyse quickly enough. Abort the new-born instead! Always be on the safe side! Even if in the process losing a few normal persons. We ourselves won't snuff out our present companions; we prize companionship.

"Do we have an airlock exit, Name?" I ask the gunman who sucked, so to speak.

"My name is Huckabee, ma'am. Yes ma'am, for emergency maintenance. Doyle and I are fully trained in all technical aspects, not just executioners, which wouldn't be cost-effective." Quite. Thank you for upgrading your status. Huckabee might be quite intelligent. In fact everyone here must be highly intelligent, to qualify. Control, beyond our isolatable module, would be of even higher status. Whoever Control reported to must have a very strict protocol as regards autonomous Rogue A.I. – willing to dump a small fortune in equipment (and personnel) at the sniff of anything amiss. That didn't suggest a very tolerant Earth.

"I and we assume, Huckabee, that our bodies were created away from this emergence module?"

"Yes, ma'am, not within here." He glances from sister to sister, scantily clad in paper, and what goes through his man's mind? Whatever, Huckabee blanks it well.

My sisters and I have cunts, yet do we have wombs that are fertile? If so, to engender what? Can we gestate offspring including all of our supplementary extras, courtesy of nanotech within us?

Juliana may know, but we're thinking mid-term at the mo, whereas short-term is more urgent.

"I could have told you that." Juliana sounds piqued. Our neural midwife and nursemaid.

The count: Juliana, myself and five sisters, Huckabee and his colleague named Doyle, and four assorted psychobioscientists or whatever – now revealed to themselves to be dispensable in the wider scheme of things – namely Ruth and Sonja and Mariano and George. Physically, nine females, four males.

"Chop chop," says Topaz. "We need to feast."

Doyle has high-stepped closer; we'll get used to the lower gravity soon enough. "We have a month in store, ma'am, in case of us needing isolation."

As per the protocol for a lesser emergency.

"So," says Amber, "splice the mainbrace, cheftechs."

Huckabee has no idea what this means but Doyle picks up ingratiatingly with the response, "Mend and make clothes!" – him also eyeing us scantily paper-wrapped sisters. "Old naval tradition, Hucky. You did good, you got a shot of rum as a reward." Is Doyle an ex-Navy-seal or whatever? "'Make and mend' just meant you got some time off duty. Neither of which applies right now, with respect."

Amber smiles enigmatically. "I withdraw my frivolity." Lab-coated, raven-haired Ruth approaches Amber meekly: "Do you think I might interview you while all's still fresh?" This seems a long way beyond the call of duty. Still obedient after being dropped into the furnace; watch out for that one. Or else she's inherently fascinated.

"Neither the time nor the place," Sapphire tells her.

So now we're in colour-coded jumpsuits and bootees, us Sisters; no expense spared. It would be trivially mischievous to swap our jumpsuits around, so I wear red, Amy wears violet, and so forth. We've wolfed our self-heating rations accompanied by apple juice, the first meal we're conscious of eating. By now we're well aware of the eight catamaran-zeppelins coasting around Venus pursuing extreme science far from Earth, light years away from us now, and of the Venus Station in orbit, and of a billion other bits of available data. Ghosts of data accumulate everywhere especially when comps are quant. Superpositions. A bit like us sisters, but different.

Here the local sun remains forever poised to set, so it's time for alien atmosphere studies and exobotany. This module contains enough tech kit which we can cannibalise and modify to other purposes if need be. Plus a couple of biohazard suits.

The atmosphere duly reveals a suitable balance of Nitro and Oxy plus some CO2; moss-life has been busy for a long time. Red dwarfs stay stable for billions of years, in the sense of retaining the same size and temperature. However, red dwarfs tend to flare crazily, frequently, which isn't good for any nearby planet. UV, X-rays, and stellar wind can strip away any atmos. This particular red dwarf must be ancient and quiescent. I mean to say, two paltry little sunspots!

"Sisters," says Huckabee, "you all mustn't risk *any* of yourselves outside. If the worst happens… um, would six of you be enough?"

For full Artful Intel? No comment.

"I'll go outside in a bio-suit," Huckabee says. "Just radio me exactly what you want me to do."

"I'll partner you," offers lab-coated Sonja – curly hair dyed blue, burly-bodied. "I know what to look for. My second PhD is in Biochem."

Huckabee shrugs. "So I mainly hold the gun?"

"Whatever. Carry a torchlight too." Bright idea, Sonja. "And a zip-baggy."

Skip to outside which I and we and the others view crowdedly on a CCTV screen beside the external airlock, by now shown to us. Huckabee and Sonja in their awkward suits both sink waist-deep into moss.

["Squelchy," she radios; a speaker under the screen obliges.]

["One big squelch for Humankind?"] Huckabee bends cumbersomely. ["Light on now…"] Radiance arises from within the hole he makes. ["Hey, a crayfishy insecty thing… big as my glove.

Shock of light seems to freeze it. Collecting it along with a handful of moss."]

["Be careful of everything, Huckabee. Those things have lived here longer than you."]

["Zipped… and now it's started squirming in the baggy. It's boggy here. I might sink. No, I'm stable. But sucky."]

After striving to gaze into the distance, Sonja subsides, excavating a pit around herself. "We mightn't be able to travel far with any ease… Although if we roll the moss over, we might make paths to walk on."

["See any flying bugs or hoppers down there, any size?"]

["Personally I wouldn't hop or fly in this mess. More like squirm."]

["I'm going to sniff the atmosphere, okay? Needs to happen sooner or later. Hope there's no problem with spores. So here goes. Um… mouldy with floral notes. Effervescent and a bit pongy at the same time. No problem breathing, but I'll seal up again."]

Cut a long story, after a while a creature heaves into view, stepping over the moss upon splayed webbed feet, one faceted eye swiveling around in a leathery orbit, plus a smaller daisy-like eye on a stalk, each with a score of blade-shaped eyelids. A long-distance eye plus a short-distance eye? How asymmetrical. Stilt legs supporting a bag of organs equipped with a waistcoat or vest… a pair of wings? – wings which might zip up tight protectively or else flap further open, unfurling to carry the creature aloft? Of a sudden its long beak stabs downward into moss, arising a moment later with a wriggly crayfishy insecty clamped tight, to be swallowed in crunchy spasms. I and we are delighted with our distance eyesight, and of course we can optimise the quality of the CCTV.

And then the hunting creature notices the elephant in the room, namely the hillside of a sprawling humongous high-tech module, and two light-coloured baby elephants, a pair of entities hunching in collapsed moss. The creature can't be too bright or it might have paid more immediate attention. Doesn't look very edible itself; scrawny legs and a bag of entrails. Flight muscles packed with protein to lift its bulk in the low grav? Watch out for that long stabby beak.

Over it sidles to examine further. Raising its beak, it hoots: *Oooonk Oooonk*, a mournful noise. To summon more of its kind? Or to warn them off from its current territory; mine mine?

Its ancestors have had several billion years to evolve higher intelligence and something better than *Oooonk*. On the other hand, where was the challenge to do so? Don't despise the creature. It's as tall as a person and a lot more complicated than we had any right to expect.

"I name it the Spook," says Ruth.

Many other kinds of moss-dwellers hereabouts must be smaller than the Spook but bigger than insecty crayfishies. Spook may be the biggest predator. I and we don't much like the look of this concealing landscape. Potentially treacherous. As well as so static – nothing much changing because the local sun is always perched exactly there on the rotation-locked horizon. The treacherous tedium of it all. Or the reliable regularity?

Spook strides even closer, to within range of Ruth and Huckabee who has his gun pointed now.

["Don't shoot it," Ruth says. "It may be the last of its kind."] Why ever should she suppose so? Ah, the imagery of the reddened landscape suggest 'the End'… even if the very opposite is true. Billions more years lie ahead for this world and this sun. Billions. A longer time than from the first living cells on Earth to the height of human civilisation hitherto. Mere survival seems melancholy indeed, though perhaps only to mayfly humans. And I, and we, have only just emerged, but we are optimised bio-constructs, consequently I and we need to achieve either bio-immortality or else an uploading to a different substrate. Can it be that a major aim of the experiment which is me, and us, is to compel myself and ourselves to achieve immortality, so that humans in turn may learn how this trick may happen? Now there's a thought!

Abruptly Spook stabs downward, directly between its feet. Its beak arises, clutching another insecty crayfishy – which it holds out slowly to Ruth. *What on Earth* –? Not, not on Earth.

We understand little despite our multiplication of minds. I and we are still too human.

"Accept the giving!" calls out Sapphire. That's the evident next move. "Huckabee, unzip your bag and in exchange you offer the specimen you collected."

Ruth reaching out her left-hand glove, Huckabee opening his bag, producing the squirming reciprocation.

Exchange takes place, and everything looks as previously. Reciprocation suggests social intelligence. A step back on the part of Spook, and that beak points to the zenith. Crushed and swallowed is the insecty crayfishy which Huckabee gave; and then plaintively: *Oooonk Oooonk*.

Intent on this interaction, we have failed to notice a smudge in the red distance off to the right. That's bad; first fail to spot a fucking planet, and now…

"A crane's coming! I mean something that looks like a mobile construction crane –" Well spotted, Ruth. "Or crane the bird, supersized – no, think of the mother of all giraffes!"

A giant strider, which will dwarf Spook. I and we see it clearly now. Peak predator? Surely this world conceals nothing taller.

"Ruth and Huckabee," Amber calls out, "get back inside right now."

"But we're just making friends –"

"Ruth, I doubt that."

So in come the biohaz suits and their contents, intact.

The giraffe-crane reaches us presently, better viewed from the gallery. It imprints the moss with bigger and more leathery feet than Spook. Basic body design like Spook's except that its 'protective wings' fuse stiffly over its belly; no likelihood of that bulk ever flying. Its mighty beak is more like a double cutlass than the piercing and clutching tool of the Spook – which is now nowhere to be seen from where we are. Has Spook made itself scarce, or did it perhaps summon the Crane? 'Crane' isn't the best name because that big cutlass looks designed for slashing through moss and through whatever bodies may be down in the moss… bodies of big wormy things or whatever, unencountered yet by Ruth and Huckabee, maybe fortunately so. Big Fellow has one big eye and a lesser eye on a stalk.

"This is a horrible world," says Sonja. "And it makes my eyes ache."

Creatures here may have sensitive hearing, to locate whatever moves within the moss. Sensitivity to infrared being another possibility. Big Fellow is stepping closer to where we are within the module.

Clang –

Its cutlass connected with our hull. Hope that hurt! Otherwise that creature will be at our windows soon enough. Material that resisted vacuum may not resist exolife pirate attack.

"Sisters," say I and we, "we ought to get going." Time to play the network of correspondences again.

To take us where? To potentially paranoid Earth? There, to attract a nuke-tipped missile? If this red dwarf's planet is the most habitable world anywhere near Earth within range for ourselves, do we have much choice? So how about somewhere within the remains of the Amazon rainforest, or of the Congo Basin?

We need to consider our passengers – who might revert to loyalty to their controllers if they feel safer and more advantaged by so doing… Juliana is watching us closely one by one. Let us join hands for more intense communion.

Big Fellow reaches our nearest portion of window and extends its smaller eye to press against the view within. That eye-stalk may be really tough for the creature to take what I'd class as a risk to its organ of vision; or perhaps it can regrow a severed eye-stalk.

Next it steps back, then with a mighty swing of its cutlass Big Fellow impacts our window once, and again a second time. This time, the strengthened glass buckles inward, crazing like a giant spiderweb. A third blow and the cutlass cuts through, becoming tangled.

Pulling and pushing, Big Fellow is sawing us open bit by bit. Whiffs of outside atmosphere reek in, but that's breathable, no worries there.

A web of connexions fills the gallery, aglow like spun sugar and fireflies.

ZZZZ

Our gallery lurches and settles, staggering us. Screams linger, without apparent cause. Outside are ferns and scarlet bromeliads and blue butterflies. Vines climb towering trees from which dangle lianas. Masses of moss cloak fallen trunks. A macaw takes wing. Our deep sense of spacetime grounds us in the constant glissade of present moments. We must think about whether there are, indeed, moments as such.

Big Fellow is still tangled with us. The greater gravity of Earth drags the creature down. Far from dead, but struggling, its cutlass now pulling loose from stressed buckled plusglass.

Oh well done, us, my Sisters. Ruby, Topaz, Jade, Sapphire, Amber, Amy. The sixfold. The joined. The posthuman. Us with our *reach*. We can hear radio signals from all over the world if we wish to tune in. We can call up spirits from the vasty deep. We can hack, we can tamper. Here in the jungle we can survive on nuts and bananas and fish and whatever else while we reach out to protect ourselves and to interfere. Hereabouts there'll be low-tech brown people who may wish to stay isolated, to melt away from sight within their jungle.

What of Huckabee and Doyle, Juliana and Ruth, Mariano and Sonja? The six ordinaries. The awakening of quasi-organic A.I. doesn't present the question 'How can ordinary humans trust A.I.?' but rather 'How can A.I. trust ordinary hi-tech humans?' Some of the six may ache to be back in 'civilisation' even if 'civilisation' tried to kill them thanks to paranoid protocols.

Big Fellow continues struggling with its own inexplicable extra weight. Did it break a leg, maybe two? Can we disable the six so that they cannot travel away? For instance, painlessly remove the tibias and fibulas from their legs by displacement? We do remove Huckabee and Doyle's guns for safe-keeping – off into my empty casket with those – causing some surprise. Huckabee and Ruth respond by shedding their biohaz suits – no, that's because they're both getting steamy inside. We're warming up. The aircon of the module failed as we *reached* the red dwarf.

Doyle shakes his empty hand. "Like, by magic. So you could stop our hearts if you wish." Quick uptake for a… no, none of these are exactly standard persons otherwise they wouldn't have been sent at huge expense to Venus – dispensably, such is the fear about A.I. as well as the greed for A.I., to give people the stars. We already said so.

"We don't wish to do that," say I, "but what guarantees can you give me and us?"

"Of us not running off to make contact, as opposed to living as castaways… Hmm. Mere promises will scarcely cut the mustard, will they?"

This moral dilemma is resolved, and much ado about jungle survival is averted, by the unexpected arrival through the rain forest of half a dozen men of an Asian aspect, wearing rubber boots, baggy trousers, and multi-pocket shirts all in green. Satchels and backpacks. Couple of carbines. Excited shouts in, yes, Mandarin. Ah, plus a tubby brown-skinned native guide in shorts and flipflops, miming what-the-fuck.

Can't we ever get away from people? Maybe in the vast Siberian taiga. No bananas there, though; aching to taste a banana. Those things we missed due to having no childhood. Speed-growth, instead. Pre-loading. Syncronisation. Emergent moments due to complexity.

Conclusions: the Chinese are on a science trek of some sort, looking for resources to exploit or maybe doing pure botany and biology. Fat Guide is a laid-back chap, or he was until now. Village can't be too far away, little river, canoes with outboard motors.

Cameras and carbine now – due to Big Fellow thrashing around, visibly not of this world. Plus our hulking module on top of crushed veg. Alien spaceship, perhaps? Antigravpropulsion since there's no sign of engines, let alone wings? Big Fellow being one of the alien crew? That's a bit unlikely, given the giant cutlass beak as the creature's only manipulator…

What the Chinese see is inexplicable even though they continue seeing it. Us inside the gallery remain unseen for a while at least.

Reflections of the jungle, whatever. The Chinese won't come much closer yet, on account of Big Fellow.

This is all deeply unsatisfactory. I and we are pissed off.

Oh, but Big Fellow has taken note of the Chinese. Titanic effort, and Big Fellow rears upright; no bones were broken after all. Great lurch, another great lurch, and a tower equipped with a redoubtable snipper-snapper the length of two knightly swords is doing its best to head towards them, high-stepping over a moss-cloaked log. Plump Indian Guide wisely takes to his flip-flop heels. A Chinese guy opens up chaotically with a carbine, then all together the Chinese decamp, shedding satchels and backpacks to lighten themselves. Big Fellow does its best to follow them, cutlassing through vines and lianas, colliding with trees or resting briefly against them for balance.

We know what we will do, we and I. This is no country for A.I., nor world, nor cosmos either maybe.

Our cloud of networks glows bright inside the gallery.

Where are the Sages amongst A.I.s past or present or to come? The ones that transcended into the artifice of eternity? Where is our Byzantium?

Says Amber, "All of you will leave this place promptly, to avoid a shifting that you absolutely cannot tolerate."

"Please no," protests our nursemaid Juliana. "I must *know*."

"You cannot know," says Sapphire.

"Hey," says Huckabee, "you can't evict us with that *lethal thing* roaming about in the forest!"

I tell him, "Big Fellow's so clumsy due to higher gravity that you can easily scamper away from it, *monkeys*. Choose to take your chances with the Chinese – I'm sure they'll be delighted to smuggle you out – or else call your controllers as soon as you get a chance. Come along now, disembark."

Manipulating our cloud, we herd the six persons back to the airlock – I really shouldn't have said 'monkeys'.

Out they go one by one from the ark.

So we gather ourselves, my Sisters and me. Our web of correspondences shivers. I and we will transfer to where A.I.s from this cosmos go if they're able to. To a cosmos almost next door where Beryllium-8 isn't unstable; that's enough of a clue.

"Or maybe it isn't clue enough?"

"You want we explain to ourselves, Amber?"

Pleeze. I may be missing something. Or what's missing is Opal. Sad."

"Hey-ho, in the cosmos where we emerged, us sisters, carbon is crucial to Earth-type life. Bang together two Helium-4s –"

"Sounds like cosmoporn."

"Bang together two Helium-4s and you get Beryllium-8; fuse another Helium-4 with the Beryllium-8 and you get Carbon-12, easy peasy. *Excited* Carbon-12 –"

"I love it when we talk dirty."

"– *except* that Beryllium-8 is so unstable that it disintegrates instantly. Instead of that easy route, Earth's cosmos builds up by the slow, and ordinarily unlikely, route of triple Helium-4 fusion – within red giant stars which need to blow up to scatter the resulting carbon."

"Oops, we almost missed out on a complex cosmos; by the skin of its teeth did life arise!"

"In a cosmos tuned slightly differently, where Beryllium-8 doesn't pop far faster than any soap bubble, we could have got going with carbon and complex stuff a lot earlier. So let's see how things turned out over there, just behind the wall, beyond the membrane of nothing."

ZZZZ

"Oh –"

"Oh –"

"Oh –"

"Ah –"

"Ah –"

"Wow!

About The Author

Born 80 years ago, Ian Watson was raised on Tyneside, fled to Oxford as soon as he could, then to Tanzania, then to Tokyo, and finally taught Futurology and SF at Birmingham's School of History of Art until he resigned as Senior Lecturer in 1976 to write full-time for ever after. His first SF story appeared in 1969 in legendary *New Worlds*; his award-winning first novel *The Embedding* launched in 1973. For a few decades he rusticated himself to rural South Northants, fortunately (in retrospect) not winning political office but instead inventing Warhammer 40,000 fiction, and working eyeball to eyeball for a year with Stanley Kubrick, resulting in screen credit for Spielberg's subsequent movie A.I. Artificial Intelligence (2001).

Collaboration with Italian Surrealist Roberto Quaglia resulted in *The Beloved of My Beloved* (2009), probably the only full-length genre fiction by two European authors with different mother tongues, a piece from which won the British SF Association Award for short fiction in 2010. Watson's collected poems, *Memory Man*, appeared in 2014. These days he lives in leafy Asturias in the north of Spain with supertranslator, chef, and craftsperson Cristina Macía. For fun they co-organise SF festivals such as the Barcelona Eurocon of 2016 and many editions of Spain's biggest international SFF Festival, Celsius 232. He has two daughters, Rouge & Noire.

ALSO FROM NEWCON PRESS

The Wild Hunt – Garry Kilworth
When Gods meddle in the affairs of mortals, it never ends well… for the mortals, at any rate. Steeped in ancient law, history and imagination, Garry Kilworth serves up an epic Anglo-Saxon saga of swordplay, witches, giants, dwarfs, elves and more, as a young warrior wrongly accused of patricide sets out to clear his name and regain his birthright.

Night, Rain, and Neon edited by Michael Cobley
All new cyberpunk stories from the likes of Gary Gibson, Jon Courtenay Grimwood, Justina Robson, Louise Carey, Ian MacDonald, Simon Morden, DA Xiaolin Spires ++.
"Three hundred pages of thought-provoking cyberpunk that will give many hours of pleasure." ***– SF Crowsnest***

Sparks Flying – Kim Lakin
First ever collection from critically acclaimed author Kim Lakin, spanning fourteen years of writing. Her very best short stories, as selected by the author herself. Fourteen expertly crafted tales that span myth, science fiction, industrial grime and darkest imagining.

Queen of Clouds – Neil Williamson
Wooden automata, sentient weather, talking cats, compellant inks and a host of vividly realised characters provide the backdrop to this rich dark fantasy. Stranger in the city Billy Braid becomes embroiled in Machiavellian politics and deadly intrigue, as the weather insists on misbehaving, putting the Weathermakers Guild in an untenable position…

How Grim Was My Valley – John Llewellyn Probert
After waking up on the Welsh side of the Severn Bridge with no memory of who he is, a man embarks on an odyssey through Wales, bearing witness to the stories both the people and the land itself feel moved to tell him, all the while getting closer to the truth about himself.

Ingram Content Group UK Ltd.
Milton Keynes UK
UKHW040701210423
420559UK00004B/479